Crime Files

Series Editor
Clive Bloom
Professor Emeritus
Middlesex University
London, UK

"The vibrant world of contemporary Irish crime fiction finally has the critical book it needs and deserves: Brian Cliff's thoughtful study tracks developments between and across genres, times and places and offers a nuanced account of the culture and history of Irish crime writing."
—Claire Connolly, *Professor of Modern English, University College Cork, Ireland*

Since its invention in the nineteenth century, detective fiction has never been more popular. In novels, short stories and films, on the radio, on television and now in computer games, private detectives and psychopaths, poisoners and overworked cops, tommy gun gangsters and cocaine criminals are the very stuff of modern imagination, and their creators a mainstay of popular consciousness. Crime Files is a ground-breaking series offering scholars, students and discerning readers a comprehensive set of guides to the world of crime and detective fiction. Every aspect of crime writing, from detective fiction to the gangster movie, true-crime exposé, police procedural and post-colonial investigation, is explored through clear and informative texts offering comprehensive coverage and theoretical sophistication.

More information about this series at
http://www.palgrave.com/gp/series/14927

Brian Cliff

Irish Crime Fiction

palgrave
macmillan

Brian Cliff
Trinity College Dublin
Dublin, Ireland

Crime Files
ISBN 978-1-137-56187-9   ISBN 978-1-137-56188-6   (eBook)
https://doi.org/10.1057/978-1-137-56188-6

Library of Congress Control Number: 2018935568

This Palgrave Macmillan imprint is published by the registered company Macmillan Publishers Ltd. part of Springer Nature.
The registered company address is: The Campus, 4 Crinan Street, London, N1 9XW, United Kingdom

For Marni: L'chayim ha'eleh imakh.
For Maura: I love you to pieces.

ACKNOWLEDGEMENTS

I am grateful to Trinity College Dublin for their research support, and for the career break that allowed me to finish this book. I am particularly indebted to the following for their support of the festival that led me to begin this book: Darryl Jones, my Head of School at the time and our current Dean; Jane Ohlmeyer in her role as the head of Trinity's globalisation efforts, through which the festival had the invaluable help of Julia Maher, whose energy and creativity elevated the event; and our student assistants for the festival, including Richard Howard, Caitlín Nic Íomhair, and Michaela Marková. That festival would not have happened without my co-organiser Professor John Waters and his colleagues at New York University's Glucksman Ireland House, which (with the support of their Dean, Professor Tom Carew) is an invaluable centre of Irish research and among the most hospitable of hosts for Irish crime fiction. The energy and profane good cheer of Joe Long and Seth Kavanagh also did much to make the weekend what it was. Above all, that event was lucky to have the contributions of nineteen novelists who gave their time, energy, and engagement. Additionally, the festival – like everyone working on or in Irish crime fiction – owes a particular debt to Declan Burke for his years of work drawing attention to the genre with his own fiction, with the books he has edited, and with his long-running blog Crime Always Pays.

Portions of this book were previously published in earlier forms as 'A "honeycomb world": John Connolly's Charlie Parker Series,' in *The Contemporary Irish Detective Novel*, edited by Elizabeth Mannion (Palgrave, 2016); and 'Genre and Uncertainty in Tana French's Dublin

Murder Squad Mysteries,' in *Twenty-First Century Popular Fiction*, edited by Bernice Murphy and Stephen Matterson (Edinburgh University Press, 2018). I am grateful for the permission to include this work here.

Much of the thought behind this book was refined through an advanced seminar I taught with my colleague Christopher Morash in the spring of 2015, with the support of our Head of School, Eve Patten. I am grateful to Chris for the collaboration, and to our students in that seminar for making the semester so rewarding. I have consistently benefited from the friendship, intellectual challenge, and professional support of numerous colleagues at Trinity, including Micheál Ó Siochrú, Mark Hennessy, and Caoimhe ní Bhraonáin in Irish Studies, and my School of English colleagues Terence Brown, Clare Clarke, Philip Coleman, Paul Delaney, Aileen Douglas, Nicholas Grene, Darryl Jones, Jarlath Killeen, Deirdre Madden, Stephen Matterson, Bernice Murphy, Brendan O'Connell, David O'Shaughnessy, Eve Patten, Ian Campbell Ross, Sam Slote, Tom Walker, and Pádraic Whyte. I'm similarly indebted to colleagues elsewhere, including Lee Behlman, Patrick Bixby, Alan Cattier, Hugh Cohen, Brendan Corcoran, Eric Falci, Renee Fox, Jon Greenberg, Geraldine Higgins, Ronan Kelly, Joseph Lennon, Patricia Matthew, Barry McCrea, Carole Meyers, Lois Overbeck, Adrian Patterson, Jessica Restaino, Ronald Schuchard, Éibhear Walshe, John Waters, and particularly Emilie Pine and Elizabeth Mannion, whose readings of early chapters were incisive and invariably right. Ellen Clair Lamb was of unfailingly good cheer as she dispensed good advice and helpful suggestions. I've also been fortunate in the editors that I've worked with at Palgrave, especially Vicky Bates, Ben Doyle, and Tom René, all of whom were warmly helpful and exceedingly patient at every turn.

I'm grateful for the support of my parents, Tom and Joan Cliff, with their Midwestern levels of positivity, and for that of my in-laws Lew and LaVonda Rothman. I was lucky to have Patrick and Betsy Cliff's encouragement, and their ability to edit with the wisdom of journalists; all excess verbiage (like the word 'verbiage') is entirely my fault. Kevin Walter, Diana Lyon, Vincent Keenan, and Jamie Kaye Walters have long been supportive and encouraging in all things. Sam Rothman, John Hankin, Shane Rothman, Whitney Ballard, Luke Rothman, and Jared Fronk: thanks, always, for being such a welcoming family. Charlie, Gus, Logan, and Ezra did me the invaluable favour of letting me know someone out there thinks I'm reliably funny. Chuey contributed just by raising everyone's spirits, as has Elven.

Above all, I am thankful beyond words for my wife Marni Rothman and my daughter Maura Cliff, for their patience, their love, their faith in my ability to see this through, and, well, just because. My world would be a greyer one without you.

CONTENTS

CHAPTER 1

Introduction

This book has its origins in a festival of Irish crime fiction, which I organised with Professor John Waters of New York University's Glucksman Ireland House, and which the School of English at Trinity College Dublin hosted in November 2013. The intent of the festival was to explore the remarkable and still-recent growth in Irish crime fiction, a growth that has only accelerated over the intervening years. Eighteen Irish crime writers (and one Irish-American) appeared on four panel discussions, and the festival closed with a public interview between John Connolly and the Irish-American author Michael Connelly.[1] The events had to move to a series of larger venues, and drew on the order of 500 discrete attendees, as well as significant print, radio, and television coverage. The success of this weekend helped confirm the impression that Irish crime fiction had reached a critical mass, for authors and readers alike.

At the time, despite increasing coverage in the book review pages and increasing sales, very little critical discussion of Irish crime fiction had yet been published. The two main exceptions were both the work of Declan Burke: his long-running website of reviews, news, and interviews, Crime Always Pays, and his edited anthology of short fiction and essays by Irish crime writers, *Down These Green Streets: Irish Crime Writing in the 21st*

---

[1] Full details of the festival are at http://irishcrimefiction.blogspot.ie (accessed 21 November 2013). A distillation of the press coverage is in the press release 'Golden Age of Irish Crime Fiction Celebrated at Festival,' https://www.tcd.ie/news_events/articles/golden-age-of-irish-crime-fiction-celebrated-at-festival/4465 (accessed 27 November 2013).

© The Author(s) 2018
B. Cliff, *Irish Crime Fiction*, Crime Files,
https://doi.org/10.1057/978-1-137-56188-6_1

1

Century (2011). These remain among the most valuable resources on the subject, providing a focal point that has been essential in establishing a sense of the genre in Ireland.

Burke aside, a number of factors contribute to the continuing paucity of scholarship. One is that Irish Studies does not yet have an enviable track record on serious and sustained consideration of *any* popular fiction for adults.[2] Some of this reflects the problematic legacy of earlier Troubles thrillers, which established several patterns that Chapter 2 examines. It also, however, reflects a cultural field in which for some time poetry and drama – as a legacy of the Irish Literary Revival of the late nineteenth and early twentieth centuries – were valorised as the prevailing genres for representing and considering Irishness. That Revival's influence on the critical discourses around Irish literature – indeed, on the very question of what constituted Irish literature – left little room for genre fiction, not when the Revival so assiduously tasked Irish literature with articulating a national identity.[3]

Just over four years and change on from the festival, more studies have begun to appear. Scattered essays have been published on individual authors, and several essays – notably those by Andrew Kincaid, David Clark, Cormac Ó Cuilleanáin, Maureen T. Reddy, and particularly Ian Campbell Ross – have provided valuable if brief overviews of Irish crime fiction, with more specialised survey essays by Keith Jeffery and Eunan O'Halpin, and by Aaron Kelly. Kelly's 2005 book about Troubles thrillers is groundbreaking in this regard, as Chapter 2 suggests, and remains to a large degree exceptional. At least two notable journal issues have also been devoted to the subject, both in 2014: a special issue of *Clues* on Tana French, and an interdisciplinary special issue of *Éire-Ireland* on Irish

---

[2] In contrast, Irish children's literature has attracted considerably more research and critical study, by scholars such as Pádraic Whyte, Anne Markey, Celia Keenan, and others, though that genre's questions of readership make it not readily comparable to crime fiction. Irish science fiction is a smaller body of work, but has also begun to attract scholarly attention, including promising work by Richard Howard, whose PhD thesis I was fortunate to supervise.

[3] This shortage is not exclusive to academic studies of Irish crime fiction, as Meier and Ross suggest that it is equally true of research on Irish crime itself: 'in comparison to other parts of Europe, thematic studies dedicated to crime history that relate wrongdoing to larger historical change are singularly lacking in Ireland.' William Meier and Ian Campbell Ross, 'Editors' Introduction,' in 'Irish Crime Since 1921,' ed. Meier and Ross, special issue, *Éire-Ireland* 49, no. 1–2 (Spring-Summer 2014): 10.

crime.[4] Elizabeth Mannion's edited collection of essays, *The Contemporary Irish Detective Novel* (2016), is the only critical book to appear so far on the subject, though more are in progress.

Little exists, however, in the way of sustained, synthesizing overviews of Irish crime fiction. While Irish Studies has not yet done much with the genre, crime fiction studies has until recently not done much more to look at Irish crime fiction *as* Irish crime fiction, rather than addressing a limited range of texts in essays about individual authors. This book seeks to remedy these shortcomings with a survey of Irish crime fiction. The intent is to provide a foundation for further study, one that begins to connect some of the dots; this book, to borrow an obvious image, is the chalk outline.

THE GROWTH OF IRISH CRIME FICTION

This book focuses for the most part on contemporary Irish crime fiction, reflecting the genre's comparatively recent coalescence on the island over the last several decades. This expansive and rapid growth has been remarked on, by the novelists themselves, by the press – 'Once upon a time, crime writers in Ireland were few and far between. These days it's not so much a case of "whodunnit", or even "who's doing it", as "they're all at it"'[5] – and by several of the overview articles that have been published, one of which fixes the genre's prominence as dating 'back only … to the publication of *Every Dead Thing* (1999), the first novel by John Connolly, Ireland's most successful and critically admired crime writer.'[6] Although one can identify various contributing factors and timelines, certainty about the precise starting point and its reasons is harder to obtain.

Even the varied attempts to provide reasons have tended to remain slightly tentative, although a number of threads recur. In particular, the genre's growth has been reductively though not untruthfully seen as reflecting the Celtic Tiger, for example, an unfortunate name for an era in which Ireland experienced a dizzying growth in prosperity from the mid-1990s followed by an even more vertiginous crash from 2008 on, with widespread corruption and newly urgent social pressures both exacerbated

[4] See Rachel Schaffer, ed., 'Special Issue on Tana French,' *Clues: A Journal of Detection* 32, no. 1 (2014), and Meier and Ross, 'Irish Crime Since 1921.'

[5] Arminta Wallace, 'Killer instinct: a golden age of Irish crime fiction,' *Irish Times*, 21 November 2013, http://www.irishtimes.com/culture/killer-instinct-a-golden-age-of-irish-crime-fiction-1.1601482 (accessed 25 March 2014).

[6] Meier and Ross, 'Editors' Introduction,' 12–13.

by and reflected in the boom and crash.[7] The narrator of Tana French's second novel, *The Likeness* (2008), for example, sees a darker range of changes in which the stresses of the boom are intensifying rather than just white-collar-ing crime in Ireland:

> Irish homicides are still, mostly, simple things … We've never had the orgies of nightmare that other countries get … But it's only a matter of time, now. For ten years Dublin's been changing faster than our minds can handle. The economic boom has given us too many people with helicopters and too many crushed into cockroachy flats from hell … and we're fracturing under the weight of it.[8]

Few passages in Irish crime fiction more bleakly assess the boom's effects. The other contributing factor most regularly cited in the genre's rise is the relative peace in Northern Ireland. As discussed more fully in Chapter 2, the end of the Troubles cleared space for wider varieties of Northern Irish crime fiction. Some of this has been explained in terms of the economic boom that followed the ceasefires, when Northern Ireland saw its own increase in prosperity, often referred to as the 'peace dividend.' North and south of the border, contributing factors in the booms included inward investment, from the EU and from transnational corporations, the latter featuring prominently in fiction by Alan Glynn, Adrian McKinty, and others. On both sides of this experience, going up and coming down, prosperity and privation left their mark on crime and consequently on crime fiction, as the central chapters here demonstrate.

Whatever the final causes of the genre's growth, these changes clearly contributed, perhaps most directly through specific economic themes that often seem tailor-made for the genre. Indeed, as Andrew Kincaid has argued, 'Noir proves a perfect genre to capitalize on' the Celtic Tiger's

---

[7] In an aside, Andrew Fox attributes the most extensive literary explorations of the boom to genre fiction, less by way of crediting such fiction than of lamenting the shortage of similar explorations in literary fiction, suggesting that as of 2010 'the Celtic Tiger, which had roared its last a little over a year before – and which had been documented to a degree in a host of crime and "chick-lit" titles – still remained curiously underrepresented in Irish literary fiction.' Andrew Fox, 'Tiger, Tiger: The Hunt for the Great Irish Novel,' *The Daily Beast*, 2 February 2014, http://www.thedailybeast.com/articles/2014/02/28/tiger-tiger-the-hunt-for-the-great-irish-novel.html (accessed 3 June 2015).

[8] Tana French, *The Likeness* (New York: Penguin, 2008; repr. 2009), 11–12.

'under-currents of melancholy, alienation, grievance, and even injustice,'[9] a capacity Shirley Peterson suggests has become all the more 'concentrated' amidst the crash.[10] These related contexts on the island – the 'Celtic Tiger,' the 'peace dividend,' the real estate boom, the economic crash – continue to inspire crime fiction about corruption and other varieties of serial human frailty. The frequency with which Dublin discussions circle back to real estate investment, home prices, and property development, for example, bewilders Declan Hughes's Ed Loy on his return to Ireland after a long absence. The boom and crash also brought other material changes to Irish society, which have in turn left their marks on crime fiction. These wider changes include an increase in immigration, a radically new experience for a country that has yet to grow back to its pre-Famine population levels nearly two full centuries later. As discussed most fully in Chapter 5, immigrants play prominent roles in contemporary Irish crime fiction by Andrew Nugent, Brian McGilloway, Arlene Hunt, Jane Casey, Michael Russell, and others. In these novels, immigrants are victims and villains and protagonists alike, roles through which they sharpen crime fiction's long-standing use of outsiders in a context where the foreign is no longer nearly as rare. As these and other examples will show, the boom may not have directly led to Irish crime fiction's growth, but its circumstances clearly nurtured certain recurring strands of interest within the genre.

Corruption and Crime

Although the boom and the crash have both been transformative in their ways, we should also acknowledge that their role in Irish crime fiction's development can be overstated. Too narrow a focus in this regard could easily overshadow slower, longer processes (or recast them in the boom's terms), resulting in a historical foreshortening that would effectively erase pre-boom Irish crime fiction. David Clark, for example, has tied Irish crime fiction's development to certain structural changes in Irish society, including those that culminated in the 1996 creation of the Criminal Assets Bureau, which he argues helped shift 'The focus of crime in the late

---

[9] Andrew Kincaid, '"Down These Mean Streets": The City and Critique in Contemporary Irish Noir,' *Éire-Ireland* 45, no. 1–2 (Spring/Summer 2010): 45.

[10] Shirley Peterson, 'Murder in the Ghost Estate: Crimes of the Celtic Tiger in Tana French's *Broken Harbor*,' in Schaffer, 'Special Issue on Tana French': 80n5.

nineties and in the first decade of the twenty-first century ... away from the old gang-based robbery and kidnappings towards the more lucrative and initially less perilous area of white-collar crime,' in particular to the 'quick profits that could be gained from' the exploding 'property market.'[11] In this view, the CAB helped fight conventional crime in Ireland, in the process reducing the gap between such crime and varieties of entrepreneurial activity that looked much more mainstream, all the more so as the boom accelerated.

One by-product of the CAB legislation, then, may have been to foster both crime and crime fiction that were less 'exotic' to some readers, and more familiar from the property, business, and society pages of the newspapers. Indeed, much crime fiction set in Ireland touches on varieties of clientelism and corruption: if an archetypal crime exists in Irish versions of the genre it may be not murder, rape, kidnapping, robbery, or drug dealing, but corruption.[12] Fintan O'Toole has described the aborted attempts to establish a Corruption Assets Bureau modelled on the Criminal Assets Bureau, attempts that reflected in part the increased prominence of corruption.[13] This corruption agency regrettably if unsurprisingly never came into existence (although Elaine Byrne argues that the Criminal Assets Bureau was nonetheless used to seize funds determined to arise from corruption).[14] Such patterns of criminal behaviour – what some of the defendants might have referred to as the 'diversification' of Irish crime – constitute a significant image in the genre, one that cannot be accounted for by the Celtic Tiger alone, but one that also reflects underlying structures of behaviour far predating the boom.

While direct causation between the economy and Irish crime fiction's growth should not be assumed, the question of corruption exemplifies ways in which a broader context – particularly one in which 'the celebrated

---

[11] David Clark, 'Emerald Noir? Contemporary Irish Crime Fiction,' in *East Meets West*, ed. Reiko Aiura, J.U. Jacobs, and J. Derrick McClure (Newcastle: Cambridge Scholars, 2014), 149.

[12] In this, Irish crime fiction shares something with corruption's long history in crime writing, a history that features in Andrew Pepper, *Unwilling Executioner: Crime Fiction and the State* (Oxford: Oxford University Press, 2016).

[13] Fintan O'Toole, *Ship of Fools: How Stupidity and Corruption Sank the Celtic Tiger* (London: Faber, 2009, repr. and updated 2010), 38–41, and Fintan O'Toole, *Enough is Enough: How to Build a New Republic* (London: Faber, 2010), 228.

[14] Elaine A. Byrne, *Political Corruption in Ireland 1922–2010* (Manchester: Manchester University Press, 2012), 170–172, 181.

warmth and friendliness of Irish culture' is linked to the social 'intimacy' that 'lies at the core of every corruption scandal that has bedevilled the Irish economy since the 1960s,'[15] as Niamh Hourigan has argued – may help explain some of that growth. Crime fiction is exceptionally well suited to engaging with experiences of the ambivalence Hourigan describes, given what Andrew Pepper has depicted as the genre's fundamental nature: 'it has always been the case that crime writing is shot through with an uneasy mixture of conflicting ideological inflections,' among them the idea that 'much, if not all, crime fiction posits the state and the law as necessary for the creation and maintenance of collective life and the public or common good and, simultaneously, as a vehicle for the reproduction of inequalities, violence and oppression.'[16] (This ambivalence is perhaps most apparent in Northern Irish crime fiction like Brian McGilloway's and Adrian McKinty's works, although Gene Kerrigan casts an eye as sceptical as any over the lines between police and criminals.) This uniquely 'uneasy mixture' may help crime fiction navigate the range of changes Ireland has faced over the past quarter century, changes that have been experienced by Irish citizens in profoundly uneasy ways. Such uneasiness is magnified by a historical moment where civic and spiritual authority in Ireland has in many ways been at a low point, for reasons both before and beyond the boom. While the cultural factors behind a genre's growth in any given place and time are complex and elusive, factors such as these have clearly contributed to making recent decades and moments acutely fertile ground for the 'uneasy' qualities of crime fiction.

ANTECEDENTS AND PRECEDENTS

Although what critical attention Irish crime fiction has received has often emphasised this recent efflorescence, the genre is not without its domestic precedents, as several critics have noted at varying length. Clark, for example, opens by refuting the mistaken perception that 'the phenomenon of crime writing' is 'a recent one in Ireland. Irish crime writing has existed for almost as long as the genre itself.'[17] He contends that the real change is in

---

[15] Niamh Hourigan, *Rule-Breakers: Why 'Being There' Trumps 'Being Fair' in Ireland* (Dublin: Gill & Macmillan, 2015), 10.

[16] Andrew Pepper, '"Hegemony Protected by the Armour of Coercion": Dashiell Hammett's *Red Harvest* and the State,' *Journal of American Studies* 44, no. 2 (May 2010): 334, 346.

[17] Clark, 'Emerald Noir?', 144.

the production of crime fiction *about* Ireland by Irish writers, which he ties to the burgeoning of true crime books in the 1970s and 1980s, books that set the table for the more recent surge.[18] Elizabeth Mannion takes a similarly long view, tracing contemporary Irish crime fiction's origins back to nineteenth-century Irish writers such as Sheridan Le Fanu, and forward again to the Golden Age author Freeman Wills Crofts.[19] Ian Campbell Ross, among the academics who helped establish crime fiction studies in Ireland, has produced the most substantive single discussion of these antecedents in his 'Introduction' to Burke's anthology *Down These Green Streets*. In that essay, Ross also looks to the Irish Gothic as a source of predecessors, as well as to some nineteenth-century texts in which Irish matters were more to the fore, including work by Samuel Lover and Lady Wilde. Despite these abundant examples, Ross also suggests that 'Old belief systems and modern nationalist politics both worked against an easy acceptance – at least among part of the population – of crime fiction as it was developing in the neighbouring island.'[20] These cultural and ideological differences had their material counterparts, not least in the differing scales of the reading public in Ireland and Britain: 'In Ireland, the market for such popular literature was much smaller, where it existed at all,' a factor that further slowed the domestic production of crime fiction for a very long time indeed.[21]

More recent antecedents are scattered across the twentieth century, by authors including Liam O'Flaherty, Freeman Wills Crofts, Cecil Day-Lewis (under his pen name Nicholas Blake), Eilís Dillon, Sheila Pim, Patricia Moyes, Brendan Behan, and Erskine Childers, whose novel *The Riddle of the Sands* (1903) is often regarded as among the first spy

---

[18] Clark, 'Emerald Noir?', 146–148. Fiona Coffey draws on Clark to make a similar argument in '"The place you don't belong": Stuart Neville's Belfast,' in *The Contemporary Irish Detective Novel*, ed. Elizabeth Mannion (London: Palgrave Macmillan, 2016), 95.

[19] Elizabeth Mannion, 'A Path to Emerald Noir: The Rise of the Irish Detective Novel,' in Mannion, *The Contemporary Irish Detective Novel*, 4–8.

[20] Ian Campbell Ross, 'Introduction,' in *Down These Green Streets: Irish Crime Writing in the 21st Century*, ed. Declan Burke (Dublin: Liberties, 2011), 19, 20. Ross's essay is even more valuable when coupled with 'Irish Crime Writing 1829–2011: Further Reading,' the bibliography he and Shane Mawe compiled for the same volume (362–368), a work for which scholars of Irish crime fiction will long be indebted.

[21] Ross, 'Introduction,' 21.

novels.[22] This is not an insubstantial collection of texts, but little suggests much of a building critical mass until the very end of the twentieth century. (Although thrillers about the Northern Irish Troubles were produced in large quantities throughout the 1970s and 1980s, they were often by non-Irish journalists, a complex and problematic case as Aaron Kelly has shown and as discussed in Chapter 2 here.) Reflecting the scattered nature of these examples, even as recently as 1985 a deeply well-informed observer like John Gray, the head librarian at Belfast's esteemed Linen Hall Library, could plausibly open a review of a reprinted Freeman Wills Crofts novel by asserting that 'The detective novel is a singularly non Irish genre. Irish ambivalence about policing has not been conducive to the emergence of police heroes, and the priorities of Irish policing have often been quite other than the methodical solution of ordinary crimes as in the British tradition.'[23] While more recent Irish writers have adapted the genre to reflect this 'ambivalence,' and while the genre has broadened far beyond 'the British tradition,' the Irish genre's uneven history – like the contexts to which Gray refers – does help give Irish crime fiction a different sense of development and different contours than can be seen in more fully established English and American traditions, as will become apparent over the course of this book.

Some thematic continuities do exist between these earlier examples and contemporary texts. One example is the distinction between revenge and justice, which has a place in crime fiction generally and a long history throughout Ireland's twentieth century, in contexts intimate enough to

[22] On Childers, see Keith Jeffery and Eunan O'Halpin, 'Ireland in Spy Fiction,' *Intelligence and National Security* 5, no. 4 (1990): 93. Like Jeffery and O'Halpin ('Ireland in Spy Fiction,' 100), Aaron Kelly discusses F. L. Green's *Odd Man Out* (1945) as another model in *The Thriller and Northern Ireland Since 1969: Utterly Resigned Terror* (Aldershot: Ashgate, 2005), 15. On Brendan Behan's work in *The Scarperer*, see John Brannigan, '"For the Readies": Brendan Behan, Crime Fiction, and the Dublin Underworld,' in Meier and Ross, 'Irish Crime Since 1921': 92–105.

[23] John Gray, review of *Inspector French's Greatest Case*, by Freeman Wills Crofts, *The Linen Hall Review* 2, no. 1 (Spring 1985): 26. Conversely, Declan Burke has argued that Ireland's colonial past means that 'Irish crime writers get to have their cake and eat it too, presenting the police as agents of oppression and terror when it suits, but also culturally attuned to tapping into the classic British perception of PC Plod as the flat-footed but utterly dependable avatar for law, order and justice.' Declan Burke, 'Raising hell in Arizona with a gripping thriller,' review of *Here and Gone*, by Stuart Neville (pseud. Haylen Beck), *Irish Times*, 29 July 2017, https://www.irishtimes.com/culture/books/here-and-gone-review-raising-hell-in-arizona-with-a-gripping-thriller-1.3164145 (accessed 29 July 2017).

blur the distinction, not least amidst internecine conflicts back well beyond the Irish Civil War, the divisions of which continue to reverberate through Irish politics. Those divisions play a significant role in some influential antecedents, like Liam O'Flaherty's classic *The Informer* (1925), and in some historical crime fiction, like Kevin McCarthy's novels set in the early 1920s, and Joe Joyce's historical trilogy, set in a neutral Ireland amidst World War II, with a central figure still motivated partly by Civil War allegiances. Perhaps ironically, more of the Irish past is dealt with in contemporary historical fiction like McCarthy's, Michael Russell's, Conor Brady's, Peter Tremayne's, Cora Harrison's, and Benjamin Black's – all of whom take significant pains to set their works in a credibly represented and specifically located Irish past – than in many of these older antecedents.[24]

CONTEXTS, PARTICULARITIES, THEMES

As this discussion of Irish contexts suggests, this book is written from an Irish Studies perspective, with such matters very much in mind. Chapter 2, for example, addresses the Troubles in Northern Ireland, while other Irish contexts both contemporary and much older – corruption, institutionalised abuse, and political infighting among them – are considered throughout the book. In this, I have sought to balance a sustained attention to Irish contexts with a broad survey of interest to both crime fiction studies and Irish Studies, in the interests of facilitating further connections

---

[24] For a focused consideration of historical crime fiction, including a discussion of the Irish author Gemma O'Connor, see Rosemary Erickson Johnsen, *Contemporary Feminist Historical Crime Fiction* (Basingstoke: Palgrave Macmillan, 2006). Numerous articles have also been published on Benjamin Black's novels, including Carol Dell'Amico, 'John Banville and Benjamin Black: The *Mundo*, Crime, Women,' in Meier and Ross, 'Irish Crime Since 1921': 106–120. See also Nancy Marck Cantwell, 'Hello *Dálaigh*: Peter Tremayne's Sister Fidelma,' in Mannion, *The Contemporary Irish Detective Novel*, 17–29. Tremayne's work has attracted the devoted fans of The International Sister Fidelma Society, and a recent essay collection, Edward J. Rielly and David Robert Wooten's *The Sister Fidelma Mysteries: Essays on the Historical Novels of Peter Tremayne* (Jefferson: McFarland, 2012). Though she is not writing about crime fiction as such, Eve Patten perceptively identifies a pattern of relations between contemporary Irish fiction in general and 'the recent past,' noting the ways in which 'novelists have put particularly intense pressure on ... the period from the 1950s to the 1970s, in which ... Ireland experienced most acutely the effects of the country's failure to keep pace with modernisation and secularisation.' Eve Patten, 'Contemporary Irish Fiction,' in *The Cambridge Companion to the Irish Novel*, ed. John Wilson Foster (Cambridge: Cambridge University Press, 2006), 263–264.

between both disciplinary areas of focus. Among these particular contexts, of course, are the experiences of the boom and the crash. As discussed in several chapters, however, while these local manifestations of wider economic crises offer some connections to international crime fiction, Ireland's specificity marks Irish crime fiction in clear ways: while it is of course deeply connected to and influenced by other forms of the genre, much Irish crime fiction also works within terms that reflect the political, cultural, and historical specificity of the island, Northern Ireland as well as the Republic of Ireland. To take just one brief example from the patterns considered in this book, these terms include very tangible matters (such as the smaller social and geographic scale of Ireland) that directly influence Irish crime fiction's characters and plots. Although it has become a cliché to point out that few Irish now live in the villages of 1950s postcards, it is true that Irish-set crime fiction cannot rely on the dense anonymity of a megalopolis, unlike novels set in London by Jane Casey and Paul Charles, or in New York by Steve Cavanagh and Adrian McKinty. Lee Child's Jack Reacher series could never happen in Ireland, for example, with all of Reacher's ceaseless motion, nor – as Arlene Hunt and others have noted – could mass serial killer novels on an American scale: in a landscape as intimate and compact as Ireland's, where can a mass serial killer hide the bodies? The scale of the stage, in other words, matters a great deal for the content and structure that are available to Irish crime fiction, as Chapter 5 argues.

These factors do not preclude serial killers in Irish crime fiction, necessarily, though they do mitigate against their plausibility. To introduce a different national context: Linnie Blake has tied American crime fiction's serial killers to what she calls that country's 'culturally vaunted doctrine of radical individualism,' while Mark Seltzer has connected such characters to the cultural growth of 'self-actualization,' not a trait exclusive to America but one nonetheless much more common there, at least until recently, than in Ireland.[25] In contrast, what Irish crime fiction offers in the way of something like serial killers often takes rather more collective paths. Adrian McKinty's Sean Duffy, for example, a Royal Ulster Constabulary officer during the Troubles, suggests that the sociopathic impulses of a fictional

---

[25] Linnie Blake, *The Wounds of Nations: Horror Cinema, Historical Trauma, and National Identity* (Manchester: Manchester University Press, 2008), 102; Mark Seltzer, from 'The Serial Killer as a Type of Person,' in *The Horror Reader*, ed. Ken Gelder (London: Routledge, 2000), 104.

serial killer are channelled through and veiled by paramilitary involvement in Northern Ireland. Similarly, other Irish crime novels run such impulses through institutions like the Magdalen laundries and the mother-baby homes, institutions that play a significant role in fiction by Benjamin Black, Jo Spain, Ken Bruen, Claire McGowan, Brian McGilloway, Gene Kerrigan, and others. Whether amidst the Troubles or at the intersection of church and state, then, serial-killing levels of violence do take place within effective Irish fictional narratives, but that violence is ascribed less to an individual sociopath and more to pathological institutions, which in turn reflect wider pathologies of the society in whose name they act. In such ways, the particularities of Ireland shape both the content and the form of Irish crime fiction.

Terminology and Subgenres

Serial killer narratives are of course but one among many possible subgenres. Crime fiction includes endlessly refracting subgenres, some of which are largely in the eye of the beholder. These range from subgenres that intersect with other genres (the romantic thriller) to established modes within the genre (like police procedurals, or like cosy amateur mysteries, of which few examples appear in contemporary Irish crime fiction, despite a number of Irish antecedents in the subgenre, discussed by Mannion, Ross, and Ó Cuilleanáin). The Agatha Christie scholar John Curran has shown in compelling detail how involved such discussions already were nearly a century ago,[26] and they have only become more so across the intervening decades. Throughout, this book uses 'crime fiction' as the most comprehensive of categorical terms for the genre. In this, as Horsley, Ascari, and others have done, I follow Stephen Knight's logic, which provides a reasonable and lucid lead:

> One of the major issues facing the author of an account of crime fiction is which terms to use to describe, and so discriminate, its varying forms. Some use the term 'detective fiction' for the whole genre, others call it 'mystery

---

[26] John Curran, 'Happy innocence: playing games in Golden Age detective fiction, 1920–45' (PhD thesis, Trinity College Dublin, 2014). See also the novelist Elizabeth George's introductory essay to her edition of *The Best American Mystery Stories 2016* (New York: Houghton Mifflin, 2016), xiii-xv, in which she distinguishes between 'mystery' and 'crime,' drawing in part on the 'rules of the game' as articulated by the Golden Age authors Curran discusses.

fiction'. But as a reader soon discovers, there are plenty of novels (including some by Christie) without a detective and nearly as many without even a mystery (like most of Highsmith's work). There is, though, always a crime (or very occasionally just the appearance of one) and that is why I have used the generally descriptive term 'crime fiction' for the whole genre. The sub-genres are as elusive to identify.[27]

Knight's terminology is persuasive in the context of Irish crime fiction, where the division of subgenres provides even less traction because so many of the texts involved draw at will on varied subgenre components. Thus, although this book uses the term 'crime fiction,' it will also of necessity touch on various subgenres and their scarcity or adaptation in Irish contexts, from the psychological thriller (Louise Phillips, Liz Nugent) to the procedural (Jane Casey, Brian McGilloway), to the supernatural or Gothic (Tana French, John Connolly), to the serial killer (Arlene Hunt, Alex Barclay), to the legal thriller (Steve Cavanagh) and the private eye (Declan Hughes).

At the same time, casting a net too widely does not question boundaries so much as it collapses meaningful differences. Both as a practical matter of scope and as a definitional matter of critical argument, drawing some lines is clearly appropriate and useful, even if Irish crime fiction has no need for a velvet rope and a doorman. With that in mind, among this book's few purposeful exclusions are texts that include a crime but do not otherwise engage with genre elements, as is often enough the case in the genre of Irish literary fiction.[28] Recent examples of this include Kevin Power's *Bad Day in Blackrock* (2008), Paul Murray's *Skippy Dies* (2010), Claire Kilroy's *The Devil I Know* (2012), Paul Lynch's *Red Sky in Morning* (2013), Emma Donoghue's *Room* (2010) and *Frog Music* (2014), and

[27] Stephen Knight, *Crime Fiction Since 1800: Detection, Death, Diversity*, 2nd ed. (Basingstoke: Palgrave Macmillan, 2010), xiii. See also Lee Horsley, *Twentieth-Century Crime Fiction* (Oxford: Oxford University Press, 2005), 3; Maurizio Ascari, *A Counter-History of Crime Fiction: Supernatural, Gothic, Sensational* (Basingstoke: Palgrave Macmillan, 2007), 7.

[28] Another example of an Irish text that draws on crime genres but cannot be described as crime fiction is the Northern Irish writer Garth Ennis's graphic novel series *Preacher* (New York: Vertigo, 1995–2000), which contains remarkable levels of graphic violence beyond almost anything in Irish crime fiction. It explicitly adapts elements of crime genres in ways both direct and less so, like it does with many other genres, including cinema and Biblical narratives. As a graphic novel first and foremost, however, *Preacher* is centred in a genre with quite particular demands, which would require a fuller and more sustained discussion.

Louise O'Neill's *Asking For It* (2015), all of which have some variety of crime playing a central role. Going even slightly farther back, literary novels by Joseph O'Connor, Hugo Hamilton, Carlo Gebler, John Banville, Dermot Bolger, and Edna O'Brien all feature narratives in which a crime is significant.

On the same grounds, much general fiction from Northern Ireland addresses crime and violence in complex and subtle ways. Both Deirdre Madden's *One by One in the Darkness* (1996) and Glenn Patterson's *The International* (1999), for example, take place in the wake of violent deaths that do not occur in the texts but that ripple throughout the narratives. This, though, does not make them crime novels, as John Connolly has argued with regard to Patrick McCabe's *The Butcher Boy* (1992), which he describes as 'a novel with a crime in it, but ... not a crime novel.'[29] Writing of *The Butcher Boy* and Flann O'Brien's *The Third Policeman* (1967), Alan Glynn rightly rejects the approach of adapting 'some elaborate theory that the book is secretly a crime novel, or even a proto-crime novel,' an exercise in which he sees little value.[30] Irish novels like those discussed by Glynn and Connolly – novels in which crime is represented, but which are themselves not crime novels – are more than numerous enough to require a separate study of their varied uses of crime and violence. Such a study, however, is beyond the scope of the present volume.

In making such distinctions, I mean to allow for a full consideration of the range of Irish crime fiction, with the divisions and genre play noted and examined, while at the same time not getting mired in the differentiation of subgenres, a potentially endless exercise. Indeed, much Irish crime fiction blurs genre boundaries promiscuously, perhaps most insistently in Tana French and John Connolly but also in the work of many of their contemporaries. An insistence on the demarcation of subgenres fails to fully recognise the impact of such multi-genre work, work that in turn allows for the consideration of the shaping influence wrought by genres like Gothic and the supernatural, an influence to which Ian Campbell Ross has notably called attention and one to which this book will return.[31]

---

[29] John Connolly, 'No Blacks, No Dogs, No Crime Writers: Ireland and the Mystery Genre,' in Burke, *Down These Green Streets*, 53.

[30] Alan Glynn, 'Murder in Mind: The Irish Literary Crime Novel,' in Burke, *Down These Green Streets*, 118–119.

[31] Ross, 'Introduction,' 21–22.

THEMATIC PATTERNS

With the goal of exploring the breadth of Irish crime fiction, this book looks at four main areas in which it has developed particular weight. These points of concentration allow the readings here to survey as suggestively as possible across texts, authors, and contexts. Doing so, in turn, facilitates a fuller exploration of diverse factors, themes, and patterns, including trauma, historical fiction, the Gothic, gender and sexuality, postcolonialism, and transatlantic cultural influence. While addressing these and other matters, this book focuses on writers about whose work less has so far been written (Tana French is an exception, for reasons discussed in Chapter 3). One result of this approach is that this book makes relatively little room for Benjamin Black, Eoin McNamee, Colin Bateman, and Ken Bruen, all of whom have written excellent, enduring novels and have made highly notable contributions to Irish crime fiction. As already noted, however, much of the scarce criticism on Irish crime fiction concentrates on individual authors, among whom these four have received degrees of comparatively significant attention. Deliberately emphasising authors whose work has not yet featured as heavily in critical discussions serves both to broaden that criticism's range and to demonstrate the genre's scope.

Over the four central chapters – respectively focused on Northern Ireland, the contemporary Republic of Ireland, women authors and protagonists, and transnational elements – a number of thematic patterns recur, around both the kinds of crimes represented and the responses accorded those crimes within their respective societies. One recurring pattern of crimes concerns property, chiefly land, homes, and development. The frequency with which this theme recurs is perhaps unsurprising anywhere with such a long and contested relationship to empire and its attendant dispossessions: as Meier and Ross argue, because of the role of crime and violence in Irish history, 'twentieth-century Irish crime continues to be marked by its colonial past' in these and other particular ways.[32] A clearly related pattern is civic corruption, much of which has to do with the planning processes related to economic and real estate development, matters often represented with profound anger or righteous satire.

---

[32] Meier and Ross, 'Editors' Introduction,' 15. Elsewhere in their essay, they argue that 'The diagnosis of "Irish crime" as premodern outrage prescribed the cure: coercive legislation to curtail civil liberties and enhance police powers. In its commission, perception, and punishment Irish crime was thoroughly colonized' (Meier and Ross, 'Editors' Introduction,' 7).

Such representations of property and corruption are also among the ways in which Irish crime fiction explores the Celtic Tiger and ties it to deeper contexts, including all of the consequent chaotic changes in class structures. This is not to say that Irish crime fiction merits consideration only in terms of 'its relationship to contemporary economic conditions in Ireland.'[33] On the contrary, as this entire book suggests, Irish crime fiction does much more than that crucial but narrow scope can acknowledge. All of the chapters demonstrate this breadth in varied ways, but Chapter 5 reflects this most directly by considering novels that engage with patterns including emigration, transnational capitalism, and settings abroad. This latter pattern is central in work by writers like Jane Casey, Conor Fitzgerald, Arlene Hunt, and John Connolly. None of Connolly's mystery fiction is set in Ireland, as is also true for Casey (whose protagonist, however, has Irish ancestry), Barclay (whose one novel set in Ireland is driven by American characters), and Fitzgerald (whose novels are set in Rome, with an expatriate American protagonist). The scant critical work on these authors – even measured against the low threshold set for studies of Irish crime fiction – speaks both to the persistent difficulty Irish literary studies has with materials that cannot be construed in terms of national identity, and to the consequent interpretative strain placed on the novels as well as the critical discussion that surrounds them.

Other recurring themes include the pronounced significance of empathy as an avowed motivation for protagonists, a matter that arises in every chapter here and the articulation of which reflects quietly important influences within the genre. American crime fiction in particular has been one such unsurprisingly large influence: at the 2013 festival at Trinity College Dublin, novelists engaged in several panel discussions about the disparity of influence between English and American writers on Irish crime fiction, the latter weighing more heavily in general. One clear influence is of course the hard-boiled style of Hammett, Chandler, and Cain, writers whose impact can be seen perhaps most clearly in Declan Burke's work, notably his protagonist Harry Rigby in *Eightball Boogie* (2003) and *Slaughter's Hound* (2012), while the influence of American police procedurals back to Ed McBain's 87th Precinct novels is apparent everywhere that subgenre has spread (which is to say, more or less everywhere).

---

[33] Moira E. Casey, '"Built on Nothing but Bullshit and Good PR": Crime, Class Mobility, and the Irish Economy in the Novels of Tana French,' in Schaffer, 'Special Issue on Tana French': 92.

Among canonical American crime writers, Ross Macdonald may have had not the flashiest but certainly among the most substantial influences on Irish crime fiction, at a different level than that of style: his insistently familial themes may simply resonate more in the context of Irish cultural patterns like the family gothic, the contours of which have been well articulated by Margot Backus and others.[34] Against an Irish backdrop, Macdonald's sense of the violence that families do within and to themselves is less alien than are Chandler's and Hammett's pre-Cold War streets of Los Angeles and San Francisco. Connolly and Hughes in particular have spoken frequently of the inspiration to be found in Macdonald, and in his protagonist Lew Archer's driving empathy, with Connolly describing Macdonald as 'the genre's first great poet of empathy and compassion,' and aptly so.[35] One marker of this influence, and a topic to which this book returns repeatedly, can be seen in how empathy has been adapted by writers as different from each other as Hughes, Connolly, Neville, French, and Casey. In their work, Irish crime fiction is strikingly alive to the ethical and aesthetic complexities of empathy, in both imaginative and moral terms.

Much more could be said about some of these writers and novels, and about others not examined here. This book, however, is a survey, not a history, and aims to be suggestive in its breadth, but does not pretend to be comprehensive. What sustains this book's approach to Irish crime fiction is the same conviction that gave rise to the 2013 festival this introduction began by discussing. That festival arose in part from a sense that one thing a field like Irish literary studies ought to do – indeed, is obligated to do – is consider what Irish people actually read, and to do so through the widest lens possible. By the same logic, this book does less to hold the texts to account for what *I* think they should be doing, and attempts rather to explore what these texts seem to be doing, or trying to do. Working from that principle, as the patterns I have noted in this introduction suggest, it becomes clear that Irish crime fiction is something other than 'mere' escapism, a charge missing the point so widely as not to merit direct rebuttal, and yet a charge so casually and reflexively made against

---

[34] See Margot Backus, *The Gothic Family Romance: Heterosexuality, Child Sacrifice, and the Anglo-Irish Colonial Order* (Durham: Duke University Press, 1999).

[35] John Connolly, '*The Chill* by Ross Macdonald,' in *Books to Die For: The World's Greatest Mystery Writers on the World's Greatest Mystery Novels*, ed. John Connolly, Declan Burke, and Ellen Clair Lamb (London: Hodder, 2012), 298.

genre fiction that it can be hard to avoid. Such charges call to mind the American novelist Michael Chabon's defence of escapism in his epic novel about Jewish-American culture and the birth of the comic book on either side of World War II:

> Having lost his mother, father, brother, and grandfather, the friends and foes of his youth … the usual charge leveled against comic books, that they offered *merely an easy escape from reality*, seemed to Joe actually to be a powerful argument on their behalf. … The escape from reality was, he felt – especially right after the war – a worthy challenge. He would remember for the rest of his life a peaceful half hour spent reading a copy of *Betty and Veronica* that he had found in a service-station rest room: lying down with it under a fir tree, in a sun-slanting forest outside of Medford, Oregon, wholly absorbed into that primary-colored world of bad gags, heavy ink lines, Shakespearean farce … *That* was magic – not the apparent magic of the silk-hatted card-palmer, or the bold, brute trickery of the escape artist, but the genuine magic of art. It was a mark of how fucked-up and broken was the world – the reality – that had swallowed his home and his family that such a feat of escape, by no means easy to pull off, should remain so universally despised.[36]

Chabon's is a powerful, novel-length argument in favour of that imaginative act and its capacity for art, and is one of the guiding lights of this book. Even the slightest of novels discussed here deserves this consideration, for – while most of the novels here move in much greyer realms than the 'primary-colored world' he describes – Chabon is right: the empathy, engagement, and art in these works constitute a kind of magic, one not to be dismissed lightly.

*   *   *

The following chapters begin with an examination of crime fiction from Northern Ireland in Chapter 2. The limited critical discussion of Ireland and crime fiction has often focused on Troubles thrillers, primarily novels from the 1970s and 1980s, habitually derided as 'Troubles trash,' relatively little of which was domestically produced. Those critical discussions allow the chapter to establish the existing critical framework around the

---

[36] Michael Chabon, *The Amazing Adventures of Kavalier & Clay* (New York: Picador, 2000), 575–576.

genre in Ireland, providing a point of reference for the following chapters, and acknowledging the impact of some of the earliest thrillers. Although it addresses the roles played by groundbreaking authors like Colin Bateman, Eoin McNamee, and Eugene McEldowney, the core of the chapter focuses on work by Stuart Neville, Claire McGowan, Brian McGilloway, and Adrian McKinty. These writers have widened the genre's potential in Northern Ireland through the quality of their work and through narratives that remain rooted in place even as they hinge on matters as varied as human trafficking, abortion, economic despair, ghosts, corporate conspiracies, and corruption.

Chapter 3 follows by examining crime fiction from and about the Republic of Ireland, continuing to consider the genre's development across the island's borders. While the prevailing context for much Northern Irish crime fiction has been – or has been assumed to be – the Troubles, the parallel context in the Republic has been the Celtic Tiger, the recent period of rapid economic growth, unprecedented in the state's history. That boom does weave in and out of much contemporary crime fiction, and is the theme on which critics have often fixed. This chapter, however, also demonstrates the breadth of what these novelists have been doing formally and thematically in works that address corruption and the state, the blurred lines between organised crime and white collar crime, and uncertainty both economic and supernatural. While drawing on the full range of contemporary crime fiction from the Republic, this chapter pays close attention to Gene Kerrigan's novels, Alan Glynn's trilogy, and Declan Hughes's Ed Loy series, before concluding with an extended discussion of Tana French's work, particularly her third novel, *Faithful Place*.

Chapter 4 moves from this focus on the island's two states to a consideration of Irish crime fiction by women and of the varied roles played by women characters. This focus introduces a specific set of ethical and political considerations, many of which are at the heart of persistent debates in crime fiction studies, including the representation of violence against and by women, and the genre's relationship to its readers. The focal points here are the works of Alex Barclay, Arlene Hunt, Claire McGowan, and Jane Casey. These authors use familiar genre elements including serial killers and medical conspiracies, but also take their characters through less genre-bound narratives around mental health and domestic abuse, as well as experiences tied directly to women's experiences in Irish society, including maternity, abortion, and the regulation of sexuality through institutions like the Magdalen laundries.

Drawing on threads from earlier chapters – including supernatural narratives, corruption, and narrative uncertainty – Chapter 5 considers the scope of Irish crime fiction against the background of traditional expectations that Irish literature will represent the nation. This chapter examines Irish crime fiction's transnational aspects through the corporate thrillers of Alan Glynn, the imperial conspiracy plots of Adrian McKinty, experiences of emigration and immigration, and non-Irish characters and settings. This chapter's capstone is a discussion of one of Irish crime fiction's best-selling authors, John Connolly, whose Charlie Parker novels are set entirely outside of Ireland. The transnational elements of Connolly's novels, like those in the other novels here, require a reconsideration of what constitutes Irish literature, and provide a new understanding of how that literature intersects with international crime fiction.

REFERENCES

Ascari, Maurizio. *A Counter-History of Crime Fiction: Supernatural, Gothic, Sensational.* Basingstoke: Palgrave Macmillan, 2007.

Backus, Margot. *The Gothic Family Romance: Heterosexuality, Child Sacrifice, and the Anglo-Irish Colonial Order.* Durham: Duke University Press, 1999.

Blake, Linnie. *The Wounds of Nations: Horror Cinema, Historical Trauma, and National Identity.* Manchester: Manchester University Press, 2008.

Brannigan, John. '"For the Readies": Brendan Behan, Crime Fiction, and the Dublin Underworld.' In Meier and Ross, 'Irish Crime Since 1921': 92–105.

Burke, Declan. *Eightball Boogie.* Dublin: Lilliput, 2003. Reprint, Kindle Original, 2011.

———. ed. *Down These Green Streets: Irish Crime Writing in the 21st Century.* Dublin: Liberties, 2011.

———. *Slaughter's Hound.* Dublin: Liberties, 2012.

———. 'Raising hell in Arizona with a gripping thriller.' Review of *Here and Gone*, by Stuart Neville (pseud. Haylen Beck). *Irish Times*, 29 July 2017. https://www.irishtimes.com/culture/books/here-and-gone-review-raising-hell-in-arizona-with-a-gripping-thriller-1.3164145 (accessed 29 July 2017).

Byrne, Elaine A. *Political Corruption in Ireland, 1922–2010.* Manchester: Manchester University Press, 2012.

Cantwell, Nancy Marck. 'Hello *Dálaigh*: Peter Tremayne's Sister Fidelma.' In Mannion, *The Contemporary Irish Detective Novel*, 17–29.

Casey, Moira E. '"Built on Nothing but Bullshit and Good PR": Crime, Class Mobility, and the Irish Economy in the Novels of Tana French.' In Schaffer, 'Special Issue on Tana French': 92–102.

Chabon, Michael. *The Amazing Adventures of Kavalier & Clay*. New York: Picador, 2000.

Childers, Erskine. *The Riddle of the Sands*. London: Smith, Elder, & Co., 1903. Reprint, London: Penguin, 1999.

Clark, David. 'Emerald Noir? Contemporary Irish Crime Fiction.' In *East Meets West*, edited by Reiko Aiura, J.U. Jacobs, and J. Derrick McClure, 144–156. Newcastle: Cambridge Scholars, 2014.

Coffey, Fiona. '"The place you don't belong": Stuart Neville's Belfast.' In Mannion, *The Contemporary Irish Detective Novel*, 91–106.

Connolly, John. *Every Dead Thing*. London: Hodder & Stoughton, 1999. Reprint, New York: Simon & Schuster, 1999.

———. 'No Blacks, No Dogs, No Crime Writers: Ireland and the Mystery Genre.' In Burke, *Down These Green Streets*, 39–57.

———. '*The Chill* by Ross Macdonald.' In *Books to Die For: The World's Greatest Mystery Writers on the World's Greatest Mystery Novels*, edited by John Connolly, Declan Burke, and Ellen Clair Lamb, 297–304. London: Hodder, 2012.

Curran, John. 'Happy innocence: playing games in Golden Age detective fiction, 1920–45.' PhD thesis, Trinity College Dublin, 2014.

Dell'Amico, Carol. 'John Banville and Benjamin Black: The *Mundo*, Crime, Women.' In Meier and Ross, 'Irish Crime Since 1921': 106–120.

Donoghue, Emma. *Room*. London: Picador, 2010.

———. *Frog Music*. London: Picador, 2014.

Ennis, Garth, and Steve Dillon. *Preacher*. 9 volumes. New York: Vertigo, 1996–2001.

Fox, Andrew. 'Tiger, Tiger: The Hunt for the Great Irish Novel.' *The Daily Beast*, 2 February 2014. http://www.thedailybeast.com/articles/2014/02/28/tiger-tiger-the-hunt-for-the-great-irish-novel.html (accessed 3 June 2014).

French, Tana. *The Likeness*. New York: Penguin, 2008. Reprint, 2009.

Glynn, Alan. 'Murder in Mind: The Irish Literary Crime Novel.' In Burke, *Down These Green Streets*, 117–129.

'Golden Age of Irish Crime Fiction Celebrated at Festival.' https://www.tcd.ie/news_events/articles/golden-age-of-irish-crime-fiction-celebrated-at-festival/4465 (accessed 27 November 2013).

Green, F.L. *Odd Man Out*. London: Michael Joseph, 1945. Reprinted with introduction by Adrian McKinty. Richmond: Valancourt, 2015.

Horsley, Lee. *Twentieth-Century Crime Fiction*. Oxford: Oxford University Press, 2005.

Hourigan, Niamh. *Rule-Breakers: Why 'Being There' Trumps 'Being Fair' in Ireland*. Dublin: Gill & Macmillan, 2015.

'Irish Crime Fiction: A Festival.' Trinity College Dublin, 22–23 November 2013. http://irishcrimefiction.blogspot.ie (accessed 21 November 2013).

Jeffery, Keith, and Eunan O'Halpin. 'Ireland in Spy Fiction.' *Intelligence and National Security* 5, no. 4 (1990): 92–116.

Johnsen, Rosemary Erickson. *Contemporary Feminist Historical Crime Fiction.* Basingstoke: Palgrave Macmillan, 2006.

Kelly, Aaron. *The Thriller and Northern Ireland Since 1969: Utterly Resigned Terror.* Aldershot: Ashgate, 2005.

———. 'The Troubles with the Thriller: Northern Ireland, Political Violence and the Peace Process.' In *The Edinburgh Companion to Twentieth-Century British and American War Literature*, edited by Adam Piette and Mark Rawlinson, 508–515. Edinburgh: Edinburgh University Press, 2012.

Kilroy, Claire. *The Devil I Know.* London: Faber, 2012.

Kincaid, Andrew. '"Down These Mean Streets": The City and Critique in Contemporary Irish Noir.' *Éire-Ireland* 45, no. 1–2 (2010): 39–55.

Knight, Stephen. *Crime Fiction Since 1800: Detection, Death, Diversity.* 2nd ed. Basingstoke: Palgrave Macmillan, 2010.

Lynch, Paul. *Red Sky in Morning.* London: Quercus, 2013.

Madden, Deirdre. *One By One in the Darkness.* London: Faber, 1996.

Mannion, Elizabeth, ed. *The Contemporary Irish Detective Novel.* London: Palgrave, 2016.

———. 'A Path to Emerald Noir: The Rise of the Irish Detective Novel.' In Mannion, *The Contemporary Irish Detective Novel*, 1–15.

McCabe, Patrick. *The Butcher Boy.* London: Picador, 1992.

McInerney, Lisa. *The Glorious Heresies.* London: John Murray, 2015.

Meier, William, and Ian Campbell Ross, eds. 'Irish Crime Since 1921.' Special issue, *Éire-Ireland* 49, no. 1–2 (2014).

———. 'Editors' Introduction: Irish Crime Since 1921.' In Meier and Ross, 'Irish Crime Since 1921': 7–21.

Murray, Paul. *Skippy Dies.* London: Hamish Hamilton, 2010.

O'Brien, Flann. *The Third Policeman.* London: MacGibbon and Kee, 1967. Reprint, McLean: Dalkey Archive, 1999.

Ó Cuilleanáin, Cormac. 'Crimes and Contradictions: The Fictional City of Dublin.' In *Crime Fiction in the City: Capital Crimes*, edited by Lucy Andrew and Catherine Phelps, 47–64. Cardiff: University of Wales Press, 2013.

O'Flaherty, Liam. *The Informer.* London: Jonathan Cape, 1925. Reprint, London: Penguin, 1937.

O'Neill, Louise. *Asking For It.* London: Quercus, 2015.

O'Toole, Fintan. *Ship of Fools: How Stupidity and Corruption Sank the Celtic Tiger.* London: Faber, 2009. Reprinted and updated 2010.

———. *Enough is Enough: How to Build a New Republic.* London: Faber, 2010.

Patten, Eve. 'Contemporary Irish Fiction.' In *The Cambridge Companion to the Irish Novel*, edited by John Wilson Foster, 259–275. Cambridge: Cambridge University Press, 2006.

Patterson, Glenn. *The International*. London: Anchor, 1999. Reprint, Belfast: Blackstaff, 2008.

Pepper, Andrew. '"Hegemony Protected by the Armour of Coercion": Dashiell Hammett's *Red Harvest* and the State.' *Journal of American Studies* 44, no. 2 (May 2010): 333–349.

———. *Unwilling Executioner: Crime Fiction and the State*. Oxford: Oxford University Press, 2016.

Peterson, Shirley. 'Murder in the Ghost Estate: Crimes of the Celtic Tiger in Tana French's *Broken Harbor*.' In Schaffer, 'Special Issue on Tana French': 71–80.

Power, Kevin. *Bad Day in Blackrock*. Dublin: Lilliput, 2008. Reprint, London: Pocket, 2010.

Reddy, Maureen T. 'Contradictions in the Irish Hardboiled: Detective Fiction's Uneasy Portrayal of a New Ireland.' *New Hibernia Review* 19, no. 4 (2015): 126–140.

Rielly, Edward J., and David Robert Wooten. *The Sister Fidelma Mysteries: Essays on the Historical Novels of Peter Tremayne*. Jefferson: McFarland, 2012.

Ross, Ian Campbell. 'Introduction.' In Burke, *Down These Green Streets*, 14–35.

Ross, Ian Campbell, and Shane Mawe. 'Irish Crime Writing 1829–2011: Further Reading.' In Burke, *Down These Green Streets*, 362–368.

Schaffer, Rachel, ed. 'Special Issue on Tana French.' *Clues: A Journal of Detection* 32, no. 1 (2014).

Seltzer, Mark. From 'The Serial Killer as a Type of Person.' In *The Horror Reader*, edited by Ken Gelder, 97–107. London: Routledge, 2000.

Wallace, Arminta. 'Killer instinct: a golden age of Irish crime fiction.' *Irish Times*, 21 November 2013. http://www.irishtimes.com/culture/killer-instinct-a-golden-age-of-irish-crime-fiction-1.1601482 (accessed 25 March 2014).

CHAPTER 2

Northern Irish Crime Fiction

Studies of fiction about the Troubles and Northern Ireland form the clos-est thing to a sustained body of scholarship on Irish crime fiction. That scholarship has largely focused on fiction produced during the Troubles, and more recently on what Michael Parker calls with some understatement 'Northern Ireland's difficult transition towards "normalisation"' amidst the post-Good Friday Agreement peace process.[1] Though 'the Troubles' has been used to describe varied historical periods and events, the term most frequently refers to the sectarian and paramilitary violence from 1969 (when the British Army was sent in to police Northern Ireland) to 1998 (when the Good Friday Agreement was signed). Despite this seem-ingly neat span, the Troubles were a complex, shifting set of events with deep roots. These roots can be seen most immediately in the civil rights movement and protest marches in Derry on 5 October 1968 and at Burntollet on 4 January 1969, more distantly in events from the Anglo-Irish War of 1919–1921 and the partitioning of the island into Northern Ireland and the Irish Free State, and still further back through a long,

---

[1] Michael Parker, *Northern Irish Literature, 1975–2006, Volume 2: The Imprint of History* (London: Palgrave, 2007), 202. In another essay, Parker and Liam Harte similarly argue that the 'peace process … opened up new artistic as well as political perspectives on the sectarian violence and religious bigotry which had plagued the province for a quarter of a century.' Harte and Parker, 'Reconfiguring Identities: Recent Northern Irish Fiction,' in *Contemporary Irish Fiction: Themes, Tropes, Theories*, ed. Liam Harte and Michael Parker (Basingstoke: Macmillan, 2000), 232.

© The Author(s) 2018
B. Cliff, *Irish Crime Fiction*, Crime Files,
https://doi.org/10.1057/978-1-137-56188-6_2

ornately complex history. Ireland has seen much prologue, and the present may not prove to be epilogue yet, but the convergence of factors that resulted in the most recent Troubles saw its clearest peak during the years 1969–1998. The genre fiction produced during this era, with the sharply critical reception it often received, is an essential starting point for discussing the subsequent growth in Irish crime fiction, north and south of the border, with which this book is concerned. The novels that emerged from this period at times gave crime fiction such a desperately bad name in Irish Studies that it has often been difficult for subsequent Northern Irish crime writers to be read in their own right outside of that very long shadow. In this regard, if the burdens placed by critical habit on contemporary Irish writers – the legacy of Joyce, for example – have a Northern equivalent, it may not be in Joyce or in Sam Hanna Bell, but in 'Troubles trash,' which has imposed a lens that Northern Irish crime fiction is still being asked to refocus.

GENRE FICTION'S STATUS AMIDST THE TROUBLES

Northern Irish crime fiction often blurs the lines between present and past, taking place in a kind of grey zone that highlights the complex relationship between an enduring past and contemporary society and culture, as Emilie Pine has demonstrated.[2] At the same time, although much literature from Northern Ireland during the Troubles engaged to varying degrees with that conflict, even when it did not clearly do so critics nonetheless found persistent ways to frame literary meaning with reference to the Troubles. As Eamonn Hughes charges, this

> habit of analogy and allegory hunting … represents a sustained and communal effort to make any piece of writing be 'about' the North. This poem is a translation from Anglo-Saxon; this novel is about a composer, this play is adapted from the ancient Greek: fine, now let's work out what they have to say about the situation in Northern Ireland.[3]

---

[2] Emilie Pine, *The Politics of Irish Memory: Performing Remembrance in Contemporary Irish Culture* (Basingstoke: Palgrave Macmillan, 2011). See particularly her chapter 'Embodied Memory: Performing the 1980–1 Hunger Strikes,' 100–126.

[3] Eamonn Hughes, 'Evasion, Engagement, Exploitation,' 30th Anniversary Special Issue, *Fortnight*, September 2000, 55.

In this context, with meaning tied ineluctably to the representations of Northern Ireland, particular criticism was levied against 'Troubles trash.'[4] Though it has also been applied to avowedly 'literary' fiction's representations of the Troubles, whether or not those representations drew on genre elements from crime or thriller novels, this term is most often taken as synonymous with Troubles thrillers of the 1970s and 1980s, many of which were produced by journalists covering the Troubles for overseas publications, and later by former members of the British armed forces.[5] Frequently successful at the time, many of these have since lost much individual place in the culture, generally possessing only a collective weight.

The term 'Troubles trash' most often encompasses novels that depict political commitment as inimical to democratic society, that attribute the violence to the incurably atavistic inhabitants of the island, or that show scant regard for local differences and particular histories. In Jack Higgins's commercially successful Liam Devlin novels, for example, discussed more fully in Chapter 5, the lead character Devlin is depicted as a 'good' republican of the old variety, as evidenced by his decision to leave 'the movement' when the Troubles become too indiscriminately violent for him. Such characterisations allow a novel to draw on the romanticism of a previous generation's nationalism while holding itself at a comfortable (and comforting) remove from the present. That present is in turn reduced to a mere landscape of blood-ridden ideologues, a landscape in which all politics are cynical, hollow, and opposed to ordinary life. In the form of such novels, 'Troubles trash' has seemed at best incapable of representing the complex ambiguities and particularities of Northern Ireland.

'Troubles trash' has been perhaps most severely judged, however, when it takes more militarised forms, the success of which is epitomised by Tom Clancy's lurid bestseller *Patriot Games* (1987) or by some of Andy McNab's work. These novels, along with a host of less spectacularly

---

[4] J. Bowyer Bell has been credited with originating this phrase with his article 'The Troubles as Trash,' *Hibernia*, 20 January 1978: 22. See Caroline Magennis, *Sons of Ulster: Masculinities in the Contemporary Northern Irish Novel* (Oxford: Peter Lang, 2010), 59n5.

[5] For a further discussion of the shift from an initial wave of novels by journalists to later works by former soldiers, see Aaron Kelly, 'The Troubles with the Thriller: Northern Ireland, Political Violence and the Peace Process,' in *The Edinburgh Companion to Twentieth-Century British and American War Literature*, ed. Adam Piette and Mark Rawlinson (Edinburgh: Edinburgh University Press, 2012), 509–511. In his earlier book *The Thriller and Northern Ireland Since 1969: Utterly Resigned Terror* (Aldershot: Ashgate, 2005), Kelly offers a valuably detailed bibliography of Troubles thrillers.

popular books, have been charged with actively distorting those particularities in the service of regressive ideologies, or as treating Northern Ireland like a canvas on which to work out the wider anxieties of American and English writers and readers.

These are patterns of representation that Irish Studies scholars have explored and dissected in detail. In particular, as Marisol Morales-Ladrón notes, such texts have been faulted for 'offering a stagnant and reductive version of the dynamics of the "Troubles", one that bases its premises on clear-cut boundaries between opposing poles with regard to nationality, religion or politics.'[6] These polarities, critics have repeatedly argued, not only misrepresented Northern Ireland in 'unreflective' ways but in doing so revealed and reinforced fundamental misunderstandings, as Eve Patten has charged:

> Recourse to the juxtaposition of vulnerable individuals with an amorphous and superficially drawn terrorist presence has supplanted the novel's function of critique with a kind of literary compensation: consolatory images which provide for an unreflective but consensual response have obliterated the need to examine the complexity and ambiguity of social conflict, while the elevation of individual sufferings has largely obscured the exploration of community, identity and motivation charted by a previous generation of writers.[7]

Absent more substantial explorations, that is, fiction about the Troubles too readily resulted in texts in which 'Terrorist violence is treated metaphysically, as the manifestation of evil and madness,'[8] or texts that seemed

---

[6] Marisol Morales-Ladrón, '"Troubling" Thrillers: Between Politics and Popular Fiction in the novels of Benedict Kiely, Brian Moore and Colin Bateman,' *Estudios Irlandeses* 1 (2006): 58. Morales-Ladrón goes on to suggest – with a long list of examples – that 'scholars almost unanimously acknowledge the thriller as the most popular form in Northern Irish literature' ('"Troubling Thrillers,"' 59). Despite this, she focuses her analysis on thrillers not by dedicated genre writers but by 'literary' authors, whose 'thrillers have been concerned with the exploration of moral, psychological and social preoccupations that were ignored in the most popular and traditional mode' ('"Troubling Thrillers,"' 60).

[7] Eve Patten, 'Fiction in conflict: Northern Ireland's prodigal novelists,' in *Peripheral Visions: Images of Nationhood in Contemporary British Fiction*, ed. Ian A. Bell (Cardiff: University of Wales Press, 1995), 132.

[8] Elmer Kennedy-Andrews, 'Shadows of the Gunmen: The Troubles Novel,' in *Irish Fiction Since the 1960s: A Collection of Critical Essays*, ed. Elmer Kennedy-Andrews (Gerrards Cross: Colin Smythe, 2006), 100.

content 'to confine their explanations to psychosexual motives.'[9] Such metaphysical and 'psychosexual' narrative patterns frequently relied on more than a hint of dark, pre-rational atavism, which served not just as atmosphere but as a substitute for explanation, as something that foreclosed further engagement.

Indeed, questions of engagement run throughout scholarship on Troubles fiction, giving that scholarship a certain energy, but an energy that at times has precluded considering other patterns in the literature. Eamonn Hughes has addressed this phenomenon, arguing that 'the literary world of the North has in many ways been an echo chamber of wider political debates.'[10] Within that chamber, a very few positions – 'evasion, engagement, exploitation' – have been 'the basis of all literary debate [in Northern Ireland] for the past thirty years,' as a result of which 'we have demanded from writers ... that they function at a mimetic level.'[11] Faced by such demands, aesthetic and political criteria can readily converge. Bernard MacLaverty's *Cal* (1983), for example, is often cited as one of the first canonical novels about the Troubles, and almost as often charged with embodying many of the literary tropes and political conceptions identified by critics as acutely problematic, a charge Joe Cleary distils sharply:

> The paralysing ambivalence that informs *Cal* is ultimately derived from its own confessional conceptualisation of the conflict in Northern Ireland as a zero-sum game of all-or-nothing territorial control, the only imaginable outcome of which is either a resigned acceptance of the Northern state (whatever one's reservations) or its violent overthrow in the name of a United Ireland. That the conflict might be susceptible to some more emancipatory political resolution is something the novel seems unable to imagine.[12]

Although Richard Haslam has mounted a thoughtful and perceptive defence of *Cal* from precisely these charges, Cleary's argument remains an incisive and emblematic example of politically engaged criticism taking

---

[9] Kennedy-Andrews, 'Shadows of the Gunmen,' 87. See also Elmer Kennedy-Andrews, 'The Novel and the Northern Troubles,' in *The Cambridge Companion to the Irish Novel*, ed. John Wilson Foster (Cambridge: Cambridge University Press, 2006), 238–258.

[10] Hughes, 'Evasion,' 54.

[11] Hughes, 'Evasion,' 55.

[12] Joe Cleary, *Literature, Partition and the Nation-State: Culture and Conflict in Ireland, Israel and Palestine* (Cambridge: Cambridge University Press, 2002), 129.

issue with Troubles clichés.[13] The connection in Troubles fiction between these modes, the aesthetic and the political, is made still more directly by Keith Jeffery and Eunan O'Halpin: 'for the most part, the Northern Ireland problem has been simplistically perceived as a violent struggle between the IRA (or some analogous republican group) and the British. This perception undermines the veracity of Irish spy novels as much as it has, at times, handicapped security policy in Northern Ireland.'[14] Jeffery and O'Halpin extend this connection strikingly, suggesting that the depiction of paramilitary 'violence ... as misguided, mindless and counter-productive ... ignores the fact that in Ireland this century politically-motivated violence, or the threat of it, has undoubtedly paid political dividends on a number of occasions.'[15] As these critical examples demonstrate, over decades of novels that have coincided with and depicted the Troubles, crime fiction and its subgenres in Northern Ireland seemed to become inseparable from several problematic patterns of representation, and indeed inseparable from the Troubles themselves.

RE-READING THE THRILLER AND NORTHERN IRELAND

Aaron Kelly has described the earliest 'attempts at depicting the conflict in the North through the thriller form' as ranging 'from the more morally serious to the meretriciously voyeuristic and the plain ridiculous,' arguing that these works established

> the prevailing terms for a mode of representing the North. Perhaps because most of the early thriller writers were British journalists, the emphasis tended to be upon explaining a strange, hostile environment to a curious or anxious external readership. ... there is equally a strong sense in which such representations in fact merely partake in the continuance of an existing sedimentation of British discourses about Ireland stretching back hundreds of years. ... In this very specific usage of aspects of the thriller form, therefore, there is a conflation between certain elements of the genre ... and a dominant

---

[13] Richard Haslam, 'Critical Reductionism and Bernard MacLaverty's *Cal*,' in *Representing the Troubles: Texts & Images, 1970–2000*, ed. Brian Cliff and Éibhear Walshe (Dublin: Four Courts, 2004), 39–54.

[14] Keith Jeffery and Eunan O'Halpin, 'Ireland in Spy Fiction,' *Intelligence and National Security* 5, no. 4 (1990): 103.

[15] Jeffery and O'Halpin, 'Ireland in Spy Fiction,' 112–113.

British view of the unravelling social conflict in Northern Ireland as the mere product of the ongoing, recidivist irrationality of the Irish.[16]

As Kelly suggests with this connection between representations and the readership for which they are produced, crime fiction during the early stages of the Troubles cemented an enduring association between that genre, Northern Ireland, and regressive aesthetic-ideological patterns (not least the image of the backwards Irish, mired in an atavistic violence that is outside history and therefore not subject to political intervention). This association still colours the genre's status in Irish Studies, long after crime fiction has developed considerably more nuanced ways of writing about Northern Ireland.

Despite the many and varied aesthetic and ideological shortcomings in these early works, from their 'disavowal of human agency in the North' to their 'image of the North as interminably traumatic,'[17] Kelly insists on the genre's potential, persuasively making the case that 'The thriller – reputedly the most throwaway of literatures – is actually the monumental form of social complexity,' despite its 'reactionary façade.'[18] The genre conveys this complexity, Kelly argues, not *despite* but *because of* its focus on crime, broadly understood, which

> in the thriller form becomes 'a connective tissue' through which to uncover concealed relationships and hidden attachments within late capitalism and the liberal democratic state. ... order is not reassuringly restored in the thriller – not least in radical thrillers which consciously strive to uncover the corruption of the state but also, just as importantly, even in the more reactionary thriller which discloses the covert violence of the democracy it would nominally defend.[19]

Here, as also in *The Thriller and Northern Ireland Since 1969: Utterly Resigned Terror* (2005) and various articles, Kelly's scholarship comprises both the most rigorously detailed critique of thrillers in Northern Ireland *and* the most sustained, suggestive defence of those novels' potential. Kelly is not alone in identifying this potential for the genre at large: as

---

[16] Kelly, 'The Troubles with the Thriller,' 508.
[17] Kelly, *The Thriller and Northern Ireland*, 147, 154.
[18] Kelly, *The Thriller and Northern Ireland*, 5.
[19] Kelly, 'The Troubles with the Thriller,' 513. Kelly is quoting Peter Messent, ed., *Criminal Proceedings: The Contemporary American Crime Novel* (London: Pluto, 1995), 1.

Andrew Pepper has detailed, critics including Mark Knight and Clare Clarke have taken related views, as has Pepper himself.[20] It is rather in Kelly's application of this extended argument to otherwise largely neglected or dismissed Irish materials that his work on crime fiction and Northern Ireland has made its most signal and lasting contribution, with a balance and a nuance that still all too few critics have brought to considering Irish forms of the genre.

LITERARY CONTEXTS FOR CRIME FICTION IN NORTHERN IRELAND

Further complicating crime fiction's status, the mid-1960s onward in Northern Ireland was not only politically turbulent, but also a cultural and social context within which critical attention and literary engagement focused on poetry. Good reasons for this focus were not hard to find amidst the still remarkable emergence of Northern poets like Seamus Heaney, Michael Longley, and Derek Mahon as well as several generations of younger poets who have followed, beginning with Paul Muldoon, Ciaran Carson, and Medbh McGuckian. If such poets were literature's accomplished eldest child, drama was the slightly more problematic middle child, despite the work of playwrights like Christina Reid, Stewart Parker, Brian Friel, and others associated to varying degrees with the Field Day enterprise. Overshadowed by poetry and drama as the prevailing genres for troubled times, fiction was the youngest sibling, left to fend for itself.

Despite peers in other genres in Northern Ireland, then, crime writers were for some time writing in relative isolation, with few domestic exceptions. The novelist Brian McGilloway has remarked, for example, that crime fiction about Northern Ireland remained largely journalistic through the early 1990s, up to which point it was still for the most part either not produced by Irish writers or even at its best overlooked amidst a crush of inferior material.[21] This can be seen with two of the earliest Northern Irish crime writers to have still active careers, Colin Bateman and Eoin

---

[20] Andrew Pepper, *Unwilling Executioner: Crime Fiction and the State* (Oxford: Oxford University Press, 2016), 110.

[21] 'Crime Fiction and Contemporary Ireland,' panel discussion with Paul Charles, Declan Hughes, Gene Kerrigan, Brian McGilloway, Niamh O'Connor, and Louise Phillips, 'Irish Crime Fiction: A Festival,' Trinity College Dublin, 23 November 2013.

McNamee. Among Troubles novels – indeed among Irish crime fiction full stop – Bateman's Dan Starkey is an unusually long-running series character, appearing in novels from *Divorcing Jack* (1995) to *The Dead Pass* (2014). The Starkey books' assertively satirical mode makes for a distinctive contribution to the genre but has also veiled some of their depth. John Connolly has noted as much, suggesting that Bateman 'recognised the tragic absurdity of what was taking place, with the emphasis on the absurd, and used that recognition to power his fiction. As with all satirists, there were times when the balance between rage and humour, between the need to confront the reality of violence and the satirist's desire to mock all involved in it, were less than perfect ... but it was brave and untypical nonetheless.'[22] One of the more fully developed assessments of Bateman's work is that of Laura Pelaschiar, who argues that by his 1995 debut Troubles thrillers were 'ripe for Bateman's comic and oblique refunctionalization of its formal elements and conventions.'[23] This praise is despite her lack of surprise 'that – given all the dangers intrinsic to this literary genre [the Troubles thriller], which seems to imprison its practitioners in all sorts of rhetorical and political traps as inescapable as the mechanisms which preside over its existence – most critics have found themselves up in arms against it.'[24] As this example suggests, even when Northern Irish crime writers were taken seriously by critics, individual writers were often isolated and read as the exception that proves the rule about 'Troubles trash.'

Like Bateman's, Eoin McNamee's reputation may have suffered from appearing ahead of his time in a literary context in which crime fiction had not really begun to coalesce as a genre on the island. This difficulty is compounded by his ambiguous blending of fact and fiction, which in some ways shares more with Truman Capote's *In Cold Blood* (1966) than with Bateman. An example of the difficult line that crime fiction in Northern Ireland is sometimes made to walk can be seen in the responses to McNamee's first full-length novel, *Resurrection Man* (1994). This revolves around the Shankill Butchers, a brutal group of Loyalist killers who were active through the late 1970s (although, as Kelly notes, 'the

[22] John Connolly, 'No Blacks, No Dogs, No Crime Writers: Ireland and the Mystery Genre,' in *Down These Green Streets: Irish Crime Writing in the 21st Century*, ed. Declan Burke (Dublin: Liberties Press, 2011), 51–52.

[23] Laura Pelaschiar, 'Troubles and Freedom Fighters in Northern Irish Fiction,' *The Irish Review* 40–41 (Winter 2009): 60.

[24] Pelaschiar, 'Troubles and Freedom Fighters,' 58.

most immediate context' for the novel's reception was the complex and tense build-up to the 1994 ceasefires, a critical stage in the peace process).[25] McNamee's novel has provoked complex and varying reactions. Where 'Troubles trash' was condemned for being subliterary exploitation, *Resurrection Man* has been charged with being too literary, too overtly *written*, as in Peggy O'Brien's review, with its concern that 'The sheer sensuality of the style, can feel like a guilty pleasure for author and reader' and her suggestion that 'maybe toning [McNamee's] rhetoric down would serve his morally tricky material more responsibly.'[26] The reception afforded McNamee's novel – too journalistic *and* too aestheticised – distils crime fiction's ambivalent location in Irish canons, particularly in Northern Ireland.

In his own fiction, most successfully in his remarkable novel *The International* (1999), Glenn Patterson offers an artistic fluidity as a curative alternative to sectarian politics' ideological rigidity. The claustrophobic intensity of a thriller can register as partaking of that rigidity, and in discussing *Resurrection Man* Patterson articulates an uneasy tension around the genre. His critique of what he sees as the novel's aestheticised violence has been quoted widely, as has his argument that the novel depicts Belfast as 'a contained, determined city, stewing in the bitterness of age-old hatreds, explicable wholly in terms of a self-induced, self-perpetuating psychopathology.'[27] Less often quoted are the sentences immediately following:

> Then again … Writing this article at the end of a week in which five more people have been murdered, four by loyalist terrorists, there might be said to be some justification for claiming that nothing has changed. … Perhaps there is indeed a need, now more than ever, for fictions which confront the violence head-on, which seek to offer insights into the minds of the terrorists.[28]

In this, the essay's hinge paragraph, Patterson acknowledges that Northern Ireland in September 1994 may not yet have changed as much as it had

[25] Kelly, *The Thriller and Northern Ireland*, 73n24.

[26] Peggy O'Brien, 'Unbalanced Styles,' review of *Walking the Dog and Other Stories*, by Bernard MacLaverty, *Resurrection Man,* by Eoin McNamee, and *Nothing is Black*, by Deirdre Madden, *Irish Review* 16 (Autumn-Winter 1994): 150, 149.

[27] Glenn Patterson, 'Butchers' Tools,' *Fortnight*, September 1994, 43.

[28] Patterson, 'Butchers' Tools,' 44.

seemed, in which case a novel like *Resurrection Man* is 'Perhaps' not mired in 'psychopathology' but engaging meaningfully with the city around it.[29] This is some way off from praising *Resurrection Man*, and yet Patterson's essay concisely enacts the persistent difficulties – ethical, political, aesthetic – surrounding genre fiction about Northern Ireland. Stark in 1994, such difficulties continue two decades later to inform the critical response to Northern Irish crime fiction.

CHANGES IN NORTHERN IRISH CRIME FICTION

Bateman and McNamee's Troubles-era novels reflect the early stages of a sustained effort to produce crime fiction in a setting as radically charged as Northern Ireland. Both writers were instrumental in enabling the development of Northern Irish crime fiction, which over the past two decades has demonstrated a quite different range of capacities than a term like 'Troubles trash' could have predicted. Of course, Irish crime fiction touching on the Troubles is by no means exclusive to Northern novels. Mary O'Donnell's *Where They Lie* (2014) is just one example of Troubles-themed mysteries continuing both to appear from and to take place in the Republic. Various splinter groups appear in other crime fiction from the Republic, where they take roles both passing and central. These splinter groups are more likely to be depicted as glorified gangs, hard men around whom other criminals tread lightly, as in several Gene Kerrigan novels, particularly *Dark Times in the City* (2009), though they play a diminished role in *The Rage* (2011) as well, where they are depicted as ridden with Special Branch informers. In Declan Hughes's fourth Ed Loy novel, *All the Dead Voices* (2009), the plot depicts conflicts in Dublin between 'ordinary decent criminals,' the INLA, and elements of the IRA, allegedly washed-up and starting to look like an easy mark. Conversely, it is not just

---

[29] Kelly suggests such meaning is the case in both *Resurrection Man* and McNamee's later work *The Ultras* (2004), novels in which 'crime is found not only amongst aberrant individuals but at the centre of the British state and its policy in Ireland as the government and secret services orchestrate a hidden network of violence, coercion, illegality and racketeering. ... This guise of the crime genre – the conspiracy thriller – therefore disrupts the conventional critical account of order disrupted by rogue criminality' ('The Troubles with the Thriller,' 513). Elsewhere, Kelly articulates a persuasive sense of *Resurrection Man*'s potential at more length, suggesting that it 'conveys how the city defeats the imposition of such a tribal cartography, setting it apart from the more reactionary thriller's criminalized zones of otherness' (*The Thriller and Northern Ireland*, 100).

authors from the Republic who depict the Troubles outside of Northern Ireland. Northern Irish writers also follow the Troubles' tendrils elsewhere: Davey Campbell in Stuart Neville's *The Twelve* is at first embedded under cover with a splinter group in the Republic, for example, while Adrian McKinty's *The Dead Yard* (2006) features a group based in the US, with the aptly self-aggrandising name The Sons of Cuchulainn.

Pushing the settings outside of Northern Ireland is one way that these and other novels connect the Troubles to a much larger framework of politics, violence, and capital that exceeds local boundaries. As these connections suggest, Northern Irish crime fiction may seem at first to paint on a small canvas, but it does so with a broad palette. Indeed, restricted neither to the Troubles nor to Northern Ireland itself, Northern Irish crime fiction is thematically and contextually diverse. This range can be seen in the novels that emerged after the Good Friday Agreement. In 1998, the Agreement set in place the conditions for what was hoped would be a durable peace process and for the power-sharing arrangement that has returned the governing of Northern Ireland to local hands for much of the intervening time, particularly after the St. Andrew's Agreement of 2006, Gerard Brennan has argued.[30] Even with their gaps and shortcomings, the ceasefires and the Agreements did clear a space in which on-going political violence no longer claimed quite so much air. This, in turn, pointed towards ways that different kinds of crime fiction could more readily be written in and about Northern Ireland, as the peace process's uneven development opened various avenues for considering corruption, the costs of compromises and of blind eyes turned, for depicting all the endless varieties of crime and human frailty. At the same time, Northern Ireland's own history has of course not disappeared: even now, Stuart Neville has remarked, it can be inordinately difficult to write about crime in Northern Ireland on any scale other than the purely individual without somehow writing about paramilitaries of some persuasion (his recent decision to publish international thrillers under the pen name Haylen Beck may in part reflect this).[31]

Despite this difficulty, in recent decades Northern Irish crime fiction has separated itself from 'Troubles trash' through, frankly, better writing as well as by taking a wider range of paths than previously seemed available,

---

[30] Gerard Brennan, 'The Truth Commissioners,' in Burke, *Down These Green Streets*, 201.

[31] Stuart Neville, panel discussion with Elizabeth Mannion, Declan Hughes, John Connolly, Fiona Coffey, and Brian Cliff, Glucksman Ireland House, New York University, 13 September 2016.

including 'ordinary decent crime' narratives. (The term 'ordinary decent criminals' has some roots in a 1972 attempt to quell an early hunger strike by granting paramilitary prisoners in Northern Irish jails a special category status distinguishing them from 'ordinary decent criminals,' or 'ODCs.'[32]) Along with fiction that directly engages with matters of the Troubles and the peace process – including books by Neville, Bateman, McKinty, McGilloway, and others – numerous novels reflect this 'ordinary decent crime fiction,' which Eamonn Hughes notes began amidst the peace process to take the place of 'the paranoid thriller, the dominant form of Troubles fiction.'[33] McKinty has similarly suggested that setting 'ordinary decent crime' fiction in Belfast was a way of 'giving Belfast something every other place in the world is allowed to have – a straightforward mystery novel with a sympathetic but dysfunctional detective, red herrings, a taut plot, and a classic well-crafted denouement.'[34] In such a light, regular crime thus becomes in fiction a sign of peace, perhaps perversely but nonetheless clearly and understandably. In Claire McGowan's Paula Maguire series, for example, her retired father – one of a statistically unlikely number of Catholic Royal Ulster Constabulary (RUC) officers in Northern Irish crime fiction – triggers an explicit reflection on this change, and the comparatively comfortable banality of ordinary decent crime: 'After so long in the RUC, every day that he woke up and someone wasn't dead was a victory for PJ. Every political gaffe story and cat-up-tree novelty item was proof they now lived in a sane society, where murder wasn't a way of life.'[35] Among other novels that engage to varying degrees with crime outside of

[32] See Rachel Oppenheimer, '"Inhuman Conditions Prevailing": The Significance of the Dirty Protest in the Irish Republican Prison War, 1978–1981,' in 'Irish Crime Since 1921,' ed. William Meier and Ian Campbell Ross, special issue, *Éire-Ireland* 49, no. 1–2 (Spring-Summer 2014): 142–163, particularly 146–147. In the same journal issue, Dale Montgomery considers the partly subjective nature of this distinction in '"Helping the Guards": Illegal Displays and Blueshirt Criminality, 1932–1936,' in Meier and Ross, 'Irish Crime Since 1921': 22–43, particularly 43.
[33] Eamonn Hughes, 'Limbo,' review of Glenn Patterson, *That Which Was* and Eoin McNamee, *The Ultras, Irish Review* 33 (2005): 139.
[34] Adrian McKinty, 'Odd Men Out,' in Burke, *Down These Green Streets*, 103.
[35] Claire McGowan, *The Lost* (London: Headline, 2013), 282. McGowan's series can generally be quite deft at depicting this normality and its particular stresses, including restrained details of recessionary times familiar across the entire island over the past ten years: 'Five days to Christmas. The ragged edge of cheer in a town with no money. Everywhere Christmas clubs; how will we pay for this plastic tat, where will we find the cash? Keep smiling for the kids. Red sale signs already in the shops, and an air of thin despair, flimsy and bright as tinsel.' Claire McGowan, *The Dead Ground* (London: Headline, 2014), 324.

the Troubles are Catriona King's Craig series, Neville's ongoing Serena Flanagan series, and a range of recent novels, including Gerard Brennan's *Wee Rockets* (2012), Kelly Creighton's *The Bones of It* (2015), and Steve Cavanagh's Eddie Flynn series, which takes place entirely abroad with little substantive reference to Northern Ireland or the Republic.[36] Brian McGilloway has offered one explanation for why so many post-Agreement novels are making such choices: depicting ordinary decent crime or not setting novels in Northern Ireland – where 'people would be looking to see how I was presenting the PSNI [Police Service of Northern Ireland]' – can avoid the insistent allegorical readings Hughes and others have described.[37] In avoiding the pressure of those readings, these ordinary decent crime novels cover much of the same range as do their counterparts from the Republic: economic boom and crash, corruption across all levels of the state, gangland violence, human trafficking, and organised crime.

Even when they focus on ordinary decent crime rather than paramilitary violence, some novels set during the Troubles at first glance may seem to conform to expectations for Northern crime fiction, but these novels are not naïve about the representational patterns, pitfalls, and problems discussed by Kelly, Patten, and others. On the contrary, a novel like Adrian McKinty's Edgar Award-winning *Rain Dogs* (2016) – the fifth of six to date in his Sean Duffy series – shows how very aware of these clichés Northern Irish crime fiction has become. McKinty's protagonist Duffy makes several direct references to these patterns, often with a characteristic facetiousness, as when he tells his girlfriend – a pop lit graduate student – that by leaving him she would 'be contributing to a stereotype which from your literary theory essays I know you hate. The policeman with dependency issues *and* girlfriend trouble. Come on, cliché city.'[38] Despite his

[36] Though it is not crime fiction as such, the Northern writer Garth Ennis's graphic novel *Preacher* (New York: Vertigo, 1995–2000, 75 issues collected in nine trade paperbacks) is almost entirely set outside Ireland, including only one Irish character, Cassidy, who was turned into a vampire when on the run from the GPO in the aftermath of the Easter Rising.

[37] 'McGilloway on the Run,' *Derry Journal*, 14 March 2008, quoted in Carol Baraniuk, 'Negotiating Borders: Inspector Devlin and Shadows of the Past,' in *The Contemporary Irish Detective Novel*, ed. Elizabeth Mannion (Basingstoke: Palgrave, 2016), 83.

[38] Adrian McKinty, *Rain Dogs* (Amherst: Seventh Street, 2016), 24. Duffy shows himself sufficiently aware of crime fiction tropes and precedents to cite them over the course of the series, including John Dickson Carr's Gideon Fell, mentioned as Duffy encounters a number of seeming locked room mysteries like those in which Carr's Fell featured. Duffy is also fully aware of the RUC's status with the public, despite being unsure why one man particularly 'disliked me. Sure, everybody hated the peelers. We were lazy and crap at best, corrupt and sectarian at worst ... but at least I was trying to solve the murder of his brother, wasn't I?' Adrian McKinty, *I Hear the Sirens in the Street* (London: Serpent's Tail, 2013), 246.

banter here, later in the same novel Duffy addresses to the reader much less playful remarks on the same topic: '*Yeah, I know what you're thinking: gun battle, rain, Ireland. But you don't know. You have no idea.*'[39] Over the course of the series, Duffy – the kind of cop who uses a word like 'Sontagian' but applies it to a thug's 'grey mohawk'[40] – develops not just the weariness of middle age, but a deeper sense of grim despair, borne of this familiarity. Although he recognises and seeks to escape this – whether through cocaine liberated from the station's evidence storage, or more healthily through his relationship with his girlfriend Beth – his growing awareness of an enmeshed web of bad actors builds throughout the series, moving across Northern Irish society, and in doing so reflects broader patterns in Irish crime fiction.

STUART NEVILLE'S *THE TWELVE*

Some of these patterns, including similarly bad actors, are prominent in Stuart Neville's *The Twelve*, among the most spectacular examples of post-Agreement crime fiction that addresses the aftermath of the Troubles.[41] This novel has been critiqued by some reviewers for what Laura Pelaschiar has termed its overabundance of clichés, which she asserts make the novel little more than 'a rehash' of 'Troubles trash.'[42] Indeed, on its surface *The Twelve* does draw on those tropes, and does contain familiar genre elements. As Fiona Coffey suggests, however, *The Twelve* clearly uses those tropes in unusual and complicating ways, allowing it to accomplish something quite different indeed. 'Although Neville operates within many of the typical conventions of the Troubles thriller, he also undermines nor-

---

[39] McKinty, *Rain*, 251.

[40] Adrian McKinty, *The Cold Cold Ground* (London: Serpent's Tail, 2012), 178.

[41] Even the title invites discussion: the original – the one under which it appeared in the US – was *The Ghosts of Belfast* (Stuart Neville, seminar discussion with the author and students, 'Imagining Ireland IV' undergraduate seminar, Trinity College Dublin, 23 November 2012). The sceptical instinct might be to assume that a less-discreet title was forced on the author by American publishers looking to reach Irish-American fetishists, and a long enough history of such marketing questions can indeed be traced, as discussed by Stephanie Rains, Diane Negra, and others. Neville's, however, is a more interesting and (within Irish Studies) less familiar case of UK publishers backing away from overt Belfast novels, in deference to their understanding of what their audience will buy, a point Brennan has also discussed ('Truth Commissioners,' 205).

[42] Laura Pelaschiar, '*The Twelve* (2009) by Stuart Neville,' *Estudios Irlandeses* 5 (2009): 196.

mative representations of the post-Agreement North and blurs distinctions between traditional binaries. … Far from showing an essentialist viewpoint locked into Troubles stereotypes,' she suggests, Neville depicts 'a symbiotic ecosystem of crime and policing where the two collapse into each other.'[43] In this, Neville's work reflects the 'increasing interpenetration between the police, informers, and criminals, and an increasing symbiosis of crime, big business and the reinforced state' that Kelly saw as part of the radical thriller's potential in Northern Ireland, and that other scholars of international crime fiction have similarly identified.[44]

The Twelve centres on Gerry Fegan, a former IRA hard man with a still-fearsome reputation who has been recently released under the terms of the Good Friday Agreement.[45] Although in this he may resemble the trope of the guilt-ridden, drink-sodden protagonist who nonetheless has well-preserved skills just beneath the surface, Gerry is haunted to the point of madness by the ghosts of twelve people for whose deaths he has some measure of responsibility. Gradually, the twelve drive him to kill the other people culpable in their deaths, killings that are central to the novel's ethical complexity, even as Gerry seeks to protect Marie, a woman he has met, and her daughter Ellen. As the novel unfolds, Davey Campbell – the British agent infiltrated into republican paramilitary groups earlier in the novel – is set on Fegan's trail to stop the murders, in the interests of both the republican political leadership and the British government, all of whom think Fegan simply mad.

It is essential to note, however, that these ghosts are in fact ghosts: they are not Fegan's feverish imaginations, not his guilt taking the form of the Freudian uncanny returned, and not just madness. Quite clearly, Fegan *is* feverish, he *is* guilt-ridden, and he *does* at least flirt with what looks very

---

[43] Fiona Coffey, '"The place you don't belong": Stuart Neville's Belfast,' in Mannion, *The Contemporary Irish Detective Novel*, 104.

[44] Kelly, *The Thriller and Northern Ireland*, 159. See also Pepper, who argues 'that the development of crime fiction as a genre is bound up with the consolidation of the modern, bureaucratic state; that is to say, with the policing, governmental, and judicial apparatuses set up to enforce law,' a dynamic that eventually includes 'The interchangeability of crime and business' in 'the flexible, networked, deregulated world of the neoliberal economy' (*Unwilling Executioner*, 1, 237).

[45] Stuart Neville, *The Twelve* (London: Harvill Secker, 2009). When Fegan bribes sailors to stow him away so he can escape Belfast at the end of the novel, however, the narrative pointedly notes that 'They had rough hands and knowing eyes; they had no fear of someone like Fegan,' as if to suggest that the hardest man in Belfast may still be a long way off from the hardest man anywhere (Neville, *Twelve*, 324).

much indeed like madness. The book even provides a clinical diagnosis of sorts from a prison psychologist with whom Fegan discussed his experiences: 'Dr Brady said it was guilt. A manifestation, he called it. Fegan wondered why people seldom called things by their real names.'[46] The novel is however at pains to make it clear that the twelve are actual, genuine ghosts, and that Fegan – who, we are told more than once, 'used to see things. People. I used to talk to them'[47] – is not delusional but literally haunted. The sequel, *Collusion* (2010), makes this even more explicit, but that is not an after-the-fact emphasis. Rather, several moments in *The Twelve* suggest that the ghosts have a reality, a presence: they warn Gerry he is being watched by Campbell, and at the novel's climax Campbell also sees some of the twelve for whose death he was responsible – 'tattooed men. They grinned at Campbell and he wanted to scream, but there was no air' – as they eagerly celebrate his imminent death.[48] Nor are these visions exclusive to men with blood on their hands: Ellen, the girl that Gerry is trying to protect throughout the later stages of the novel, also sees the remaining ghosts.[49] Spread throughout the text, these details affirm the ghosts' existence independent of Fegan's own guilty psyche. Their existence removes the novel's plot from a simple mechanism of a remorseful-but-vengeful man, or a broken, flawed hero seeking redemption. Through this, the novel makes Fegan's violence not simple redemptive atonement but something slightly stranger, less familiar, and less subject to the same binaries and clichés that plagued older Troubles thrillers, the 'Troubles trash' of J. Bowyer Bell.

A still more recent novel dealing in less Gothic terms than Neville with post-Agreement matters of revenge is Claire McGowan's third Paula Maguire book, *The Silent Dead* (2015). The plot concerns a splinter group of anti-ceasefire terrorists who trigger an Omagh-like bomb. Freed after a failed trial, they are hunted down and killed by the victims' survivors. In the end, the novel offloads much – though not all – of the moral responsibility for these gruesome acts of revenge onto a lone madman who has manipulated the other survivors in their grief. The novel thereby provides the gratification of that revenge while largely sheltering its more sympathetic characters from the worst ethical excesses of the violence.

[46] Neville, *Twelve*, 7.
[47] Neville, *Twelve*, 138; see also 39, 114.
[48] Neville, *Twelve*, 297–298.
[49] Neville, *Twelve*, 323.

Crucially, the book mitigates the risk of seeming to have its cake and eat it too through Paula's narration, which expresses both a deep horror at the violence and an equally deep empathy with the survivors' rage, describing them even when she is their captive as 'good people, if hopelessly damaged.'[50] At the conclusion, Paula makes this damage explicit: 'She thought about what Guy had said – how you could lose your ability to judge, to say who was right and who was wrong, and that was why we had the law, so we didn't have to make those choices ourselves, in all our human weakness and pain.'[51] McGowan, however, has Paula do more than acknowledge empathy for 'human weakness and pain' on the way to reaffirming the rule of law. Hers is more than a passing empathy, for it persists despite Paula being subjected to her captors' horrifying rage as the book attempts to navigate a thin line between revenge and justice. That thin line recurs throughout crime fiction, but its thinness is, as *The Silent Dead* and much other Northern Irish crime fiction suggest, all the more fragile in a society emerging from a traumatic period.

A pain and rage like that of McGowan's survivors also colours Neville's ghosts, drawn from varied positions across Northern Irish society:

> Of the five soldiers three were Brits and two were Ulster Defence Regiment. Another of the followers was a cop, his Royal Ulster Constabulary uniform neat and stiff, and two more were Loyalists, both Ulster Freedom Fighters. The remaining four were civilians who had been in the wrong place at the wrong time. [Fegan] remembered doing all of them, but it was the civilians whose memories screamed the loudest.[52]

The hint of a moral hierarchy here, one in which some sins and some injuries weigh more heavily – and scream more loudly – plays out in the present tense killings as well. Perhaps the most complex example of these ghosts driving Fegan to kill others involved in their murders involves a local priest on the IRA payroll, Father Coulter, whose involvement opens up still greyer shades of responsibility and complicity. As one of Fegan's flashbacks shows, another IRA man, Eddie Coyle (a nicely overt reference to George V. Higgins's classic crime novel, *The Friends of Eddie Coyle*) mistimed a bomb meant to kill a British patrol, leaving three of the six

[50] Claire McGowan, *The Silent Dead* (London: Headline, 2015), 365.
[51] McGowan, *Silent*, 365.
[52] Neville, *Twelve*, 4.

soldiers on patrol wounded but alive. When Fegan prepares to kill them, Coulter tries to intervene, only to leave the soldiers to be shot when Fegan challenges him: 'Tell me to take the other way and I'll do it. But you better be ready to stand over it. You better be ready to answer to the boys who run these streets. … Have you the guts to practise what you preach? Or will you shut your eyes and say nothing like you always do?'[53] Fegan initially refuses the ghosts' insistence that he kill Father Coulter, seeming to forgive the priest's weakness as borne of real fear of Fegan himself. This changes when Coulter delivers threats as the former IRA commander-turned-politician McGinty's messenger boy, and when he breaks the seal of confession in order to tell McGinty that Fegan has admitted killing others at the behest of the ghosts. Father Coulter's case extends the killings from those who had actual blood on their hands to those who had a less direct involvement, and a different kind of culpability, less tangible but no less real for that.

After a climactic and dramatic shoot-out, with baroque violence, betrayal, and tension, the conclusion does much to underscore this unresolved complexity, returning the narrative to a murky realm in which mercy and forgiveness, revenge and justice, are all entangled. *The Twelve*'s distance from Troubles clichés is further affirmed in this conclusion, with the final ghost releasing Fegan from her demand that he kill himself. When she does so, the novel describes it explicitly, twice, as 'Mercy.'[54] Crucially, then, Fegan is not redeemed, and not really forgiven, for mercy is of its nature bestowed rather than earned. This precludes *The Twelve* being read as a heroic journey of redemption-through-violence, a sub-Pádraig-Pearse blood sacrifice, or a simple thriller plotted around acts of vengeance.[55] Instead, to the extent that Fegan, alive through mercy alone, finds some kind of contingent peace, he does so not through the people he kills, or the ghosts whose bidding he does, but rather through the young girl Ellen, through the person he protects, and saves, here and again for a last time in the sequel *Collusion*.

[53] Neville, *Twelve*, 88.

[54] Neville, *Twelve*, 322–323.

[55] In this sense, although Eunan O'Halpin and Keith Jeffery are right to identify among 'the classic genre types' in Irish thrillers that of 'the loner who has lived by violence ultimately facing nemesis' and right to suggest the 'type recurs repeatedly in novels set in the … Irish troubles,' Fegan himself cannot quite be classed with that type ('Ireland in Spy Fiction,' 101).

In place of a closed treatise on justice and revenge, *The Twelve* depicts real ambiguity, befitting the complexity of its narrative and its contexts. Neville's deft combination of genre elements – including thrillers and the supernatural – keeps the novel unstable and ambivalent, undermining any reading of *The Twelve* that relies on the patterns from any of these constituent genres, or from earlier Troubles thrillers. In a conventional crime novel, for example, as Neville has suggested, the hero would not be Gerry Fegan, but Davey Campbell, the intelligence services mole in the republican hierarchy.[56] Neville is right to see this as a departure from the genre's conventions: in her granular, quantified study of Troubles thrillers during the 1980s, Pauline Rafferty traces the development of conventions according to which 'The heroes will tend to be members of the British Security Services, villains will be IRA operatives, and women will be depicted as girlfriends or victims.'[57] These patterns were quickly familiar and established 'by the end of the 1970s.'[58] Despite this, Rafferty concludes that nearly half – 43 percent – of the numerous Troubles thrillers she examines show significant signs of modifying the inherited conventions of the Troubles thriller.[59] This suggests the Troubles thriller clichés are somewhat less rigid than is often assumed, and that familiar critical models for reading them risk oversimplifying the genre, missing essential nuances and modulations within the genre. A reading that starts with these clichés, taking them as a presumptive lens or a point of departure, will misread Neville's novel. *The Twelve* has a certain *sui generis* quality: little in the Irish crime fiction genre quite resembles it, and even its sequel, *Collusion*, is more conventional in some ways. However, by maintaining such complexities without premature resolution – without the conservative comfort of closure so often imputed to the genre – *The Twelve* exemplifies what Northern Irish crime fiction has begun to do, in blurring genres, in stretching the genre's form, and in writing about the Troubles and its aftermath without the reductive binaries of 'Troubles trash.'

---

[56] Stuart Neville, seminar discussion with the author, Christopher Morash, and students, 'Irish Crime Fiction' undergraduate seminar, Trinity College Dublin, 11 February 2015.

[57] Pauline Rafferty, 'Identifying Diachronic Transformations in Popular Culture Genres: A Cultural-Materialist Approach to the History of Popular Literature Publishing,' *Library History* 24, no. 4 (December 2008): 266.

[58] Rafferty, 'Identifying Diachronic Transformations,' 267.

[59] Rafferty, 'Identifying Diachronic Transformations,' 268.

REVENGE IN ADRIAN MCKINTY'S SEAN DUFFY SERIES

Neville has suggested that, 'When it comes to Northern Irish crime fiction, Adrian McKinty forged the path the rest of us follow. The Sean Duffy series is the culmination of a career spent examining our darkest moments, and McKinty is the only crime writer who can do justice to our singular history.'[60] Where the distinction between private revenge and public justice is largely implicit and unsettled in *The Twelve*, which acknowledges the particular complexity of that distinction amidst a peace process that has often required the surrender of the personal to the public, McKinty makes that same distinction a persistent undercurrent in his Duffy series, using it to open other avenues as the series develops. These avenues include in particular McKinty's depiction of Northern Ireland as set indifferently adrift on the seas of others' convenience. This representation emerges through Duffy's entanglement with British intelligence operatives, an entanglement that in turn begins with his pursuit of revenge.

In *The Cold Cold Ground* (2012), Freddie Scavanni is ostensibly the head of the IRA's much-feared internal investigations unit, but really a corrupt double agent code-named 'Stakeknife,' kept on the payroll by MI5 only as long as the hunger strikes – running through the background of this novel – threaten to destabilise the North even further.[61] After discovering Scavanni's identity, and his role behind the core killings in the novel, Duffy is debriefed by MI5 and 'made to sign The Official Secrets Act. ... They asked me if I understood the big picture. I told them I understood the big picture.'[62] However, shortly thereafter, the hunger strikes end and Duffy is visited by Peter Evans, a British security official who in classic Le Carré mode over tea and biscuits discreetly warns Duffy against telling the truth about Scavanni and the killings. Without naming names, Evans – who evokes the tropes of Troubles thrillers past, laying them at the feet of his own government when he declares that in his 'world

---

[60] This is from a blurb that appears on several of McKinty's Duffy novels, including the US edition of *Rain Dogs*.

[61] According to the *Irish Times*, the real 'Stakeknife' was an informant for British military intelligence who was also a member of the IRA's internal security group, responsible for finding informers and spies: see, for example, John Ware's articles on the subject, including 'Exposed: The Murky World of Spying During the Troubles,' *Irish Times*, 11 April 2017, updated 20 April 2017, https://www.irishtimes.com/news/ireland/irish-news/exposed-the-murky-world-of-spying-during-the-troubles-1.3043818 (accessed 17 May 2017).

[62] McKinty, *Cold*, 289.

everything is binary. Black and white. Friend and enemy. Traitor and hero' – refers to James Angleton, the post-war head of the CIA's counter-intelligence efforts, who 'became convinced that everyone working in that agency was a traitor. Everyone was in a conspiracy except for him. The President, the Vice-President, they were all working for the Russians. Poor chap. He couldn't trust anyone in the end.'[63] This offhand bit of chat, however, is just a prelude: Evans casually gives Duffy a copy of an *Architectural Digest* spread on Scavanni's vacation home in Italy, suggesting Duffy should consider a European trip as part of his recuperation from being shot.[64] Quite clearly, MI5 – in the archetypal language of unspoken conniving – uses Duffy's desire for vengeance, inducing him to kill Scavanni on their behalf, cleaning up their loose ends. Through this extended plot thread, McKinty depicts Northern Ireland being treated like the flotsam and jetsam of the British Empire, tossed around on seas of someone else's making.

When Duffy finds his target, Scavanni pleads '"This isn't justice, Duffy, this is revenge!"', only to get the bluntly noir rejoinder: '"What's the difference?"'[65] Despite the pithiness, McKinty gives the consequences significant moral weight for Duffy, no slouch as far as self-critique goes, like the good Jesuit boy he is. These consequences, for Duffy's state of mind and for his career, reverberate throughout the series, up to and including the most recent novel, *Police at the Station and They Don't Look Friendly* (2017). Duffy having come to their attention, MI5 gradually attempt to recruit Duffy, but a helicopter crash kills his main contact, along with 'all the top MI5, MI6 and Special Branch agents in Northern Ireland' – the 'entire intelligence cohort.'[66] This relationship with MI5 becomes a central thread in the Duffy series, over the course of which McKinty deftly weaves a sense of his protagonist's increasing unease with violence, vengeance, and complicity.

---

[63] McKinty, *Cold*, 303.

[64] McKinty, *Cold*, 304, 305.

[65] McKinty, *Cold*, 328.

[66] Adrian McKinty, *Gun Street Girl* (London: Serpent's Tail, 2015), 318. The clear reference is to the 1994 Chinook helicopter that crashed on the Mull of Kintyre, but McKinty's novel is set considerably earlier, primarily in 1985, as the text notes repeatedly. In an epilogue set a year and a half after Duffy hears of the crash, he sees televised coverage of US Senate testimony on the Iran-Contra scandal by an Oliver North figure who has been part of Duffy's case in this novel. News of the scandal first broke in late 1986, with hearings following in 1987.

While Scavanni is thus Duffy's gateway to further entanglements, he also leaves a more interior mark on Duffy. As early as the conclusion of *The Cold Cold Ground*, Duffy observes of Belfast: 'After Italy I saw the city anew. A fallen world. A lost place.'[67] This is partly a function of the contrast between Northern Ireland and his glimpses of a more conventionally functional society in Italy, but it also suggests that Duffy is beginning to see his world in a grimmer light, with a changed vision, one darkened by what he did while there.[68] In the second novel, *I Hear the Sirens in the Street* (2013), as Duffy prepares to follow a lead by flying to the States, he decides – despite claiming that he is 'not a superstitious arsehole' – to go to confession and seek penance.[69] Duffy could (and does) confess to ample things, but he emphasises his killing of Scavanni:

> Revenge is the foolish stepbrother of justice. I understood that. I had lived with that thought for eight months. *Ever since that night on the shores of Lake Como.* What I had done then was a crime, and it was also a sin. No one cared about the crime, but tonight I was going to confess to the sin. To the act itself and to the feeling of satisfaction I got when I thought about what I'd done.[70]

Duffy 'did not regret what I had done and I told [Father O'Hare] that I would do it all again. ... Technically, he should not have offered me absolution until I had explained that I was sorry for these and all the sins of my past life, but Father O'Hare was no sea lawyer and couldn't afford to be too harsh with his tiny congregation.'[71] For better and for worse, Duffy's Jesuit education is evident in his concise distinction between crime and sin, in his pragmatically flexible approach to confession and absolution, and perhaps above all in his recognition that the revenge he took is not to be confused with justice.

By *In the Morning I'll Be Gone* (2014), Duffy's awareness of such complexities has become a touchstone. A main subplot in the novel includes Mary Fitzpatrick, a woman from a strong republican family whose youngest daughter's murder remains unsolved. In desperation, knowing that she cannot obtain legal justice, Mary offers to inform on a republican hero – a

---

[67] McKinty, *Cold*, 331.
[68] McKinty, *Cold*, 306.
[69] McKinty, *Sirens*, 266, 267.
[70] McKinty, *Sirens*, 268.
[71] McKinty, *Sirens*, 269.

profoundly dangerous act, as she knows well – if Duffy finds her daughter's killer. Before Duffy gives her the name, however, he warns her:

> 'Revenge is a mug's game, Mary. The person getting revenge injures himself far worse by the act of vengeance than he was ever suffering before. He ends up living miserably. I've seen this first hand. A few years ago I revenged myself on a man who did terrible wrongs and it has brought me no satisfaction and considerable regret.'[72]

This is no small observation from a man whose scant faith in justice divine or legal persists throughout the series. Duffy at times treats such questions with sardonic levity, at least briefly. By the later stages of *Rain Dogs*, however, he shows much less in the way of such levity.

The plot of *Rain Dogs* revolves around a Finnish telecom whose executives are on a trade mission to explore setting up shop in Northern Ireland, a mission the British government is eager to see succeed. Those executives, however, are implicated in a murder and in the sexual abuse of underage boys in a group home while on the trade mission. Late in the novel, Duffy receives yet another visit from yet another Le Carré-esque government operative, seeking to persuade him to let the matter drop, in the interests of trade, employment, and consequent increases in stability for Northern Ireland. In time, the Finns set up in the Republic anyway – 'because the corporation tax is that much lower down there,' a still-resonant matter[73] – and the executives escape prosecution, until Duffy learns that the murderer, Ek, has died in a 'hunting accident.'[74] In his shadowy way, the operative makes it clear that British intelligence found a path it thought it could control, much as it had done when it set Duffy on Scavanni's trail. Despite bristling at the operative's veiled threats, Duffy finds some comfort in seeing Ek's death as 'delayed justice.'[75] This view reflects his consistent investment in justice, however qualified or compromised, in a system and place that often seemed to make legal justice difficult to secure, not least because so much faith had been lost in the system, as Duffy often and insistently remarks. The result, six books into the series, is a remarkable depth of character and sustained ethical investment within

[72] Adrian McKinty, *In the Morning I'll Be Gone* (Amherst, NY: Seventh Street Books, 2014), 258.
[73] McKinty, *Rain*, 111.
[74] McKinty, *Rain*, 321.
[75] McKinty, *Rain*, 322.

the compressed landscape and timeframe of Northern Ireland during the Troubles. Genuinely rare is the series that can accomplish this, and that, in so doing, makes such a contribution to both its immediate genre and to the wider sense of contemporary Irish literature.

Northern Ireland and International Forces

As British intelligence's involvement in Duffy's initial act of revenge and in the Finnish telecom case suggests, these questions of revenge, justice, and ethics are neither compartmentalised nor abstract in McKinty's work. If the intimate scale of Northern Ireland intensifies such matters, with revenge and justice all the more difficult to separate in a small community, that same scale also leaves Northern Ireland subject to larger external forces, as much crime fiction suggests. In the background of the Duffy series, for example, Britain – spoken for by the security operatives with whom Duffy repeatedly crosses paths – seeks to conduct 'as orderly a retreat as possible from the apogee of empire.'[76] While the intelligence agents project an aura of competence and historical prescience about this, Duffy remains at best sceptical, with concisely pointed observations about their wisdom, as when he encounters an operative who had 'been recruited at St. Andrews because of his proficiency in foreign languages. He'd been studying Russian literature but could also read Czech, Polish, and Serbo-Croat— no doubt these skills were why they had put him on the Northern Ireland desk.'[77] Duffy's tentative relationship with MI5 is one of several ways in which the series depicts Northern Ireland's vulnerability to trans-national exploitation and depredation amidst the power struggles of competing empires, whether they are American, British, or nationally agnostic corporations.

Along with the Finnish telecom and MI5's varied interventions, McKinty also makes use of DeLorean's brief manufacturing enterprise in Northern Ireland, handled with considerable and acute historical irony in *I Hear the Sirens in the Street*. Until the novel's epilogue, DeLorean's own downfall is beyond the horizon. In the main narrative, what registers is that 'He had done what everybody said couldn't be done and Dunmurry was the only place in Ulster where heavy industry worked, where people

---

[76] McKinty, *Morning*, 307.
[77] McKinty, *Morning*, 267–268.

actually made things.'[78] This factory is an almost overwhelming source of hope for people living in a town where the local Salvation Army 'sold dozens of suitcases every month, especially now that everyone was trying to emigrate,' and at a time when 'Anybody with any brains was getting out. The destination wasn't important. ... the great thing was to go.'[79] The resulting tension – between the locals' hopes, the economically disastrous moment, and the collapse the reader knows is coming – generates a poignantly doomed air throughout the main narrative. This is compounded by the fact that DeLorean falls through an FBI sting, which the novel implies the UK government went along with to keep America on side in the midst of the Falklands War (depicted as good for the circulation of the *Daily Mail* and little else).[80] Yet again, Northern Ireland in McKinty's novels is depicted as subject to the shifting exigencies of external forces, a situation that the Duffy novels repeatedly make central to their narratives.

Through all of this, the series builds a sense of Northern Ireland as 'less an anachronism of Europe's bellicose past and more a prophecy of the coming future.'[81] In this remarkably bleak reading, 'Belfast is the prototype of a new way of living. In 1801 it was a muddy village, by 1901 it was one of the great cities of the Empire, and now Belfast is the shape of things to come. Everywhere is going to look like this soon enough after the oil goes and the food goes and the law and order goes.'[82] In a striking inversion of the 'Troubles trash' critiqued by Patterson for depicting Belfast as ceaselessly and irreparably 'stewing in the bitterness of age-old hatreds,'[83] Duffy's Northern Ireland is not simply an atavistic backwater, gazing

---

[78] McKinty, *Sirens*, 231.

[79] McKinty, *Sirens*, 72, 20.

[80] McKinty, *Sirens*, 212, 81. As one blunt indicator of his views, Duffy memorably remarks, 'I went to my office and pretended to work, but really spent time drawing glasses and moustaches on every wanker in the *Daily Mail*, and that is a lot of wankers' (McKinty, *Sirens*, 179). The line is comically in keeping with Duffy's tone, but its utter contempt functions more quietly as a remark not only on the *Mail*, but on the Falklands War and Duffy's general sense of it as one of the Empire's last gasps. McKinty is not the only Northern Irish writer to have addressed the DeLorean scandal. The poet Paul Muldoon scripted a BBC Northern Ireland television film, *Monkeys* (1989), directed by Danny Boyle, and most recently Glenn Patterson has published *Gull* (London: Head of Zeus, 2016).

[81] McKinty, *Gun*, 319.

[82] McKinty, *Rain*, 307.

[83] Patterson, 'Butchers' Tools,' 43.

endlessly inward, but contemporary capitalism's canary in the coalmine, enmeshed in a much wider transnational web.

This depiction of Northern Ireland in ways that emphasise its international connections more than its parochialism plays a significant role in fiction by others as well. Claire McGowan's books touch on the region's economic fragility, and the acute pressure to find external investment from multinational corporations. Brian McGilloway's Benedict Devlin novels, despite their protagonist's distance from the metropolis, as Carol Baraniuk notes centrally address 'issues criminal and social that arise from international drug running, trafficking and exploitation of migrants, illegal adoption rackets, the Celtic Tiger economic boom, and the bust of the global banking crisis.'[84] By focusing on Northern Ireland's particular experiences amidst competing international forces, such narratives model twenty-first century Irish crime fiction's ability to develop substantive, material engagements with Northern Ireland without lapsing into the dichotomous clichés critiqued by Kelly, Patten, and others. Moreover, these novels are able to do so without subordinating character to plot or rhetoric, because these narrative elements arise from the characters' immediate, intimate, and personal experiences. Work from the Republic, discussed in later chapters, shares this international thematic pattern.

Conflicting Ethics

In a quieter but no less insistent way, McGilloway's Devlin series draws from the same deep well of vulnerability and exploitation, framed through Devlin's private faith and his characteristic sense of conflicting ethical choices, which shapes the series' unresolved and even irresolvable narratives. Though McGilloway himself is from Derry, the Devlin series is based in the Republic's side of the borderlands, with Devlin as a Garda Inspector working in Lifford, County Donegal, just across the River Foyle from Strabane, Northern Ireland. Devlin regularly crosses the border during the novels, and frequently cooperates with his PSNI counterpart in Strabane, Jim Hendry. The series quietly uses the mundaneness of this cooperation to suggest the post-Agreement degrees of change, though the first book, *Borderlands* (2007), goes so far as to have Devlin comment directly:

---

[84] Baraniuk, 'Negotiating Borders,' 77.

As I had expected, Hendry didn't care about our people going across the border to question bar owners, though it was technically not allowed. Some policemen on both sides of the border could be sticky about it, but generally we all knew that we were chasing the same people. The bad old days, when collusion and suspicion had prohibited any contact, were passing, if not yet past.[85]

Here, Devlin sounds a characteristic note of hope tempered by caution, something that gives the series a tone quite distinct from many other Northern Irish crime writers: the violence and loss in the Devlin books weighs as heavily and is committed as brutally as almost any in Northern Irish crime fiction, but the books themselves largely are not as dark – more *gris* than *noir* – and Devlin himself rarely as pessimistic.

This relatively unpessimistic tone perhaps reflects Devlin's deep, abiding Catholic faith, a trait unusual to this degree in Irish crime fiction from either side of the border, and one established early in the series. His beliefs have a markedly personal, intimate cast throughout the series: as he tells one character in *Gallows Lane* (2008), 'My faith is private, Reverend.'[86] Though he attends Mass, his faith is marked in the novels not primarily through interactions with priests or contemplation of doctrinal matters. In McKinty's novels, by contrast, Duffy's reflections on penance and absolution are more doctrinally inflected than are Devlin's here, despite Duffy generally behaving more like Hunter S. Thompson than Thomas Aquinas. Instead of through official practices, Devlin's faith surfaces through private reflection and habit, to the point of saying a remarkably forgiving Act of Contrition for a woman shot by his colleague just as she was about to kill him.[87] When Devlin mentions penance and feels 'the familiar catharsis of confession' in *Borderlands*, it is in a discussion with his wife, not a visit to a priest.[88] In the same book, as he watches a mother grieve over her son's violent death, Devlin turns to uncertain but deep and silent prayer: 'I found myself both questioning His existence and praying all the harder that He would transcend time and space and bring comfort both to this

[85] Brian McGilloway, *Borderlands* (London: Macmillan, 2007; repr. London: Pan, 2007), 80.

[86] Brian McGilloway, *Gallows Lane* (London: Macmillan, 2008; repr. London: Pan, 2009), 101.

[87] McGilloway, *Borderlands*, 287. This is explicitly a sympathy he does not extend to every dead character, as is made clear a few pages later (McGilloway, *Borderlands*, 293).

[88] McGilloway, *Borderlands*, 142.

woman and to her son, who surely did not deserve to die in such a manner.'[89] This 'questioning' is deeply characteristic, and remains important in the most recent Devlin book, *The Nameless Dead* (2012), in which outdated concepts of limbo conflict with Devlin's understanding of his faith's charity and mercy. Better reflecting his empathy in *The Nameless Dead*, Devlin lights 'seven candles beneath the statue of the Blessed Virgin, for the seven children we had recovered' from a burial ground.[90] Although this follows his attendance at a Requiem Mass for another victim, that Mass and its formal, public elements are not part of the narrative, which focuses rather on Devlin's personal acts, in keeping with the rest of the series.

This private faith is part of Devlin's characteristic earnestness, which runs deep enough that it seems a fault to other characters, who find his ethical reflections frustrating at times, as they make clear to him more than once. This is most true of his wife Debbie, who repeatedly expresses a profound frustration with him over it: 'you've put us at risk just so you can prove your rectitude.'[91] While Debbie expresses an immediate anger at a threat to her family's safety, she later draws a considered distinction between righteousness and what it can become when vanity interferes: 'honesty isn't always a virtue, Ben. Don't delude yourself into self-righteousness.'[92] At the same time, Devlin is more than capable of self-critique, for things like petty cruelty to a woman he interviews about a case:

> It was almost as though I had confirmed for her all that she believed. We may talk of equality and serving the community, but sometimes, despite ourselves, we treat people badly because we can, because we tell ourselves that we do it in the name of justice or virtue, or whatever excuse we use to hide the fact that we want to hurt someone, to get at them in any way we can to compensate for their total lack of respect for our job and all that we have sacrificed to do it.[93]

[89] McGilloway, *Borderlands*, 69–70.
[90] Brian McGilloway, *The Nameless Dead* (London: Macmillan, 2012), 376.
[91] McGilloway, *Gallows*, 149.
[92] McGilloway, *Gallows*, 199.
[93] McGilloway, *Borderlands*, 235.

Despite such self-critique, and his recognition that Debbie is right,[94] in a string of cases across the series Devlin's earnestness brings him into conflict with others as well as with himself, at times leaving him torn between a formally righteous solution and an informally empathetic one.[95] Strikingly, McGilloway makes ethical conflicts in the series not a binary choice between an upright protagonist and a compromised opponent, rather between incompatible options that only come in shades of grey.

In *Bleed a River Deep* (2009), Devlin struggles with a number of these conflicting, partially ethical options when he realises he cannot report the exploitation of immigrants without putting those same immigrants at further risk: 'If I do nothing, I'm letting whoever is fleecing these people get away with it. If I report it, I'll be handing them over to send home.'[96] Later in the case, Devlin is distraught at not being able to pursue a rapist because doing so would imperil the attempt to catch a ring of human smugglers, as a PSNI counterpart argues: 'there are other women involved here. We believe this guy … is involved in several brothels between here and Strabane, all involving eastern Europeans. If we can get him – and whoever is behind him, more importantly – we'll achieve a hell of a lot more.' Though Devlin is 'sickened' he 'had to concede that Gilmore was making a sound operational judgement. That didn't make it any less unpalatable.'[97] In *The Nameless Dead*, one of several interlocking plots concerns the Independent Commission for the Location of Victims' Remains, created in 1999 by a joint UK-Irish governmental agreement and subsequent laws passed in both jurisdictions. The Commission is tasked with gathering information 'which may lead to the location of' the bodies of the Disappeared, defined by the Commission as 'those murdered and buried in secret arising from the conflict in Northern Ireland.'[98] In order to encourage people to come forward with information, the relevant laws prohibit that information from being disclosed by the Commission or being used in any criminal proceeding.[99] When a Commission dig involving

[94] McGilloway, *Gallows*, 152.

[95] See for example McGilloway, *Nameless*, 43–44.

[96] Brian McGilloway, *Bleed a River Deep* (London: Macmillan, 2009; repr. London: Pan, 2010), 47.

[97] McGilloway, *Bleed*, 186.

[98] Independent Commission for the Location of Victims' Remains, http://www.iclvr.ie (accessed 19 December 2017).

[99] Independent Commission for the Location of Victims' Remains, 'Confidentiality,' http://www.iclvr.ie/en/ICLVR/Pages/Confidentiality (accessed 19 December 2017).

Devlin discovers the unrelated body of a baby, Devlin struggles to reconcile the Commission's task of locating remains and returning them to survivors, with the injustice of not being able to pursue the case of the dead baby. He and Millar, the Commission's investigator, share degrees of unease, as Millar says to Devlin: "'It is shit thinking that people get away with this. But at the end of the day, all we can hope to do is bring some peace to those who've been left behind. That has to be enough, you know?" He squinted at me as he spoke, though I suspected the words were as much for his own benefit as mine.'[100] These two distinct ethical goals – justice for those who have been killed, and the return of the bodies to their families – come into irreconcilable conflict here. In *The Rising* (2010), these ethical conflicts take a more immediately personal form, when Devlin cannot bring himself to arrest Vincent Morrison, a man he knows to be guilty, because Morrison saved his daughter's life.[101] In all of these cases, McGilloway gives narrative space and weight to both positions, and offers little in the way of unambiguous, definitive narrative resolution. Reflecting this, Devlin's ethical victories are often at best partial, as he reflects in the final line of *Gallows Lane*: 'On such small victories must the future be built.'[102] A long way, this, from the closure on which some forms of the genre have depended.

Like McKinty and McGowan, McGilloway at times ties his protagonist's particular challenges to a sense of the region's economic vulnerability, the exploitation of which heightens the books' sense of ethical division. *Bleed a River Deep* assembles another ornate plot involving the discovery of a female bog body by an archaeological excavation that is part of a gold mine developed by an American company. The mine turns out to be a money-laundering front for the profits from illegal military software sales through a company partly owned by a conservative American senator, Cathal Hagan, who had also run a charity that was in reality a source of funds for Northern republican paramilitaries. As one protester complains, "'He's an arsehole. He funded terrorism over here for years, and now he's trying to stifle debate in the US over Iraq.'"[103] Even Devlin, considerably more tempered than the protester, reflects with frustration on his inability

---

[100] McGilloway, *Nameless*, 109.
[101] Brian McGilloway, *The Rising* (London: Macmillan, 2010; repr. London: Pan, 2011), 297, 346, 352.
[102] McGilloway, *Gallows*, 321.
[103] McGilloway, *Bleed*, 115.

to 'stop people like Cathal Hagan delivering hawkish speeches about the need for military intervention while lining his pockets with the profits of such action.'[104] After a protestor tries to attack Hagan at the mine's opening ceremony, the sacrificial bog victim is shipped off to Hagan in the States for 'a gift.'[105] As the archaeologist on her case complains, '"Was her being sacrificed once not enough? ... We have to sacrifice her again for fucking gold."'[106] (Not for nothing is the title of the German edition *Blutgold*, or *Blood Gold*.) Further complicating the plot – detailed enough that it requires a two-page summary near the conclusion – are various schemes including human trafficking and fuel laundering.

These seemingly scattered elements are woven together by a deep underlying empathy with the exploited and victimised, from the economically vulnerable people who throng the area around the gold mine in the hopes of panning for riches, to the illegal immigrants preyed upon by traffickers. This empathy with those who are sacrificed or exploited for economic goals or desperate needs is among the book's defining notes. Echoing the final line of *Gallows Lane*, *Bleed a River Deep* concludes with Devlin reflecting on a character who, after all of the book's suffering, may finally be able 'to return to his family, to face his children with a sense of dignity. That is, perhaps, the best for which any of us may aim.'[107] Here as so often in the series, Devlin ends with at best a qualified justice and a partial resolution, which may never be enough but which may be all we may receive. Such characteristic endings powerfully reflect the complexities and the conflicting ethical imperatives that are central to the Devlin series. In this, it is hard not to see an image of the borderlands setting, with all of the enduring uncertainty and literal ambivalence that has long surrounded the region,[108] or a ripple moving out from the Good Friday Agreement, with all the varieties of compromise it required, the laying aside of revenge and sometimes justice in the interests of a broader peace.

---

[104] McGilloway, *Bleed*, 120.

[105] McGilloway, *Bleed*, 110.

[106] McGilloway, *Bleed*, 271.

[107] McGilloway, *Bleed*, 295.

[108] For a detailed overview of intra-insular smuggling around the borderlands during World War II – an issue that appears in McGilloway's Devlin series, as well as in Neville's *The Twelve* and *Collusion*, and that has its parallel in McKinty's and McGowan's representations of abortion restrictions – see Bryce Evans, '"A Pleasant Little Game of Money-Making": Ireland and the "New Smuggling", 1939–1945,' in Meier and Ross, 'Irish Crime Since 1921': 44–68.

From these contexts arise the 'small victories' with which Devlin struggles throughout the series in ways personal and professional.

ABORTION, NORTHERN IRELAND, AND CRIME FICTION

Troubles thrillers may have been prone to reductive binaries – politics or 'real life,' ideology or 'truth,' engaged or absent – but the past two decades of crime fiction in Northern Ireland at its best works through disjunction and contradiction, through the 'concealed relationships and hidden attachments' Kelly identified as part of the thriller's potential.[109] McKinty's Sean Duffy and McGowan's Paula Maguire, for example, both represent the abortion laws in Northern Ireland as a deep disjunction of state and identity, as evidence that in certain meaningful ways conservative Protestants there have more in common with the Republic's Catholicism than with the United Kingdom with which they may otherwise identify: 'If there was one thing which united Catholic and Protestant in Ireland,' Maguire thinks, 'it was a firm hatred of abortion.'[110] In the first Maguire novel, a clipping of a twenty-five-year-old editorial from the local newspaper addresses the abortion incongruity in rather more pointed terms, its age underscoring the endurance of the matter:

> For years in the North we have followed events South of the border, often priding ourselves on our moral superiority. Many cases have come to light in recent years that seem to prove this. Abuse scandals. Cover-ups by the Catholic Church. Pregnant women banned from leaving the country for an abortion by a government more concerned with bowing the knee to men in cassocks than protecting the vulnerable. Many will have been raped, or told that giving birth was likely to kill them, and yet there is no choice at all. We may well have felt smug. That could never happen here, in the more enlightened North. Yet abortion is just as illegal in the North, despite being part of the United Kingdom and subject to the laws and principles of that domain. Unless, of course, you happen to be young and female.[111]

[109] Kelly, 'The Troubles with the Thriller,' 513.

[110] McGowan, *Dead Ground*, 92.

[111] McGowan, *Lost*, 292–293. This editorial echoes Rose's speech from Christina Reid's 1989 play *The Belle of the Belfast City*. Amidst an argument with her sister about ending the partition of Northern Ireland and the Republic of Ireland, the radical journalist Rose insists that Loyalism's 'right-wing Protestant Church is in total agreement with the right-wing Catholic Church on issues like divorce and abortion, on a woman's right to be anything

Paula offers little reaction beyond blinking at the sternness of the prose, but when she is struggling with her own unplanned pregnancy in the next novel, she expresses no small unease: 'She imagined this happening in London, how no one would bat an eyelid … But here – the idea of having to fly to England, stay in a hotel somewhere, sore and bleeding – she shrank from it. … The ties of family, home, community – they bound you tight and kept you safe but they were almost impossible to sever.'[112] Maguire does not get the abortion, a decision that impacts the rest of the series in significant ways, but this passage suggests that the decision reflects not only her own internal uncertainty but also practical material barriers: were she still living in London, she might already have had the abortion, but in Northern Ireland she is both comforted and restrained by the conflicted security of home.

This, too, is a series in which the first novel hinges on compulsory adoptions in a Magdalen home for unwed mothers,[113] and the second novel's nemeses include an alleged spiritualist seer who helps her sister 'save' babies from abortion by killing their mothers in forced, crude caesarean sections. These villains' vision of women as mere vessels is one of their distinguishing evils, and converges darkly with their particular crimes in the novel. Through such thematic patterns, McGowan's novels avoid any prematurely celebratory 'end of history' normalisation, instead depicting post-Agreement Northern Irish society as still marked by both its recent and its more distant histories. The fourth novel, for example, expresses some optimism about these changes: '"There's no such thing as sides in the police now, remember," said Gerard, himself Catholic. And that was an achievement, Paula thought. The PSNI was not seen, as the RUC had been, as the tool of the Protestant majority. Rather it disgruntled everyone equally, as should probably be the case.'[114] Before long, however, this is juxtaposed with a brief but tense interaction over whether the proper name of the city is the nationalist-favoured Derry or the unionist-favoured Londonderry, suggesting that, whatever about the RUC becoming the PSNI, 'sides' have not yet disappeared from the

---

other than a mother or a daughter or a sister or a wife. Any woman outside that set of rules is the Great Whore of Babylon.' Christina Reid, *Plays 1* (London: Methuen, 1997), 221.

[112] McGowan, *Dead Ground*, 92–3.

[113] McGowan, *Lost*, 58.

[114] Claire McGowan, *A Savage Hunger* (London: Headline, 2016), Chapter Twenty-Five, Kindle.

landscape.[115] Like McGilloway's Inspector Devlin series, which also touches on the Disappeared, McGowan's Maguire books are set in the borderlands where Northern Ireland and the Republic meet, and include significant though at times complicated cross-border police cooperation, particularly in the missing persons squad for which Paula works. While McGowan's series, then, is invested in the meeting ground between cultures, states, classes, in the points where these groupings rub up against each other, her narratives also overtly and consistently foreground other crimes and conflicts, notably those around abortion and abuse, pregnancy and poverty. Together, these narrative patterns minimise the presumptive centrality of Troubles themes without erasing those themes from the landscape or from her characters' lives.

The disjunction Maguire recognises between proclaimed identity and practiced regulation recurs in McKinty's Duffy novels, which are set in the early 1980s, roughly three decades before McGowan's. In the series debut, Duffy observes that 'Everybody in Ireland understood this particular trope. Girl gets pregnant out of wedlock, runs away, gives birth, kills herself. Happened all the time. Abortion was illegal on both sides of the Irish border.'[116] Indeed, later in the novel, with a poignantly spare language otherwise little on display, Duffy maps the route a woman had to travel for an abortion: 'Train to Larne. Ferry to Stranraer. Train to Glasgow. Abortion. Overnight in the hospital. Train to Stranraer. Ferry to Larne. Train to Carrickfergus. Home for Christmas.'[117] In the fifth novel in the series, Duffy and his pregnant girlfriend Beth follow a similar route, travelling what he calls 'the Great Abortion Trail walked by thousands of Irish women and girls every year.'[118] As he drives to pick her up for the morning ferry, he thinks, *'Look at you. Aren't you supposed to be a policeman? Aren't you supposed to enforce the law? Abortion is illegal on the island of Ireland. On both sides of that porous, wiggly-line border. Assisting someone in the procurement of an abortion is a criminal offense under the catch-all clause of the Offenses Against the Persons Act (1861).'*[119] As well as demonstrating Duffy's uncertainty, which matches much of the series' tone, this passage bluntly reminds the reader of precisely how illegal this is, and precisely

---

[115] McGowan, *Savage*, Chapter Twenty-Eight, Kindle.
[116] McKinty, *Cold*, 118.
[117] McKinty, *Cold*, 193–4.
[118] McKinty, *Rain*, 315.
[119] McKinty, *Rain*, 307.

how difficult the state has made it, while also underscoring exactly how – literally – Victorian these restrictions are.

Though Duffy and Beth leave Liverpool after she decides not to get the abortion, these two chapters – part of a long epilogue to the novel, concerning Beth's pregnancy and Duffy's response, but bearing little overt connection to the surface plot that occupies most of the novel – are among the most fragile and haunting in the Duffy series, and carry an emotional weight undeflected by the hard-boiled banter in which Duffy otherwise often revels. This is particularly true in a brief encounter on the ferry to Liverpool, when Duffy goes to the cafeteria for a morning cup of tea:

> This side of the cafeteria has at least a dozen single women staring at cups of tea and coffee, tears in their eyes, ciggies in their hands. One of them approaches. She's about fifteen.
> 'I couldn't get a smoke, could I?'
> I give her the entire packet and go up on to the freezing observation deck. Stand there for a long time, getting cold.[120]

Such moments confirm crime fiction's capacity to explore a full range of lives in Northern Ireland, amidst and after the Troubles, and to do so while depicting one of the island's most fraught issues with an empathy as acute as it is understated. In doing so, McKinty, McGowan, and the other authors discussed here demonstrate the emotional and social scope of Northern Irish crime fiction as it is now practiced. Never so generic as to imply 'we're just like anywhere else,' and never dependent just on tangential details (the brand of tea, the background music, the cultural ephemera) to mark their place's distinctness, their writing models how the genre can produce 'ordinary decent' narratives in Northern Ireland. This in turn allows Northern Irish crime fiction to depict their societies' historical complexities without subordinating the entire scope of meaning to those complexities, and without returning to the fatalistic determinism of earlier Troubles thrillers.

CONCLUSION

Northern Irish crime fiction and its subgenres interact productively and powerfully with the material particularities of Northern Ireland. The novels discussed here represent crime that is both ordinary, like that in many

---

[120] McKinty, *Rain*, 312.

other places, as well as crime that is often intimately entangled with Northern Ireland's complex historical contexts, not least its contested relationships to the United Kingdom and to the Republic of Ireland (most recently highlighted by the border's ongoing prominence in Brexit talks). These particularities span the public and the intimate, ranging from the well-known and dramatic (the Troubles and lingering paramilitary violence) to some less well-known outside of the island (the legal status of abortion), from Northern Ireland's experiences of transnational capitalism to organised crime that takes advantage of the border's opportunities for smuggling and trafficking. By engaging with such particularities in the ways this chapter has discussed, these novels enable a specific kind of crime fiction that is often distinct – in its themes and in its relationship to its society – from the crime fiction written in and about the Republic of Ireland. These same contemporary Northern Irish texts demonstrate an even wider separation from the 'Troubles trash' that gave genre fiction such a problematic reputation in Irish Studies, and that did so by fetishising Northern Ireland's otherness while simultaneously reducing it to a secondary actor in its own story, substituting the merely generic for meaningful difference. The novels discussed here, in contrast, demonstrate clearly that crime fiction from and about Northern Ireland has developed far beyond the point where critical and scholarly habits generated in response to those Troubles clichés can remain persuasive or insightful. Writers from Neville to McGowan model how the genre can rise from and reflect that very particular society, without covering its specificity in a half-baked soufflé of indifferent clichés or prematurely restoring an artificial sense of order. These novels instead conclude with a profound uncertainty (characteristic of much Irish crime fiction) that preserves the ambiguities and ambivalences of a complex society.

Whether these novels are set in the past or present, and whether they involve active paramilitary groups or garden-variety civic corruption, they powerfully illustrate some of the ways in which Northern Ireland is subject not just to the political machinations of empires, or to intransigent sectarianism, but to the endlessly varied yet obsessively repetitive depredations of transnational capitalism in the 20th and 21st centuries. This broader narrative framework has been essential to the genre's thematic diversity. At the same time, the narrative investment in representing matters from experiences of abortion to 'ordinary decent crime' also shows how writers have used crime fiction to examine the particularities of Northern Ireland, the social, civic, and intimate experiences fostered by its anomalous qualities, much as their peers in the Republic do, as Chapter 3 will suggest. Addressing such patterns of power and economy with consistent empathy, these novels use their genre to demonstrate what Irish crime fiction can at its best offer in narrative sophistication, ethical engagement, and emotional investment.

REFERENCES

Baraniuk, Carol. 'Negotiating Borders: Inspector Devlin and Shadows of the Past.' In Mannion, *The Contemporary Irish Detective Novel*, 73–90.

Bateman, Colin. *Divorcing Jack*. New York: Arcade, 1995.

———. *Mystery Man*. London: Headline 2009.

———. *The Dead Pass*. London: Headline, 2014.

Bell, J. Bowyer. 'The Troubles as Trash.' *Hibernia*, 20 January 1978, 22.

Brennan, Gerard. 'The Truth Commissioners.' In Burke, *Down These Green Streets*, 201–210.

———. *Wee Rockets*. Edinburgh: Blasted Heath, 2012. Kindle.

Burke, Declan, ed. *Down These Green Streets: Irish Crime Writing in the 21st Century*. Dublin: Liberties, 2011.

Capote, Truman. *In Cold Blood*. New York: Random House, 1966. Reprint, New York: Vintage, 1994.

Cavanagh, Steve. *The Defence*. London: Orion, 2015.

———. *The Plea*. London: Orion, 2016.

———. *The Liar*. London: Orion, 2017.

Cleary, Joe. *Literature, Partition and the Nation-State: Culture and Conflict in Ireland, Israel and Palestine*. Cambridge: Cambridge University Press, 2002.

Coffey, Fiona. '"The place you don't belong": Stuart Neville's Belfast.' In Mannion, *The Contemporary Irish Detective Novel*, 91–106.

Connolly, John. 'No Blacks, No Dogs, No Crime Writers: Ireland and the Mystery Genre.' In Burke, *Down These Green Streets*, 39–57.

Creighton, Kelly. *The Bones of It*. Dublin: Liberties, 2015.

'Crime Fiction and Contemporary Ireland.' Panel discussion with Paul Charles, Declan Hughes, Gene Kerrigan, Brian McGilloway, Niamh O'Connor, and Louise Phillips. 'Irish Crime Fiction: A Festival.' Trinity College Dublin, 23 November 2013.

Ennis, Garth, and Steve Dillon. *Preacher*. 9 volumes. New York: Vertigo, 1996–2001.

Evans, Bryce. '"A Pleasant Little Game of Money-Making": Ireland and the "New Smuggling", 1939–1945.' In Meier and Ross, 'Irish Crime Since 1921': 44–68.

Harte, Liam, and Michael Parker. 'Reconfiguring Identities: Recent Northern Irish Fiction.' In *Contemporary Irish Fiction: Themes, Tropes, Theories*, edited by Harte and Parker, 232–254. Basingstoke: Macmillan, 2000.

Haslam, Richard. 'Critical Reductionism and Bernard MacLaverty's *Cal*.' In *Representing the Troubles: Texts & Images, 1970–2000*, edited by Brian Cliff and Éibhear Walshe, 39–54. Dublin: Four Courts, 2004.

Higgins, George V. *The Friends of Eddie Coyle*. New York: Knopf, 1972. Reprint, New York: Picador, 2010.

Hughes, Declan. *All the Dead Voices*. New York: William Morrow, 2009. Reprint, New York: Harper, 2010.

Hughes, Eamonn. 'Evasion, Engagement, Exploitation.' 30th Anniversary Special Issue, *Fortnight*, September 2000, 54–55.

———. 'Limbo.' Review of *That Which Was*, by Glenn Patterson, and *The Ultras*, by Eoin McNamee. *Irish Review* 33 (2005): 138–141.

Independent Commission for the Location of Victims' Remains. http://www.iclvr.ie (accessed 19 December 2017).

———. 'Confidentiality.' http://www.iclvr.ie/en/ICLVR/Pages/Confidentiality (accessed 19 December 2017).

Jeffery, Keith, and Eunan O'Halpin. 'Ireland in Spy Fiction.' *Intelligence and National Security* 5, no. 4 (1990): 92–116.

Kelly, Aaron. *The Thriller and Northern Ireland Since 1969: Utterly Resigned Terror*. Aldershot: Ashgate, 2005.

———. 'The Troubles with the Thriller: Northern Ireland, Political Violence and the Peace Process.' In *The Edinburgh Companion to Twentieth-Century British and American War Literature*, edited by Adam Piette and Mark Rawlinson, 508–515. Edinburgh: Edinburgh University Press, 2012.

Kennedy-Andrews, Elmer. 'Shadows of the Gunmen: The Troubles Novel.' In *Irish Fiction Since the 1960s: A Collection of Critical Essays*, edited by Elmer Kennedy-Andrews, 87–117. Gerrards Cross: Colin Smythe, 2006.

———. 'The Novel and the Northern Troubles.' In *The Cambridge Companion to the Irish Novel*, edited by John Wilson Foster, 238–258. Cambridge: Cambridge University Press, 2006.

Kerrigan, Gene. *Dark Times in the City*. London: Harvill Secker, 2009. Reprint, New York: Europa, 2013.

———. *The Rage*. London: Harvill Secker, 2011. Reprint, New York: Europa, 2012.

King, Catriona. *The Keeper*. Belfast: Hamilton-Crean, 2015. Kindle.

MacLaverty, Bernard. *Cal*. London: Jonathan Cape, 1983. Reprint, New York: Norton, 1995.

Magennis, Caroline. *Sons of Ulster: Masculinities in the Contemporary Northern Irish Novel*. Oxford: Peter Lang, 2010.

Mannion, Elizabeth, ed. *The Contemporary Irish Detective Novel*. Basingstoke: Palgrave, 2016.

McGilloway, Brian. *Borderlands*. London: Macmillan, 2007. Reprint, London: Pan, 2007.

———. *Gallows Lane*. London: Macmillan, 2008. Reprint, London: Pan, 2009.

———. 'McGilloway on the Run.' *Derry Journal*, 14 March 2008. http://www.derryjournal.com/news/mcgilloway-on-the-run-1-2122496 (accessed 30 May 2017).

———. *Bleed a River Deep*. London: Macmillan, 2009. Reprint, London: Pan, 2010.

———. *The Rising*. London: Macmillan, 2010. Reprint, London: Pan, 2011.

———. *The Nameless Dead*. London: Macmillan, 2012.

McGowan, Claire. *The Lost*. London: Headline, 2013.

———. *The Dead Ground*. London: Headline, 2014.

———. *The Silent Dead*. London: Headline, 2015.

———. *A Savage Hunger*. London: Headline, 2016. Kindle.

McKinty, Adrian. *The Dead Yard*. New York: Scribner, 2006.

———. 'Odd Men Out.' In Burke, *Down These Green Streets*, 96–105.

———. *The Cold Cold Ground*. London: Serpent's Tail, 2012.

———. *I Hear the Sirens in the Street*. London: Serpent's Tail, 2013.

———. *In the Morning I'll Be Gone*. Amherst, NY: Seventh Street Books, 2014.

———. *Gun Street Girl*. London: Serpent's Tail, 2015.

———. *Rain Dogs*. Amherst: Seventh Street, 2016.

———. *Police at the Station and They Don't Look Friendly*. Amherst: Seventh Street, 2017.

McNamee, Eoin. *Resurrection Man*. London: Picador, 1994. Reprint, New York: Picador, 1995.

———. *The Ultras*. London: Faber, 2004.

Meier, William, and Ian Campbell Ross, eds. 'Irish Crime Since 1921.' Special issue, *Éire-Ireland* 49, no. 1–2 (2014).

———. 'Editors' Introduction: Irish Crime Since 1921.' In Meier and Ross, 'Irish Crime Since 1921': 7–21.

Montgomery, Dale. '"Helping the Guards": Illegal Displays and Blueshirt Criminality, 1932–1936.' In Meier and Ross, 'Irish Crime Since 1921': 22–43.

Morales-Ladrón, Marisol. '"Troubling" Thrillers: Between Politics and Popular Fiction in the Novels of Benedict Kiely, Brian Moore and Colin Bateman.' *Estudios Irlandeses* 1 (2006): 58–66.

Muldoon, Paul, screenwriter. *Monkeys*. Directed by Danny Boyle. Belfast: BBC Northern Ireland, 1989.

Negra, Diane, ed. *The Irish in Us: Irishness, Performativity, and Popular Culture*. Durham: Duke University Press, 2006.

Neville, Stuart. *The Twelve*. London: Harvill Secker, 2009.

———. *Collusion*. London: Harvill Secker, 2010. Reprint, New York: Soho, 2010.

———. Seminar discussion with the author and students. 'Imagining Ireland IV' undergraduate seminar. Trinity College Dublin, 23 November 2012.

———. Seminar discussion with the author, Christopher Morash, and students. 'Irish Crime Fiction' undergraduate seminar. Trinity College Dublin, 11 February 2015.

———. *Those We Left Behind*. London: Harvill Secker, 2015.

———. *So Say the Fallen*. New York: Soho, 2016.

———. [Haylen Beck, pseud.]. *Here and Gone*. New York: Crown, 2017.

Neville, Stuart, Brian Cliff, Fiona Coffey, John Connolly, Declan Hughes, Elizabeth Mannion. Panel discussion at launch of Elizabeth Mannion, ed., *The Contemporary Irish Detective Novel* and Stuart Neville, *So Say The Fallen*. Glucksman Ireland House, New York University, 13 September 2016.

O'Brien, Peggy. 'Unbalanced Styles.' Review of *Walking the Dog and Other Stories*, by Bernard MacLaverty, *Resurrection Man*, by Eoin McNamee, and *Nothing is Black*, by Deirdre Madden. *Irish Review* 16 (Autumn-Winter 1994): 148–152.

O'Donnell, Mary. *Where They Lie*. Dublin: New Island, 2014.

Oppenheimer, Rachel. '"Inhuman Conditions Prevailing": The Significance of the Dirty Protest in the Irish Republican Prison War, 1978–1981.' In Meier and Ross, 'Irish Crime Since 1921': 142–163.

Parker, Michael. *Northern Irish Literature, 1975–2006, Volume 2: The Imprint of History*. Basingstoke: Palgrave, 2007.

Patten, Eve. 'Fiction in conflict: Northern Ireland's prodigal novelists.' In *Peripheral Visions: Images of Nationhood in Contemporary British Fiction*, edited by Ian A. Bell, 128–148. Cardiff: University of Wales Press, 1995.

Patterson, Glenn. 'Butchers' Tools.' *Fortnight*, September 1994, 43–44.

———. *The International*. London: Anchor, 1999. Reprint, Belfast: Blackstaff, 2008.

———. *Gull*. London: Head of Zeus, 2016.

Pelaschiar, Laura. 'Troubles and Freedom Fighters in Northern Irish Fiction.' *The Irish Review* 40–41 (Winter 2009): 52–73.

———. Review of *The Twelve*, by Stuart Neville. *Estudios Irlandeses* 5 (2009): 195–196.

Pepper, Andrew. *Unwilling Executioner: Crime Fiction and the State*. Oxford: Oxford University Press, 2016.

Pine, Emilie. *The Politics of Irish Memory: Performing Remembrance in Contemporary Irish Culture*. Basingstoke: Palgrave Macmillan, 2011.

Rafferty, Pauline. 'Identifying Diachronic Transformations in Popular Culture Genres: A Cultural-Materialist Approach to the History of Popular Literature Publishing.' *Library History* 24, no. 4 (December 2008): 262–272.

Rains, Stephanie. *The Irish-American in Popular Culture 1945–2000*. Dublin: Irish Academic Press, 2007.

Reid, Christina. *Plays 1*. London: Methuen, 1997.

Ware, John. 'Exposed: The Murky World of Spying During the Troubles.' *Irish Times*, 11 April 2017, updated 20 April 2017. https://www.irishtimes.com/news/ireland/irish-news/exposed-the-murky-world-of-spying-during-the-troubles-1.3043818 (accessed 17 May 2017).

CHAPTER 3

Crime Fiction and Contemporary Ireland

Contemporary crime fiction from the Republic of Ireland shares numerous concerns and themes with Northern Irish crime fiction, not least in its depictions of economic vulnerability, whether that economy is aspirationally ascendant or going under for a third time. Novels from the Republic are, however, more likely to emphasise crimes around housing and contemporary land ownership. Coloured by this fraught relationship to homes and land, corruption is a prominent theme – perhaps to a unique degree – in Irish crime fiction, a significant amount of which engages with corrupt planning processes and other crimes related to economic and real estate development. With such matters in mind, this chapter pays particular attention to Gene Kerrigan's depictions of gangland Dublin and corrupt civic authorities (2005–2011),[1] Alan Glynn's trilogy of corruption and conspiracy (2009–2013), and Tana French's ongoing Dublin Murder Squad series (2007-), especially *Faithful Place* (2010). Works by a number of additional authors contribute further thematic emphases to this focus and to the depictions of contemporary Ireland discussed here,[2] as other authors find their own ways to move crime fiction across the different

---

[1] One of few scholarly articles to address Kerrigan at length is Rosemary Erickson Johnsen's 'Crime Fiction's Dublin: Reconstructing Reality in Novels by Dermot Bolger, Gene Kerrigan, and Tana French,' in 'Irish Crime Since 1921,' ed. William Meier and Ian Campbell Ross, special issue, *Éire-Ireland* 49, no. 1–2 (Spring-Summer 2014): 121–141.

[2] Some novels draw in *all* of these contexts, as does Declan Burke's *The Lost and the Blind* (2014), which includes historical episodes from World War II, the post-Celtic Tiger crash, and the Troubles, all in an ambitiously plotted set of events.

© The Author(s) 2018
B. Cliff, *Irish Crime Fiction*, Crime Files,
https://doi.org/10.1057/978-1-137-56188-6_3

strata and locations of Irish society, in works as distinct from each other as Niamh O'Connor's bridging of true crime and fiction in *If I Never See You Again* (2010), or Declan Burke's metafictional author-protagonist in *Absolute Zero Cool* (2011).

The scale and intimacy of a small nation can make it difficult for some crime fiction to avoid being read (or misread) as a *roman à clef*: Cormac Millar's novel *The Grounds* (2006), for example, acerbically applies the boom era's prevailing language of entrepreneurial activity to an old Irish university, which as a concluding 'Author's Note' takes pains to say is very much *not* Millar's employer Trinity College Dublin, but a university drawn from his mother Eilís Dillon's *Death in the Quadrangle* (1956).[3]

A number of subgenres generally prominent in crime fiction, cinema, and television are somewhat rarer in Irish crime fiction. Beginning with *Red Ribbons* (2012), Louise Phillips has so far produced four novels with the protagonist Dr Kate Pearson, who as a forensic psychologist is a figure less familiar within Irish crime fiction than in television crime dramas, or American crime fiction. Similarly, medical thrillers are represented primarily by Paul Carson, though Claire McGowan, Arlene Hunt, Alex Barclay, and Alan Glynn have also drawn on that subgenre to various degrees. The cosy village mystery is relatively thin on the ground as well, despite elements of it in works like Andrew Nugent's *The Four Courts Murder* (2006) and Andrea Carter's *Death At Whitewater Church* (2015), with its small-town amateur drama society. Such small-town settings are a relative rarity for Irish crime fiction, with notable exceptions including Northern crime fiction set along the border by McGowan, Paul Charles, and Brian McGilloway.

Amidst these diverse modes, themes, and subgenres, the novels discussed here all reflect in different ways a society that has struggled with massive changes, including those around the boom and crash that bridged the end of Ireland's twentieth century and the start of its twenty-first. These changes were at once belated and accelerated, like so much of Ireland's experience of modernity.[4] Addressing such experiences – among the most central to mark Irish public life over recent decades – in one of the first substantial articles to synthesise a broad view of Irish crime fiction,

---

[3] Cormac Millar, *The Grounds* (Dublin: Penguin, 2006; repr. London: Penguin, 2007), 368.

[4] For more on this history of economic modernisation, see Conor McCarthy, *Modernisation, Crisis and Culture in Ireland, 1969–1992* (Dublin: Four Courts, 2000).

Andrew Kincaid concludes that the genre has been particularly well suited to recent times:

> Much, of course, has changed in Ireland over the past months, and it remains to be seen how this genre, and popular literature more generally, will respond to the current global financial recession. I suspect that noir will lend itself to this outward despair. As a matter of fact, Irish emigration to London and America has increased recently, a trend many thought was finally behind us. This goes hand in hand with a new Irish phenomenon, large-scale regret among those who had returned from the United States and elsewhere, lured back by what they thought would be lasting economic success. Noir proves a perfect genre to capitalize on these undercurrents of melancholy, alienation, grievance, and even injustice.[5]

These 'undercurrents' reflect experiences of new kinds and degrees of prosperity, as well as the relative withering of clerical authority (despite its persistent strong hold in uneven and idiosyncratic ways) and the injustices to which Kincaid refers, including the era's blurred line between entrepreneurial and criminal, the crises of immigration and emigration, and familiar forms of corruption. The convergence of these complex and at times confounding experiences and changes has been one of Irish crime fiction's clear focal points.

COMMUNAL CORRUPTION: GLYNN AND HUGHES

Among the authors to make the most acute use of contemporary Ireland's economic changes is Alan Glynn, in his trilogy of novels: *Winterland* (2009), *Bloodland* (2011), and *Graveland* (2013). One hallmark of Glynn's trilogy is its deft skill at spinning complex narratives around the interplay of transnational capital. Glynn's fiction, however, also demonstrates a striking ability to explore the diffuse web of connections that both flow from and give rise to corruption within Ireland, particularly as that corruption revolves (as is often the case in Irish politics) around property development and land. Tangled in that web are characters who suffer from the loss of control it brings, a loss the scope of which exceeds the characters' grasp. In *Winterland*, for example, most of the murders are in some sense accidents: instead of going as planned, they are rather events where

---

[5] Andrew Kincaid, '"Down These Mean Streets": The City and Critique in Contemporary Irish Noir,' *Éire-Ireland* 45, no. 1–2 (Spring/Summer 2010): 45.

the villains of the piece – none of Moriarty's omnipotence, here – make things worse for themselves, eventually losing even the illusion of control. Read by the glow of the crash's burning embers – or, as Declan Hughes's Ed Loy has it, 'amid the rotting entrails of the Celtic Tiger'[6] – such patterns reflect gradual but voluminous revelations about the seemingly massive ineptitude among Ireland's ostensible leadership, as well as the correspondingly profound uncertainty that comes with being out of one's depth.

That leadership is figured in *Winterland* through Larry Bolger, who is belatedly made to understand the corrupt parish pump machinations that put him into the political office left vacant when his upstanding brother died in another mysterious accident, and that eventually make him *Taoiseach*, the Irish political equivalent of Prime Minister, despite his own petty corruption.[7] Bolger rises to this office with the support of the Dublin developer Paddy Norton and of the shadowy American financier James Vaughan, whose company is an investor in and anchor tenant for a new Dublin skyscraper Norton is building as the jewel in his portfolio's crown. The novel's intricate plot is set moving by Norton's attempt to hide a fatal architectural flaw in this skyscraper, itself loaded with some allegorical weight, overtly suggestive of the frailty at the heart of the Celtic Tiger and the bluster used at times to hide that.[8] While Glynn's trilogy is unique in Irish crime fiction for the extent of its global conspiracies, discussed more fully in Chapter 5, even this brief discussion shows that he attends at the same time to local experiences of political and civic corruption, embodied not only in Norton and Bolger but in exchanges throughout *Winterland*.

Such corruption is also central to Declan Hughes's novel *The Wrong Kind of Blood* (2006), in which one character's actions concisely distil the way that corruption, petty or grand, can become communal: 'if everyone was on the take, it cancelled itself out; as good as if no-one was'.[9] Indeed, this novel emphasises the long-standing, repetitive nature of such corruption, depicting it not as an exclusive failing of the Celtic Tiger, but as a

---

[6] Declan Hughes, *City of Lost Girls* (London: John Murray, 2010; repr. 2011), 179. Earlier in the same novel, Loy has already made it clear that he has begun to find the crash an enervating topic, at least as it is discussed by his friend Tommy (Hughes, *City*, 87).

[7] Alan Glynn, *Winterland* (London: Faber, 2009; repr. 2010), 144, 156.

[8] Alan Glynn, seminar discussion with the author and students, 'Imagining Ireland I' undergraduate seminar, Trinity College Dublin, 10 February 2014.

[9] Declan Hughes, *The Wrong Kind of Blood* (London: John Murray, 2006; repr. 2007), 334.

practice with generational roots stretching well back before recent years.[10] Reflecting this, Hughes has his character Aileen Williamson, the daughter of a famously wealthy developer, defend long-established Irish clientelist politics: 'Local politicians are the people's direct connections to power – especially for those who have little else in the way of wealth or status.'[11] This is in the abstract a noble enough assertion insofar as it echoes the role of the hard-boiled private eye in securing justice within a corrupt system. Particularly coming from the daughter of a developer known for cutting corners and for cosy friendships with civic officials,[12] however, it is also an assertion that does little to acknowledge the way in which, as Elaine Byrne and others have shown, this clientelism is open to the kind of corruption that hides the venal behind the benignly local.[13]

The Wrong Kind of Blood is the first of five novels featuring Ed Loy, a private eye recently returned to Dublin after 'over twenty years'[14] in Los Angeles. Although he published the first Loy novel in 2006, Hughes had mentioned the idea of the character over a decade earlier.[15] The intervening boom years were rife with opportunities for writing about social observation, justice, and corruption, opportunities that proved well-suited for nurturing a character like Loy, a classically hard-boiled narrator who couples a weary scepticism with a sentimental core and an angry eye for justice. The weariness and the anger both colour Loy's sharp sidelong glances at Irish prosperity during the boom, often following observations about

[10] For a more formal discussion of corruption in Ireland, see an article by Conor Brady, the former editor of the *Irish Times* and author of a series of historical crime novels: 'The Journalist and the Policeman: Seekers for Truth or Rivals in the Game?', in Meier and Ross, 'Irish Crime Since 1921': 193–204, particularly 200–201. See also Niamh Hourigan, *Rule-Breakers: Why 'Being There' Trumps 'Being Fair' in Ireland* (Dublin: Gill & Macmillan, 2015), and Elaine Byrne, *Political Corruption in Ireland 1922–2010: A Crooked Harp?* (Manchester: Manchester University Press, 2012).

[11] Hughes, *Wrong*, 139.

[12] Hughes, *Wrong*, 84–85.

[13] See Byrne, *Political Corruption*, particularly 9–11, 215. Byrne argues that 'favourable planning decisions at local government level' were vital for developers' profits, particularly in an administrative context where 'Local councillors' – such as those bribed in Hughes's *The Wrong Kind of Blood* – 'now had the extraordinary power to override management decisions on land rezoning and planning permission decisions' (*Political Corruption*, 215).

[14] Hughes, *City*, 200.

[15] Hughes mentioned Loy to Alan Glynn as long ago as 1995, as Hughes explained during 'Crime Fiction and Contemporary Ireland,' a panel discussion with Paul Charles, Declan Hughes, Gene Kerrigan, Brian McGilloway, Niamh O'Connor, and Louise Phillips, 'Irish Crime Fiction: A Festival,' Trinity College Dublin, 23 November 2013.

the crassest displays of new wealth, like the 'sleek sheen' and newly 'brash, unapologetic confidence' of Grafton Street's upscale shopping, with images of those left behind and cast aside, like the 'derelict in every door-way' on the same street, 'gathering up their cardboard boxes and bedding, ready for another day of whatever you did when you had nowhere to go and nothing to do once you got there'.[16] Still more pointedly, as Loy visits a woman in the working-class area near his old home, he notices the adver-tisements on her television for

> property investment opportunities in Budapest and Sofia. The English absentee landlord who exploited his tenants was a much-vilified figure in Irish history; little wonder, I suppose, that we had internalized our colonial master's methods and sought to emulate them, buying up cheap property in recovering countries so we could make a profit at the local population's expense. It was our turn now.[17]

While some wheels may have turned, giving the Irish a chance to exploit rather than be exploited, others remain fixed, as another character acidly tells Loy, speaking of her ill and impoverished mother, giving the lie to the old saw about a rising tide lifting all boats: 'Not that she was the only one on pills round here, sure there still does be women in their bathrobes at lunchtime, even in the midst of our great economic boom.'[18] Here and throughout the series as a whole, Loy is continually attuned to the ways that Dublin's prosperity is akin to a thick coat of spray-tan over centuries of pasty insecurity.[19]

After a brief prologue, the main narrative opens in laconically dramatic fashion: 'The night of my mother's funeral, Linda Dawson cried on my shoulder, put her tongue in my mouth and asked me to find her husband. Now she was lying dead on her living-room floor, and the howl of a police siren echoed through the surrounding hills.'[20] As the novel quickly estab-lishes, Loy has returned to bury his mother and settle her estate, before – he thinks – returning to Los Angeles, where he plans to pick up the fragments of his life after a painful divorce and the death of his daughter, the full details of which are withheld until the novel's final pages. Instead,

---

[16] Hughes, *Wrong*, 29.
[17] Hughes, *Wrong*, 192.
[18] Hughes, *Wrong*, 281.
[19] See, for example, Hughes, *Wrong*, 32–33.
[20] Hughes, *Wrong*, 5.

he gradually decides to stay in Dublin, after becoming enmeshed in Linda Dawson's case. That case sprawls out until it takes in Loy's own father's death, several murders, gangland Dublin, childhood friends, civic corruption, blurred family ties, hidden lineage, and the desperate attempts of some murderously ambitious characters to legitimise their recent social-financial standing by erasing their past.

As the novel proceeds through these interwoven layers, Loy finds himself solving a different mystery than he had thought, uncovering one intersecting detail after another, like a Russian nesting doll that has at its centre not a tiny figure but a festering secret. His search for Linda's husband first brings him to face ongoing corruption in boomtime Dublin, with the planning process subverted in the interests of developers and land speculators at the expense of homeowners and stable development, a theme in crime fiction stretching back at least as far as Dashiell Hammett's *Red Harvest* (1929).[21] This contemporary corruption in turn has very specific, inbred family roots, which lead Loy deeper down the path of buried legacies and into an earlier generation's civic corruption in the 1960s. Following these threads, Loy gets ample opportunities to voice his sense of justice, and to work with the archetypal private eye's commitment to see that one character will pay for murdering another.[22]

Amidst the narrative's social and familial complexities, Loy's time in the States makes him an insider who is simultaneously an outsider, someone who can register for the reader the changes Dublin has experienced

---

[21] On Hammett's *Red Harvest*, see Andrew Pepper, *Unwilling Executioner: Crime Fiction and the State* (Oxford: Oxford University Press, 2016), particularly Chapter 5, '"No Good for Business": States of Crime in the 1920s and 1930s,' 131–165.

[22] Elsewhere, in some of the series' most hard-boiled language, Loy comments with a kind of pride on the public's low regard for his profession: 'you hired a private detective, and no-one wants to know who a private detective is. He's too shabby and disreputable and hustle-a-buck ordinary to make the grade at your charity balls and grand-a-plate dinners and that suits him fine, because that way, he can get on with what he's been hired to do. That's the only point of him really, like a dog that's been bred to work, he can't relax by sitting around. He's got to be prying and poking and stirring things up until somehow, out falls the truth, or enough of it to make a difference' (Hughes, *Wrong*, 200). In *City of Lost Girls*, however, a woman Loy is interviewing questions his ethics: 'Dublin's a small town, Mr Loy. I happen to *know*, was at *school* with someone whose husband divorced her because you provided him with evidence of her infidelity. And there was a pre-nup, and she landed hard on her ass with fuck all. So don't paint yourself as some kind of service to widows and orphans, some knight in shining armour.' Nor does Loy mount a defence: 'I don't think I blush, but I can feel the heat on my brow' (Hughes, *City*, 141).

without the acclimatised rationalisations of one who has remained. After such a long absence, Loy experiences the shock of sudden revelation, not for nothing describing himself as 'feeling utterly bewildered' on his return to Dublin, 'like George Bailey in Pottersville'.[23] Through Loy, Hughes introduces a cast of characters who are interconnected in a familial tangle dense enough for a Russian play. This complexity, as Loy notes wearily, befits the novel's setting in Dublin, a place 'where everyone was someone's brother or cousin or ex-girlfriend and no-one would give you a straight answer, where my da knew your da and yours knew mine, where the past was always waiting around the next corner to ambush you.'[24] This cast of characters is shot through with thwarted love, with familial damage, with paternity absent or denied or hidden. These patterns give depth to the novel's use of hard-boiled tropes, and lead Loy to take the case against some of his instincts, because doing so could 'close one broken circuit, remake one connection that had been broken. And even if I didn't, it was good to feel the stir of blood in my veins again.'[25]

Some of these hard-boiled tropes are gratifyingly familiar, but they are never inert, instead expressing the uneasy ambivalence around so many of Loy's encounters. Grappling with the pain of his mother's funeral, and the complicated confusion of returning home after a long absence, Loy returns to the pub he had last visited as a teenager, where, on ordering his second double Jameson, he is queried by the bartender:

> 'Drinking to forget?' he asked.
> 'I can't remember', I said.[26]

Tonally, this echoes William Powell's alcoholic wit in W.S. Van Dyke's 1934 film adaptation of Hammett's *The Thin Man*, as might Loy's line 'If you want the truth, maybe a private detective is the last person you should come to.'[27] Other bits of banter are more barbed, though, and sharply observant, as Loy voices judgements with a wryness that somehow both masks and intensifies the depth of their conviction:

[23] Hughes, *Wrong*, 52.

[24] Hughes, *Wrong*, 127. By *City of Lost Girls*, the fifth novel in the series, Loy is still sounding this note, if more numbly so: 'In Dublin, it sometimes seems as if more than one degree of separation is too much to hope for' (Hughes, *City*, 89).

[25] Hughes, *Wrong*, 48.

[26] Hughes, *Wrong*, 87.

[27] Hughes, *Wrong*, 127.

Compared to his brothers, George gave the closest impersonation of a human being, but it was an impersonation, nothing more. I looked at his shirt: pale blue with white collar and French cuffs. Only two kinds of men wore that shirt: CEOs and gangsters. I still had enough in common with Tommy Owens not to be sure which kind I disliked more.[28]

This eye for socially ambitious veneers runs through the novel, as when Loy describes a vast nouveau riche living room decorated in 'a riot of styles ... It was as if whoever lived here refused, or had been afraid, to make a decision about what kind of room it was, what kind of house it was. It was a study in visual uncertainty, in social insecurity. It was a mess.'[29] Indeed, one of the undercurrents of this novel is the sense – unnerving for some characters, freeing for others – of the fluidity of class, an issue that also runs throughout Tana French's and Gene Kerrigan's fiction. Loy uses this same sceptical tone about class throughout *The Wrong Kind of Blood*, often implicating himself in its complexities: 'She said she thought I'd have too much integrity to make a habit of taking money from the rich. I said I preferred my integrity with a roof over its head, and anyway, who better to take money from than people who had too much of it?'[30] It may be veiled here by the genre's penchant for banter, but throughout the series Loy displays a blunt if ambivalent pragmatism about the nature of his work and its relationship to matters of class.

Near the conclusion, the novel's threads of class and family intersect in a confessional letter from Peter Dawson, a developer whose family is at the centre of the narrative. Intending to send it to newspapers for publication, Dawson wrote the letter shortly before his death, detailing his own corruption, his father's criminal 'inclination and greed,' and his mother Barbara's criminality, which Peter suggests was inherited through her hidden 'blood' relationship to the 'dangerous' Halligan crime family. The letter, however,

was never made public. There was something glorious about its recklessness and its honesty, something terrifying about its nihilism. I think he wanted to die, but only if his family was publicly shamed in the process. But it's sometimes hard to imagine what would be deemed shame in Ireland: financial crimes don't seem to figure. Murdering your son and daughter-in-law

[28] Hughes, *Wrong*, 94.
[29] Hughes, *Wrong*, 314.
[30] Hughes, *Wrong*, 342.

would certainly qualify. But ... juries returned open verdicts. Nobody wanted to believe a mother would do such a thing, so nobody did. ... It was as if it had never happened. Whatever you say, say nothing.[31]

Here, with a pained weariness that lands somewhere between a cynic's confirmation and an optimist's frustration, Loy weaves together *The Wrong Kind of Blood*'s central elements, particularly the bitter roots of family legacies and the public corruption of civic culture, the latter often enough blurring with the former. Through this weaving, Loy identifies the damage wrought by the characters' farrago of Marian maternalism and their well-honed ability to think wishfully, which Hughes has elsewhere called a susceptibility to 'magical thinking.'[32] Amidst all of this, facilitated by what he has called Macdonald's particular 'southern-Californian family Gothic,' Hughes merges his novel's sceptical distaste for the Celtic Tiger's disabling excesses with a long Irish literary tradition of 'the troubled family plot' (also sharpened to a razor's edge by Tana French).[33] Through such connections to the buried guilt of previous generations, *The Wrong Kind of Blood* undermines contemporary pretences of legitimacy, implying that the boom itself is suspect in the most literal ways, an amplified echo of earlier sins. Indeed, much of this novel's power is not in the baroquely complex set of murders that arise from its characters' corruption and social ambition, but rather in Loy's gradual uncovering of this internal rot, spreading down the generations in a warped chain of familial legacies.

As the novel closes with Loy contemplating his decision to stay and make his home anew in Dublin, he observes that 'Your past is always waiting for you, and the longer you leave it, the less prepared you are. I had left it long enough.'[34] This is not a novel that merely allegorises the Celtic Tiger as fraught with the psychological failures of a nation that has rushed to forget itself: this is a novel that engages meaningfully with its place and time as a means of opening up a wider, deeper consideration of family, community, and the corruption of both. In this regard, the Ed Loy series

---

[31] Hughes, *Wrong*, 336.

[32] Declan Hughes, 'Irish Hard-Boiled Crime: A 51st State of Mind,' in *Down These Green Streets: Irish Crime Writing in the 21st Century*, ed. Declan Burke (Dublin: Liberties, 2011), 161.

[33] Hughes, 'Irish Hard-Boiled Crime,' 164. Macdonald is the source of epigraphs in both *The Wrong Kind of Blood*, 131, and the second Loy novel, *The Colour of Blood* (London: John Murray, 2007), 129.

[34] Hughes, *Wrong*, 345–346.

is one of the best models yet for how prominent traditions and tropes of crime fiction, particularly of American hard-boiled crime fiction, can be adapted to Ireland without subordinating to each other either the genre's capacity for emotional depth or its equal capacity for social observation. Instead, in hands like Hughes's and novels like *The Wrong Kind of Blood*, those crime fiction traditions can be repurposed and revised to provide both the emotional power of Macdonald's work and a passionate, even quietly profound sense of personal and social justice.

EMPATHY, CRIMINALS, AND SOCIAL CRITIQUE

Late in the series, Loy refers to another character being 'very clear-cut about the ethics surrounding associating with gangsters' before noting his own deep 'sympathy with clear-cut ethics along those lines; unfortunately my chosen line of work meant I couldn't hang that sympathy out on display.'[35] Irish crime fiction's ability to express social critique, and to serve social justice, finds some of its most overt expressions in novels set amidst gangland Dublin, and novels that inhabit the intersection of fiction with journalism or true crime writing. Niamh O'Connor, in novels like *If I Never See You Again* (2010), produces crime fiction with an insistent and overt current of social justice. Already known as a journalist and a true-crime writer in books of her own and in her role as the true crime editor of the *Sunday World* newspaper, O'Connor brings the energy of advocacy op-eds to fiction, which she has described as allowing her to write the fuller version of a story than would a newspaper,[36] and as a way 'to get around the restrictions of libel law.'[37]

Other gangland novels work through criminal characters who, if not conventional protagonists, are at the very least sympathetic central characters portrayed with considerable nuance and meaningful ambivalence. A notable example is Frankie Gaffney's *Dublin Seven* (2015). Set at the peak of the Celtic Tiger's fever dreams, Gaffney's novel is heavily coloured by the use of free indirect discourse as it follows the central character, Shane, and his developing career as a dealer (in tandem with his developing habit as a user). Despite the immersive specificity of the novel's settings, *Dublin*

---

[35] Declan Hughes, *All the Dead Voices* (New York: William Morrow, 2009; repr. New York: Harper, 2010), 207.

[36] 'Crime Fiction and Contemporary Ireland' panel discussion.

[37] Niamh O'Connor, 'The Executioners' Songs,' in Burke, *Down These Green Streets*, 200.

Seven could almost be a gangster novel set anywhere, insofar as it depicts – carefully, sympathetically, and in detail – Shane's gradual slide downwards through recognisable steps in a familiar arc. In this regard, Gaffney's novel straddles the line between generic and universal. Much as novels like Alan Glynn's find their own ways of navigating this line, Gaffney is able to touch on the universal without succumbing to the generic by insistently grounding the narrative in the particularities of Shane's life amidst the more common trajectory of his experiences. Although none of the novels discussed here cross it, this can be a hard line for authors – Irish and otherwise, genre or not – to navigate, perhaps particularly when working in a genre with such globally recognisable tropes and forms.

Few Irish crime novelists are as immersed in the granular details of crime across Irish society as is Gene Kerrigan, who has suggested that 'To write fiction about Irish crime is to write about Irish society – in its brutality, its irrationality and its injustice.'[38] Kerrigan's novels emphatically reflect this view, with an acute empathy (also evident in Irish crime writers from Jane Casey to Brian McGilloway to John Connolly) and with a commitment to the genre's capacity for concrete, specific social critique that is among the most insistent in Irish crime fiction. His fourth novel, *The Rage* (2012), has a Chandler epigraph – 'The law was something to be manipulated for profit and power. The streets were dark with something more than night' – that not only signals his relationship to the genre but distils his central themes, of empathy, justice, and corruption.[39] Reflecting these patterns as well as his reputation as a dogged journalist, Kerrigan's novels from the very first sceptically describe the boom of the Celtic Tiger era almost as though it were already over. (Of course, he is not alone in such reflections – a character in Paul Murray's first novel, *The Evening of Long Goodbyes* (2003), worries that the boom will end and people will realise that 'all anyone'll have done is eaten a lot of expensive cheese'[40] – but Kerrigan's ability to write as though the boom were already over is distinct.) His first novel, *Little Criminals*, was published in 2005, but necessarily written earlier, when the public discourse of the boom was almost relentlessly optimistic, and property prices were not yet at their peak –

[38] Gene Kerrigan, 'Brutal, Harrowing and Devastating,' in Burke, *Down These Green Streets*, 262.

[39] Gene Kerrigan, *The Rage* (London: Harvill Secker, 2011; repr. New York: Europa, 2012), 9.

[40] Paul Murray, *An Evening of Long Goodbyes* (London: Hamish Hamilton, 2003; repr. London: Penguin, 2011), 234.

though the certainty of overvaluation and the likelihood of a bubble had already been identified publicly, albeit with considerable dissent from the government.[41] Early in *Little Criminals*, Kerrigan describes a magazine article about 'ten up-and-coming entrepreneurs who made fortunes during the boom years,' a phrasing that quietly suggests those years are clearly past, not a mainstream suggestion by any means in 2005's Ireland. The novel quickly makes this more explicit, describing the nature of Irish business mergers 'since the economic boom peaked.'[42] By *The Midnight Choir* (2006), Kerrigan is already depicting not just the crash but ongoing desperate denials of its reality: 'the country had been a decade in love with its own prosperity and everyone agreed that even though the boom years were over there was no going back. We might, Synnott thought, be card-carrying members of the new global order, but we're still committing the same old crimes.'[43] *Dark Times in the City* (2009) opens on a yet more insistent note, as two unnamed criminals searching for a potential burial site in the Dublin mountains turn to look back at the cityscape and its inhabitants:

> Many of them were wealthy and wealth is detachable. In that shallow, glittering bowl there were a million opportunities. ... It used to be that the chattering classes were never done boasting about how many cranes there were on the Dublin skyline. The cranes were badges of national pride, and they talked about them in the same respectful tones that the old folk used when they remembered the sacred patriot dead. *Not so much boasting these days.*[44]

Indeed, by the publication of *The Rage*, this note has moved from an observation in mid-stream to a more fully articulated analysis of how

---

[41] On 4 July 2007, for example, *Taoiseach* Bertie Ahern famously remarked of people 'moaning' about the economy, 'I don't know how people who engage in that don't commit suicide,' a remark that his subsequent apology did little to prevent symbolising the official response to those who were questioning the Irish economy. For a discussion of this remark and its contexts, see Fintan O'Toole, *Ship of Fools: How Stupidity and Corruption Sank the Celtic Tiger* (London: Faber, 2009; reprinted and updated 2010), 119–124.

[42] Gene Kerrigan, *Little Criminals* (London: Vintage, 2005; repr. New York: Europa, 2008), 50.

[43] Gene Kerrigan, *The Midnight Choir* (London: Harvill Secker, 2006; repr. New York: Europa, 2007), 23.

[44] Gene Kerrigan, *Dark Times in the City* (London: Harvill Secker 2009; repr. New York: Europa, 2013), 16.

people assumed this 'money-go-round would keep spinning as long as two or three bad things didn't happen simultaneously – then four or five bad things happened at once' as 'house prices went through the floor, jobs evaporated, factories and businesses that had been around for decades folded overnight,' until 'The knowledge that all the backslapping and arrogance of the previous decade was nurtured in bullshit made the country blush like a teenager caught posing in front of a mirror.'[45] Not that Kerrigan's writing lacks a grimly dry humour about the Celtic Tiger's various excesses ('If the new Irish aristocracy had an emblem,' one Garda observes of an oversized chess set, 'that's it – a swanky, overpriced version of a game they can't play'[46]) and failings ('Designed for relaxed shopping. The place had everything, including lots of *To Let* signs'[47]). Whether couched through such sardonic passages, or less leavened by humour, the consistency of Kerrigan's critiques in these novels stands out for its earliness and intensity alike.

Particularly in his first two novels, *Little Criminals* and *The Midnight Choir*, Kerrigan's fiction creates a continual motion in the narrative, with rapid and frequent cuts from one section to the next, from one character

---

[45] Kerrigan, *Rage*, 23. In a later passage that echoes Hughes's depiction of the rationale for succeeding generations of civic corruption – 'if everyone was on the take, it cancelled itself out; as good as if no-one was' (Hughes, *Wrong*, 334) – a highly ranked Garda accuses a Detective Sergeant of 'throwing around allegations about the very people who have an important role in getting this country up from its knees' (Kerrigan, *Rage*, 277). Anticipating such rationales, the novel preemptively undercuts the senior officer in an earlier scene, when James Snead, a retired construction worker, gives one acidly concise view of Irish politics: 'After all the bullshit about the fight for freedom, about throwing off the foreign yoke – they gave the country away. The politicians fell in love with the smart fellas – gave them any law they wanted. The smart fellas made speeches and gave interviews about how smart they were, and the journalists kissed their arses. And in the end it was the smart fellas broke the country in pieces, without any help at all from the red brigades' (Kerrigan, *Rage*, 88). This argument has its precedents in the earlier *Dark Times in the City*, where the crime boss Lar Mackendrick defends himself against an IRA man's accusation that he is 'part of what's wrong with this country.' Mackendrick smiles in reply: 'Half this city was built on crooked land deals and politicians selling bent planning permission. ... All those big-time tax frauds the banks organized – you see any bankers in jail? The difference is I steal thousands, they steal millions' (Kerrigan, *Dark*, 226). Lar eventually rebuts the IRA man's point in more personal terms that echo Snead: 'Thirty years you spent blowing things up, shooting people dead in front of their wives and their kids – and you're lecturing *me* on the spirit of the fucking nation?' (Kerrigan, *Dark*, 227).

[46] Kerrigan, *Rage*, 128.

[47] Kerrigan, *Rage*, 56.

to the next, allowing for telling juxtapositions. These juxtapositions lend a certain density to the depiction of Irish society, reinforcing the point without the overt intrusion of an authorial voice. This rhythm also gives weight to Kerrigan's otherwise light touch with telling details. In *The Midnight Choir*, for example, a minor character who has been badly beaten by criminals has to spend 'the evening on a trolley in the A&E corridor,' a glancing reference to one of the defining images associated with Ireland's healthcare crises, mounting even amidst the peak boom years.[48] Similarly, in describing the gangster Lar Mackendrick's estate, an aside notes that previously 'it had been owned by an undistinguished local councillor who suddenly sold off an extensive property portfolio and moved his family to Spain,' cashing out only part way into the boom, and short of the market's peak.[49] This detail is suggestive at once of the corruption likely to have led an 'undistinguished local' politician to amass such a portfolio in the first place, as well as of intimidation or risk of prosecution leading him to sell 'suddenly' in a rising market. In this one sentence, Kerrigan deftly hints at a deep reservoir of contexts, including Ireland's history of planning corruption, detailed by Hourigan and Byrne among others, and the involvement of criminals like Mackendrick in that corruption. Such brief details are frequently mentioned only in passing, left to speak to the era's conditions without narrative comment from Kerrigan. These knowing contextual references establish the novel's intimate credibility without making it in any simplistic way *about* the Tiger era.[50]

Kerrigan's novels also include more overtly contextual passages, as when *Little Criminals* refers to Ireland's shockingly expensive sea of tribunals in the early 2000s, mired as they were in corruption both petty and

[48] Kerrigan, *Midnight*, 246. Other writers make similarly intimate references to the social pressures of the time. Declan Hughes, for example, has Ed Loy's friend Detective Inspector Dave Donnelly complain about the 'hit on his salary because of the public service pension levy,' a very specific reference indeed to the austerity regime that followed the economic crash in Ireland, when the levy served as a back-door pay cut on public sector salaries (Hughes, *City*, 92). Loy responds with characteristically bone-dry sarcasm: 'There's no room any more for the politics of envy, as you know, Dave. We should just sit back and wait for the bankers and developers who got us into this mess to get us out of it, as of course they will, in due course, once they've figured out a way to screw us all over again' (Hughes, *City*, 92).

[49] Kerrigan, *Midnight*, 285.

[50] *Dark Times in the City* is more overt in titling Part 2 of the novel '*Entrepreneurs*,' among the most totemically Celtic-Tiger-ish of words, both for its marking of elevated status in that era and for the way it grew to signify a vapidly self-congratulatory kind of entitlement (Kerrigan, *Dark*, 117).

grand in scale, leaving in their wake crowds of 'barristers looking to put tribunal money to profitable use.'[51] The narrative ties this to a broader, subtler undermining of justice, reminding the reader of the scale of the money involved when the barrister Desmond Cartwright bribes his way out of a drunk driving charge, which he justifies by claiming that facing the charge would prevent him from utilising his 'intellect' and 'guts to do what's right for this country' once he becomes a judge.[52] Over the course of the scene, however, the narrative specifies with an almost Dickensian use of physiognomy that 'Cartwright had made a solid reputation' in his early years, when 'His fees grew in proportion to his experience, and his girth in proportion to his fees. Representing a leading businessman at a long-running tribunal of inquiry, Cartwright graduated from merely very wealthy to unassailably rich.'[53] Another businessman similarly benefits from the bulwark of his wealth, grown great enough 'that his skirmishes with legality took on the glow of youthful frolics.'[54] In such passages, characteristic of his fiction, Kerrigan concisely and deftly conveys the texture of Irish political and civic life from the mid-1990s through to the novel's publication, and does so not through the mechanisms of plot but through these concise sketches of character. (In doing so, Kerrigan shows himself to be yet another Irish writer who challenges the assumption that crime fiction is necessarily only about plot.) This texture was characterised by what insiders rationalised as the way of doing business, but what by any other name was widespread, petty corruption that gradually had corrosive effects across its society and its culture.[55]

Despite the aura of omnipotence around characters such as Cartwright, Kerrigan's fiction, like Glynn's, depicts a system characterised by little sense that *anyone* is in control, or that anyone really knows quite what they are doing. It is a context, in his telling, in which almost everyone is out of their depth. *Little Criminals*, for example, revolves around a kidnapping that goes awry, with motives misunderstood at one point or another by

---

[51] Kerrigan, *Little*, 109. Byrne argues, however, that despite the enormous expense of the tribunals they still worked to the government's material advantage: 'the financial yield to the exchequer as a direct consequence of the inquiries is twice their estimated cost. When indirect revenue is considered, the yield to the exchequer is over four times their outlay' (*Political Corruption*, 181).

[52] Kerrigan, *Little*, 134.

[53] Kerrigan, *Little*, 132–133.

[54] Kerrigan, *Little*, 207.

[55] See O'Toole, *Ship of Fools*; Byrne, *Political Corruption*; and Hourigan, *Rule-Breakers*.

most of the characters, good and bad alike. As the Assistant Garda Commissioner sighs at one point, 'what we know for certain – fuck all.' This is not – or not just – a critique of the Gardaí. Instead, that same scene makes it clear that journalists (including Dublin's 'leading investigative journalist') are also ill-informed about the story, while opposition politicians are piling on to the Government, and 'the public found the killings more exciting than shocking' because 'it was an internal gangland affair' in which 'No civilians had been hurt.'[56] This is more than a mockery of criminal and official errors and ineptitude: it constitutes a much broader critique of a flawed system and a damaged civic culture, a critique that depicts these failures as serially interrelated.

This systemic view is a far cry from any emptily cynical view that 'sure, they're each as bad as the next': *Little Criminals* has ample fingers to point, ample judgements to make. From the opening page, which puts the reader *in medias res* until near the conclusion, the novel's ethical focus is framed in terms at once broadly ranging and precisely specific, encompassing characters from those who rob a pub through to the Celtic Tiger's speculators, as Stephen, a witness to the pub robbery, thinks: 'There were people who took shortcuts through other people's lives, didn't give a damn what harm they did. Sometimes, what mattered wasn't just the damage they left after them, it was the reckless contempt of it. It's like some lives matter and other people exist just to populate the landscape.'[57] A more central character, veteran Detective Inspector John Grace, pointedly tracks this disregard across classes: 'The way things were, when people didn't get the things they wanted or needed, some of them became beaten and sour, others just took what they could, where they could. All of them, whether they lived in ghettos or mansions, had their own vision of the life they were entitled to.'[58] Grace here touches on one of Kerrigan's recurring themes, the parallels between the crimes of Dublin's poor and the crimes of its burgeoning bourgeoisie. In all of Kerrigan's novels, these parallels consistently level the presumed and habitual distinctions of class, undermining the financial elites' pretensions of grandeur, competence, and merit while simultaneously extending degrees of empathy and understanding to street criminals, shrinking the gap between tabloid crimes and *Irish Times* crimes. When a wealthy man tries to interfere with his son's

---

[56] Kerrigan, *Little*, 89.
[57] Kerrigan, *Little*, 11–12.
[58] Kerrigan, *Little*, 181.

prosecution for rape by sending a junior employee to pose as a lawyer and warn the victim against the humiliations of a trial, the investigating sergeant, Rose Cheney, discovers the ruse and identifies the junior employee through his staff profile, which lists him as a 'B.Comm., M.P.R.I.I.', i.e., as someone who earned a Bachelor's degree in communications and who is a Member of the Public Relations Institute of Ireland. '*These days*,' Cheney thinks, '*even the hoodlums come with letters after their names.*'[59] Indeed, the experiences of those who suffer under the narrowly selfish contempt of others' urges are central to Kerrigan's ethics and aesthetics, leading his work towards precisely such critiques, which he then supports through his novels' diffused structures. For Kerrigan, as for Glynn, the broad ethical interest in the specific crimes of corruption draws his novels towards narrative structures built around large casts of characters, woven together through shifts, cuts, and jumps, with little sense of a single centre in one character or another.

For Kerrigan's fiction, the spine that allows these structures and characters to cohere is not the tight continuity of plot's momentum but a core empathy, exhibited by veteran police as much as anyone else, notably Grace. While waiting in the courthouse hallway for a verdict in a manslaughter trial, Grace views a shoplifter he knows as a woman who 'might be technically a habitual criminal but in truth … was a decent sort who did her best with one of the few income-producing options open to her.'[60] This passing moment, indicative of the series' commitment to engaging meaningfully with society's castoffs, is quickly contrasted with the prosperous lawyer Justin Kennedy's birthday dinner with his family. As he and his children finish their cake in the dining room, and his wife 'Angela left the kitchen, carrying two cups of coffee, there was something on the TV about a verdict in a manslaughter trial. The kitchen door swung closed behind her as the screen showed a fat little man with a sweaty face being

---

[59] Kerrigan, *Midnight*, 303. The phrase 'these days' recurs throughout the series, typically as an indicator of the boom-era hubris of thinking everything had changed. In this same novel, for example, the vain and shallow Minister for Justice vacuously asserts that 'These days … we get things done. On the streets at home, or on the world stage' (Kerrigan, *Midnight*, 236). Kerrigan quickly juxtaposes this with a woman who, unhappy with her latte, gets the server fired by complaining that 'the customer expects certain standards these days' (Kerrigan, *Midnight*, 240). This juxtaposition underscores the self-congratulatory vapidity of the phrase, putting a particular point on the novel's criticisms of the Celtic Tiger's excesses.

[60] Kerrigan, *Little*, 95.

led out in handcuffs, climbing cautiously into a van.'[61] Kerrigan offers no further comment beyond this juxtaposition, which is nonetheless enough to suggest that the lives involved in that trial – those of the dead man and his attacker, along with those of the families they leave behind – amount to no more than unnoticed background noise in lives like Justin and Angela's, lives that for the moment seem more placidly settled. With its unspoken but unambiguous point about the disconnection from empathy, this scene is emblematic of how Kerrigan's writing works, modelling the value his fiction places on empathy and the ways in which he attends to its absence.

In its most basic sense, empathy as Kerrigan expresses it is about imagining the experiences of other people as *they* experience them. At times, this empathy receives a broad, almost universal voicing, as when Grace helps put his young grandson to bed, observing 'The simple beauty and innocence' of the boy: 'He'd seen that quality in his own children, and watched as it was washed away by incremental waves of maturity. There wasn't a face on the planet, no matter how hardened, weary or cruel, that hadn't at one time, and however briefly, glowed with that same beauty and innocence.'[62] This is soon amplified when Angela, imprisoned by her kidnappers, describes her childhood recognition of 'the size and the complexity of the world, and that she wasn't the centre of it all, and that it didn't stop when she went to bed and fell asleep,' a recognition that seems to evade many characters here.[63] Such basic empathy underlies other varieties throughout Kerrigan's work. When Gardaí shoot a kidnapper during a rescue, Kerrigan devotes several pages to the kidnapper's thoughts and rationalisations as he bleeds in the street, never quite aware that he is himself dying: 'As consciousness melted into something else, Milky thought, Gone nowhere, I'm right here. Just resting.'[64] Amidst the narrative tension of the kidnapping, this passage exemplifies his novels' attention to character and to individual experiences within a social structure, an attention that functions first through the workings of empathy, over and above the dictates of plot, dictates little served by the narrative space given to Milky. The seemingly abrupt ending of *Little Criminals* confirms the weight of this attention, as Stephen – the elderly witness to the pub

[61] Kerrigan, *Little*, 98.
[62] Kerrigan, *Little*, 141–142.
[63] Kerrigan, *Little*, 147.
[64] Kerrigan, *Little*, 292.

robbery that opened the book – confesses to killing the gang's leader in protest at the damage he so casually inflicted on people in Stephen's town. Fully in keeping with the narrative that precedes it, Stephen's role suggests again that the real focus of the novel has been on questions other than those made explicit at the level of plot. In particular, empathy is integral to *Little Criminals*, both structurally (with its continual shifts amongst different characters' perspectives) and thematically (with its enduring interest in the after effects of violence on characters at all levels of society, characters who inhabit all shades of culpability for the narrative's crimes, from bystander to victim to violator). This centrality in *Little Criminals* establishes the foundation on which the rest of Kerrigan's novels build.

Indeed, while Kerrigan's novels register their engagement with the downtrodden and outcast, they also attend to others more likely to receive scorn and judgement, often enough including righteous judgement. This includes Maura Coady, an elderly nun ridden with guilt about having beaten children in her care, and robbers whose deaths in a shootout lead Detective Sergeant Bob Tidey to feel 'regret for the two gobshites in the morgue, and for whatever policeman put them there.'[65] Such examples are characteristic of Kerrigan's work, which holds empathy for the individual in tension with often scathing critiques of the system those individuals find themselves inhabiting. This tension enables a real moral depth and complexity, one that sees all of the characters' choices in connection to and contrast with each other. These connections between crooks and cops, junkies and politicians, are all the more powerful for their seemingly unmediated presentation, through which Kerrigan implies – forcefully, and yet quietly, with very little overt authorial commentary – an analysis across social strata, an analysis coloured by a kind of righteous outrage that is anchored in a thoroughgoing sense of empathy. Here, as so consistently elsewhere, Kerrigan's fiction is at a bone-deep level structured centrally around that empathy, for the good and bad alike.

That structure often contains significant police procedural elements, but rather than adhering to the procedural subgenre Kerrigan's novels move continually between characters, classes, and professions, having more in

---

[65] Kerrigan, *Rage*, 171; for Maura's confession to Bob Tidey, see Kerrigan, *Rage*, 176, 178–183, 307. Declining Church authority is also mentioned in *The Midnight Choir*, through a brief encounter with a priest who 'still received from his parishioners the regard that used to be the birthright of all priests, before the scandals broke the Church' (Kerrigan, *Midnight*, 258)

common with the structure and scope of a show like *The Wire* – also, not coincidentally, the work of veteran journalists – than with any single-genre heading. Other novelists have worked these intersections (like Niamh O'Connor), or have rooted their novels in gangland Dublin (like Frankie Gaffney), or have decentred their narratives in thematically significant ways (like Alan Glynn and Lisa McInerney). No one, however, has really written Irish crime fiction with quite the same mix of characteristics as Kerrigan's, with the focused range of Dublin geography it encompasses, the extensive use of narratives that cut across classes, and the reliance on juxtaposition (particularly of the underworld gangster and the white collar criminal) to create a commentary all the more powerful for being pointed and spare.[66]

The power of this commentary should not, however, be confused with certainty, closure, or resolution. On the contrary, for Kerrigan as for Brian McGilloway, empathy – used as a method rather than a solution – can put characters in a seemingly irresolvable conflict about what to do when they can find 'No moral thing to do. But something had to be done.'[67] Such narrative uncertainty recurs in Irish crime fiction from John Connolly to Tana French, whose work uses ambivalence and loss to create a thorough-going and unresolved uncertainty, one with which characters at best make a contingent peace.

Uncertainty in Tana French's Dublin

A related sense of at-best contingent certainty shapes the core of Tana French's fiction. French's drama training leaves traces throughout her novels, which are framed largely by first-person narrators with strong, sus-

---

[66] Kerrigan's novels make this point more than once. When the Minister for Justice questions Synnott in *The Midnight Choir* about the 'ambitions' of gangland criminals, Synnott thinks – but does not say – '*Same as yours, minister, same as your horsey friend's. They want position and wealth with the least amount of sweat possible. They do whatever it takes*' (Kerrigan, *Midnight*, 235). A strand of contemporary Irish crime fiction – including Hughes, Glynn, and Kerrigan – has regularly depicted little meaningful difference between gangsters and white collar criminals, as suggested by panellists at Trinity's 2013 festival of Irish crime fiction. Recent Irish history has lent itself well to perceiving criminality across class and occupation, with no particular exemption – quite the opposite – carved out for the upper classes during the boom.

[67] Kerrigan, *Rage*, 16. This same character, Bob Tidey, comments in the best attempt he can muster to give some hope to a suspect's relative, 'There's no happy ending to this, but let's see what we can see, right?', a cautiously balanced assessment, at once frank and, within its limits, encouraging (Kerrigan, *Rage*, 55).

tained individual voices.[68] The immersive quality of these first-person narratives makes the reader particularly dependent on narrators who withhold, and even dissemble, or who remember only fragments, creating a problematic reliability that keeps the reader both immersed and off-balance. Across her first six novels – *In the Woods* (2007), *The Likeness* (2008), *Faithful Place* (2010), *Broken Harbour* (2012), *The Secret Place* (2014), and *The Trespasser* (2016) – this sense of voice shapes not only the narrators but also French's use of the police procedural subgenre, a crucial element of scenes such as the long interrogations from *In the Woods*, or the extensive forensic detail in *Broken Harbour*, scenes distilled until they resemble extended stage dialogues, slowing the narrative while heightening the tension.

Although her novels are structured and marketed as part of the Dublin Murder Squad series, French evades the fundamental genre convention of the recurring series protagonist: each novel has a different protagonist-narrator, often a secondary character from the immediately preceding novel. Through this pattern, distinct like Kerrigan's books from a conventional single-protagonist series, the novels amplify each other without making a reader's understanding of one entirely dependent on the others. French's emotionally and psychologically rich novels proceed essentially through these different characters.

French's novels have developed a market status as both literary fiction and genre fiction, winning numerous awards and generating significant sales, domestically and abroad. This position speaks to a central goal in French's work, as she makes clear in discussing Donna Tartt's *The Secret History*, which

> wasn't marketed as a mystery novel at all; it was presented as literary fiction, but I think it would be ridiculous to claim that it isn't both. The book itself is one of the best arguments I've ever seen against that tired, lazy distinction … Sure, it's about the mystery surrounding a murder; but it refuses to go along with the convention that says the real mystery is whodunnit. For this book, the true mystery is deeper, buried inside the hidden places of the human mind: why the murder happened; what consequences it has, for everyone it touches.[69]

---

[68] French has commented on this in several interviews, including Clare Coughlan, 'Paper Tiger: An Interview with Tana French,' in Burke, *Down These Green Streets*, 343.

[69] Tana French, '*The Secret History* by Donna Tartt (1992),' in *Books to Die For: The World's Greatest Mystery Writers on the World's Greatest Mystery Novels*, ed. John Connolly and Declan

This view of 'the real mystery' shaped her own sense of the possible, French suggests, particularly her 'aim to write mysteries that take genre conventions as springboards, not as laws ... books where the real murder mystery isn't whodunnit, but whydunnit and what it means.'[70] This distinction, and French's emphasis on the 'why,' is part of how her books sustain their baseline uncertainty, as if suggesting that any understanding of such an intimate 'why' as these books involve must necessarily be at best partial or oblique. French's fiction generates further unease by shifting subtly between genres, supernatural, Gothic, and crime among them. Her characters acknowledge those genres' conventions with a wry self-awareness, as the narrator Rob does in the first book: 'I could get a fedora and a trench coat and a wisecracking sense of humor; she could sit poised at hotel bars with a slinky red dress and a camera in her lipstick, to snare cheating businessmen.'[71] As her essay on Tartt suggests, however, genre conventions rarely determine the arc of French's novels.

In the Dublin Murder Squad series, French crosses Gothic and other genres with Irish literary traditions, from pookas and fairy lore (*In the Woods*) to Big House novels (*The Likeness*), from the Celtic Tiger to Irish Gothic novels and Irish theatre's family traumas (*Faithful Place* and *Broken Harbour*). Among other effects, these crossings allow the series to convey experiences of fundamental uncertainty, as when *Faithful Place*'s narrator Frank Mackey feels 'the earth rippling and flexing underneath me like a great muscle, sending us all flying, showing me all over again who was boss and who was a million miles out of his depth ... The tricky shiver in the air was a reminder: everything you believe is up for grabs, every ground rule can change on a moment's whim.'[72] Virtually French's only Irish counterpart on such unstable ground is John Connolly, whose work (see Chapter 5) is 'fascinated by the possibility of combining the rationalist traditions of the mystery novel with the antirationalist underpinnings of supernatural fiction.'[73] Like Connolly, French's importance lies not just in her popularity (though that does shape perceptions of the genre, and does draw readers to other Irish authors) but also in the unsettling power she

Burke (London: Hodder, 2012), 568–569.

[70] French, '*The Secret History*,' 572.

[71] Tana French, *In the Woods* (New York: Penguin, 2007, repr. 2008), 274.

[72] Tana French, *Faithful Place* (New York: Penguin, 2010; repr. 2011), 247.

[73] John Connolly, *I Live Here* (Dublin: Bad Dog, 2013), expanded and reprinted in *Night Music: Nocturnes 2* (New York: Atria, 2015), 422.

generates by blurring genre boundaries, in the way she maintains what Eve Patten has described in another context as 'a purposeful inconclusiveness.'[74]

The specifics of contemporary Ireland, the economic boom among them, have been central in varying ways throughout French's fiction, perhaps especially in her first four novels, though all six frame their narratives in relation to the wider society, with protagonists who have sharp eyes for subtle class distinctions, which they readily manipulate in working their cases. The Tiger era's direct impact on lives is most overt in *Broken Harbour*, which centres on a family that has murderously imploded under the strains of the economic collapse. Here, the economy is an essential plot engine, even as the desperately positive narrator Kennedy defends the developers of half-finished ghost estates (like the titular one): 'if it wasn't for them thinking big, we'd never have got out of the last' recession.[75] However, despite this prominent contemporary context, French's novels also insistently ground themselves in deeper histories, whether those are of 1980s working-class Dublin poverty and economic emigration (*Faithful Place*), the post-1960's aspirational but abortive growth of Dublin's suburbs (*In the Woods*), or the colonial legacy of aristocratic estates (*The Likeness*). Even when the present looms large, these pasts are at the heart of the matter, magnifying the uncertainty in the series.

This uncertainty is often illustrated in French's use of what should be the most stable elements of our lives: our homes. The Celtic Tiger centred in many ways on property, and her first four novels revolve around private homes.[76] These homes have at best a fragile role in the lives of the protagonists, most of whom are haunted by a desire to belong and by their own regrets, missed chances, and turning points. Along with this fragile hold on being at home, other patterns sharpen the sense of instability across the series. One is a kind of retrospective foreshadowing that highlights – without mediating – the gap between what the narrator regrets and the reader does not yet know. Halfway through *Broken Harbour*, for example, without fully elaborating on what exactly went wrong, the nar-

---

[74] Eve Patten, 'Contemporary Irish Fiction,' *The Cambridge Companion to the Irish Novel*, ed. John Wilson Foster (Cambridge: Cambridge University Press, 2006), 261.

[75] Tana French, *Broken Harbour* (Dublin: Hachette, 2012), 13.

[76] Rosemary Erickson Johnsen has suggested that French's first four novels comprise an 'alternate ... tour' of Dublin, with 'different levels of the housing market explored one book at a time' ('Crime Fiction's Dublin,' 132). Shirley Peterson elaborates on this theme in 'Homicide and Home-icide: Exhuming Ireland's Past in the Detective Novels of Tana French,' *Clues: A Journal of Detection* 30, no. 2 (2012): 97–108.

rator and lead investigator Kennedy remarks that, 'When I think about the Spain case, from deep inside endless nights, this is the moment I remember. Everything else, every other slip and stumble along the way, could have been redeemed. This is the one I clench tight because of how sharp it slices.'[77]

He is not alone in such memories, for French's narrator-detectives are frequently wrong, their mysteries solved almost in spite of their blind spots, their mistakes, their intimate and at times dysfunctional attachment to the cases. During *In the Woods*, for example, Rob makes the case virtually un-prosecutable by hiding his connections to it and by woefully misreading a central character, while Conway and Moran draw critically mistaken conclusions even at the end of *The Secret Place*, as pointedly underlined in that novel's final chapter,[78] and as they do again at critical points in *The Trespasser*. This pattern is so clear as to suggest that something in the world fundamentally exceeds the grasp of reason and stands outside of rational comprehension: 'Caught the edge of understanding,' as Stephen puts it, 'swung by my fingertips, before I lost hold and it soared up and away again.'[79] Indeed, as critics have noted,[80] French's are rarely if ever logical mysteries in which everything is explained, everything understood, neither by the detectives nor by the other characters. Kennedy's compulsive 'Positive Mental Attitude,' for example, leaves him bereft before the possibility that '*There isn't any why*.'[81] His urgent need to believe in order is part of what makes the Spain case so destabilising for him: 'This case was different. It was running backwards, dragging us with it on some ferocious ebb tide. Every step washed us deeper in black chaos, wrapped us tighter in tendrils of crazy and pulled us downwards.'[82] Here, only the barest outlines are grasped, and these only tenuously.

The central means of fostering this pervasive narrative instability, however, is the weight French gives to Gothic and supernatural elements. These elements can be sensory – like the 'atavistic prickle' that 'went up [Rob's] spine,' or the visceral 'presence of evil ... strong and rancid-sweet in the air, curling invisible tendrils up the table legs, nosing with obscene

---

[77] French, *Broken Harbour*, 267.
[78] Tana French, *The Secret Place* (New York: Viking, 2014), 432, 450–452.
[79] French, *Secret*, 424.
[80] See, for example, Johnsen, 'Crime Fiction's Dublin,' 133.
[81] French, *Broken*, 351.
[82] French, *Broken*, 363.

delicacy at sleeves and throats'[83] – but they also take the less impressionistic form of the actual magic seemingly forged by Holly and her friends in *The Secret Place*. Building on such elements, French articulates her own particular version of crime fiction, characterised by the series' fundamental uncertainty, which is in turn magnified by the play between the tropes, genres, and contexts on which she draws.

A closer look at *Faithful Place*, the novel to date through which most of the Dublin Murder Squad series' threads intersect, illustrates this. More than other series entries, it draws on the preceding novels while echoing in ways both overt and delicately implicit throughout the subsequent novels. Of its secondary characters, two ('Scorcher' Kennedy and Stephen Moran) serve as narrators in later books. A third (Holly Mackey) is an important catalyst in *The Secret Place*, where she occupies almost as much space on the page as does Stephen, who in turn appears a third time in *The Trespasser*, as the partner of that novel's protagonist-narrator Antoinette Conway. Continuing the pattern set in preceding novels, *Faithful Place* is narrated by Frank Mackey, who was Cassie's undercover supervisor in *The Likeness*, where – despite limited space on the page – French established him as a dramatically strong voice. In *Faithful Place*, however, the performativity of Frank's voice is pared back, and the reader encounters a more nuanced character.

One of the central themes that presses on Irish crime fiction – including novels by McKinty, Hughes, and others – has been the stresses reflected in and wrought by the economic boom and by the subsequent crash, in the varied shapes those experiences have taken on both sides of the border. Though its present-tense narrative takes place amidst the early days of the most recent crash, *Faithful Place* is set in motion by events decades in the past, the meaning of which emerges gradually over the present-tense narrative's course, triggering further crimes as it does so. The defining narrative strand from the characters' past concerns the teenaged Frank's plan to emigrate with his girlfriend Rosie, seeking to escape his brutally dysfunctional family. This plan, borne of desperation, speaks explicitly and pointedly to the bleakness of Ireland's 1980s, in which Frank and Rosie saw no hope, no opportunities beyond the dole and emigration, seemingly a way of life for their generation. Thus, despite the novel's present-tense setting amidst the end of the recent boom, it is in the first instance the experience of 1980s deprivation that drives the central characters and,

---

[83] French, *In the Woods*, 77, 374.

through them, the narrative. In broadening the focus from the Tiger and its aftermath to the 1980s recession, French gives a different kind of social depth to the experiences that drive her characters, who have a decades-long arc tied to Ireland's extreme swings between experiences of prosperity and poverty. This arc also stretches back beyond Frank and Rosie, to the 1960s unemployment and poverty that distorted their parents' lives: Frank's father's alcoholic, abusive rages are insistently tied to not just the 1980s deprivation his children experienced, but the 1960s poverty that, along with some of the last vestiges of peak clerical authority, trapped him on Faithful Place.

Frank and Rosie's plan to escape to a bright new life in London fell apart when Rosie did not make their rendezvous on the fateful night. Frank, thinking she had abandoned him to go to London on her own, simply moved across Dublin and never went home again. He returns only when Rosie's suitcase – with its poignant, spare collection of the few belongings she planned to take to London – is discovered mouldering in the chimney of a long-vacant house being gutted by developers. This disturbing discovery quickly becomes still more grim when her body is found under the basement floor of the same house, bearing signs of the violent act that killed her. The rest of the novel centres on Frank's efforts – despite this not being his case – to determine what happened, and to untangle the ramifications of her death.

In certain ways, this third novel is quite distinct from the rest of the series. The conclusion, for example, is comparatively upbeat (in fairness, crime fiction does set a low bar for what constitutes 'upbeat'), while the central mystery is, as Rachel Schaffer has argued,[84] more intimately connected to the narrator's past than earlier books in the series, a tighter focus that enriches the text. Similarly, although the entire series draws from the deep well of Irish Gothic and supernatural fiction, it does so least overtly in *Faithful Place* and *The Trespasser*. As a result, though it is no less 'sunk in local history,' one reviewer aptly observed, *Faithful Place* 'isn't as eccentric as French's previous novels.'[85] Nonetheless, the novel taps into that same 'eccentric' well in its own way, evincing Ross Macdonald's postwar California of tainted, twisted familial legacies as much as the

---

[84] Rachel Schaffer, 'Tana French: Archaeologist of Crime,' in 'Special Issue on Tana French,' ed. Rachel Schaffer, *Clues: A Journal of Detection* 32, no. 1 (2014): 36.

[85] Marilyn Stasio, 'The Old Neighborhood,' *New York Times*, 16 July 2010, http://www.nytimes.com/2010/07/18/books/review/Crime-t.html?_r=0 (accessed 5 March 2016).

nineteenth-century Irish writer Sheridan LeFanu's more ornate work: 'Blood tells, sonny boy. Blood tells,' we hear from Frank's abusive father Jimmy.[86] In its choice and construction of its narrator, and in its particular use of genre elements, then, this third novel is an important bridge in French's work, one that connects the series' different genres and narrative strands.

An essential continuity amidst these intersecting threads is the series' use of turning points and hinge moments, often colouring the novels with a sense of glowing, immanent potential, particularly with adolescence's 'too-tender-to-touch gold' aura.[87] This aura is tinged by an acute awareness of alternate, unrealised possibilities, and frequently by a stunning loss like Rob's: 'it almost knocked me over: all the things we should have had … I had been robbed blind.'[88] Drawing on this sense of loss, *Faithful Place* presents itself as centred on Frank's experience of 'that riptide change … much too strong to fight.'[89] As he elaborates later,

> All my signposts had gone up in one blinding, dizzying explosion: my second chances, my revenge, my nice thick anti-family Maginot line. Rosie Daly dumping my sorry ass had been my landmark, huge and solid as a mountain. Now it was flickering like a mirage and the landscape kept shifting around it, turning itself inside out and backwards; none of the scenery looked familiar any more.[90]

It is this kind of experience that French has described as 'what I'm interested in writing about – those enormous turning points that you only get a couple times in your life. … These moments strip people down to their essentials: You get to find out what you're really made of and what is really important to you.'[91] Indeed, every French novel includes such 'enormous turning points,' and she is adept at depicting those moments' pained and often remorseful qualities, as when Kennedy contemplates 'the ghosts of things that never got the chance to happen.'[92] More insistently and imme-

[86] French, *Faithful*, 328.
[87] French, *Secret*, 206.
[88] French, *In the Woods*, 185.
[89] French, *Faithful*, 2.
[90] French, *Faithful*, 109.
[91] 'Interview with Tana French,' July 2010, Goodreads.com, http://www.goodreads.com/interviews/show/536.Tana_French (accessed 5 March 2016).
[92] French, *Broken*, 187.

diately than the books before or after it, *Faithful Place* – overflowing with near misses, with brass rings that someone *almost* caught – pivots on this pain.

With this capacity for sweeping pathos, the hinge moments at the heart of French's novels – characterised as they are by the past's persistent haunting of the present – are most central in *Faithful Place*, with the series' closest integration of turning points, narrator, and plot. As we have seen, Frank's early life is marked by two related turning points, one of his own making and one not. The former is his choice to escape his family in Dublin for an adventurous life in London with Rosie, and the latter is Rosie's disappearance, which eclipsed the future he had envisioned. *Faithful Place* amplifies the weight of these turning points by having the central events ripple through not just Frank's life but the lives of his entire family, indeed of his entire street. His father, for example, crippled by his own grievances, directly related to Frank's, tells Frank that 'There's things went wrong fifty years ago, and they just kept going. It's time they stopped. If I'd've had the sense to let them go a long time back, there's a lot would've been different. Better.'[93] Despite this prominence, the novel eventually gives Frank's turning points a less heavily determined inflection by allowing him to revise his understanding of his past. With the qualified exception of Antoinette Conway in *The Trespasser*, the other narrators typically do not quite get enough information about their own pasts to enable such a recalibration, one that would allow them, like Frank, to shed at least some of the distorting weight of those pasts. Where Rosie had been Frank's 'own secret magnetic north' long after her disappearance, he learns that she did not abandon him just before emigrating alone.[94] On the contrary, she was murdered, as Maureen T. Reddy notes, '*because* she was faithful to him and *because* she was helping him get away.'[95] This revelation allows him to see his life anew and to reorient himself around tragedy rather than any betrayal by Rosie.

Near the conclusion, the novel suggests (as *The Secret Place* later confirms) that he will reunite with Olivia, the wife from whom he had separated but whom he sees as his saving beacon: 'I let myself out; maybe I said good night, I don't remember. All the way out to the car I could feel her

---

[93] French, *Faithful*, 331.

[94] French, *Faithful*, 395.

[95] Maureen T. Reddy, 'Authority and Irish Cultural Memory in *Faithful Place* and *Broken Harbor*,' in Schaffer, 'Special Issue on Tana French': 86.

behind me, the heat of her, like a clear white light burning steadily in the dark conservatory. It was the only thing that got me home.'[96] Such openness at the conclusion – Frank has direction but not a definite destination beyond his own bed for the night – jars with any traditional expectations of resolution, as does so much other Irish crime fiction. This ending is, however, fully in keeping with French's series, which paints cynicism and certainty as costumes, ones that no character wears gracefully, ones that are adopted as defensive poses, but that are never really integral to the book or the character in quite the way that hard-boiled conventions would sometimes have it.

French is not alone in this. Hughes's Ed Loy – for all of his weary banter – concludes *The Wrong Kind of Blood* with a precisely ambivalent view of human nature: 'I was in two minds anyways about why I liked Delaney when there was so much to dislike. Maybe it's just that the good in him seemed to outweigh the bad. I always thought that was worth taking a chance on. I was often wrong.'[97] Here, in the gap between 'always' and 'often,' Loy, among the most archly hard-boiled of Irish crime fiction narrators, implicitly acknowledges that his pessimism is a veneer over the hope, much like Frank's hard-boiled poses in *Faithful Place*.

It would be wrong to suggest that *Faithful Place* provides anything like full 'closure,' and not only because Frank dismisses the word as 'a steaming load of middle-class horseshite invented to pay for shrinks' Jags.'[98] Even approaching the conclusion, the novel introduces further notes of grey without resolving them: the guilty party in Rosie's death had done awful, unforgivable things, but is presented with empathy, even intimacy, in a way that complicates Frank's credibility. A clearly flawed narrator, Frank had neglected to mention telling events in his past, events that, as the reader learns in the climactic scene, qualify the self-image he projects. These late revelations demonstrate the novel's commitment to preserving an essential ambiguity, in keeping with the series' blurring of genres; as Meier and Ross perceptively note, 'Tana French is also concerned with crimes that go unpunished – so much so that her novels lack the reassurance of resolution, inviting the reader to share with her characters in the

---

[96] French, *Faithful*, 385.
[97] Hughes, *Wrong*, 303.
[98] French, *Faithful*, 133–134.

not-knowing.'[99] While family Gothic's antirational elements and mystery's rational impulses cross each other's orbits, Frank makes his way through the narrative, reaching little more certainty than the bittersweet rhapsody of the novel's closing line, in which he hopes 'to God that somehow or other, before it was too late, we would all find our way back home.'[100] In this tentative embrace of an uncertain hope, fully in keeping with the tenor and structures of French's work, the conclusion of *Faithful Place* models how Irish crime fiction working with the materials of contemporary Ireland can use the genre to reflect back and convey its society with as much sustained depth as any Irish writing.

CONCLUSION

Because Irish crime fiction is still emerging as an area of study, critics seem at times torn between emphasising either the Irish contexts of that fiction or genre-focused studies, often without really reconciling these strands. The novels of Tana French, however, require a less divided approach, and do so in ways that also challenge us to open our reading of her peers in Irish crime fiction, from Kerrigan's juxtapositions to Hughes's adaptations of hard-boiled forms. Within Irish crime fiction, novels like those by French, Kerrigan, Hughes, and their contemporaries are helping broaden the scope in every way, stretching habitual assumptions about the genre's boundaries and about their work's various contexts. French's novels inhabit uncertainty to an especially acute degree, for example, as do Glynn's, and this awareness of uncertainty's inescapability runs throughout Irish forms of the genre, as Chapter 5 considers. Like the pathos in *Faithful Place*, Irish crime fiction's adaptation of this uncertainty exceeds the bare requirements of the plot: rather than serving as mere ornamentation, it rises to the level of a world view. Despite the wider genre's association with closure and resolution, of course, many crime fiction plots require at least a temporary lack of certainty, but through some of its recurring patterns, including the blurring of genres by French and others, contemporary Irish crime fiction makes this lack fundamental, even existential. This is a defining feature of the work discussed here, one through which Irish crime fiction plays with many of the potent expecta-

---

[99] William Meier and Ian Campbell Ross, 'Editors' Introduction,' in Meier and Ross, 'Irish Crime Since 1921': 19.

[100] French, *Faithful*, 400.

tions that accompany the genre, as do the women protagonists discussed in the next chapter.

REFERENCES

Barclay, Alex. *Killing Ways.* London: HarperCollins, 2015.
Brady, Conor. 'The Journalist and the Policeman: Seekers for Truth or Rivals in the Game?' In Meier and Ross, 'Irish Crime Since 1921': 193-204.
Burke, Declan. *Absolute Zero Cool.* Dublin: Liberties, 2011.
———. ed. *Down These Green Streets: Irish Crime Writing in the 21ˢᵗ Century.* Dublin: Liberties, 2011.
———. *The Lost and the Blind.* Surrey: Severn, 2014.
Byrne, Elaine. *Political Corruption in Ireland 1922–2010: A Crooked Harp?* Manchester: Manchester University Press, 2012.
Carson, Paul. *Cold Steel.* London: Heinemann, 1998.
———. *Ambush.* London: Heinemann, 2004. Reprint, London: Arrow, 2005.
Carter, Andrea. *Death at Whitewater Church.* London: Constable, 2015.
Connolly, John. *I Live Here.* Dublin: Bad Dog, 2013. Expanded and reprinted in *Night Music: Nocturnes 2*, 399–443. New York: Atria, 2015.
Coughlan, Clare. 'Paper Tiger: An Interview with Tana French.' In Burke, *Down These Green Streets*, 335–344.
'Crime Fiction and Contemporary Ireland.' Panel discussion with Paul Charles, Declan Hughes, Gene Kerrigan, Brian McGilloway, Niamh O'Connor, and Louise Phillips. 'Irish Crime Fiction: A Festival.' Trinity College Dublin, 23 November 2013.
Dillon, Eilís. *Death in the Quadrangle: An Irish Mystery.* London: Faber, 1956. Reprint, Boulder: Rue Morgue, 2010.
French, Tana. *In the Woods.* London: Hodder & Stoughton, 2007. Reprint, New York: Penguin, 2008.
———. *The Likeness.* New York: Penguin, 2008. Reprint, 2009.
———. *Faithful Place.* New York: Penguin, 2010. Reprint, 2011.
———. 'Interview with Tana French.' Goodreads.com, July 2010. http://www. goodreads.com/interviews/show/536.Tana_French (accessed 5 March 2016).
———. *Broken Harbour.* Dublin: Hachette, 2012. Reprint, New York: Penguin, 2012.
———. '*The Secret History* by Donna Tartt (1992).' In *Books to Die For: The World's Greatest Mystery Writers on the World's Greatest Mystery Novels*, edited by John Connolly, Declan Burke, and Ellen Clair Lamb, 567–572. London: Hodder, 2012.
———. *The Secret Place.* New York: Viking, 2014.
———. *The Trespasser.* New York: Viking, 2016.

Gaffney, Frankie. *Dublin Seven*. Dublin: Liberties, 2015.

Glynn, Alan. *Winterland*. London: Faber, 2009. Reprint, 2010.

———. *Bloodland*. London: Faber, 2011.

———. *Graveland*. London: Faber, 2013.

———. Seminar discussion with the author and students. 'Imagining Ireland I' undergraduate seminar. Trinity College Dublin, 10 February 2014.

Hammett, Dashiell. *Red Harvest*. New York: Knopf, 1929. Reprint, New York: Vintage/Black Lizard, 1992.

Hourigan, Niamh. *Rule-Breakers: Why 'Being There' Trumps 'Being Fair' in Ireland*. Dublin: Gill & Macmillan, 2015.

Hughes, Declan. *The Wrong Kind of Blood*. London: John Murray, 2006. Reprint, 2007.

———. *The Colour of Blood*. London: John Murray, 2007.

———. *All the Dead Voices*. New York: William Morrow, 2009. Reprint, New York: Harper, 2010.

———. *City of Lost Girls*. London: John Murray, 2010. Reprint, 2011.

———. 'Irish Hard-Boiled Crime: A 51st State of Mind.' In Burke, *Down These Green Streets*, 161–168.

Hunt, Arlene. *Blood Money*. Dublin: Hachette, 2010.

Johnsen, Rosemary Erickson. 'Crime Fiction's Dublin: Reconstructing Reality in Novels by Dermot Bolger, Gene Kerrigan, and Tana French.' In Meier and Ross, 'Irish Crime Since 1921': 121–141.

Kerrigan, Gene. *Little Criminals*. London: Vintage, 2005. Reprint, New York: Europa, 2008.

———. *The Midnight Choir*. London: Harvill Secker, 2006. Reprint, New York: Europa, 2007.

———. *Dark Times in the City*. London: Harvill Secker, 2009. Reprint, New York: Europa, 2013.

———. *The Rage*. London: Harvill Secker, 2011. Reprint, New York: Europa, 2012.

———. 'Brutal, Harrowing and Devastating.' In Burke, *Down These Green Streets*, 249–263.

Kincaid, Andrew. '"Down These Mean Streets": The City and Critique in Contemporary Irish Noir.' *Éire-Ireland* 45, no. 1–2 (2010): 39–55.

McCarthy, Conor. *Modernisation, Crisis and Culture in Ireland, 1969–1992*. Dublin: Four Courts, 2000.

McGowan, Claire. *Blood Tide*. London: Headline, 2017.

Meier, William, and Ian Campbell Ross, eds. 'Irish Crime Since 1921.' Special issue, *Éire-Ireland* 49, no. 1–2 (2014).

———. 'Editors' Introduction: Irish Crime Since 1921.' In Meier and Ross, 'Irish Crime Since 1921': 7–21.

Millar, Cormac. *The Grounds*. Dublin: Penguin, 2006. Reprint, 2007.

Murray, Paul. *An Evening of Long Goodbyes.* London: Hamish Hamilton, 2003. Reprint, London: Penguin, 2011.

Nugent, Andrew. *The Four Courts Murder.* London: Headline, 2006.

O'Connor, Niamh. *If I Never See You Again.* London: Transworld, 2010. Reprint, 2011.

———. 'The Executioners' Songs.' In Burke, *Down These Green Streets*, 195–200.

O'Toole, Fintan. *Ship of Fools: How Stupidity and Corruption Sank the Celtic Tiger.* London: Faber, 2009. Reprinted and updated 2010.

Patten, Eve. 'Contemporary Irish Fiction.' In *The Cambridge Companion to the Irish Novel*, edited by John Wilson Foster, 259–275. Cambridge: Cambridge University Press, 2006.

Pepper, Andrew. *Unwilling Executioner: Crime Fiction and the State.* Oxford: Oxford University Press, 2016.

Peterson, Shirley. 'Homicide and Home-icide: Exhuming Ireland's Past in the Detective Novels of Tana French.' *Clues: A Journal of Detection* 30, no. 2 (2012): 97–108.

Phillips, Louise. *Red Ribbons.* Dublin: Hachette, 2012.

Reddy, Maureen T. 'Authority and Irish Cultural Memory in *Faithful Place* and *Broken Harbor*.' In Schaffer, 'Special Issue on Tana French': 81–91.

———. 'Contradictions in the Irish Hardboiled: Detective Fiction's Uneasy Portrayal of a New Ireland.' *New Hibernia Review* 19, no. 4 (2015): 126–140.

Schaffer, Rachel, ed. 'Special Issue on Tana French.' *Clues: A Journal of Detection* 32, no. 1 (2014).

———. 'Tana French: Archaeologist of Crime.' In Schaffer, 'Special Issue on Tana French': 31–39.

Stasio, Marilyn. 'The Old Neighborhood.' *New York Times,* 16 July 2010. http://www.nytimes.com/2010/07/18/books/review/Crime-t.html?_r=0 (accessed 5 March 2016).

Van Dyke, W.S., dir. *The Thin Man.* Hollywood: Metro-Goldwyn-Mayer, 1934.

CHAPTER 4

Women and Irish Crime Fiction

One of the clear strengths of Irish crime fiction is the prominence not only of female authors, who have emerged in tandem with their male peers, but of rewardingly complex female protagonists. Among the relatively few mid-century authors who produced crime fiction set in Ireland are Sheila Pim and Eilís Dillon. In novels like *Common or Garden Crime* (1945), which takes place in Ireland during World War II, Pim wrote village mysteries set in small Irish towns, a number of which have more recently been republished by the Rue Morgue Press. Dillon wrote a series of arch mysteries, including *Death in the Quadrangle: An Irish Mystery* (1956), also republished by Rue Morgue Press. This novel eventually inspired the setting for her son Cormac Millar's *The Grounds* (2006), and has many trappings of cosy crime fiction, but also has a number of barbed moments demonstrating the often-maligned subgenre's capacity for more treacherous emotional currents. (These moments include some acute satire on mid-century male academics' fear of women, something with which Dillon – married to an academic – was presumably only too familiar.) Pim and Dillon are to some extent, however, the exceptions that prove the rule: as with Irish crime fiction more generally, it is not that no precedents exist, nor that the genre sprang fully formed from the head of Ken Bruen or Colin Bateman in the 1990s. Rather, it is that only comparatively recently has a sustained sense of an active group of crime writers emerged, before which Irish literary history offers scattered and unjustly overlooked examples, but little critical mass.

© The Author(s) 2018
B. Cliff, *Irish Crime Fiction*, Crime Files,
https://doi.org/10.1057/978-1-137-56188-6_4

In contrast, since the late 1990s crime novels by Irish women have become both numerous and successful: at the annual Bord Gáis Energy Irish Book Awards, seven out of the nine Irish crime fiction awards through 2017 have been won by women.[1] The prominence of women authors in Irish crime fiction may be partly a function of the Irish marketplace, where a real boom in genre fiction followed the work of Maeve Binchy and other writers of what was marketed as women's literature. This strength may also reflect some of the broader developments in crime fiction – developments less familiar within Irish Studies – that Maureen T. Reddy has identified, particularly the 'astonishing number of series with female protagonists' that began to appear on the path cleared by Sue Grafton, Sara Paretsky, Marcia Muller and others from the late 1970s onward.[2] In an admirably lucid and detailed essay surveying feminist approaches to crime fiction and the critical responses to women crime writers, Lee Horsley quantifies some of this change. Making the important qualification 'that in examining the "regendering of the genre" we are not talking simply about the substitution of a female for a male detective,' she describes 'the number of fictional female investigators soaring from thirteen in the late 1970s to over 360 in the mid-1990s.'[3] This, the crucial role played by women crime novelists, touches on a recurring scholarly debate about whether the genre is fundamentally masculine and conservative, and whether the hard-boiled crime novel in particular is 'so *unavoidably* male that the whole project of feminist transformation seems a lost cause'[4] for progressive feminist critics and novelists. Horsley answers such questions with characteristic lucidity:

> For the better part of the twentieth century, writers who have wanted to subvert the conservative assumptions and practices of their society – whether with respect to class, race, or gender – have found a ready instrument in the crime novel, the narrative structure of which *requires* the disruption of

[1] Bord Gáis Energy Irish Book Awards, http://www.irishbookawards.irish/crime-fiction-award (accessed 3 December 2017).

[2] Maureen T. Reddy, 'Women Detectives,' in *The Cambridge Companion to Crime Fiction*, ed. Martin Priestman (Cambridge: Cambridge University Press, 2003), 200.

[3] Lee Horsley, *Twentieth-Century Crime Fiction* (Oxford: Oxford University Press, 2005), 243. Horsley is citing Priscilla L. Walton and Manina Jones, *Detective Agency: Women Rewriting the Hard-Boiled Tradition* (Berkeley: University of California Press, 1999), 28–30. See also Stephen Knight, *Crime Fiction Since 1800: Detection, Death, Diversity*, 2nd ed. (Basingstoke: Palgrave, 2010), 164.

[4] Horsley, *Twentieth-Century Crime Fiction*, 246.

apparently stable social arrangements. Just as the detective interrogates the guilty individual, the genre as a whole interrogates the collective guilts that society conceals under what looks like an orderly surface.[5]

This is an argument closely related to those discussed in Chapter 2: much as Aaron Kelly's work modelled an Irish criticism that could simultaneously identify the Troubles thriller's failings and underscore its more radical potential, feminist criticism has provided fierce critiques while exploring progressive capacities.

Late twentieth-century developments in crime writing by women have explicitly revised the genre, as many scholars have documented. Margaret Kinsman is not alone in arguing that 'the modern female private eye has proved to be … transformative of the genre' and that 'it is not only safe to say, but perhaps imperative to understand, that crime and mystery fiction really has not been the same since the birth of these three gumshoes [Sharon McCone, Kinsey Millhone, and V.I. Warshawski], and many more like them.'[6] She rightly includes in this indebtedness male novelists 'such as Ian Rankin, Robert Crais, [and] Lee Child … [who] have opened up the emotional and domestic lives of their tough cops and private eyes; and their novels now include interesting women characters who range well beyond the old stereotypes.'[7] Other scholars have extended this reading back into a deeper history, resisting any implication that female crime writers played a secondary role or that their only significance – outside of cosy or Golden Age novelists like Agatha Christie and Dorothy L. Sayers – has been in more recent revisions of the genre. Adrienne E. Gavin has documented how, as

> detective fiction took root in the nineteenth century, female crime writers and sleuths challenged general expectations about both women's writing

---

[5] Horsley, *Twentieth-Century Crime Fiction*, 287. Susan Rowland makes a similar argument in suggesting that 'crime fiction … crucially supplements the culturally authoritative texts of the law. … all crime fiction … is offering a story that the laws cannot or will not tell. It is saying, in effect, that there is more to crime than the institutionalized stories told in courts and police stations … Crime fiction is the *other* of the powers of legal institutions to *represent* crime to the culture.' Susan Rowland, *From Agatha Christie to Ruth Rendell: British Women Writers in Detective and Crime Fiction* (Basingstoke: Palgrave Macmillan, 2001), 17.

[6] Margaret Kinsman, 'Feminist Crime Fiction,' in *The Cambridge Companion to American Crime Fiction*, ed. Catherine Ross Nickerson (Cambridge: Cambridge University Press, 2010), 158, 148.

[7] Kinsman, 'Feminist Crime Fiction,' 161.

and female characters. The standard critical inclination has been to see female crime writers and detectives as also subverting a specifically male 'norm' for crime fiction. Women crime writers and investigators, however, while clearly expressing issues of female concern, have from the start been an integral part of the history of crime writing rather than simply an adjunct or reaction to it.

Gavin extends this argument to suggest that in the century between 'Victorian originators' and their more recent 'rebellious goddaughters ... a female and feminist vision of crime became a clear norm.'[8] Flipping such readings of women's place in a history seen as dominated by male authors and archetypes, Susan Rowland strikingly argues that 'detective fiction is structurally gendered as feminine. Perhaps critics should rather be concerned to explain how anxious male writers may engender a fundamentally unruly femininity in the genre, rather than start from the position of women authors as anomalous.'[9] Megan Abbott arrives at a related conclusion, arguing persuasively that even the appearance of masculinity in the genre is less stable than it seems. In the classic novels that establish the mode, Abbott suggests, already the hard-boiled

> figure's masculinity is shown to require constant maintenance and reconstitution. These men repeatedly find themselves dissembling, fainting, unconscious, overpowered, and out of control while their ideals of masculinity continue to require of them self-discipline, toughness, and the quintessential hardness that gives the genre its name. ... far from generic and stable, masculinity in these novels is a fraught and tentative thing, and not merely as a result of the femme fatale's betrayal. Indeed ... the protagonists' reaction to the femme fatale derives from an already existing threatened and threatening configuration of masculinity.[10]

Thus, through both literary-historical approaches and more theorised readings, scholars have done much to refute arguments about the genre's

---

[8] Adrienne E. Gavin, 'Feminist Crime Fiction and Female Sleuths,' in *A Companion to Crime Fiction*, ed. Charles J. Rzepka and Lee Horsley (Chichester: Blackwell, 2010), 258.

[9] Rowland, *From Agatha Christie to Ruth Rendell*, 17.

[10] Megan E. Abbott, *The Street Was Mine: White Masculinity and Urban Space in Hardboiled Fiction and Film Noir* (Basingstoke: Palgrave, 2002), 7–8. See also Horsley's chapter on 'Regendering the Genre' in *Twentieth-Century Crime Fiction*, 242–289, particularly her discussion of Sally Munt's *Murder by the Book? Feminism and the Crime Novel* (London: Routledge, 1994).

normativity and to challenge the habits of reading that both fostered and reflected those assumptions. In doing so, they have revised understandings of the genre and its history along feminist lines while simultaneously suggesting that such revisions reveal what was already happening under the accrued misreadings. As we have seen with the Troubles thriller, then, crime fiction in general and its hard-boiled mode in particular are at times constructed as monolithic, but – despite the problematic issues such constructions sometimes identify – the genre is much less stable, and consequently much more open to revision and to radical potential, than its critics have at times suggested.

Perhaps reflecting general readers' ability to perceive the genre's capacity for doing something other than reinscribing patriarchal values, crime fiction is frequently understood to have a disproportionately female readership. This is almost a truism, with largely experiential evidence. The British journalist and crime writer Melanie McGrath, for example, has described her experiences of seeing crime fiction festivals approaching an 80/20 balance of female/male audience members, against something more like a 50/50 ratio among the festival authors.[11] Similar numbers were apparent at the festival of Irish crime fiction I co-organised at Trinity College Dublin on 22–23 November 2013: approximately 70 per cent of ticket orders were made by women, which was in turn in line with the audiences at the festival itself. A number of novelists on the panels at this festival made points very similar to McGrath's, particularly about graphic violence against women, in books frequently written by women and frequently read by women.

A rare data-based study of this readership is *The Mystery Book Consumer in the Digital Age*, a study done for the organisation Sisters in Crime (founded by Sara Paretsky and others) by Bowker PubTrack, the American company that issues ISBNs. At least in the US, the report suggests, 68 per cent of mystery book sales are to women, a figure slightly higher than for fiction in general (64 per cent) or for espionage (59 per cent), though significantly lower than for romance (87 per cent).[12] The data also suggests

---

[11] Melanie McGrath, 'Women's appetite for explicit crime fiction is no mystery,' *Guardian* (Manchester), 30 June 2014, https://www.theguardian.com/books/booksblog/2014/jun/30/women-crime-fiction-real-anxieties-metaphorical (accessed 5 May 2017).

[12] Carl Kulo and R.R. Bowker, *The Mystery Book Consumer in the Digital Age*, www.sistersincrime.org/resource/resmgr/imported/ConsumerBuyingBookReport.pdf (accessed 5 May 2017), 6–7.

that women are slightly more likely (41 per cent) to value a 'Dark/ Suspenseful' mystery than are men (37 per cent),[13] and that women remain significantly more likely to read a book irrespective of the author's gender, with 21 per cent of men less likely to read a mystery written by a woman against only 7 per cent of women less likely to read one by a man.[14] Some caveats should restrict undue generalising to other cultures, including Ireland and the UK: the study is from 2010, shortly before the peak of electronic book reader sales; it is entirely US-based; and it separates 'Espionage' and 'Mystery,' but otherwise does not track subgenres of crime fiction. Nonetheless – particularly when taken with experiential accounts like McGrath's and those of many other authors, and with data from the 2013 festival in Dublin – this study seems to confirm that crime and mystery readers are in fact more likely than not to be women.

This readership alone does not insulate the genre from the critiques made by Sally Munt and others, of course, nor is this brief consideration sufficient to explain exactly why such numbers arise. Gavin offers one partial defence for some of the genre's representations of gender and violence, arguing that 'The central concern of feminist crime fiction remains violence against women. Women are victims: captured, raped, murdered, butchered and in the hands of forensic detectives dissected into evidence. In emphasizing violence against women, feminist detective fiction makes a gendered protest.'[15] Where Gavin and other critics address the fiction's generation and intent, the novelist McGrath emphasises rather its relationship to its readers: 'The trend towards ever-more explicit accounts of murder, rape and torture in crime novels, often involving a female victim, is led not by men but by women … partly because we understand what living with fear feels like.'[16]

---

[13] Kulo and Bowker, *The Mystery Book Consumer*, 33.

[14] Kulo and Bowker, *The Mystery Book Consumer*, 35. The study notes an interesting 'generational shift in perception and blurring of the lines' between genres and subgenres, suggesting perhaps that readers may be increasingly disinterested in subgenre divisions, such as that between the thriller and the cosy, or the noir and the comic, or the procedural and the PI (Kulo and Bowker, *The Mystery Book Consumer*, 43). With exceptions like John Connolly, Colin Bateman, and Declan Burke, the most conspicuous examples of blurring genres in Irish crime fiction tend to be women writers, drawing on the supernatural (French), romance (McGowan), or cosy mysteries (Catriona King and Andrea Carter), often while including pronounced elements of the procedural.

[15] Gavin, 'Feminist Crime Fiction,' 268.

[16] McGrath, 'Women's appetite for explicit crime fiction is no mystery.'

This invocation of the reader's relationship to the text touches on some longstanding issues in studying crime fiction, including those addressed by the Agatha Christie scholar John Curran, who has exhaustively catalogued the 'rules of the game' in Golden Age detective fiction between the wars.[17] These rules regularly include a contract between the reader and the author, in which the author is taken to promise 'fair play' in structuring the mystery, giving the reader access to what she may need to solve the mystery without authorial deception. As these 'rules' suggest, modern crime fiction has long had a particularly intimate and highly articulated relationship between the author and the reader, in principle and in practice. This intimacy necessarily shapes the relationship between the genre's female readership and its female authors, in a process that has only intensified as publishers increasingly rely on authors to do much of their own promotional work, particularly through social media, which with its aura of immediacy further compounds the perceived intimacy of the author-reader relationship.

These are important questions that need sustained discussion beyond the scope of this book. Clearly, however, the genre and its readers have a complicated, subjective relationship, within which difficult and violent content can register in intricate ways. Indeed, the novels discussed in this chapter contain ample such content, including a great deal that ranges from unnerving to disturbing: domestic violence and its aftermath, sexual assault, murder, incest, corruption, burning, serial killing, and kidnapping.

Just as Irish women novelists – including Arlene Hunt, Alex Barclay, Tana French, Jo Spain, and Nicola White – have produced novels with male protagonists, a number of Irish crime novels by men have featured female protagonists, including Stuart Neville's Serena Flanagan books, Brian McGilloway's Lucy Black series, Andrew Nugent's Molly Power, Declan Hughes's Clare Taylor in *All The Things You Are* (2014), and several central characters in Alan Glynn's novels. This chapter will however for the most part focus on crime novels by Irish women and featuring female protagonists, whether they are profilers (Louise Phillips's Kate Pearson and Claire McGowan's Paula Maguire), private eyes (Arlene Hunt's Sarah Kenny), detectives in the Metropolitan Police (Jane Casey's Maeve Kerrigan) or An Garda Síochána (Tana French's Antoinette

---

[17] See John Curran, 'Happy innocence: playing games in Golden Age detective fiction, 1920–45' (PhD thesis, Trinity College Dublin, 2014).

Conway, Niamh O'Connor's Jo Birmingham, and Sinéad Crowley's Claire Boyle), bipolar FBI agents (Alex Barclay's Ren Bryce), journalists (Anna Sweeney's Nessa in *Deadly Intent*),[18] small-town lawyers (Andrea Carter's Benedicta O'Keeffe), or schoolteachers on the run (Arlene Hunt's Jessie Conway).[19] The best of these novels have very little indeed in the way of suspiciously unflawed female characters, reflecting a pattern that Lee Horsley has identified in noir crime novels by women: their 'refusal to offer positive female role models. … Through the sympathetic representation of "transgressive" female desire and insecure, fragmented female identities, [women's noir] subverts the idealized cultural possibilities of stereotypical femininity.'[20] Although these novels are discussed throughout this book, this chapter's focus on these specific qualities further develops questions about the representation of violence against (and by) women, including ways this violence intersects with particularly Irish tropes of femininity. Alex Barclay's Ren Bryce series models the psychological depth that Irish crime fiction can give to female protagonists, as Barclay's portrait of Ren develops over the course of the series. Similarly, both Arlene Hunt's QuicK Investigations series and Jane Casey's Maeve Kerrigan series move their female protagonists through a full range of experiences with regard to violence and crime, in a way that few male protagonists share in Irish crime fiction.

Violence and Women Characters

Violence against women, particularly as written by women authors and narrated by women protagonists, takes varied forms within Irish crime fiction. One can identify, of course, stock women characters who are depicted as passively in need of protection, and other women characters who

---

[18] Published under the name Anna Sweeney, *Deadly Intent* (Sutton: Severn House, 2014) is an English-language version of Anna Heussaff's *Buille Marfach* (Gaillimh: Cló Iar-Connacht, 2010), one of the relatively rare examples of crime novels written in Irish. Other examples are discussed in Ian Campbell Ross, 'Introduction,' in Burke, *Down These Green Streets*, 14–35, particularly 20–21.

[19] Though the focus here is on contemporary settings, Irish women have of course also written historical crime fiction, of which Gemma O'Connor's and Cora Harrison's novels are significant examples. For a detailed consideration of O'Connor's work, see Rosemary Erickson Johnsen, *Contemporary Feminist Historical Crime Fiction* (Basingstoke: Palgrave Macmillan, 2006), particularly Chapter 6, 'Women and the Ever-Present Past,' 127–149.

[20] Horsley, *Twentieth-Century Crime Fiction*, 252.

primarily illustrate the masculinity of male protagonists, serving as the blank field on which those protagonists play out their games. This chapter, however, focuses on more actively articulated expressions through women characters who seek and find vengeance; through actively malignant women villains; and through women who are abused, dead, or missing as well as those who themselves inflict violence. With characters like those in novels by Arlene Hunt, Jane Casey, and Alex Barclay, Irish crime fiction also offers numerous women protagonists who are at least as effective as the male characters, and frequently more so. Such characters develop not just as strong leads, but as flawed and physically capable protagonists, at times willing to use violence in the course of their narratives. These narratives frequently involve crimes against women and significant attention to the protagonists' private and interior lives. One recent successful example is Liz Nugent's *Unravelling Oliver* (2014), a deftly structured multi-narrator novel in which the psychological and emotional violence women suffer (at the hands of both men and other women) is central, albeit in a way unsettled by multiple narrators who scatter perspectives and fragment the knowledge of exactly what has happened.

Complex representations of violence against women are, of course, not limited to Irish crime novels by women: Stuart Neville makes human trafficking central to *Stolen Souls* (2011) and abuse to *Those We Left Behind* (2015), for example, while Brian McGilloway writes with emotional eloquence about domestic abuse in his Lucy Black books and about human trafficking in *Bleed a River Deep* (2009). McGilloway conveys a particularly deep anger about mother and baby homes in his fifth Inspector Devlin book, *The Nameless Dead* (2012), which insistently emphasises the horrific loss of agency inflicted on the women forcibly held in such institutions.[21] Beginning with the adoption schemes uncovered in the series' first book, *Christine Falls* (2006), John Banville's Benjamin Black novels, too, engage with these issues in nuanced ways, as Carol Dell'Amico has

---

[21] A further plot strand concerns drug trials being run in the homes, as McGilloway explains in an 'Author's Note': 'Two hundred and eleven girls in Mother and Baby homes in Ireland were used, without parental consent, to test trial vaccines during the sixties and seventies.' Brian McGilloway, *The Nameless Dead* (London: Macmillan, 2012), 381. Declan Hughes also references the Magdalen laundries when a character in *City of Lost Girls* (2010) links Dublin's red-light district as depicted by Joyce to contemporary human trafficking, and then back to the Magdalen laundries, which serve in his speech as another example of trafficking, 'where women and children were trapped and abused for decades.' Declan Hughes, *City of Lost Girls* (London: John Murray, 2010; repr. 2011), 18.

demonstrated.[22] John Connolly's Charlie Parker series includes a number of novels that address similar crimes, and has a central thread running through the series concerning the abuse of children.

Similarly, graphic representations of violence against women are by no means limited to Irish crime fiction written by men. Indeed, Alex Barclay's *Killing Ways* (2015) – the fifth in her Ren Bryce series, discussed more fully below – contains among the most graphic scenes of violence against women anywhere in Irish crime fiction. Barclay balances the horror of these scenes with an acutely articulated sense of empathy for women as individuals and as experiencing violence, exploitation, and the vulnerabilities enabled by social invisibility, particularly at the intersection of class, gender, and sexuality. *Killing Ways* illustrates this dynamic through the contrast between the killer's first two victims in this book, Stephanie Wingerter and Hope Coulson. Where Hope was 'a sweet, blonde, kind-hearted kindergarten teacher, a volunteer for everything' who 'had captured the public's hearts,' Stephanie was 'a twenty-three-year-old meth-addicted prostitute' with 'a skinny, washed-out face dotted with scabs.'[23] As the narrative notes, in contrast to the intense publicity Hope's case has received, Stephanie 'had scarcely registered in the media. She was the type to be considered a victim-in-waiting by people who could never see her as a young woman struggling to survive or desperately feeding a habit that was never on her list of life's goals.'[24] Here, particularly given this passage's placement at the very end of the chapter, Barclay draws the reader's attention not just to graphic sexual violence but to the invisibility that class and appearance inflicted on Stephanie.

Even amidst the violence, *Killing Ways* emphasises Hope's and Stephanie's experiences, their own senses of the lives being taken from them. This emphasis gives them significantly more emotional weight in the narrative than is given to the killer as a character, despite the prominence of his violence. In thinking about these women suffering, Ren feels 'a step closer to a world she didn't want to know, a world that these women

---

[22] Carol Dell'Amico, 'John Banville and Benjamin Black: The *Mundo*, Crime, Women,' in 'Irish Crime Since 1921,' ed. William Meier and Ian Campbell Ross, special issue, *Éire-Ireland* 49, no. 1–2 (Spring-Summer 2014): 106–120, particularly 113–117, where Dell'Amico examines how 'the Black novels are a refashioning of the entire panoply of recently uncovered postindependence state crime' (114).

[23] Alex Barclay, *Killing Ways* (London: HarperCollins, 2015), 11, 49.

[24] Barclay, *Killing*, 50.

were likely never to have imagined.'[25] When she addresses the investigative team, for example, Ren draws righteous attention to the possibility that in these women's dying moments they might have been questioning what they had done to bring this on themselves, a self-doubt that reflects familiarly gendered experiences of guilt. Ren's response on their behalf is a kind of intimate rage, which finds its verbal outlet in her response to Gaston, a colleague who makes an appallingly callous remark on viewing the latest crime scene:

> 'I just can't listen to your fucked-up, disrespectful bullshit any more. ... It blows my mind,' said Ren, 'that a woman gave birth to you and you can still come out with some of the shit you come out with. I don't give a fuck if it's a defense mechanism or if you're just a massive prick in all your waking hours, but if for one more second of *my* waking hours, *I* have to listen to your horrible, cruel and nasty remarks, I will beat you to within an inch of your pathetic fucking life.'[26]

Though Ren is rebuked by her boss for this speech, she also receives numerous congratulatory texts from other colleagues who found Gaston similarly noxious. Through the close juxtaposition of these passages, Barclay's novel draws a straight line from Gaston's repeated performance of disregard for these women's suffering to the loathing and rage that the killer exercised upon them, both of which stand in stark contrast to Ren's almost overwhelming empathy and to the women themselves. Such passages are emblematic of the depth of detail that Irish crime fiction brings to its representations of women's experiences.

MOTHERS IN IRISH CRIME FICTION

The line between an archetype and a cliché may be nowhere thinner in crime fiction than with the *femme fatale*. Figures of the *femme fatale* appear across Irish crime fiction, including Rosalind in Tana French's *In the Woods* (2007), who is – with little if any mitigation – evil, as most of the other characters viscerally recognise.[27] In Declan Hughes's *The Wrong Kind of Blood* (2006), the narrator Ed Loy is brought into the case by Linda Dawson, described early on by Loy's friend Tommy as 'Big trouble.

---

[25] Barclay, *Killing*, 116–117.
[26] Barclay, *Killing*, 151.
[27] Tana French, *In the Woods* (New York: Penguin, 2007, repr. 2008), 374.

Poor little rich girl, black widow spider.'[28] *The Wrong Kind of Blood*'s strongest version of the *femme fatale*, however, is Linda's mother-in-law Barbara Dawson, who 'always argued like it was the last throw of the dice. She'd cry, or rage, slam doors, the whole Joan Crawford routine.'[29] Barbara, the unacknowledged child of the local crime boss, willed her way up from the town's poorest housing in Fagan's Villas, and made her bid for social legitimacy, successfully for a time. By the novel's end, to maintain that veneer she has killed her husband as well as their son, his wife, and her own lover. In Barbara, Hughes gives the reader a woman for a villain, one who does truly awful things that register as awful to other characters in part because of the extent to which they violate images of maternity, Irish or otherwise. At the same time, the narrative also invests considerable energy in establishing the brutal life that has been part of her character development, with all of her struggles. Just before her final act of violence, Loy notices 'a moment where Barbara Dawson's face seemed to collapse back through time until it was the tear-stained face of a child again, hurt and smarting from yet another humiliation; a moment when Barbara's journey from Fagan's Villas to the top of Castlehill finally ended, right back where it began.'[30] This is a long way short of enough to excuse her, but it is more than enough to involve empathy in assessing the evil she has done.

Barbara is one of many challenging maternal figures in Irish crime fiction. In French's *Faithful Place* (2010), Ma is a much more developed character than she first seems. She is introduced as 'your classic Dublin mammy: five foot nothing of curler-haired, barrel-shaped don't-mess-with-this, fueled by an endless supply of disapproval,'[31] and is possessed of 'a black belt in guilt-tripping.'[32] As the novel progresses, though, French circles around, gradually weaving Ma's story until the novel conveys a deep empathy for all she has suffered, including the years of abuse from an alcoholic husband as she grinds to keep the family together, fed, and

---

[28] Declan Hughes, *The Wrong Kind of Blood* (London: John Murray, 2006; repr. 2007), 23.

[29] Hughes, *Wrong*, 224.

[30] Hughes, *Wrong*, 325.

[31] Tana French, *Faithful Place* (New York: Penguin, 2010; repr. 2011), 19.

[32] French, *Faithful*, 217.

housed.[33] This, all while knowing she was her husband's distant second choice to the woman living across the street: telling her son this story, 'The solid weight of grief in her voice could have sunk ships,' as Frank eventually notices.[34] Irish images of mothers play an even more determining role in French's *Broken Harbour* (2012), when Jenny is the only survivor in a house where her children and husband have been murdered. Among the many things happening in *Broken Harbour*, a novel bursting with grim energy, is what at first appears to be almost a version of a locked room mystery, with the detectives spending much of the book looking for an intruder of whom few traces can be found.[35] Eventually, Jenny is revealed to have killed her family and wounded herself in what she meant to be a murder-suicide. French gives much space to the stresses that fracture Jenny's family, breaking her husband's psyche and in turn her own. In the process, the book fosters a deeply pained but profound empathy for their suffering, coloured but not diminished by the horror of their deaths. Through all of this, it is in no small part Jenny's status as a mother that prevents the male detectives from seriously considering her culpability until they are presented with irrefutable physical proof. In contrast, as any number of crime novels and real statistics would suggest, had her husband Pat been the sole survivor, he would have been a serious suspect much sooner. Jenny's maternity, however, makes her guilt unimaginable, as French deftly uses expectations around that maternity for emotional ballast and for a plot device that draws out the narrative tension by misdirecting the detectives for so long.

Although many are not mothers (Jane Casey's Maeve Kerrigan, Tana French's Cassie Maddox and Antoinette Conway, and Arlene Hunt's Sarah Kenny among them), a number of Irish series protagonists have or are expecting children. Sinéad Crowley's Sergeant Claire Boyle is pregnant in *Can Anybody Help Me?* (2014), as is Claire McGowan's Paula Maguire by the end of the first novel in her series. Maguire's relationship first to that fact and later to her daughter remains a core element of a series in which pregnancy, maternity, paternity, IVF, and infertility are prominently

---

[33] Two novels later, Frank's daughter Holly feels a 'pulse of wariness' around her parents after their split and reconciliation, echoing Frank's and his siblings' constant vigilance around their dad, implicitly suggesting – across several books in what is more an anthology than a traditional series – how experiences of domestic violence ripple down through the generations. Tana French, *The Secret Place* (New York: Viking, 2014), 442.

[34] French, *Faithful*, 274.

[35] Along with McGilloway's *The Nameless Dead*, French's *Broken Harbour* is one of the Irish crime fiction novels that makes the most of the recession's ghost estates – housing developments abandoned, unfinished by their builders – as a phenomenon and a setting.

recurring themes, at times serving as plot devices or cliffhangers.[36] In McGowan's *The Dead Ground* (2014), these themes are interwoven extensively with the plot's central crimes, and in *Blood Tide* (2017) Maguire experiences direct conflict between parenthood and her professional commitment. This conflict is not exclusive to women authors: Neville's Serena Flanagan has appeared in three novels so far, in which her career and her family come into conflict more than once, not least when she miscarries after being cautioned not to work such intensely long hours.[37] In *Those We Left Behind* (2015), Flanagan goes to see her husband Alistair in the hospital, where he is recovering from an assault at their home related to one of her cases. She considers waiting in the room so she can 'Be there for him when he wakes,' or going 'to my children,' 'the things I *should* do' as a wife and mother, but leaves and goes back to work on her case.[38] Despite some of Serena's regrets,[39] this is not represented as an exclusively maternal failure: in Neville's earlier novels *Stolen Souls* and *The Final Silence* (2014), the protagonist Jack Lennon is a deeply flawed man, one who frequently prioritises his work at the expense of time with his daughter, a choice for which other characters judge him severely, as he does himself.

PSYCHOLOGY AND FEMALE PROTAGONISTS

As these examples suggest, varieties of developed female protagonists and characters appear throughout contemporary Irish crime fiction, where their characters are at times amplified by Irish social patterns, including those regarding maternity, sexuality, and femininity, to which the best of these series give a sustained psychological depth. This includes a number of series featuring female profilers, whose profession makes them not quite detectives, and not quite private citizens, a positioning that enables productive ambiguity. Louise Phillips and Claire McGowan have both written series with profiler/criminal psychologist protagonists, for example, though their novels are quite distinct. Some of Phillips's work reaches

---

[36] A surprise, even miraculous pregnancy is also revealed near the end of Mary O'Donnell's *Where They Lie* (Dublin: New Island, 2014). Marketed as something of a crime novel, much of the book revolves around two brothers who were 'disappeared' – murdered, for the presumed crime of informing, their bodies never found (141–142).

[37] Stuart Neville, *Those We Left Behind* (London: Harvill Secker, 2015), 140, 203.

[38] Neville, *Those*, 325.

[39] Neville, *Those*, 355–356.

towards Irish family gothic material, with a profound sense of tangled and interwoven lives, as in *The Doll's House* (2013).[40] McGowan's Paula Maguire is often a less ominous character, with distinct strains of comedy and romance in even quite bleak narratives like *The Dead Ground*, *The Silent Dead* (2015), and *Blood Tide*. McGowan also makes wry nods to genre tropes, such as the male colleague who wishes he inhabited an older, televised version of policing, 'skulking about in stakeout cars, slamming his fist against interview-room tables, smoking in the office while wearing a trench coat.'[41]

Perhaps the most intensely flawed female protagonist in Irish crime fiction, however, and consequently the one for whom psychology is most intimately woven into the series, is Alex Barclay's Ren Bryce, who has been the centre of six novels to date, many of them dotted with their own wryly acknowledged genre tropes. These are frequently dark novels that address acutely difficult material in serious ways, and it may be that their setting outside of Ireland facilitates this. As Chapter 5 considers more fully, Barclay's American-set novels – like works by John Connolly, Jane Casey, and others – are able to explore these matters without the added weight of home, where they would encounter the particular representational expectations with which Irish culture is often freighted.

Bryce is an FBI agent in rural Colorado with a deep trauma in her background that comes primarily not from childhood or her personal life, but from her work as an undercover agent in a drug ring run by a particularly vicious woman, Domenica.[42] Bryce is also diagnosed with and treated for bipolar disorder over the course of the series. This treatment involves unusually realistic encounters with her psychiatrist, far more closely tied to professional standards than Tony Soprano and Dr Melfi.[43] Ren's diagnosis has a striking effect on the trope of the rogue, out-of-control cop – behaviours that her colleagues do see in Ren at times – and on sexist clichés about 'female unpredictability.' In Barclay's novels, it is as if those tropes and clichés are integrated and amplified, or as if the cliché is turned up to 11 until it burns out and leaves a new space for a richly articulated

---

[40] For a theorised discussion of Irish family gothic, see Margot Backus, *The Gothic Family Romance: Heterosexuality, Child Sacrifice, and the Anglo-Irish Colonial Order* (Durham: Duke University Press, 1999).

[41] Claire McGowan, *The Silent Dead* (London: Headline, 2015), 91.

[42] For an account of Ren's trauma and Domenica's violence, see Alex Barclay, *Blood Runs Cold* (London: Harper, 2008), 458.

[43] See, for example, Barclay, *Blood Runs Cold*, 255–257.

character.[44] The care with which Barclay accomplishes this is apparent when tracing the arc of the series to date.

The Bryce series signals its play with crime fiction tropes almost from the very beginning of the first novel, *Blood Runs Cold* (2008). In an early scene, explaining the background to the relationship between the local sheriff and his undersheriff, the narrative recalls 'The first night they worked together' and went 'on a domestic violence call-out.'[45] This is a depressingly common scenario, but it becomes clear that the abuser was the wife, who beat 'the shit out of that poor husband.' Cutting across a reader's expectations, as if to underscore that the novel will depart from some of the usual gender tropes, this is a less familiar representation of domestic violence. However, violent women, particularly mothers, appear across Barclay's work. Her first novel, *Darkhouse* (2005) – one of several with a different protagonist, Joe Lucchesi – gives a recurring villain's origin story, which includes horrific violence inflicted on him by his mother, while another character briefly refers to a childhood friend with an abusive mother.[46] In the second Ren Bryce novel, one male character comments directly and profanely on this pattern: 'And my mother was clearly insane. And violent. Who has a violent mother, for Christ's sake? Probably point zero five per cent of the population. Lucky fucking me.'[47] Despite this character's assumption about maternal violence, Barclay's novels return to the image at a somewhat higher rate than .05 per cent, and never with the allure of the *femme fatale*.

Though her own mother has nothing like that level of dysfunction, Ren herself is introduced in a hung-over mess, waking up to find herself hugging her toilet and late for work, with her partner breaking up with her as she tries to leave. This is almost immediately framed as part of a pattern for her, not an exception, and Ren is painfully self-aware enough to recognise her problem even as she tries to minimise it. After another late night, and a morning aided by coffee, 'Visine and extra foundation,' she is on one of her temporary upswings, with the feeling of 'instant mental clarity,' one of the first signs of something more nuanced than the archetypal troubled

[44] Leroy L. Panek discusses some of these tropes of the police procedural in 'Post-war American Police Fiction,' in Priestman, *The Cambridge Companion to Crime Fiction*, 155–171, particularly 157.

[45] Barclay, *Blood Runs Cold*, 16.

[46] Alex Barclay, *Darkhouse* (London: HarperCollins, 2005; repr. New York: Dell, 2008), 34–35, 133.

[47] Alex Barclay, *Time of Death* (London: HarperCollins, 2010), 321.

cop.[48] Soon enough, though, after she has to leave a crime scene with a crippling headache, she has swung in the other direction, coursing not with optimism but shame: 'She was thinking about self-sabotage – not for the first time. *Altitude sickness could happen to anyone.* But she had drunk a lot of contributory factors' at the bar the night before.[49] These passages quickly establish Bryce's recurring up-and-down patterns, building a careful foundation for the eventual bipolar disorder diagnosis that comes later in the novel and reverberates throughout the series.

Barclay establishes these patterns in part through Ren's frequent internal dialogues. More than an internal monologue, these include her running commentaries on herself and her interactions with others. These are often ambivalent in the most literal sense, enacting for the reader Ren's internal divisions, impulses, and uncertainties in a visceral way that is all the more powerful for its contrast with the more conventional third person narrative voice. This can lend the novels a dark kind of humour. Interviewing a victim's neighbour, Ren – who has a Native American background, with her full name (Orenda) taken from an Iroquois spirit[50] – is told she does not look like an FBI agent, before the neighbour continues:

> 'You could be...'
> *Don't say anything that will scar me.*
> '... well, you have those eyes, so ...'
> *Don't say squaw.*
> '... one of those *Disney on Ice* people.'
> *Original.*[51]

Other italicised asides and internal dialogues are more scathing. After getting drunk and sleeping with an unusually attractive person of interest in her case, Ren

> stopped in the bathroom on her way out. She looked in the mirror and saw her hangover face: the skin, paler than her neck, mascara slightly smudged. She spent good money on makeup to withstand a night's drinking ... she also saw her mistake face, her eyes slightly haunted and asking that question

[48] Barclay, *Blood Runs Cold*, 78.
[49] Barclay, *Blood Runs Cold*, 94.
[50] Barclay, *Blood Runs Cold*, 229.
[51] Barclay, *Blood Runs Cold*, 117.

she could never answer. *What the fuck were you thinking?* She ran her middle finger under each eye and fixed her mascara. She scraped her nails through her hair and stared at her reflection. *What the fuck were you thinking?* She frowned. She smiled. *But WTF?*[52]

These internal dialogues continue throughout the series, as when Ren struggles with the idea of telling a friend about her diagnosis:

> *Just tell her.*
> *No.*
> *Do.*[53]

Through such passages, Ren's mind is less explained than it is enacted. Again, genre tropes are at work here – the hard-drinking, boundary-pushing cop – but Barclay is building something both more nuanced and more psychologically knotty than the familiar neurotic mess of a cop from any number of films and television shows.

Barclay does this with considerable acuity, describing Ren's internal experience of the symptoms before (and more than) she describes the external evidence:

> Her heart beat too quickly, her breathing was off. Rushes of heat and nausea swept over her. The clock read one a.m., then two, then three. And as it finally flashed four, every negative sensation sharpened and spiraled and became connected and expanded and hammered at her. … There was a lavender candle [on the nightstand]. *Do these really work?* She lit it anyway. But the flame was so small, it was swallowed into the dark.[54]

Indeed, much of the establishing work on Ren's character is internal in this way, and captures her experience of being at the mercy of her brain, an experience repeated all too frequently for Ren: '*Does any of this matter?* Ren wondered if all this thinking, the inability to switch off her brain, was the thing that one day would take her down. Something so terrible would happen that she wouldn't be able to stop thinking about it, and she would

---

[52] Barclay, *Blood Runs Cold*, 233–234.
[53] Barclay, *Killing*, 52.
[54] Barclay, *Blood Runs Cold*, 248–249. These late-night spirals recur throughout the book, as she thinks obsessively about various details almost against her will: 'The theories continued, nauseating and paralyzing, until she eventually fell asleep, half an hour before her alarm woke her' (Barclay, *Blood Runs Cold*, 366).

implode. *Shut up.*[55] This builds to an explosive monologue in another confrontation at work:

> 'Sanity is bullshit. ... I'm serious,' said Ren. 'People prize sanity because of how much they fear *in*sanity. Sanity is like happiness; it comes, it goes, it feels good, it means one thing to me, something else to someone else, but, boy, do we all want it. So bad. It's what keeps people showing up in shrinks' offices every day all over the world. It's like paying a weekly subscription to the Sanity Club. And all that happens there is a lot of talk. Well, screw that. It's all wrapped up in negativity. And losing: lose your grip, lose the plot, lose perspective.'[56]

Despite this fierce denial, within pages Ren is at her therapist's office, insisting that she is 'on an even keel right now' as 'Tears flowed down her face.'[57] Through all of these fears and denials, Barclay insistently invests Ren with a complex, grounded psychology, one that shows considerably more authorial acuity than could be gleaned from any quick reading of the *DSM-5*, the latest edition of the American Psychiatry Association's *Diagnostic and Statistic Manual of Mental Disorders* (2013). This psychological acuity manifests not just in Ren's actions – not just in the external plot – but in who she is, both when she is directly involved in the plot and when she is simply herself. The work *Blood Runs Cold* does to establish Ren in such a full way, well beyond the exigencies of plot, offers further strong evidence that crime fiction at its best is about character before plot.

In the second novel, an ornately plotted affair, Ren's diagnosis becomes part of the case itself when her therapist is murdered. When the therapist's anonymised case notes are read by her colleagues as part of the investigation, she recognises herself: '*Thirty-seven, single, psychotic episodes, bipolar, law-enforcement officer, Rx Zyprexa,*' the last a brand-name medication for bipolar disorder and schizophrenia, among other conditions.[58] Her discomfort is so great that, in her inner dialogue mode, she has to remind herself '*I am talking about this too much.*'[59] Despite this discomfort, as

---

[55] Barclay, *Blood Runs Cold*, 403–404.

[56] Barclay, *Blood Runs Cold*, 459.

[57] Barclay, *Blood Runs Cold*, 473.

[58] Barclay, *Time*, 113. Her brother Beau, we learn, committed suicide, something about which Ren is remarkably insightful in a passage that stands out even in a book like this, which gives more serious and sustained attention to mental illness than do most novels of whatever genre (Barclay, *Time*, 267).

[59] Barclay, *Time*, 115.

Time of Death (2010) establishes, Ren believes that her unique mind benefits rather than inhibits her work.[60] Indeed, having been reminded of her 'triggers for mania: you need to avoid stress, get a lot of rest, reduce your caffeine intake,' Ren realises that she has been using that knowledge to bring about a manic phase that, she thinks, makes her more effective: the phase 'had slowly built – late nights, fear, stress, travel, caffeine … and then, she knew. Her mind sharpened, her thoughts sped. Connections jumped off the page, her fingers worked quicker on the keyboard, she drove faster, she got everywhere quicker.'[61] This is an ongoing temptation for Ren, sacrificing stability for the rush of 'living the best, most productive day of your life on a loop. … by the time the mania comes around again, you've forgotten the depth of the low that will follow. You kid yourself – this time, the high won't end; this time will be painless.'[62] Despite passages such as this, the series does not romanticise Ren's psyche: as Barclay has written elsewhere, Ren has a 'skewed sense that the darkness was something brilliant and glowing, when, in fact, it was engulfing and suffocating.'[63] This oscillation between 'glowing' and 'suffocating' runs throughout the books, with Ren struggling to find a way of sustaining her life. Clearly, Barclay is not writing an episodic series in which character changes minimally and is unaffected by plot. Instead, the Bryce books gradually deepen, unfolding a fully dimensional character, in large part through her bipolar condition and the personal and professional complications that intersect with it. The plots are never unimportant, and tend to be intricately layered, but Ren's character is inseparable from that intricacy to an unusual extent, consistently matched in Irish crime fiction perhaps only by John Connolly's Charlie Parker, Jane Casey's Maeve Kerrigan, Declan Hughes's Ed Loy, and Adrian McKinty's Sean Duffy.

Immediately highlighting the increasingly tighter integration of Ren's character and the novel's plot, the third novel, *Blood Loss* (2012), begins with a Gothic description of an abandoned asylum. In a way that seems to speak to Ren's experiences, this description gains its power from deep sympathy with the inmates, who suffered 'an imprisonment, twice over. Minds captured first by insanity were captured a second time by Kennington

[60] Barclay, *Time*, 257.

[61] Barclay, *Time*, 310.

[62] Barclay, *Time*, 290–291.

[63] Alex Barclay, 'How a line you hear, read or write can light a fuse,' *Irish Times*, 7 April 2015, http://www.irishtimes.com/culture/books/how-a-line-you-hear-read-or-write-can-light-a-fuse-1.2167392 (accessed 1 May 2017).

Asylum for the Insane. ... In appearance, [the building] stood for its promises. ... In contrast, the grounds were overrun, choked by nature untended, as if the twisted roots of madness, ignored for over a century, were finally unbound.'[64] Against such a backdrop, and reflecting the series' informed investment in Ren's psychology, this is a book grim enough that banal domestic happiness registers as ominous foreshadowing.

Ren's own emotional state has grown correspondingly more fragile, emphasising the revolving extremes of 'Her trickster mind' and their wearing effect on her life.[65] Here, Ren's internal dialogue continues in a trial appointment with a new psychiatrist, underscoring not just her ambivalence amidst this novel's increasing swings and turns but her conscious understanding of that ambivalence:

> 'What are your concerns about coming here?' said Dr Lone.
> *Let me think: I'm not sure I like you. Or you're right for me. Or there's any need for me to be here.* 'I don't want to be put on medication.' *You said that last part out loud.*
> 'We've only just met,' said Dr Lone. 'I won't be handing you a prescription today.'
> 'And ... any other day?' said Ren.
> 'I don't necessarily believe in medication,' said Dr Lone.
> *What? But I want you to. Even though I don't want to take any. I just want to know it's there. And that you believe there's a quick fix. If, at some point, I need one. Which I don't right now.*[66]

Dr Lone's credibility on such matters is validated within the novels partly by Ren's growing trust of him, and partly by contrast with other, less impressive therapists, including one who runs a group home for teens and bizarrely claims 'They're in therapy ... They have no need to act out.'[67] Through Lone's preference in most cases for talk therapy over continual medication (as distinct, he carefully explains in a later book, from 'short term' use 'to get people back on their feet'[68]), this entry in the series marks a compelling shift in the narrative role played by Ren's emotional state. For the novels and particularly for Ren, this shift opens her to the possibility

---

[64] Alex Barclay, *Blood Loss* (London: HarperCollins, 2012), 1.
[65] Barclay, *Blood Loss,* 29–30.
[66] Barclay, *Blood Loss,* 133.
[67] Alex Barclay, *Harm's Reach* (London: HarperCollins, 2014), 91.
[68] Barclay, *Blood Loss,* 135.

of a more gradual, fluid existence rather than the extremes of both her behaviour and her relationship to that behaviour.

In the scenes with Lone and across the novel, *Blood Loss* connects Ren's character more intimately to the central plot than did earlier novels, making for an increasingly focused narrative. The particular villain is corporate: Lang Pharmaceuticals, a company that has marketed the antidepressant Cerxus to young children, thereby replacing the profits from other antidepressants whose patents were about to expire. Lang was purchased by MeesterBrandt, who have been engaged in wide-scale corruption and problematic clinical trials as they seek to hide the profound side effects of Cerxus. These side effects are particularly acute when it is taken in combination with Ellerol, another drug the company was also marketing to children with disastrous effects: 'kids were committing suicide, harming themselves, lashing out. The drug was banned in Europe.'[69] The plot begins with crimes familiar from other police procedural novels: kidnapping, home invasion, rape, missing children. As it moves forward, however, the connections between those crimes, the medications, their side effects, and a tangled set of corruptions unfold, turning *Blood Loss* into something more like a conspiracy thriller, one not out of place with Alan Glynn's novels, but one tied intimately to Ren's specific character.

The first crime in the novel is a brutal rape committed by a teenage boy, who later attacks Ren with terrifying and sudden violence and who had been prescribed the Cerxus-Ellerol cocktail. Most of the crimes and violent acts in the novel are related either to this drug cocktail, or to the company's efforts to corrupt the patenting and prescription processes, cover up the side effects (by blackmailing and framing potential leakers for murder, prostitution, and child pornography[70]), and erase their own tracks. This corporate conspiracy unfolds gradually: for much of the novel, the crimes seem unrelated, until a series of late revelations weave them together in a quick but impressively tight conclusion.[71] The themes and issues in this novel are particularly well suited to the conspiracy subgenre: with its overarching sense of unseen evils all around, that subgenre maps perfectly onto the emotional and psychological effects of widely prescribed and wildly profitable antipsychotic drugs, a phenomena that manifests in

---

[69] Barclay, *Blood Loss*, 328; see also 171.

[70] This provides a thematic continuity with the leverage brutally manipulated by Domenica in the previous Ren Bryce book, *Time of Death*.

[71] Barclay, *Blood Loss*, 345–347 contains the core revelations.

initially unobtrusive but increasingly disturbing ways. The novel ultimately ascribes these evils to the corporate drive for profits, however, rather than to an evil inherent in the medications when it concludes with Ren back on mood stabilisers after a manic phase that has gone on for over a month.[72] In this tentative, fragile conclusion, Barclay's Ren Bryce series reaches its tightest fusion of plot and character, deftly balancing the bleak misery its characters experience with a glimpse of tentative stability for Ren. Well short of an assured order, this glimpse is made both plausible and palatable by being woven into – rather than just set against – a sustained, nuanced character, and by being leavened with Ren's symptomatically difficult internal dialogue, in which every state of mind is at risk of being temporary.

Indeed, in the following novel, *Harm's Reach* (2014), Ren continues to struggle with stability, at times not wanting it even when she has it, worrying that the medications that stabilise her also take away what makes her good at her job.[73] Amidst a tangled plot of deception and violence, much of it inflicted on or by women, Ren judges herself severely for missing clues and misreading people involved in the case.[74] The novel's closing lines show her blaming these failures on her medications making her '*repressed. ... Inhibited. Reined in,*'[75] as she drops her dose down the drain, explicitly welcoming the return of the manic state that she hopes will follow. This reaffirms the centrality of Ren's character to the series: although the plot still matters, and gives the novel much of its shape and momentum, here at the end of *Harm's Reach* the narrative is pulled back into the whirlpool of Ren and her very particular psyche.[76] Across the series, then, Barclay develops an astute and clinically informed sense of her character's deeply elaborated psychology. This sustained depiction of mental health,

[72] Barclay, *Blood Loss,* 368–372, 376.

[73] See Barclay, *Harm's,* 276.

[74] No one else does so: her boss pointedly says 'this is the first time at the end of a big case that I haven't almost fired you' (Barclay, *Harm's,* 391).

[75] Barclay, *Harm's,* 401.

[76] In the unremittingly dark following novel, *Killing Ways,* Ren spends much of the narrative avoiding her medication and immersed in a manic phase, replete with continual self-aware internal dialogues – '*But I'm fine. You're off the rails. No, I'm not*' (Barclay, *Killing,* 173) – and angrier moments where she is protective of the accelerating mania. *Killing Ways* ends with a remarkably unrelieved sense of desolation as Ren bottoms out, convinced (not without reason) that the decisions she made in that manic state led to a catastrophic end to the case. The killer's guilt is clear and explicit, but closing with such a bleak, repeated insistence hardly refutes Ren's feelings of culpability.

with all of Ren's swings from despair to euphoria, is impressive for any genre, and is indicative of the complexity that women protagonists have in the most effective Irish crime fiction.

WOMEN AS VICTIMS, VILLAINS, AND AVENGERS

A similar interweaving of character, genre, and narrative emerges in several quite different series protagonists for whom this interweaving is framed more overtly in terms of gender: Jane Casey's Maeve Kerrigan and Arlene Hunt's Sarah Kenny, both of whom directly experience violence, abuse, and harassment by men in ways that fundamentally shape their characters and their series' plots. Casey's series protagonist Maeve Kerrigan is a detective in a murder squad of the London Metropolitan Police. As Elizabeth Mannion has demonstrated,[77] Casey makes Maeve's gender central to her character and many of her experiences, from lingering (and baseless) gossip that she slept her way onto the murder squad to acts of physical violence.

Perhaps the chief example of this centrality is a plot thread that runs throughout the series. In the second novel, *The Reckoning* (2011), Maeve moves to a new apartment, where one of her neighbours is Chris Swain, a computer specialist who introduces himself as reviewing 'games and technology for a couple of magazines' and as running a 'pretty popular' blog.[78] Chris quickly takes an unnerving interest in Maeve. By the end of the novel, this has escalated to Chris being on the run, revealed as the stalker who had been sending her surveillance photos, along with a video of her and her boyfriend in bed. When Maeve's colleagues investigate further, they discover that he is behind a horrific dark web site with videos of 'actual slavery, torture, rape. Snuff films too, it seems.'[79] Over the next four novels – *The Last Girl* (2012), *The Stranger You Know* (2013), *The Kill* (2014), and *After the Fire* (2015) – Swain regularly reaches out from the shadows, ratcheting up Maeve's levels of suspicion, whether by sending her more pictures and lingerie, or by stalking her through a public

---

[77] Elizabeth Mannion, '"Irish by blood and English by accident": Detective Constable Maeve Kerrigan,' in *The Contemporary Irish Detective Novel*, ed. Elizabeth Mannion (Basingstoke: Palgrave, 2016), 121–134.

[78] Jane Casey, *The Reckoning* (London: Ebury, 2011), 79. In *After The Fire* (London: Ebury, 2015), another hacker expands on this, describing Swain's legendary status in his world (256).

[79] Casey, *Reckoning*, 469.

park.[80] As Maeve reflects, Swain 'had marked me out as a victim and I couldn't seem to shake off the role, no matter how much I hated it, and him. He was a sneak, a voyeur, a rapist whose style was to drug his victims to avoid the possibility of them fighting back. A coward. Dangerous.'[81] Even while on the run, then, Swain remains a ghosting presence in Maeve's life, influencing her decisions about finding a new, more secure flat and varying her route home.[82]

By the closing lines of the fifth novel, *The Kill*, Maeve 'had had enough of it. … I was tired of running away. One way or another, I was going to end this.'[83] She follows through in *After the Fire* by luring Swain out of hiding, with the help of another recurring central character, her immediate superior Josh Derwent. In explaining her plan to Derwent, she forcefully articulates the perspective of someone being stalked while waiting for police assistance:

> no one is going to make it a priority. Some overworked detective will turn up and take a statement. They'll take the letters away. They'll tell me to note every incident of harassment. And if he kills me, they'll use it all to build the case against him. But I'll still be dead. … I've been waiting for them to find him for years and they've done nothing.[84]

Heightened by Casey's deeply researched and forensically detailed writing, Maeve's authority here reflects the knowledge she has gained from her experiences as both a detective and the stalker's target. Her righteous anger carries through to the novel's grim coda, one that initially appears surplus to a plot that had already seemed to conclude, and that therefore pulls the reader's focus away from plot and towards the character's series-long arc. In an extended final scene, Maeve, having taunted Swain into the open, is kidnapped while wearing a tracking device, so that she and Derwent can first beat and then arrest Swain, stopping just short of killing him in the process.[85] Part of Maeve revels in unleashing her anger, but she also expresses unease about the violence and unofficial methods she and Derwent used. This unease is compounded when she learns that in the act

---

[80] Jane Casey, *The Last Girl* (London: Ebury, 2012), 204, 356.
[81] Jane Casey, *The Stranger You Know* (London: Ebury, 2013), 325.
[82] Casey, *Stranger*, 31.
[83] Jane Casey, *The Kill* (London: Ebury, 2014), 455.
[84] Casey, *Fire*, 197.
[85] Casey, *Fire*, 425–433.

of kidnapping her Swain killed her colleague Mal, a death for which she feels responsible. These conflicted feelings of shame, rage, and guilt prevent the revenge from providing any simple resolution, here or in the following book, *Let the Dead Speak* (2017). Even in this most recent title, Maeve tries to tell herself that '*The past can't hurt me any more*. I knew it was a lie, but it was a comfort all the same.'[86] Through these moments, the series makes it clear that the suffering inflicted by Swain's crimes does not end with his arrest, and depicts Maeve's very human mix of a need for comfort and a realism that gets in the way of such comfort.

The centrality that Casey gives these traumatic experiences for Maeve's character is rare. By contrast, among male protagonists in Irish crime fiction perhaps only John Connolly's Charlie Parker has at the heart of his character quite such intimate, enduring experience of victimisation. In Casey's work, however, this narrative thread connects Maeve and all of her conflicted feelings directly to a specific kind of crime aimed predominately against women, by Swain and others like him for their own profit and pleasure. Through these extensive connections, as Mannion has argued, the series 'reveals [Maeve's] own susceptibility to harm, unifying her with women citywide, including victims of the crimes she investigates.'[87] This deep connection is a central feature of Maeve's character in a series that compellingly depicts her conflicting but linked responses, from terror to rage to revenge. These experiences allow Casey to anchor Maeve at the intersection between being victimised by a crime and being the agent of justice who stops criminals, an intersection that is given particular form here by Maeve's experiences as a woman.

This particular form is also clear in the way that character and plot articulate each other – through a male abuser and a female protagonist – in Arlene Hunt's QuicK Investigations series. To date, this series includes five novels: *False Intentions* (2005), *Black Sheep* (2006), *Missing Presumed Dead* (2007), *Undertow* (2008), and *Blood Money* (2010). Hunt's writing in this series has a deceptive ease, a fluidity and a breezy wit that can veil some of the narratives' increasingly bleak matters. The main protagonists are Sarah Kenny and John Quigley – hence, the capitalised Q and K in their agency's name – who in their early adulthood had a brief relationship, which ended when John cheated on Sarah and she left for England. Sarah returns suddenly just as John was considering setting up a private

---

[86] Jane Casey, *Let the Dead Speak* (London: HarperCollins, 2017), 93.
[87] Mannion, '"Irish by blood and English by accident,"' 121.

eye firm, which, early in *False Intentions*, is described as their 'two-year-old, slipshod, failing detective agency.'[88] Along with Declan Hughes's Ed Loy series, Hunt's QuicK Investigations series is one of the few Irish-set PI series. It also stands out for being a mixed-gender PI team (although police procedurals are increasingly likely to feature mixed-gender squads in general). Addressing other examples of women investigators, Horsley has argued that just as much significance should be seen in less known 'revisionings of the female transgressor – and indeed victim.'[89] As do Casey's books, Hunt's QuicK series uses this full range of 'revisionings,' for 'transgressor' and 'victim' alike, particularly through Sarah, a strong protagonist with a veiled past, one that amplifies and is amplified by several of their investigations.

Appearing during the full rush of Ireland's turn-of-the-century economic boom, *False Intentions* is replete with passing references to that era's panoply of tropes. Characters admire and lament the reckless spending and the unsustainable housing prices (it's a spectral prosperity, John notes, if you can't afford to buy anywhere after cashing in your own house). *False Intentions* also includes the strains of corruption that shape so much of Irish crime fiction from this era, as when John's much younger girlfriend complains – with an unnerving sense of normality – that her friend insulted her by saying 'the only reason Daddy bought *my* apartment was for tax reasons, and that the one *her* daddy bought wasn't ... Everyone knows her father barely escaped without a prison sentence for having all those offshore accounts.'[90] The novel's plot revolves around a nightclub that distils such excesses in the figures of its cocaine-addled owner and the wealthy young women who crowd his club, one of whom – Ashley Naughton – disappears, setting the plot in motion.

Amidst the Naughton case, this first novel already contains hints of Sarah's unexplained interval in England, as when Sarah claims 'she was happy alone,' clearly an innocent preference on its own, but one that takes on murkier shading as the series progresses.[91] When the novel describes John and Sarah's agreement to form a partnership for the agency, however, she insists forcefully that her name appear on no legal documents: 'I don't want my name on anything ... I'll be a silent partner. I'll draw a

[88] Arlene Hunt, *False Intentions* (Dublin: Hodder Headline, 2005), 17.
[89] Horsley, *Twentieth-Century Crime Fiction*, 244.
[90] Hunt, *False*, 28.
[91] Hunt, *False*, 22.

salary, but I want my name on nothing.'[92] Along with this need for privacy that verges on secrecy, other hints of her past emerge, including Sarah's 'pinched and serious' insistence that John not group Ashley in with other women who 'disappear into thin air in this country.'[93]

The dramatic conclusion to *False Intentions* builds on these hints to establish two points that shape the rest of the series. The first: during a shootout, Sarah has to kill a man in order to save John's life, an act that comes with a persistent psychic cost to her. This traumatic experience establishes what becomes crucial later in the series: Sarah's knowledge that she can kill a man, and that she has done so.[94] The second point, quieter but no less insistent, is in the contrast that arises when Ashley visits Sarah's hospital room to thank her and John. This young woman – whose father has been murdered, and who herself has barely survived a brutal kidnapping – displays deep reservoirs of strength: 'John held his tongue. He stared at Ashley with raw admiration. This slip of a girl had had her whole world shattered. She was holding herself together with sheer willpower.'[95] Her 'willpower' starkly contrasts with her dead father, 'a weak, stupid man,' as she bluntly puts it in an assessment shared by John, Sarah, and the novel. The difference between the older man and the younger woman passes with no narrative comment, but it articulates the series' insistent characterisation of women who are victimised, even brutalised, and who yet display, villain and victim alike, a profound strength.

The third novel, *Missing Presumed Dead*, finally reveals the story of Sarah's time in England, when – as none of her friends or family yet knows – she was trapped in a deeply abusive relationship that ended only when, desperate to escape her partner Victor and their life in England, she had framed him for criminal possession of drugs, ensuring that he was jailed.[96] For much of *Missing Presumed Dead*, Sarah is unaware that he is out of jail and has come to Dublin, let alone that he is the one who is stalking her and terrorising her family, forcing one sister's car to crash, smashing Sarah's car windows, and brutally beating Sarah and John's friend and office neighbour. The kind of abuser beyond even the pretence of remorse,

[92] Hunt, *False*, 118.
[93] Hunt, *False*, 251.
[94] See Arlene Hunt, *Missing Presumed Dead* (Dublin: Hodder Headline, 2007), 404–405.
[95] Hunt, *False*, 530.
[96] Hunt, *Missing*, 397–398. *Undertow* (Dublin: Hachette, 2008; repr. 2009) calls him 'her deranged ex-boyfriend' (20), but *Blood Money* (Dublin: Hachette, 2010) calls him her 'husband' (157).

as these actions show, he is not in Dublin to get Sarah back, but for revenge. Unsurprisingly, Sarah's trauma surfaces in memories of 'Days when you didn't need to glance over your shoulder to make sure you were safe,'[97] and in nightmares about her time with Victor, nightmares that despite the harrowing physical details of his brutality emphasise rather the psychological consequences of the abuse.

Once Sarah learns that Victor is in Dublin, she moves through several responses before deciding emphatically that 'She had run before and she wasn't going to run again. She could take care of this before it destroyed her life. She could do it. She could stop him.'[98] Despite this resolve, she comes close to panic, and to calling John back from his case in London for help, before stopping herself:

> The fear. This was how he wanted her.
> No. She didn't need anything. She had to take care of something. Victor was a malignancy. She had cut him out before, but this time she would cauterise the wound. This time he would not return, she would make sure of it.[99]

Sarah is scared, and scarred, but never a damsel in distress (nor does she have anything quite as slapstick as a few of John's scenes, including his miserably failed attempt to break into an apartment, which by contrast sharpens the depiction of Sarah's determination).[100] Instead, Hunt consistently depicts Sarah as neither superhuman in her abilities and her bravery, nor as frail and incapable, but as very human, if particularly strong-willed.

Hunt captures this quality when Sarah discovers that Victor has destroyed the QuicK Investigations office: 'She was angry now – angry that her door had been broken down, angry that she was rooted to the stairs with fear.'[101] Strikingly, the fear leads to the anger, which in turn

---

[97] Hunt, *Missing*, 93.

[98] Hunt, *Missing*, 281.

[99] Hunt, *Missing*, 286.

[100] Hunt has described John as 'that kind of *laissez-faire* detective that I quite enjoy. He's not a detective because he's the smartest guy ever to walk the streets. He's a detective because he doesn't want to do a nine-to-five job … He's a bit of a shyster, really. If he can avoid work, he will.' 'Irish Crime Fiction Abroad' panel discussion, 'Irish Crime Fiction: A Festival,' Trinity College Dublin, 23 November 2013.

[101] Hunt, *Missing*, 369.

drives Sarah's actions through the remainder of the novel, bringing with it not hope, as Sarah reflects, but an eerie calm borne from determination.[102] Despite this, killing Victor is still traumatic, both because of the violence he inflicts on her and her horror at her own actions, which she describes as unambiguously 'premeditated'[103] in the next novel, *Undertow*, where she seems markedly more cynical to those around her. As John reflects there, 'Whatever had gone on, it had totally changed Sarah.'[104] Her trauma is long-term, not just a flicker in the immediate wake of Victor's abuse or of his death, and is much more foundational than the anxiety that comprises its surface.

Weighed down by these experiences, she leaves Dublin at the end of *Undertow*, telling neither her family nor John where she is going, hinting only that she is too damaged to be around them. Leaving doesn't end her story, though: in *Blood Money*, the next novel, Victor haunts the narrative even in her absence, when his body is discovered and identified, posthumously revealing their relationship to John and her sisters. The novel – and, to date, the series – ends with John leaving to find Sarah in England. Throughout Sarah's arc in the series, her characterisation remains consistent: a deeply human victim of violence and agent of vengeance, but one who is conflicted and guilty, even ashamed, about both poles of her experience. Much like Barclay's Ren Bryce, then, Hunt's Sarah Kenny inhabits a full range of emotional and practical capacities, a representation that Hunt, like Barclay, achieves without succumbing to the polarised gender clichés that shadow the genre's reputation. On the one hand, it is hardly breaking news that novels develop characters as rounded as Sarah and Ren. On the other hand, the point bears making – and repeating – because of both the genre's reputation for reductive and misogynistic narratives, and because of the genre's still-developing standing in Irish Studies.

Where Sarah's character is concisely but richly developed, the investigations in Hunt's QuicK novels reflect a similar dynamic, depicting women neither as essentially victims – despite the sexual assaults in *False Intentions* and the human trafficking in *Undertow* – nor as exclusively *femmes fatales*, but as individuals with rather more shades of grey, working within problematic structures or institutions. In this sense, what Nickerson has argued regarding genre precedents is equally true of Hunt's novels, novels in

---

[102] Hunt, *Missing*, 393.
[103] Hunt, *Undertow*, 59.
[104] Hunt, *Undertow*, 56.

which 'Crime and danger serve to throw the vulnerabilities *and* strengths of women into high relief.'[105] The central investigation in *Missing Presumed Dead* echoes some of these issues, providing a female villain in Lizzie, who for decades had very profitably been selling babies, at least some of them kidnapped, under the false guise of a charity called The Cradle Foundation, as Sarah learns from a woman who 'said "poor" in the same way that John said "non-alcoholic beer."'[106] This investigation echoes the belated revelations about the Magdalen laundries, mother and baby homes, and other institutions of incarceration in Ireland, institutions that, although not exclusive to Ireland, nonetheless served there overtly to preserve 'the respectability of the normative Irish family' by containing 'the threatening embodiment of instability' represented by the women and children sent to these institutions.[107]

Such institutions appear throughout Irish crime fiction, often reflecting wider narrative patterns – like those in novels by Brian McGilloway, Benjamin Black, Jo Spain, Claire McGowan, Nicola White, and others – that concern the regulation of female sexuality in Ireland, from forced adoption schemes (both illicit and with governmental collusion), to abor-

---

[105] Catherine Ross Nickerson, 'Women Writers Before 1960,' in Nickerson, *Cambridge Companion to American Crime Fiction*, 39, emphasis added.

[106] Hunt, *Missing*, 318.

[107] James M. Smith, *Ireland's Magdalen Laundries and the Nation's Architecture of Containment* (Notre Dame: University of Notre Dame Press, 2007), xviii. While Smith is at pains to note that these institutions' 'punitive nature is not unique to the Irish context' (*Ireland's Magdalen Laundries*, xv), he concisely describes the laundries as part of 'Ireland's architecture of containment,' which also 'encompassed an assortment of interconnected institutions, including mother and baby homes, industrial and reformatory schools, mental asylums, adoption agencies ... These institutions concealed citizens already marginalized by a number of interrelated social phenomena: poverty, illegitimacy, sexual abuse, and infanticide ... Those incarcerated included unmarried mothers, illegitimate and abandoned children, orphans, the sexually promiscuous, the socially transgressive, and, often, those merely guilty of "being in the way". This bureaucratic apparatus operated as a bulwark to the state's emerging national identity' (*Ireland's Magdalen Laundries*, xiii). Smith is also careful not to conflate the Magdalen laundries with these other institutions, each of which had discrete characteristics (*Ireland's Magdalen Laundries*, 48, 224n12). For further astute discussion of Irish culture's representation of these and related institutions, see Emilie Pine, *The Politics of Irish Memory: Performing Remembrance in Contemporary Irish Culture* (Basingstoke: Palgrave Macmillan, 2011), particularly 36–51.

tion restrictions, to shaming of sexual activity.[108] Claire McGowan's second Paula Maguire novel, *The Dead Ground*, for example, has as one of its villains a woman named Magdalena, a name that in an Irish context cannot but be suggestive of the laundries. This is clearly apt for a character whose crimes include the murderously forced removal of babies from their mothers, crimes inseparable from her view of women as 'nothing but a husk' for reproduction.[109] McGowan's first Paula Maguire novel, *The Lost* (2013), includes a closed Magdalen laundry as part of the central mystery. In the novel's contemporary present tense, the laundry's former existence in Paula's (fictional) hometown Ballyterrin comes as news to her, particularly the fact that 'it was open till the eighties.'[110] Closed though the laundry may be, the misogynistic shaming of sexuality remains depressingly familiar, as when one girl is taunted by others because her 'mum … she'd been a slut too and they'd sent her away to a home to have a baby.'[111] Both of these moments register as disturbing for Paula, and together prevent readers from either blaming a 'degraded' contemporary culture or isolating the problem solely in the past. Instead, through this juxtaposition, the novels tie the crimes inflicted by the laundries very much to long-enduring patterns that persist in the present, where they continue to generate further suffering, through official policies and less official social conventions alike. It is through such juxtapositions, anchored as they are in the central narratives rather than merely providing window dressing, that Irish crime novels with female protagonists take an issue in crime fiction in general – violence against women, whether fetishised *à la* Mike Hammer, or examined by more progressive authors – and tie it to particular Irish experiences.

In this context, it says much that the *licit* explanation Hunt's Lizzie gave clients – one that did more rather than less to let them sleep at night – was that the babies 'came from an orphanage, one of them … what do you call 'em? Them homes where they put girls who were knocked up.'[112]

---

[108] For an extended historical examination of this regulatory activity, see Diarmaid Ferriter, *Occasions of Sin: Sex and Society in Modern Ireland* (London: Profile, 2009). In this work, Ferriter details an 'enduring theme in relation to perceived sexual transgression – the collusion of state, society and religious orders in seeking to remove from public circulation perceived threats to a conservative moral order' (*Occasions of Sin*, 16). See also Laura Weinstein, 'Unlawful Carnal Knowledge of Teenage Girls: Performing Femininity and the Myth of Absolute Liability,' in Meier and Ross, 'Irish Crime Since 1921': 69–91, particularly 75–81.

[109] Claire McGowan, *The Dead Ground* (London: Headline, 2014), 377.

[110] Claire McGowan, *The Lost* (London: Headline, 2013), 58.

[111] McGowan, *Lost*, 314.

[112] Hunt, *Missing*, 241.

Lizzie herself does nothing to mitigate the horror of these still unfolding scandals: 'And half the silly bitches who dropped the brats out could hardly feed themselves, let alone anyone else. Sluts and tramps, the lot of them.'[113] Here, crass and brutal as she is, Lizzie's role engages a thorny, problematic dynamic around these institutions, a dynamic that Emilie Pine has described in which, 'as the laundries prove, women were not merely acquiescent in a male system in which women were powerless, but were drivers of the cruelty themselves' as well.[114] As Pine notes, and as a recent novel like Jo Spain's *With Our Blessing* (2015) suggests, priests frequently outranked nuns in the institutional hierarchies, but that framework also left room for significant female agency in these institutions, agency that was no guarantor of benign influence. On the contrary, Lizzie and Hunt's other female villains – like her male villains – are figures for whom everyone else's lives are either impediments or instruments.

A capacity like Lizzie's for selfish evil, barely hidden within a woman whose profession was ostensibly one of caring, is most explicit in Hunt's fifth QuicK Investigations novel, *Blood Money*. Like Barclay's *Blood Loss*, Hunt's *Blood Money* is in part a medical thriller, but one that highlights the vulnerability of women in relation to certain crimes, and the complicity of other women. Here, the *femme fatale* is literalised in the figure of Frieda Mayweather. Described by one character as 'a demon in human form,' she is a plastic surgeon who runs an upscale clinic in post-Celtic Tiger Dublin, devoted largely to 'the Irish lady' inclined and able to make 'a small investment' so that 'a waist made thick by childbearing could be whittled away, sagging breasts could be lifted, noses straightened, prominent veins blasted away, lips plumped, and chins carved to perfection.'[115] Amidst the economic crash, however, slower sales and haggling customers lead Frieda to develop a sideline in black market transplants, using organs bought or otherwise 'acquired' abroad for clients who cannot wait on the transplant lists, or who had been excluded from the lists on mental or physical grounds, and who had the money to pay for a new organ by other means. She becomes the focal point of two investigations: John meets her in the course of investigating another Dublin doctor's mysterious death, and she is targeted by Pavel Sunic, after his sister sells her kidney – and dies from the resulting infection – so that she can bribe the police to free him from a Bosnian jail. Pavel, a Rom who makes his familiarity with exclusion and

[113] Hunt, *Missing*, 276.
[114] Pine, *Politics*, 41.
[115] Hunt, *Blood Money*, 170, 141–142.

victimisation clear, sets out to find 'people who use people like cattle … who will be God, who will pick lives to live and lives to condemn,' wreaking a trail of vengeance all the way to Dublin and to Frieda's doorstep.[116]

Before Pavel kills her, Frieda blackmails, threatens, and has people killed. All the while, she echoes Lizzie's disingenuous pleas to be seen as a facilitating angel, offering a rationale that she is only helping people in need of a transplant:

> They sense their time running out in days, hours, minutes. They've tried everything but to no avail. The lucky ones are waiting on lists for donors, trying to hang on, but every day is one day closer to the grave and they know that. … I became a doctor to save lives, not to take them, but if it's any consolation your death will mean life to several others. How many of us can be that special?[117]

The persuasiveness of this plea, however, is more than a little undermined by its narrative context: she delivers this speech while Pavel is sedated and strapped to an operating table, waiting for his organs to be harvested for the clinic's profit. Frieda's self-justifying malignancy is highlighted by the contrast with Alison Cooper, another doctor who tried to force Frieda to provide *pro bono* transplants for those who could not afford the black market. Where Frieda is 'The real monster … stalking the corridors' of the clinic, Cooper is consistently devoted to her clients, a professional whose '*compassion* was true.'[118] This contrast helps keep the novel's image of Frieda's villainy away from the clichéd *femme fatale*, locating her evil not in any version of femininity but in the utter lack of empathy that allows her to use everyone who crosses her path, a train she shares with the other villains in the series, most notably the abusive Victor.

Frieda may be an unmitigated horror, and Allison the closest thing to a purely good character, but Sarah – who has already inhabited a richly ambivalent series of positions – herself never appears directly on the page in *Blood Money*. Nonetheless, her absence ghosts the entire novel, particularly given that it has to do with Victor's death at her hands, a case the police are pursuing throughout the narrative. Both Frieda's presence and Sarah's absence, then, reflect Hunt's narrative investment in women's vulnerability and simultaneously in their agency, without essentialist claims

---

[116] Hunt, *Blood Money*, 233.
[117] Hunt, *Blood Money*, 264–265.
[118] Hunt, *Blood Money*, 292, 291.

for woman's nature, like those that blinded French's detectives in *Broken Harbour* to that novel's actual murderer. As with the earlier QuicK novels, and the scope of Sarah's character they explore, *Blood Money* gives its female characters the varied shades of human goodness, frailty, and evil.

CONCLUSION

Tana French's character Antoinette Conway bluntly expresses the urgency behind the issues and representations this chapter has examined:

> I don't get rescued. I'll take help, no problem … Rescue – where you're sinking for the third time, you've tried everything you've got and none of it's enough – rescue is different.
>
> If someone rescues you, they own you … because you're not the lead in your story any more. You're the poor struggling loser/helpless damsel/plucky sidekick who was saved from danger/dishonour/humiliation by the brilliant brave compassionate hero/heroine, and they get to decide which, because you're not the one running this story, not any more.[119]

What Conway describes is something other than just control: it is agency in and over one's own life, an agency frequently under threat. The novels at the core of this chapter – particularly those by Alex Barclay, Claire McGowan, Jane Casey, and Arlene Hunt – are among those that show how Irish crime fiction has developed credibly complex, ambivalent female protagonists who are often characterised by their efforts to preserve and exercise this agency. As scholars of women's roles in the genre have argued, such efforts carry particular weight when characters' gender intersects with the specific crimes they both experience and investigate, as happens frequently in these novels: the attempted rape of Ren, who is categorised as 'crazy'; the stalking, assault, and kidnapping of Maeve; the domestic abuse Sarah suffers; the premature caesarean almost forced on an abducted Paula.

Building on these intersections and the genre's wider questions of agency, the novels in this chapter also draw on specifically Irish cultural patterns, modelling how Irish culture can shape the genre and how the genre can in turn be adapted to explore that culture's intricacies. In novels by McGowan, Spain, Hunt, and others, for example, the pressure exerted

---

[119] Tana French, *The Trespasser* (Dublin: Hachette, 2016), 268.

on women's agency is perhaps at its most stark in the depiction of institutions such as the Magdalen laundries and mother and baby homes. By representing through these institutions some of the most disturbing, most fraught experiences around Ireland's regulation of sexuality and gender, these novels are able to link the crimes in their narratives to particular Irish contexts without crass exploitation. This link sharpens the focus of broader questions about agency and gender in crime fiction, and it further demonstrates the wide-ranging ways in which Irish adaptations of the genre have been able to sustain significant engagements with some of the most intimate, fundamental crises of Irish society.

References

Abbott, Megan E. *The Street Was Mine: White Masculinity and Urban Space in Hardboiled Fiction and Film Noir.* Basingstoke: Palgrave Macmillan, 2002.

American Psychiatry Association. *DSM-5: Diagnostic and Statistic Manual of Mental Disorders.* Fifth Edition. Arlington: American Psychiatry Association, 2013.

Backus, Margot. *The Gothic Family Romance: Heterosexuality, Child Sacrifice, and the Anglo-Irish Colonial Order.* Durham: Duke University Press, 1999.

Barclay, Alex. *Darkhouse.* New York: Delacorte, 2007.

———. *Blood Runs Cold.* London: Harper, 2008.

———. *Time of Death.* London: HarperCollins, 2010.

———. *Blood Loss.* London: HarperCollins, 2012.

———. *Harm's Reach.* London: HarperCollins, 2014.

———. *Killing Ways.* London: HarperCollins, 2015.

———. 'How a line you hear, read or write can light a fuse.' *Irish Times*, 7 April 2015. http://www.irishtimes.com/culture/books/how-a-line-you-hear-read-or-write-can-light-a-fuse-1.2167392 (accessed 1 May 2017).

———. *The Drowning Child.* London: HarperCollins, 2016.

Black, Benjamin. *Christine Falls.* London: Picador, 2006. Reprint, 2007.

Bord Gáis Energy Irish Book Awards. http://www.irishbookawards.irish/crime-fiction-award (accessed 3 December 2017).

Burke, Declan, ed. *Down These Green Streets: Irish Crime Writing in the 21ˢᵗ Century.* Dublin: Liberties, 2011.

Casey, Jane. *The Reckoning.* London: Ebury, 2011.

———. *The Last Girl.* London: Ebury, 2012.

———. *The Stranger You Know.* London: Ebury, 2013.

———. *The Kill.* London: Ebury, 2014.

———. *After the Fire.* London: Ebury, 2015.

———. *Let the Dead Speak.* London: HarperCollins, 2017.

Connolly, John. *A Time of Torment*. New York: Emily Bestler/Atria, 2016.

Crowley, Sinéad. *Can Anybody Help Me?* London: Quercus, 2014. Reprint, 2015.

Curran, John. 'Happy Innocence: Playing Games in Golden Age Detective Fiction, 1920–1945.' PhD thesis, Trinity College Dublin, 2014.

Dell'Amico, Carol. 'John Banville and Benjamin Black: The *Mundo*, Crime, Women.' In Meier and Ross, 'Irish Crime Since 1921': 106-120.

Dillon, Eilís. *Death at Crane's Court*. London: Faber, 1953. Reprint, Boulder: Rue Morgue, 2009.

———. *Death in the Quadrangle*. London: Faber, 1956. Reprint, Boulder: Rue Morgue, 2010.

Ferriter, Diarmaid. *Occasions of Sin: Sex and Society in Modern Ireland*. London: Profile, 2009.

French, Tana. *In the Woods*. London: Hodder & Stoughton, 2007. Reprint, New York: Penguin, 2008.

———. *Faithful Place*. New York: Penguin, 2010. Reprint, 2011.

———. *Broken Harbour*. Dublin: Hachette, 2012. Reprint, New York: Penguin, 2012.

———. *The Secret Place*. New York: Viking, 2014.

———. *The Trespasser*. Dublin: Hachette, 2016.

Gavin, Adrienne E. 'Feminist Crime Fiction and Female Sleuths.' In *A Companion to Crime Fiction*, edited by Charles J. Rzepka and Lee Horsley, 258–269. Chichester: Blackwell, 2010.

Horsley, Lee. *Twentieth-Century Crime Fiction*. Oxford: Oxford University Press, 2005.

Hughes, Declan. *The Wrong Kind of Blood*. London: John Murray, 2006. Reprint, 2007.

———. *City of Lost Girls*. London: John Murray, 2010. Reprint, 2011.

———. *All the Things You Are*. Surrey: Severn House, 2014.

Hunt, Arlene. *False Intentions*. Dublin: Hodder Headline, 2005.

———. *Black Sheep*. Dublin: Hodder Headline, 2006. Reprint, 2007.

———. *Missing Presumed Dead*. Dublin: Hodder Headline, 2007.

———. *Undertow*. Dublin: Hachette, 2008. Reprint, 2009.

———. *Blood Money*. Dublin: Hachette, 2010.

'Irish Crime Fiction Abroad.' Panel discussion with Declan Burke, Jane Casey, John Connolly, Conor Fitzgerald, Alan Glynn, and Arlene Hunt. 'Irish Crime Fiction: A Festival.' Trinity College Dublin, 23 November 2013.

Johnsen, Rosemary Erickson. *Contemporary Feminist Historical Crime Fiction*. Basingstoke: Palgrave Macmillan, 2006.

Kinsman, Margaret. 'Feminist Crime Fiction.' In Nickerson, *The Cambridge Companion to American Crime Fiction*, 148–162.

Knight, Stephen. *Crime Fiction Since 1800: Detection, Death, Diversity*. 2nd ed. Basingstoke: Palgrave, 2010.

Kulo, Carl, and R.R. Bowker. *The Mystery Book Consumer in the Digital Age*. www.sistersincrime.org/resource/resmgr/imported/ConsumerBuyingBookReport.pdf (accessed 5 May 2017).

Mannion, Elizabeth, ed. *The Contemporary Irish Detective Novel*. Basingstoke: Palgrave, 2016.

———. '"Irish by blood and English by accident": Detective Constable Maeve Kerrigan.' In Mannion, *The Contemporary Irish Detective Novel*, 121–134.

McGilloway, Brian. *Bleed a River Deep*. London: Macmillan, 2009. Reprint, London: Pan, 2010.

———. *Little Girl Lost*. London: Macmillan, 2011. Reprint, London: Pan, 2012.

———. *The Nameless Dead*. London: Macmillan, 2012.

———. *Hurt*. London: C&R Crime, 2013. Reprinted as *Someone You Know*. New York: Witness Impulse, 2014.

———. *Preserve the Dead*. London: Corsair, 2015. Reprinted as *The Forgotten Ones*. New York: Witness Impulse, 2015.

———. *Bad Blood*. London: Corsair, 2017.

McGowan, Claire. *The Lost*. London: Headline, 2013.

———. *The Dead Ground*. London: Headline, 2014.

———. *The Silent Dead*. London: Headline, 2015.

———. *Blood Tide*. London: Headline, 2017.

McGrath, Melanie. 'Women's appetite for explicit crime fiction is no mystery.' *Guardian* (Manchester), 30 June 2014. https://www.theguardian.com/books/booksblog/2014/jun/30/women-crime-fiction-real-anxieties-metaphorical (accessed 5 May 2017).

Meier, William, and Ian Campbell Ross, eds. 'Irish Crime Since 1921.' Special issue, *Éire-Ireland* 49, no. 1–2 (2014).

Millar, Cormac. *The Grounds*. Dublin: Penguin, 2006. Reprint, 2007.

Neville, Stuart. *Stolen Souls*. London: Harvill Secker, 2011.

———. *The Final Silence*. London: Harvill Secker, 2014.

———. *Those We Left Behind*. London: Harvill Secker, 2015.

Nickerson, Catherine, ed. *The Cambridge Companion to American Crime Fiction*. Cambridge: Cambridge University Press, 2010.

———. 'Women Writers Before 1960.' In Nickerson, *The Cambridge Companion to American Crime Fiction*, 29–41.

Nugent, Liz. *Unravelling Oliver*. Dublin: Penguin Ireland, 2014.

O'Donnell, Mary. *Where They Lie*. Dublin: New Island, 2014.

Panek, Leroy L. 'Post-war American Police Fiction.' In Priestman, *The Cambridge Companion to Crime Fiction*, 155–171.

Phillips, Louise. *The Doll's House*. Dublin: Hachette, 2013.

Pim, Sheila. *Common or Garden Crime*. London: Hodder & Stoughton, 1945. Reprint, Boulder: Rue Morgue, 2001.

Pine, Emilie. *The Politics of Irish Memory: Performing Remembrance in Contemporary Irish Culture*. Basingstoke: Palgrave Macmillan, 2011.

Priestman, Martin. *The Cambridge Companion to Crime Fiction*. Cambridge: Cambridge University Press, 2003.

Reddy, Maureen T. 'Women Detectives.' In Priestman, *The Cambridge Companion to Crime Fiction*, 191–207.

Ross, Ian Campbell. 'Introduction.' In Burke, *Down These Green Streets*, 14–35.

Rowland, Susan. *From Agatha Christie to Ruth Rendell: British Women Writers in Detective and Crime Fiction*. Basingstoke: Palgrave Macmillan, 2001.

Smith, James M. *Ireland's Magdalen Laundries and the Nation's Architecture of Containment*. Notre Dame: University of Notre Dame Press, 2007.

Spain, Jo. *With Our Blessing*. London: Quercus, 2015.

Sweeney, Anna. *Deadly Intent*. Surrey: Severn House, 2014. Originally published in Irish as Anna Heussaff, *Buille Marfach*. Inverin: Cló Iar-Chonnacht, 2010.

Weinstein, Laura. 'Unlawful Carnal Knowledge of Teenage Girls: Performing Femininity and the Myth of Absolute Liability.' In Meier and Ross, 'Irish Crime Since 1921': 69–91.

CHAPTER 5

Transnational Irish Crime Fiction

Irish crime fiction's transnational aspects reflect the international reach of the wider genre, with its enduring propensity for insistently national subdivisions.[1] These subdivisions nonetheless connect in considerable ways that are in explicit dialogue with each other, as Andrew Pepper has argued, describing crime fiction as a genre that 'has always been a resolutely transnational phenomenon.'[2] Some of the factors in this transnational quality are bluntly material, such as the unrelenting consolidation of publishing firms. The genre is also transnational in its readership and its settings, of course, as is clear from the voluminous attention paid to Scandinavian crime fiction in Anglophone markets, or from the clearly significant appetite for the ever-expanding Akashic Noir series of short story anthologies, from *Beirut Noir* to *Belfast Noir* to *Buenos Aires Noir*, collections that affirm the genre's particular need for recognisably specific (and at times exoticised) settings.

We have already seen some of these forces play out in Irish crime fiction, particularly in Chapter 2: despite the reputation 'Troubles thrillers' devel-

---

[1] The term 'transnational' is used here in its most immediate sense: 'Extending or having interests extending beyond national bounds or frontiers; multinational.' *Oxford English Dictionary*, s.v. 'Transnational, adj.,' http://www.oed.com.elib.tcd.ie/view/Entry/204944?rskey=qXuyG1&result=1#eid (accessed 23 March 2017).

[2] Andrew Pepper, *Unwilling Executioner: Crime Fiction and the State* (Oxford: Oxford University Press, 2016), 168.

© The Author(s) 2018
B. Cliff, *Irish Crime Fiction*, Crime Files,
https://doi.org/10.1057/978-1-137-56188-6_5

oped for being narrow or atavistic, Northern Irish crime fiction displays a number of fundamentally transnational elements. This is true not only of Adrian McKinty's Sean Duffy novels, with their corporate and imperial conspiracies, but more generally as well, with those novels that represent the Troubles as a conflict between multiple nation-states, and that in some cases explicitly invoke comparisons to other conflicts with roots in political, racial, and religious differences.[3] This final chapter, however, will focus on several further patterns of transnational connection in Irish crime fiction.

An examination of these patterns moves us towards a conclusion about the current state of Irish crime fiction, about that fiction's significance within Irish culture and about its significance for wider literary-cultural matters, both within and beyond international crime fiction. With this in mind, this chapter first briefly considers the influence of other national (and international) crime fiction on Irish crime fiction. It then turns to novels that send their Irish characters abroad, that bring their Irish characters back 'home' from abroad, and that address the experiences of immigrants to Ireland. (This is apart from Irish-American settings, which do play significant roles in Declan Burke's *The Lost and the Blind* [2014], Adrian McKinty's Michael Forsythe series [2003–2007], and Stuart Neville's *Collusion* [2010], among others.) After considering Irish crime novels that build their narratives around a sense of globalised, international crime, the chapter then concludes with a closer examination of John Connolly's Charlie Parker series, the content of which has no overt or allegorical connection – neither characters nor plot, neither settings nor themes – to Irish matters, an absence that contributes to (rather than detracts from) the Parker novels' meaning. Through Connolly and other authors, this chapter argues that these transnational and extra-insular elements allow space for a yet wider thematic range. One crucial effect of this range is to develop the genre in further directions when freed from some of Ireland's weighty representational burden.

Transnational Influences

Of course, one immediate sign of the genre's transnational qualities in Ireland is the matter of influence, including connections to other national traditions. Here, it is worth nothing that Irish Americans constitute a disproportionate amount of the best-selling American crime fiction,

---

[3] In this regard, see Joe Cleary's comparative work on *Literature, Partition and the Nation-State: Culture and Conflict in Ireland, Israel and Palestine* (Cambridge: Cambridge University Press, 2002).

through writers like Peter Quinn, Dennis Lehane, and particularly Michael Connelly, many of whom have significant readerships in Ireland and have maintained professional connections with Irish crime writers.[4] Irish-American crime fiction, however, is such a substantial body of work, with such particular contexts, that it merits its own distinct study.

More immediately material is Irish crime fiction's heavy disposition to American modes of the genre, something noted and critiqued by Maureen T. Reddy.[5] Indeed, with a few exceptions that seem to prove the rule, some hallmarks of the more traditionally British Golden Age modes – the brilliant amateur, the locked room, the cosy village mystery – are notably less common in Irish crime fiction than are the counterpart American traditions and tropes, which have in general shown more (and more overt) influence on Irish crime fiction than have the British traditions. It's been suggested that some of this resistance to those British modes may reflect a well-developed Irish scepticism about the trustworthiness of the official forces of law and order.[6] This scepticism maps very well on to (for example) American private eye traditions, with their roots in the corrupt California of the early 20th century (and, farther back, in the Western), providing an *ad hoc* justice for those left behind by official law and order.[7] This American influence appears most immediately in formal, stylistic, and linguistic patterns, such as the banter-heavy dialogue of McKinty's Sean Duffy series and his Michael Forsythe books, or the vernacular narrative patter of the hard-boiled P.I. Ed Loy, the protagonist of five Declan Hughes novels to date. Such narrative and verbal influences

[4]Declan Hughes did the main public interview in Ireland with Lehane on his 2015 book tour, for example, while Connelly was the special guest at the Irish crime fiction festival held at Trinity College Dublin in 2013.

[5]See Maureen T. Reddy, 'Contradictions in the Irish Hardboiled: Detective Fiction's Uneasy Portrayal of a New Ireland,' *New Hibernia Review* 19, no. 4 (2015): 126–140.

[6]Several panellists at Trinity's 22–23 November 2013 festival of Irish crime fiction suggested as much.

[7]As Pepper notes in discussing Hammett's *Red Harvest*, 'Much has been written about the interpenetration of the western and hard-boiled detective fiction forms.' Andrew Pepper, '"Hegemony Protected by the Armour of Coercion": Dashiell Hammett's *Red Harvest* and the State,' *Journal of American Studies* 44, no. 2 (May 2010): 336n10. On Hammett, see also Lee Horsley, *Twentieth-Century Crime Fiction* (Oxford: Oxford University Press, 2005), 166–169. Another example is Elmore Leonard, who began as a Western writer before moving on to patent his particularly laconic version of crime fiction, but who returned to something more like Westerns at the end of his career, with the Raylan books and stories, the basis for the TV series *Justified*.

lend themselves to a heightened sense of style, the postmodern boundaries of which are perhaps most fully explored by Irish crime fiction's most energetic adapter of hard-boiled language, Declan Burke, particularly in his novel *Absolute Zero Cool* (2011). With echoes, too, of Flann O'Brien, this novel sets Billy – a character from an uncompleted novel – in conflict with his author, as Billy tries to force the narrative towards publication. (Less overt is the influence of a later novelist, Ross Macdonald, particularly in his sense of family and of empathy, an influence to which we will return.)

CRIME FICTION'S RELATIONSHIP TO IRISH LITERARY STUDIES

These basic questions of influence are important to acknowledge at least briefly, in part because Irish literary studies has largely overlooked crime fiction, leaving such questions little explored. Particularly for a few individual authors, most notably Tana French, that paucity of attention has started to change, as the bibliography here suggests and as books like Elizabeth Mannion's *The Contemporary Irish Detective Novel* (2016) and Maureen T. Reddy's forthcoming book on the subject demonstrate. This paucity remains an issue, however, particularly for novels *not* set in Ireland, and those not featuring the Irish abroad: without some kind of toehold on reading these texts in terms of Irishness, they often remain effectively ignored by scholars. Apart from some works that reviewers and academics have classed as somehow 'transcending the genre' – like John Banville's work as Benjamin Black – Irish Studies has tended to associate crime fiction with literature of the Celtic Tiger and its aftermath, giving such fiction little more meaning than as a footnote to that traumatic period. Paula Murphy has astutely traced the ways in which Ken Bruen's Jack Taylor series charts social change surrounding the Celtic Tiger, for example, but in a sparsely populated critical field such a chart implicitly constitutes the novels' main interest.[8] This line of inquiry has also shaped much of the attention paid to writers like Gene Kerrigan, Niamh O'Connor, and Alan

---

[8] Paula Murphy, '"Murderous Mayhem": Ken Bruen and the New Ireland,' *Clues* 24, no. 2 (Winter 2006): 3–16. More broadly, Murphy suggests that Bruen's Taylor books 'employ the "foreign" characteristics of crime fiction with Irish settings and characters, realising the collision of the local and the global that is at the heart of contemporary Irish literature' ('"Murderous Mayhem,"' 15). See also Andrew Kincaid, 'Detecting Hope: Ken Bruen's Disenchanted P.I.,' in *The Contemporary Irish Detective Novel*, ed. Elizabeth Mannion (London: Palgrave Macmillan, 2016), 57–71.

Glynn, often deservedly so and to good effect, if sometimes at the price of simplifying those novels. Despite these exceptions, Irish Studies remains unsure of how to study fiction that cannot be construed – however obliquely or allegorically, whether as a between-the-lines symptom or an above-the-fold diagnosis – to be *about* Ireland and Irishness, unsure of how to locate such fiction within prevailing views of what Irish literature is and what Irish literature does, a gap that is all the more clear with popular genre work like crime fiction.

This shortcoming in part reflects the fact that, as Conor McCarthy has argued, 'nationalism' has provided 'the presiding Irish metanarrative since the early nineteenth century.'[9] Because that metanarrative's vocabulary has been centred on the nation as the point of gravity around which all art is presumed to orbit, texts that do not fall into that orbit can simply fail to register. This is something John Connolly – whose career highlights some of these questions – has commented on, not without frustration:

> As a modern state, the Irish Republic has been in existence for less than a century, and a young nation is compelled to engage in a period of questioning its identity, of coming to terms with the forces that created it in an effort to determine what shape it should take for the future. Writers as much as politicians, and economists, and historians, are involved in this act of interpretation, and a very serious business it is too, so serious, in fact, that any writing that is not actively contributing to this discussion may be disregarded entirely or at best relegated to a position of irrelevance. Such an environment actively discourages experimentation with genre, unless that experimentation is perceived to be commenting upon the process in hand.[10]

This habit of overlooking texts that are less readily interpretable as informing discussion of Irish identity and Irish society may help explain the relative silence in Irish Studies on – for example – Connolly's work, a

---

[9] Conor McCarthy, *Modernisation, Crisis and Culture in Ireland, 1969–1992* (Dublin: Four Courts, 2000), 33.

[10] John Connolly, 'No Blacks, No Dogs, No Crime Writers,' in *Down These Green Streets: Irish Crime Writing in the 21st Century*, ed. Declan Burke (Dublin: Liberties, 2011), 41–2. Indeed, while fiction by Patrick McCabe and others plays with or adapts genre elements, Flann O'Brien's novels *At Swim-Two-Birds* (1939) and *The Third Policeman* (1968), and perhaps Beckett's *Molloy* (1951, trans. 1955), are among the few post-Revival fictions to give themselves over fully to genre experimentation and still to have a secure place in the academic canon.

silence that starkly contrasts with his impact on the marketplace for crime fiction by Irish writers, domestically and abroad (it is at best difficult to think of another living Irish writer who has sold more than 10 million books and yet received so little critical commentary within Irish Studies). For both its relevance to this discussion and for the merits of the series, a fuller discussion of Connolly's work concludes this chapter, tying together many of these matters.

IRISH CHARACTERS ABROAD, STRANGERS AT HOME

Irish crime fiction has used diverse characters, settings, and plots to move in some outward-looking directions, and to separate itself from some of the tropes of Irish fiction in general. To good effect, Irish characters are sent abroad in a wide range of Irish crime fiction including Michael Russell's Stefan Gillespie series, Stuart Neville's *Collusion*, Adrian McKinty's Michael Forsythe novels, and Eoin Colfer's *Plugged* (2011), which centres on a former sergeant in the Irish army now working as a bouncer in New Jersey.

In *The Eagle Has Landed* (1975) and *The Eagle Has Flown* (1991), Jack Higgins's Liam Devlin is an ex-IRA man co-opted into WWII German intrigues in Britain. In both novels, several varieties of plausibility are severely strained (for academic readers, not the least of these comes when the novel claims that he has 'a job waiting as professor of English at Trinity College in Dublin whenever' he wants, a claim unlikely to amuse anyone who has ever sought a faculty position).[11] Devlin seems mostly to offer some grain of local particularity to speculative 'what if...?' plots that use Ireland and World War II less for moral complexity than for narrative tension and bits of colour. We learn in one scene, for example, that Himmler is 'annoyed' by Devlin's stereotypical Irish flippancy, which Devlin blames on, of course, 'the rain.'[12]

A similar but far more effective mechanism appears in Michael Russell's recent *The City in Darkness* (2016), the third in his series with the protagonist Stefan Gillespie, who is of mixed German and Irish heritage, while his mother 'still gets Christmas cards from her cousins' in Germany.[13] Unlike the Liam Devlin novels, Russell's series immerses itself more fully

---

[11] Jack Higgins, *The Eagle Has Flown* (New York: Pocket, 1991), 334.
[12] Higgins, *Eagle*, 106.
[13] Michael Russell, *The City of Shadows* (London: HarperCollins, 2012), 200.

in its various overseas contexts – including Danzig in 1934, New York in 1939, and Spain at the tail end of 1939 – bringing those contexts together as part of the series' sustained and serious exploration of the moral conflicts around Irish neutrality (an effort also made to good effect by Joe Joyce's *Echoland* trilogy, 2013–2015). In Russell's third novel, Stefan Gillespie has to – among other plot threads – track down the ex-IRA man Frank Ryan. Not unlike the real Frank Ryan, Russell's character fought for the Spanish Republic, has been imprisoned by Franco, and is in the novel freed through the intervention of Spain's German allies, in the hope that they can use Ryan to disrupt neutral Ireland and thereby further complicate Britain's position early in the war. In the earlier novels in the series, Gillespie travels abroad on official business, notably to Danzig in 1934 when it was still under the authority of the League of Nations despite Germany's pre-war attempts to gain control over the border town.

Although Russell's novels do so with a great deal more nuance than Higgins's Devlin novels, and with considerably more in the way of sustained ethical consideration, both series reflect this approach of tying domestic Irish contexts to larger European intrigues. Similar approaches were adapted by other precursors, including Elizabeth Bowen's darkly elegant/elegantly dark *The Heat of the Day* (1948) and John Welcome's *Run For Cover* (1958), as well as by more recent novels such as Stuart Neville's *Ratlines* (2013). Of course, World War II and all of the hazy allegiances that ran through it have long presented a dramatically tempting context for thriller writers, perhaps most notably in recent years Alan Furst and David Downing. Reflecting this temptation, historical Irish crime fiction does seem to cluster around the era and its transnational entanglements, as the above examples suggest.[14]

Other novels have instead brought immigrants to Ireland. As outsiders immersed in a new social and cultural landscape, these characters both document an Ireland changing rapidly (not least in its relationship with the larger world) and facilitate a changed view *of* Ireland. In Joe Joyce's *Echobeat*, for example, the Austrian-Jewish refugee Gertie tells the protagonist 'You Irish ... you think you're the only ones with history,' an astutely delivered observation about one of insularity's downsides, and an observation facilitated by the inclusion of her immigrant voice.[15] Alex

---

[14] The most wide-ranging recent study of Ireland's neutrality during World War II is Clair Wills's excellent *That Neutral Island* (London: Faber, 2007).

[15] Joe Joyce, *Echobeat* (Dublin: Liberties, 2014), Chapter Ten, Kindle.

Barclay's *Darkhouse* (2005) revolves around an expatriate American family that settles in rural Ireland. The central character, Joe Lucchesi, is a semi-retired FBI agent, who returns later in Barclay's career in one novel of his own, *The Caller* (2010), and in one of her Ren Bryce novels, *Killing Ways* (2015). Importing the Lucchesi family, along with some familiar crime fiction tropes, gives the novel some of its tension, and does allow for the narrative conflict with a small village's understaffed and under-resourced police force, who are then faced with Duke, another American and a much more dangerous criminal than they would normally encounter. Much of the novel's tension also arises from Joe's fish-out-of-water Americanness, which marks his dislocation in Ireland, while Duke's serial-killer violence contrasts the small scale of the Irish village with the wide-open prairie landscape from which he emerged. In the end, however, *Darkhouse* does relatively little to suggest any sustained sense that it is using these outsiders to generate particular insights about Ireland, which provides more setting than focus.

A different approach is offered in Andrew Nugent's engaging and thoughtful but uneven novel *Second Burial* (2007), which revolves around an immigrant who has been brutally murdered.[16] Like Nugent's first novel, *The Four Courts Murder* (2006), *Second Burial* strains plausibility at times, partly as a by-product of squeezing too many coincidences and missed observations into one plot, going some ways towards illustrating the particular challenges of setting certain crime plots in a country as small as Ireland. The detectives' case in *Second Burial* concerns Shad, an Igbo immigrant from Nigeria, who is found dying after he is dumped in Wicklow, with his leg inexplicably severed and missing, his wound crudely bandaged. To an extent relatively rare in Irish literature of any genre, the detectives spend significant time exploring elements of Igbo and Yoruba cultures (including an extended visit to Nigeria), and the Nigerian characters are by no means passive objects of contemplation. Instead, the novel gives these characters something approaching equivalent agency on the page, as the narrative explicitly remarks at one point: 'As two Irishmen sat in Nigeria discussing the Nigerians, two Nigerians sat in Dublin discussing

---

[16] For a more extensive account of immigrants in Irish crime fiction, see David Clark, 'Mean Streets, New Lives: The Representations of Non-Irish Immigrants in Recent Irish Crime Fiction,' in *Literary Visions of Multicultural Ireland: The Immigrant in Contemporary Irish Literature*, ed. Pilar Villar-Argáiz (Manchester: Manchester University Press, 2013), 255–268.

what to do next about the Irish.'[17] Much of the novel revolves around Shad's surviving brother, Jude, and others in the African community north of the Liffey in Dublin, including Pita, a younger boy who arguably does more to solve the crime than do the Gardaí. The third-person narrative voice includes substantial amounts of free indirect discourse, and gives much space to Jude's thoughts and experiences, clearly investing itself in the immigrant characters' perspectives and experiences amidst a rapidly changing Dublin, an investment suggested by the sometimes awkwardly broad explanations of cultural difference that are studded throughout the book, such as this: 'In Africa, unlike Europe, irrespective of gender assortment, such extreme physical proximity, indeed promiscuity, occasions neither embarrassment nor lubricity.'[18] Indeed, for a crime novel, *Second Burial* spends relatively little time on the police or the criminals, instead investing on the whole more heavily in this narrative and cultural attempt at empathy, for the individual victims and survivors as well as for the broader cultural experience of emigration and immigration.[19]

Chris Binchy's novel *Open-Handed* (2008) is similarly refracted through the perspectives of several immigrant characters from Eastern Europe, now working various service and hospitality jobs in Dublin. Though neither a mystery nor a crime novel as such, *Open-Handed* revolves around corruption and varieties of crime, including prostitution, and touches on human trafficking, a particularly transnational crime that also appears in novels including Stuart Neville's *Stolen Souls* (2011), Brian McGilloway's *Bleed a River Deep* (2009), Jane Casey's *After the Fire* (2015), and Arlene Hunt's *Vicious Circle* (2004) and *Undertow* (2008), while Hunt's *Blood Money* (2010) depicts illegal international traffic in human organ transplants and Declan Hughes touches on related ground with the vulnerable, rootless victims in *City of Lost Girls* (2010) and Ukrainian women in *The Colour of Blood* (2007). Among the interesting things that Binchy's novel does is to consider his characters in such a light that they might be better understood not as immigrants, with Dublin at the centre of their present tense lives, but as emigrants, with the homes

---

[17] Andrew Nugent, *Second Burial* (London: Headline 2007), 146. This novel was published earlier in the US than in Ireland and the UK, under the more ornate title *Second Burial for a Black Prince* (New York: Thomas Dunne, 2006).

[18] Nugent, *Second Burial*, 176.

[19] Nugent's first novel, *The Four Courts Murder* (London: Headline, 2006), also contains a number of passages touching on varieties of bigotry and anti-Semitism in Ireland.

they left behind (and to which some of them return) instead taking the emotional focus. With a real complexity to its sense of home and one's relationship to it, *Open-Handed* thus shifts the centre away from the Dublin that it depicts, pointing quietly instead towards extra-insular, global dynamics of trade, movement, emigration, and economic change. Although these dynamics all intersect in these characters' Ireland, they are for the most part not depicted as uniquely Irish, a representation that is shared by much of Alan Glynn's work, as I will discuss shortly.

At a slight angle to these patterns of the Irish abroad and immigrants in Ireland is the figure of the returned detective. As discussed in Chapter 3, Declan Hughes gives the reader a protagonist – Ed Loy – who grew up in a very recessionary Dublin, but who has spent much of his adulthood in the sunnier (and more noir climes) of southern California.[20] When Loy returns from years in Los Angeles, he finds a Dublin at the height of the Celtic Tiger, awash in a prosperity alien to Loy, such that one old friend 'must have been the fifteenth person to reassure me about the vibrancy of the local property market.'[21] This is an inescapable topic, even at his mother's funeral, but one in which Loy as a returned emigrant sees deep wells of anxiety just behind the thin, satisfied veneer.[22] An internal emigrant of sorts is Frank in Tana French's *Faithful Place* (2010), who returns from suburban Dublin to the insistently working-class street in Dublin's Liberties neighbourhood where he grew up but which he has not visited in decades, and to the family with which he has largely not communicated since he left.[23] Now, however, despite his partial claim on being an insider, he is at the same time very much an outsider, to his family (with whom he had severed relations), to his former socioeconomic class (from whom he was distanced by marrying a posh suburban career woman), and to his neighbourhood (from whom he is alienated by virtue of his taboo-breaking status as a cop, and an undercover cop at that). This positioning allows French – as Hughes did with Loy – to provide her readers with an ambivalent perspective, one estranged like that of the

[20] Charlotte Headrick suggests that this 'exploration of the returning emigrant' is 'something Hughes has also worked through in his drama,' from 1991's *Digging for Fire* through at least to 2003's *Shiver*. Charlotte Headrick, '"Where no kindness goes unpunished": Declan Hughes's Dublin,' in Mannion, *The Contemporary Irish Detective Novel*, 47.

[21] Declan Hughes, *The Wrong Kind of Blood* (London: John Murray, 2006, repr. 2007), 11.

[22] Hughes, *Wrong*, 15.

[23] Tana French, *Faithful Place* (New York: Penguin, 2010, repr. 2011), 28.

immigrant characters in Joyce's *Echobeat* and Nugent's *Second Burial*, but one that also has a different kind of intimate insight gained from having gone away and then returned. Through both returned emigrants and new immigrants in these and other novels, Irish crime fiction merges the genre's outsider traditions with Ireland's particular histories and the movement of people across borders, in the process helping give Irish versions of the genre a very broad scope indeed.

Transnational Crime

Other examples of Irish crime fiction engage more overtly with transnational crime. David Graham's *Incitement* (2013), for example, is set amidst an international drug war, ranging from Mexico to Miami to Kosovo, with a DEA agent and a mercenary as the central figures. Paul Carson's fourth novel *Ambush* (2004), a relatively rare example of an Irish medical thriller, follows a Dublin widower and his murdered American wife's surviving brother as they chase down her killer, part of an international drug conspiracy ranging from Chicago to Thailand. Cormac Millar's protagonist – with the coyly literary name Seamus Joyce – also finds himself at the centre of, first, an Irish conflict around the international drug trade in *An Irish Solution* (2004) and then the scarcely less duplicitous internationalisation of for-profit colleges in *The Grounds* (2006). Similarly, other novels with strong thriller elements – from Ed O'Loughlin's Booker Prize-nominated *Not Untrue & Not Unkind* (2009) to Vincent Banville's *An End to Flight* (1973) – ground Irish characters in international conflicts well beyond Ireland and Europe. Much as serial killer novels can be difficult to set plausibly in Ireland, conspiracy novels may be difficult to set in Ireland for the same reason: Ireland's vastly reduced sense of scale is likely to mean that a conspiracy thriller will often require implausible and unsustainable levels of coincidence. Alan Glynn is an obvious and excellent exception, but he manages that in part by making the frame of reference very international from the start.

Glynn's loose trilogy – *Winterland* (2009), *Bloodland* (2011), and *Graveland* (2013) – constitutes the pre-eminent example of Irish novels rooted in transnational crime narratives. In these novels, Glynn begins with an Irish version of globalisation's depredation, which then allows him to reflect larger, more widespread experiences, thereby straddling the global and the local in ways relatively few crime novels are able to do so successfully. Although *Winterland* and *Bloodland* have narrative or character anchors in Ireland, these globe-spanning novels reflect the amorphous flow of capital and crime through a cast of characters who move in and out of the foreground over the trilogy. This structure is perfect for engaging with the precise nature of the crimes, conspiracies, and corruptions with which they are concerned: these novels are structured in shifting, inter-locked ways that resonate acutely with experiences of international capitalism's and globalised finance's dislocations.

The trilogy's narrative roots in Irish characters and affairs can best be shown by tracing the plot strands backwards, against the grain of their increasingly international settings and dimensions. The third novel, *Graveland*, opens with the murder of two New York financiers and quickly refers to both the Tea Party and Occupy Wall Street before turning to another American character, Frank Bishop, who lost his job in the crash, of which he – like many Glynn characters – has only a 'fragile understanding.'[24] At the centre of *Graveland*'s narrative is James Vaughan, a nearly mythic investor and archetypal American insider. With connections and a reputation going back to JFK's Camelot, for more than one character 'It's like he's the very *embodiment* of money. Cash made carnate.'[25] Vaughan's status and reputation are undone in the end when a New York-based magazine publishes an exposé by Jimmy Gilroy, an Irish journalist introduced in the second novel, *Bloodland*, where he is writing a quick biography of Susie Monaghan, 'a tabloid celebrity, a bottom-feeding soap-star socialite'[26] who died in a helicopter crash at a resort in Donegal. As Gilroy learns, Vaughan's company was centrally involved with this crash, plotted to prevent the discovery of their illicit involvement in extracting 'thanaxite,' an exceedingly 'rare metallic ore,' from an African mine.[27] Gilroy is set on Vaughan's trail when, in an attempt to prevent him from uncovering the real story behind the crash, interested parties offer him the chance to ghostwrite the memoirs of Larry Bolger, a lightweight Irish politician who backed his way into becoming *Taoiseach* (the equivalent of a Prime Minister in the Irish system). Bolger, amidst drunken bouts of self-pity and resentment after he lost that office and fell out of Irish power's inner circle, lets slip to Gilroy that Susie was '"collateral damage" ... A nice

---

[24] Alan Glynn, *Graveland* (London: Faber, 2013), 275.
[25] Alan Glynn, *Bloodland* (London: Faber, 2011), 128.
[26] Glynn, *Bloodland*, 27.
[27] Glynn, *Bloodland*, 287; 288–297 spells out the core details of this tangled conspiracy.

piece of misdirection is all.'[28] Bolger's rage and self-loathing, in turn, go back to the previous novel, *Winterland*, where his entanglement with the corrupt developer Paddy Norton helps bring Bolger to Vaughan's attention.

This narrative structure – at once intricate and fluid – proceeds through a gradual unfolding, one that keeps the characters largely in the dark. The novels' deferral of resolution is consistent with the genre's need for suspense, but these novels exceed that baseline need, offering little narrative centre, little sense that anyone knows anything more than a contingent piece of the answers. Indeed, even *Winterland*'s conclusion – amidst all of the revelations, amidst all of the individual narratives that are tied up with the finality of death – offers little in the way of resolution or closure, to an extent matched in Irish crime fiction perhaps only by John Connolly's and Tana French's novels. No mere coy cliffhanger, this lack of resolution is directly tied to the trilogy's subject matter: while individual chapters or side stories may reach contingent conclusions or find fragmentary answers, Glynn implies no broader relief from the larger forces driving these narratives. Instead, the scope and nature of these forces puts their total comprehension continually beyond the reach of any of Glynn's characters. By depicting this dynamic so consistently – at the levels of structure, of plot, and of character – Glynn's novels demonstrate crime fiction's ability to sustain profound uncertainty, an ability sometimes masked by genre imperatives. As does French, whose work is examined in Chapter 3, Glynn builds on this expressive capacity, enabling his trilogy to reflect in a fundamental way – not assuage with narrative resolution, but genuinely reflect, in however fragmentary a fashion – the experience of uncertainty, of unresolved lives.[29] Glynn's novels are at their most transnational in so acutely reflecting the overwhelming complexity of such global affairs.

---

[28] Glynn, *Bloodland*, 118.

[29] Aaron Kelly has described 'the conspiratorial thriller' in terms relevant here: 'the confrontation within earlier detective fiction of the organic community with the criminal individual ... is fundamentally overhauled and historically rewritten in the conspiratorial thriller by the confrontation of the individual with the criminal collective, the mystery of the social. In such thrillers one crime often leads not to its resolution but rather its attachment to other seemingly interminable concatenations and labyrinths of crime and conspiracy. Nevertheless ...this conspiratorial mode also harnesses a utopian desire to uncover and trace the social totality and its complexity in however degraded or skeletal a manner through such criminal patterns and intrigues.' Aaron Kelly, *The Thriller and Northern Ireland Since 1969: Utterly Resigned Terror* (Aldershot: Ashgate, 2005), 22.

One way in which the trilogy maintains this uncertainty is by dividing the focus between characters conspiring to maintain or extend their hold on power, and characters struggling – to the point of what others see as obsession – to understand some part of those conspiracies, haunted like Frank Bishop in *Graveland* by the feeling 'that deep inside ... if only he could find and unravel it, is the key to the whole thing, the answer.'[30] The novels' structures oscillate continually between these two main groups of characters, further evincing the trilogy's investment in decentred narratives, experiences, and contexts. Introduced in the first novel, *Winterland*, Vaughan is the closest thing the novels have to a central character, though still not that in any conventional sense. The sort of man who 'has been at or near the centre of power in Washington ... for the best part of fifty years' and 'Manna to conspiracy theorists,'[31] over the course of the trilogy Vaughan is increasingly the crossroads through which the trilogy's various plots, sub-plots, characters, and forces intersect.

This role is most apparent in *Graveland*, the sections of which are prefaced with epigraphs from the fictional biography *House of Vaughan*, later revealed to be a work-in-progress by Jimmy Gilroy, the Dublin journalist from *Bloodland* whose reappearance is the only overt Irish strand in *Graveland*, otherwise set primarily in Manhattan. Gilroy's brief but crucial appearance is enough to remind a reader of the trilogy that core events in *Graveland* have roots in earlier novels, particularly the murders that put him on Vaughan's trail.

This is not to suggest *Graveland* is secretly about Ireland. On the contrary, this connection works to strengthen Glynn's recurring theme of almost incomprehensibly large and stateless forces that shape and sometimes destroy people's lives. As Jimmy says of his work on Vaughan, 'the subject matter was vast, octopus-like, and it expanded exponentially the more he researched it.'[32] As a journalist, but also simply as a character, Gilroy connects what Vaughan seems to have regarded (if at all) as just another necessary business measure – the murder of Susie and others he did not know before the outset of *Bloodland* – to the eventual unravelling, years later, of Vaughan's own life and his violently guarded desire for anonymity within the veil of power. The line between Susie's death at the margins and Vaughan's downfall from the centre is constituted out of

---

[30] Glynn, *Graveland*, 275; cf. 277.
[31] Glynn, *Bloodland*, 331; see also Glynn, *Graveland*, 95.
[32] Glynn, *Graveland*, 314.

indirect, even glancing connections of the most passing and yet most impactful sort. This fusion of direct causation and fragmentary knowledge is essential to Glynn's trilogy, both as crime novels and as novels immersively engaged with characters' experiences amidst the tumbling, uneven flow of transnational capital and crime.

As this suggests, Glynn's intricately plotted novels remain centrally invested not so much in the external events that take place around the machinations of wealth and power, and more in the individual experiences of both the victims who bear the brunt of those machinations and the agents of power who move their levers. This is perhaps most overt with Frank Bishop, 'an ordinary guy who's suddenly living the unimaginable nightmare of having his personal life – family tragedy, professional failures, character flaws, the lot – projected onto the Jumbotron screen of public consciousness.'[33] In this pattern, Glynn confirms a breadth of interest that is also evident in the scope of his novels and in their dynamic movement from one character's perspective to another, shifting continually across the range of characters. Again, this wide cast of competing characters contributes to keeping the novels off-centre, reflecting the experience of transnational power, wealth, and corruption. This sense of scale is furthered by Glynn's ability to maintain tiny interconnections between the novels in the trilogy, at times on a scale as small as the fictional game console LudeX, mentioned in *Bloodland* and again at the outset of *Graveland*,[34] or with more material details like the pharmaceutical company Eiben, which becomes significant in *Graveland*[35] after brief mentions in the preceding two novels, and after a significant role in Glynn's otherwise distinct first novel *The Dark Fields* (2001).[36] Such passing connections create a sense of continuity within a fictional universe for the reader, of course, one recognisably mapped on to our own world. In a less immediately apparent way, however, these connections between novels also serve to amplify the sense of a world, fictional *and* real, in which the scope of wealth and power's web – like the scale of interconnectedness across the trilogy – is beyond the grasp of any one character or any one reader. As the journalist Ellen

---

[33] Glynn, *Graveland*, 256–7.
[34] Glynn, *Bloodland*, 269; Glynn, *Graveland*, 9.
[35] Glynn, *Graveland*, 3, 230, 258.
[36] This was republished as *Limitless* (New York: Picador, 2011) after the film adaptation of that name was released.

Dorsey observes in *Graveland*, 'No one's an expert … Isn't that part of the problem?'[37]

Glynn's books have been successful at home and abroad, and part of the trilogy's power is its ability to show how contemporary Ireland's experiences *are* global experiences in readers' daily, political, and communal lives, not provincial narratives or family secrets. It is surely in part because of this that these novels have found a readership invested – necessarily so, given the trilogy's settings and concerns – not just with the internecine details of Irish corruption in recent decades but also with larger-scale forces that are experienced locally, intimately, even as they are seen to be anchored in a much wider scope. The climactic confrontation near the end of *Winterland*, for example, distils the potential difference between Irish events – like the public revelation of the glittering skyscraper's fatal structural flaw – registering anecdotally abroad and those same events mattering existentially at home: 'Outside of Ireland, the story has a kind of train-wreck fascination, and proves irresistible to cartoonists and joke writers. But at home the whole business is seen as something altogether more urgent – because as far as the public at large is concerned … this shiny new forty-eight-storey glass box is, in the words of one vox pop contributor, "just sitting there waiting to keel over."'[38] Glynn's fiction works in this suspended space between home and abroad, with roots in Irish circumstances but with an arc that spreads to these global conspiracies. Writing in this space allows Glynn's work to reject any choice between Irish writing and international writing, and to follow the threads of transnational capital's interventions in individual lives, a kind of navigation that Glynn does uniquely well.

Settings Elsewhere

While Glynn engages with sprawlingly transnational conspiracies and crimes across a trilogy that nonetheless originates in Ireland, other novels with little or no materially significant Irish content, and few if any Irish characters, also expand our understanding of Irish crime fiction's scope. Through their range of content, contexts, and settings, these novels demonstrate Irish crime fiction's varied ways of participating in the 'resolutely transnational

[37] Glynn, *Graveland*, 329.
[38] Alan Glynn, *Winterland* (London: Faber, 2009), 407.

phenomenon' that is crime fiction.[39] As noted with Hughes and others, some of this transnational quality is a matter of cultural influence. Glynn's particular strand of crime fiction, for example, shows the impact of 1970s American conspiracy cinema that saw some of its fullest flowering in films such as Francis Ford Coppola's *The Conversation* (1974), with Gene Hackman playing a surveillance expert, or Sydney Pollack's *Three Days of the Condor* (1975), starring Robert Redford as a CIA analyst who stumbles onto a far-reaching conspiracy (albeit one less unambiguously illicit than in the source novel, James Grady's 1974 *Six Days of the Condor*).[40]

Along with Glynn's, among the most effective Irish crime novels to conjure this acutely tense atmosphere are Steve Cavanagh's *The Defence* (2015), *The Plea* (2016), and *The Liar* (2017). Cavanagh's books are all tightly plotted – and rare examples of Irish legal thrillers – with the con man/lawyer Eddie Flynn as their narrator, forced into ticking-clock scenarios full of shadowy authority figures and powerful criminals. Where Glynn's trilogy spans the globe, however, Cavanagh's books are insistently set in and around a gritty New York City, itself redolent more of Pollack's paranoia than Giuliani's family-friendly Times Square. The main characters, too, are American and the novels contain little or nothing that could give any meaningful traction to a more allegorical reading of the texts' Irishness. The most prominent exception is New York City's St. Patrick's Day parade, which forms the backdrop to *The Plea*'s climax but which carries no real explanatory force within the narrative. As discussed earlier in this chapter and in the introduction, the field of Irish literary and cultural studies often struggles with material that does not somehow frame itself in terms of representing Ireland. Consequently, I argue, novels like Cavanagh's and like Connolly's Charlie Parker series carry more rather than less weight – and deserve more rather than less attention – precisely because crime novels lacking Irish settings and characters pose such an interpretative challenge to the field's established frameworks of meaning.

Other Irish crime fiction at least as far back as the many books of Freeman Wills Crofts, or J.B. O'Sullivan's *Don't Hang Me Too High* (1954), have also been set primarily or entirely abroad, for varied settings, for integral plot elements (William Ryan's Captain Alexei Korolev books set in the Stalin-era Soviet Union, for example, give themselves over

---

[39] Pepper, *Unwilling Executioner*, 168.

[40] Glynn comments on precisely these films in the interview appended to the UK/Irish release of *Bloodland* (416).

wholly to their respective contexts), or for yet more articulated and individual reasons. Recent examples include Adrian McKinty, who has written an excellent series of Northern Irish crime novels discussed in Chapter 2 and has also written standalone novels set abroad: *The Sun is God* (2014), set in the South Pacific, and the Cuba-to-Colorado *50 Grand* (2009), which, despite its transnational span, powerfully creates an almost claustrophobic sense of obsessive pursuit. Declan Hughes's *All the Things You Are* (2014) is a departure from his Ed Loy series, and takes place in Wisconsin. Like McKinty and Hughes, Ken Bruen has set his main series (the Jack Taylor novels) in Ireland, but has also published a series of novels featuring the London police officers Brant and Roberts. In a quite different series, Paul Charles's affectingly humane protagonist Christy Kennedy is Irish-born but works most of his cases in London, and has only had one case to date (2003's *I've Heard the Banshee Sing*) taking place partly in Ulster.

Like Kennedy, Jane Casey's protagonist Maeve Kerrigan has Irish roots. Kerrigan, a young police detective whose cases take place in and around metropolitan London, where she was born and bred, has an extended family in Ireland. Although Kerrigan's Irishness never quite generates a plot of its own, Elizabeth Mannion has developed a suggestive reading of the ways in which Maeve's experiences of her Irishness – from her complex pride in that identity, to her bristling at the casual prejudices that she often has to navigate at work and in London – amplify and reinforce some of the series' central themes. In particular, Mannion argues, Kerrigan's heritage allows her specific character to anchor the series' investment in considering 'cultural otherness,' an investment that makes 'Distinctions of race, class, and gender ... central to each volume in the series, along with a running commentary on social inequities along these boundaries.'[41] This commentary, in turn, connects Kerrigan to others – women, minorities, victims of crimes – who also encounter those boundaries, in ways both violent and mundane. These connections not only mark her as inhabiting 'something of the alienated space so common to' detective fiction but, with greater significance for the quality of the series, also give a particular focus to 'the depth of her empathy.'[42] That empathy is amplified by the ambivalence of Kerrigan's belonging: 'I was Irish by blood and English by accident and I

---

[41] Elizabeth Mannion, '"Irish by blood and English by accident": Detective Constable Maeve Kerrigan,' in Mannion, *The Contemporary Irish Detective Novel*, 121.

[42] Mannion, '"Irish by blood and English by accident,"' 123, 128.

didn't belong to either tradition, or anywhere else,' a claim supported by its juxtaposition with the quite different views of her father, who had 'little time for the Empire and less sympathy for the country he lived in.'[43] The novels' setting outside of Ireland is part of what gives these questions such a sharp edge for Kerrigan, with subtle effects throughout the series.

Settings outside of Ireland also allow for a wider scale, and for crimes and mysteries that would strain plausibility in Ireland's smaller landscape, where certain plots would quickly require an unsustainable level of coincidence. Conversely, some kinds of coincidence, notably those involving an intimately small, even inbred, social elite, as in Glynn's trilogy, require a kind of interconnectedness that would be implausibly coincidental elsewhere, but that make sense on an Irish scale, as Glynn's characters lament: 'How many degrees of separation? Never too many in this fucking town, that's for sure. Never *enough*.'[44] Much as representations of sexual violence can tie into both genre tropes and particularly Irish experiences, as discussed in Chapter 4, this matter of scale is one of the recurring particularities of Irish crime fiction, as a brief consideration of work by Alex Barclay and Arlene Hunt suggests.

Alex Barclay's main series, also discussed in Chapter 4, is set entirely in North America. With an unusually deft ear for psychological nuance, and a level of colloquially psychotherapeutic conversation that is – to speak generally – *far* more American than it is Irish, Barclay builds her series around Ren Bryce. Bryce is a highly driven FBI agent who mostly works in Colorado, but who has also gone undercover in a long-running drug case involving Mexican cartels and has followed a case to Oregon in *The Drowning Child* (2016). The Bryce books frequently involve some kind of serial killer or crimes on a larger scale, beyond the scope local enforcement would plausibly face. With these plots in this setting, Barclay's work

---

[43] Jane Casey, *The Stranger You Know* (London: Ebury, 2013), 10, 9. A less centrally ambivalent approach can be seen in Zane Radcliffe's *London Irish* (2002), a comic thriller that uses its protagonist-narrator Bic (who 'was born in Bangor, lived there till I was ten, then moved to Scotland') to anchor its narrative amidst London's Irish expats and their descendants. Zane Radcliffe, *London Irish* (London: Black Swan, 2002), 129.

[44] Glynn, *Winterland*, 435. Declan Hughes's Ed Loy is just as explicit: 'Dublin is a small place for a private detective to be a public figure, and I'm already too well known for my own good. The city is shrinking, and I wonder, not for the first time, whether I'm running out of road.' Declan Hughes, *City of Lost Girls* (London: John Murray, 2010; repr. 2011), 142. Nor is this just Loy's perspective: his girlfriend says in passing 'God, that was a coincidence. Or rather, that was Dublin for you' (Hughes, *City*, 128).

exemplifies comments Arlene Hunt has made regarding her own grim novel, *The Chosen* (2011, republished in 2016 as *Last to Die*), when she suggested some creative and practical reasons for setting a novel abroad. Set in the US, primarily in the small towns and massive forests that sprawl across the junctions of North Carolina, Tennessee, Kentucky, Virginia, and West Virginia, *The Chosen*'s hero is Jessie Conway, a teacher who stops a school shooting, only to attract the attention of a serial killer, Caleb, who has kidnapped, hunted, and killed numerous women in the region's vast backwoods. Such plots, Hunt suggested, are not viably set in Ireland, the size of which mitigates against the numerous and repetitive nature of a serial killer's crimes.[45] Caleb's particular crimes, for example, require a different geography – Tennessee alone is substantially larger in area than the entire island of Ireland – and a different, more primeval landscape in which to target women without fear of detection. This applies not just to the villain, but to the hero Jesse as well, who has her own secret past in another small Southern town, one from which she has been able to hide in ways that would be less persuasive amidst Ireland's relative geographic and social intimacy.

Serial killer plots may also have less tangible cultural reasons for being set outside of Ireland: Linnie Blake has suggested that the iconic variants of the serial killer are most at home in the US, and reflect a particular nexus of social, cultural, and political forces that are best emblematised in the contemporary US, outside of which serial killers lack the same (relative) plausibility and the same resonance.[46]

---

[45] Seminar discussion with the author and students, 'Irish Crime Fiction' undergraduate seminar, Trinity College Dublin, 11 March 2015. This point is also on display in Jane Casey's fiction, where London provides potential anonymity because of its sheer scale, a very different urban landscape even from Dublin, sprawling enough for one to disappear into it. In Casey's seventh Maeve Kerrigan novel, *Let the Dead Speak* (London: HarperCollins, 2017), Maeve reflects on this metropolitan sprawl, in which she could hear 'a jumble of accents around us – English, Eastern European, Irish, Jamaican, Glaswegian … London, basically' (*Let the Dead Speak*, 272).

[46] Linnie Blake, *The Wounds of Nations: Horror Cinema, Historical Trauma, and National Identity* (Manchester: Manchester University Press, 2008), 102. Blake further argues that factual and fictional murder narratives reflect ingrained American 'binarisms that pit the transgressive individual against the common good, the lone frontiersman against the machinery of urban-industrial life under capitalism' (*The Wounds of Nations*, 108). In contrast to such national imagery, modern Irish culture has for better and worse frequently carried with it a stronger, more overt strain of communitarian discourse. Despite the setting of Hunt's *The Chosen*, these American binaries do not quite apply in that novel, because Jessie and her allies do not themselves neatly map on to them: instead, *everyone* in *The Chosen*, villain and protagonists alike, is some variety of outsider relative to 'the machinery of urban-industrial life under capitalism.'

Non-Irish settings are thus more than a question of thrillers that co-opt international locales for their potential glamour, more than simply varying the palette or avoiding the familiar terrain of Irishness (though they can also partake of those things). For Hunt's novel *The Chosen*, as for Barclay's series, the setting outside of Ireland matters materially, directly affecting the plot and the characters alike. Casey's Maeve Kerrigan in London, or McKinty's Michael Forsythe in North America, function as outsiders in part because of their distance from Ireland, a distance that gives a particular force to this familiar role for a crime fiction protagonist. Nor is that outsider quality limited to the Irish abroad: Conor Fitzgerald's novels take place in Rome, for example, where his protagonist Alec Blume is a police commissioner. The orphan of two American parents, Blume grew up in Rome, and – like Casey's Kerrigan – is reminded at work that he remains not quite an insider, but other, foreign.

The most sustained series set outside of Ireland, with no significant Irish characters, however, is John Connolly's Charlie Parker series, novels in which outsiderness and otherness are fundamental to the protagonist, a character who is in essential ways profoundly unlike and apart from those around him.

JOHN CONNOLLY'S CHARLIE PARKER SERIES

As I have suggested, Irish literary studies has often seemed unable to readily address Irish texts that cannot be understood as somehow about Irishness. Connolly's Parker series, in contrast, exemplifies how the kind of Irish crime fiction discussed in this chapter can be transnational, can be both Irish and elsewhere, without needing to be *about* Ireland. At once sprawling and almost obsessively focused, the series exhibits a dizzying range of concerns from which a number of patterns emerge, among them the novels' blurring of genres and modes, particularly the supernatural and crime fiction, which in turn informs the novels' insistent empathy.[47] These connections and tensions are central both to the Parker books in

---

[47] Lee Horsley is not alone in noting a 'shared history, linking crime fiction from its inception to the gothic representation of excess, violence, and transgressions of the boundaries of reason and law' (*Twentieth-Century Crime Fiction*, 4). For an important and detailed discussion of some of these issues in the genre, see Maurizio Ascari, *A Counter-History of Crime Fiction: Supernatural, Gothic, Sensational* (Basingstoke: Palgrave Macmillan, 2007). See also Michael Cook, *Detective Fiction and the Ghost Story: The Haunted Text* (Basingstoke: Palgrave Macmillan, 2014).

particular and to Connolly's work more generally, which often stands on the borders of the various traditions in which it participates. It is in this sense that the Parker novels, in their transnational elements and their blurring of genres, challenge habits of reading within both Irish fiction and mystery fiction. In this, they are a model of the way in which such texts can contribute to and even revise traditions and genres such as this book has discussed. They do so not just through overt thematic interventions at the level of content, but also simply by being what they are: texts that cannot be subsumed within a single national tradition or a single way of understanding their genres.

Connolly spent several years as a journalist at the *Irish Times* before beginning his career as a novelist. Since then, he has sold well over ten million books in 29 languages. Among them are three young adult novels in the Samuel Johnson series;[48] the standalone novels *Bad Men* (2004), *The Book of Lost Things* (2006), and *he* (2017); two collections of short stories, *Nocturnes* (2004) and *Night Music: Nocturnes 2* (2015); and, with his partner, Jennifer Ridyard, a science fiction trilogy, *The Chronicles of the Invaders.*[49] The bulk of his published fiction, however, has been his Charlie Parker series, in which fifteen novels, one novella, and a collection of miscellany have been published to date. The protagonist-detective Parker's series stretches from *Every Dead Thing* (1999), the first non-American winner of the Shamus Award from the Private Eye Writers of America, to the most recent Parker novel, *A Game of Ghosts* (2017). Like other Connolly novels, *A Game of Ghosts* was a *Sunday Times* bestseller, appearing at number one on the list, and characteristically spending over a month on the Irish bestseller lists.

The Parker series is marked by the way in which it blurs genre distinctions, drawing heavily on both crime and supernatural fiction, alternately fusing one's themes with the other's structures and rhythms. In identifying his influences, Connolly has often cited the California novels of Ross Macdonald and the Louisiana novels of James Lee Burke, both canonical standard-bearers in crime fiction. More surprisingly, however, he has also invoked the British fantasy writer M.R. James, not an influence widely cited in crime circles but one whose work bespeaks its own variety of abiding and mysterious unease. Indeed, as noted in Chapter 3, Connolly has

---

[48] *The Gates* (2009), *The Infernals* (2011), and *The Creeps* (2013).
[49] *Conquest* (2013), *Empire* (2015), and *Dominion* (2016).

characterised his own work as from the beginning 'fascinated by the possibility of combining the rationalist traditions of the mystery novel with the antirationalist underpinnings of supernatural fiction.'[50] This fusion becomes an increasingly essential element as the series develops, such that even the seemingly 'normal' crimes and the underlying supernatural patterns amplify each other. This play with generic conventions is essential to the strengths of Connolly's work, not least for the ways in which it underpins the substantial ethical core of the series and helps Connolly's work extend the boundaries of Irish writing.

This blurring has not always appealed to genre readers: not unlike a certain kind of jazz (or blues, or punk) fan, some crime readers see the genre's conventions as central to its appeal.[51] Viewed from this perspective, the Parker novels may represent something of a misfit, even a kind of betrayal of the genre's rational inclinations. In one of the few academic considerations of Connolly's work to date, for example, Bill Phillips argues that the author 'became increasingly obsessed with the devil and his novel *The Black Angel* (2005) can more fairly be described as a horror story than a crime novel.'[52] A more receptive reading, which makes fewer assumptions about Connolly's own beliefs, is in Charles De Lint's highly favourable review of the same novel that Phillips dismisses, *The Black Angel*, on precisely the grounds that this work 'for the interstitial crowd' adeptly draws on multiple genres.[53] (It is perhaps unsurprising that De Lint is an established author of fantasy/science fiction, a genre at times more welcoming than crime fiction to experimentation and to free adaptation of genre writing.)

Much as Connolly's fiction does not quite fit crime conventions, his place in Irish writing can be hard to locate. In this regard, his work raises

[50] John Connolly, 'I Live Here,' *Night Music: Nocturnes 2* (New York: Atria, 2015), 420.

[51] This is perhaps particularly true in discussions of Golden Age crime fiction, as John Curran, Martin Priestman, Stephen Knight, and others have all demonstrated. See also Connolly, 'I Live Here.'

[52] Bill Phillips, 'Irish Noir,' *Estudios Irlandeses* 9 (2014): 175. Some of Phillips's assertions suggest that, while his praise of Ken Bruen and Benjamin Black reflects more sustained reading, he has given relatively little attention to Connolly's work. For example: the claim that violence is something about which Parker feels 'little need for regret' (Phillips, 'Irish Noir,' 169), overlooks a great deal of nuance about Parker's empathy and his clear ambivalence around violence.

[53] Charles De Lint, 'Books to Look For,' *Fantasy & Science Fiction* 110, no. 6 (2006): 28.

in detail many of the transnational issues presented by the other novels here. None of the novels for which he is best known are set in Ireland, for example, and they contain almost no overt Irish themes or references. (The Parker novels do contain a few minor examples of Irish diction, such as 'tutorial' rather than the American 'seminar' or 'class,'[54] and 'fairy lights' rather than 'Christmas lights,'[55] which are however more in the order of exceptions that prove the rule.) In this context, the Irish-American characters in *The Lovers* (2009) stand out: Charlie's father's 'closest friend, Jimmy Gallagher...bled Irish green and cop blue,' while Parker spent some of his adolescence in Pearl River, a town 'where all the Irish cops lived.'[56] Even here, however, though Catholic, Parker's father explicitly 'was not himself Irish.'[57] Some scattered textual fragments across the series – including one from Le Fanu's *Uncle Silas*,[58] and Oscar Wilde's epigrammatic assertion that 'sentimentality is the bank holiday of cynicism'[59] – similarly stand out, as does this wry passage: 'The tall one was named Mackey, the short one was Dunne. Anybody hoping to use them as proof that the Irish still dominated the NYPD was likely to be confused by the fact that Dunne was black and Mackey looked Asian.'[60]

[54] For instances of 'tutorial,' see John Connolly, *Dark Hollow* (New York: Simon & Schuster, 2001), 318, 321; John Connolly, *The Killing Kind* (New York: Atria, 2002), 54; John Connolly, *The White Road* (New York: Atria, 2003), 46; John Connolly, *The Unquiet* (New York: Atria, 2007), 196; and John Connolly, *The Wolf in Winter* (New York: Atria, 2014), 365. Except where otherwise noted, Connolly references are to the American editions of his novels, which often have different pagination and sometimes small textual differences, though the UK first editions are also listed in the bibliography for reference purposes.

[55] John Connolly, *The Reapers* (New York: Atria, 2008), 45, 46; and John Connolly, *The Wrath of Angels* (New York: Atria, 2013), 49, 119.

[56] John Connolly, *The Lovers* (New York: Atria, 2009), 25, 20.

[57] Connolly, *Lovers*, 20.

[58] John Connolly, *A Game of Ghosts* (London: Hodder, 2017), 91.

[59] This phrase appears twice, in Connolly, *Lovers*, 188, and John Connolly, *The Burning Soul* (New York: Atria, 2011), 61. In the latter, it is spoken by an expatriate Irish gangster, indignant that his companion does not know who Oscar Wilde is. A quotation from Wilde's 'Requiescat' also appears in Connolly, *Wrath*, 387:

Tread lightly, she is near
    Under the snow,
Speak gently, she can hear,
    The daisies grow.

[60] John Connolly, *The Black Angel* (New York: Atria, 2005), 111.

Although the supernatural elements that run throughout the Parker series could be seen as marking a Catholic heritage, a point Connolly himself has raised, even the most prominent Catholic priest in the series – the Cistercian Martin Reid in *The Black Angel* – is not Irish but Scottish. Moreover, the supernatural elements in the Parker series are less likely to feature priestly influence than rabbinical commentary and Kabbalistic figures, including a golem, a dybbuk, and dark angels with obscure Old Testament roots, like Kittim in *The White Road* (2002), who has 'An unusual name, a scholarly name,' one referring to 'the tribe destined to lead the final assault against the sons of light, the earthly agents of the powers of darkness.'[61] Connolly has given this absence of Irish material a purposeful air at times, noting that 'As a young writer, I could think of few subjects with which I wanted to engage less than the nature of Irishness, or the Irish situation, and now, as a slightly older writer, that position has not changed.'[62]

In place of such engagement with Irishness, Connolly focuses the series on questions that are explained through an idiosyncratic fusion of genres, figured in Parker himself. Indeed, as an extended consideration of these matters will suggest, it is most powerfully through his protagonist Parker as a character – and not just through the novels' plots – that Connolly's books draw together their different genre elements, from the supernatural hauntings of M.R. James and the familial burdens of Macdonald's Californian noir, to the more generally familiar avenging detective of crime fiction. Parker's empathetic relationship with the supernatural evolves over the course of the series. In the first novel, *Every Dead Thing*, the supernatural initially emerges through the Traveling Man, a serial killer who poses his victims' flayed bodies as *écorchés*, tableaux from medieval and Renaissance medical texts, with overtones drawn from the Book of Enoch. Throughout subsequent novels, this supernatural element gradually builds to include 'dark angels' who remember the trauma of the Fall. By inhabiting a human form – like a parasitic wasp controls its host[63] – these beings look for others of their kind as they roam the earth, 'dark passengers on the human soul, carried unawares for years, even decades,

---

[61] Connolly, *White*, 364.
[62] Connolly, 'No Blacks, No Dogs, No Crime Writers: Ireland and the Mystery Genre,' 44.
[63] Connolly, *Lovers*, 272–5.

until it came time to reveal their true natures.'[64] First hinted at in *Every Dead Thing*, where Parker and his friends suspect the Traveling Man 'believes he's a demon…Or the offspring of an angel,'[65] images of dark angels are explicit as early as the third novel, *The Killing Kind* (2002).[66] By *The Black Angel*, it is clear that – while their particular nature remains shrouded in mystery – these are neither hallucinations nor religious delusions, a point Connolly confirms in his introductions to the recent reprints of the Parker series.[67] Gradually, these dark angels become convinced that Parker may be one of them, one they thought lost, and they rage at him for his betrayal in seeking to atone. As the monstrous Brightwell thinks upon encountering (or, as he thinks, re-encountering) Parker in *The Black Angel*:

> Parker. Such sadness, such pain, and all as penance for an offense against Him that you cannot even recall committing. Your faith was misplaced. There is no redemption, not for you. You were damned, and there is no salvation.
> You were lost to us for so long, but now you are found.[68]

Despite the absolute conviction of Brightwell and other characters – and Parker's own recognition that 'Now I spanned two worlds, the worlds of the living and the dead'[69] – his precise nature still remains open to question.

That nature is tied in narratively complicated ways to Parker's own grievous losses. *Every Dead Thing* introduces him amidst the discovery

---

[64] Connolly, *Wrath*, 174–5. As Connolly notes in his introduction to the reprint edition of *The Wrath of Angels* (London: Hodder & Stoughton, 2015), the novel 'is completely in thrall to the supernatural' (II). This essay, like all of Connolly's author introductions for the Parker books, along with other non-fiction prose of Connolly's, has been collected in *Parker: A Miscellany* (Dublin: Bad Dog, 2016).

[65] John Connolly, *Every Dead Thing* (New York: Simon & Schuster, 1999), 252.

[66] The early pages of the second Parker novel also contain a brief mention of a sound 'like the beating of dark, leathery wings' (Connolly, *Dark*, 71). Though *Dark Hollow* does not freight this image with supernatural weight, it nonetheless is so specific as to anticipate the explicitly supernatural 'leathery wings' – central to the imagery of the dark angels as the series progresses – first mentioned in Connolly, *Killing*, 65.

[67] See in particular his introduction to the reprint edition of *The Black Angel* (New York: Atria, 2015), collected in Connolly, *Parker: A Miscellany*.

[68] Connolly, *Black*, 216.

[69] Connolly, *White*, 61.

that his wife Susan and daughter Jennifer have been brutally murdered in their Brooklyn home, and later reveals that Parker's father took his own life under grimly mysterious circumstances. (In the seventh novel, *The Lovers*, Parker discovers that his father had encountered an evil presence, some of the series' parasitic beings, which led to his suicide and which the novel connects to the same dark angels Parker would later fight.) Throughout the subsequent novels, Parker continues to see Susan's and particularly Jennifer's spirits, which leave physical traces on his world and are clearly more than just manifestations of grief. This tangle of physical and metaphysical origins becomes an emotionally affecting, narratively complex mythology that is dealt with most fully in *The Lovers* but develops further in each of the most recent novels, from *The Wolf in Winter* (2014) through to *A Game of Ghosts*. By the time of *A Song of Shadows* (2015), Parker's second daughter, Sam, has taken on an unambiguously super-natural role, clearly connected to the mythos developed in the preceding novels, with the implication that she even has some ordering power over ghostly presences like those of Susan and Jennifer.

These experiences of loss and the empathy that drive Parker in their wake are central to the series.[70] As he moves forward, Parker perceives what he calls the honeycomb world, initially and most elaborately in the third novel, *The Killing Kind*:

> This is a honeycomb world…The stability of what is seen and felt beneath our feet is an illusion, for this life is not as it seems. Below the surface, there are cracks and fissures and pockets of stale, trapped air…a labyrinth of crystal tumors and frozen columns where history becomes future, then becomes now.[71]

Parker later elaborates, connecting the image to the series' sense of empa-thy in describing his 'first glimpse of the honeycomb world,' which reveals 'an interconnectedness to all things, a link between what lies buried and what lives above, a capacity for mutability that allows a good act commit-ted in the present to rectify an imbalance in times gone by.'[72] Crucially, this is not just Parker's perception. He repeatedly has encounters with

---

[70] Connolly is not the only Irish mystery writer for whom empathy is not just about present suffering but also about absence, as examples like the death of a young man in Gene Kerrigan's *The Rage* (2011) make clear.

[71] Connolly, *Killing*, 3.

[72] Connolly, *Killing*, 264–5.

others who also recognise that honeycomb quality, for example, beginning with *Tante* Marie Aguillard in *Every Dead Thing* and continuing with Sam in novels from *The Black Angel* forward. Nor is this image exclusive to Catholic or Christian characters: Rabbi Epstein, Parker's frequent guide to such matters, refers to Kabbalah, which

> speaks of harmony between the upper and lower worlds, between the visible and the unseen, between good and evil. World above, world below, with angels moving in between. Real angels, not nominal ones…Perhaps [Parker] is such an angel…An agent of the Divine: a destroyer, yet a restorer of the harmony between worlds. Perhaps, just as his true nature is hidden from us, so too it may be hidden even from himself.[73]

Such passages depict a 'honeycomb' view of the supernatural world's layered interconnectedness not as uniquely or particularly Irish Catholic, but rather as a deeper, older view, one voiced in different ways by different traditions, which Epstein in particular helps Parker synthesise.

The honeycomb imagery at times does describe a physical place quite literally, as in *The White Road*, which prominently features the limestone karsts of the South Carolina swamps, a landscape 'honeycombed by underwater streams and caves.'[74] At the same time, however, such a landscape also serves as a figure for empathy as well as for the broader spiritual and moral landscape of the world. Earlier in *The White Road*, for example, Parker makes this more metaphorically toned observation:

> When I look out on the Scarborough marsh from the windows of my house and see the channels cutting through the grass, interlinking with one another, each subject to the same floods, the same cycles of the moon, yet each finding its own route to the sea, I understand something about the nature of this world, about the way in which seemingly disparate lives are inextricably intertwined.[75]

This vision of the world's honeycomb nature – of the way in which 'seemingly disparate lives' are, like distinct geographical features, connected by hidden pathways – amplifies the role of empathy in Parker's life, a force by which he is defined, even haunted. Particularly from *Dark Hollow* (2001)

---

[73] Connolly, *White*, 277.
[74] Connolly, *White*, 323.
[75] Connolly, *White*, 39–40.

on, Parker is overtly shaped by this empathy, however idiosyncratically expressed: 'I saw and heard my dead wife and child, and I saw and heard others too...I think that it may be a kind of empathy, a capacity to experience the suffering of those who have been taken painfully, brutally, without mercy.'[76]

The specific supernatural form this 'capacity' takes for Parker marks him out not only from other Irish series protagonists but also from his own friends, colleagues, and enemies. In this 'capacity,' the transnational elements of setting, character, and theme – more overt in Glynn and others, but just as central here – converge with the way the series travels across genres, the acute and individual form of the detective Parker's empathy marking him as an outsider who imagines his way into connection through this supernatural empathy.

Empathy and the honeycomb world are thus suggestively interwoven across the series. As Parker says in *The Killing Kind*, linking empathy to the images of the honeycomb world with which the novel opens:

> I'd been hurt, and in response I had acted violently, destroying a little of myself each time I did so, but that wasn't the worst of it. It seemed to me that as soon as I became involved in such matters, they caused a fissure in my world. I saw things: lost things, dead things. It was if my intervention drew them to me, those who had been wrenched painfully, violently from this life. Once I thought it was a product of my own incipient guilt, or an empathy I felt that passed beyond feeling and into hallucination.
> But now I believed that they really did know, and they really did come.[77]

This is a crucial distinction: Parker does not resolve this fissure by disavowing the force of empathy in favour of accepting the reality of the supernatural 'things' he sees, nor by dismissing those 'things' as 'hallucinations.' Instead, he accepts *both* the empathy *and* the realness of his visions, disavowing neither. His bone-deep empathy signals others, the suffering and the dead, drawing them to him and impelling him forward across the 'fissures' that 'such matters' bring to his life. Indeed, throughout the series, *contra* Phillips, Connolly's depiction of violence emphasises this complex empathy, characteristically drawing attention to the experience of the victim over and above the act of violence itself, as when Parker viscerally envisions Curtis Peltier's experience of dying in *The Killing Kind*.

[76] Connolly, *Dark*, 121.
[77] Connolly, *Killing*, 27–8.

This foundational empathy is one of the ways in which Connolly's work intersects with the overtly transnational-themed plots discussed here and in Chapters 2 and 4, particularly with sex trafficking and associated crimes. As an *Irish Times* reporter, Connolly covered the Christmas 1996 murder of a young woman in Dublin, which was initially viewed sympathetically in the press, as the tragedy of a young visitor. When it became known that she had been a sex worker, however, the 'public attitude' shifted and 'one tabloid newspaper began routinely to refer to her as "the Sri Lankan hooker, Belinda Pereira,"' both assigning her a non-Irish otherness and suggesting 'in some bleak, appalling way' the view that 'it should not have come as a complete surprise to Belinda when some harm eventually befell her.'[78] This experience shaped the development of *Every Dead Thing*, which Connolly was then writing and which 'became more about the importance of empathy and the necessity of acting on behalf of the vulnerable and the abused,' including the foreign and the transient.[79] Under the crucial influence of such experiences and of Ross Macdonald – who, through his 'profoundly empathetic' protagonist Lew Archer, conveyed in his novels an 'intensely humane view of people and how they suffer' – Parker 'became a being defined not simply by anger and the desire for revenge, but by his own sufferings. Because he has suffered, he is unwilling to allow others to suffer in turn. It is his capacity for empathy that ultimately ensures he does not destroy himself with selfishness and grief.'[80] This empathy extends throughout the novels, and their frequent sense of rootedness in a specific political-social moment, including the struggles of American Iraq War veterans in *The Whisperers* (2010), homelessness in *The Wolf in Winter*, and the images of economic decline that open *A Song of Shadows*.

In depicting Parker, the series continually suggests that his empathy is not without a certain ambivalence, as he himself observes. His empathy is entangled in his own 'reservoir of hurt and pain and anger upon which we can draw when the need arises,' such that

---

[78] John Connolly, 'Author Introduction,' *Dark Hollow*, reprint edition (New York: Emily Bestler/Atria, 2015), xiv, reprinted in Connolly, *Parker: A Miscellany*, 10.

[79] Connolly, *Parker: A Miscellany*, 10.

[80] John Connolly, 'Charlie Parker,' in *The Lineup: The World's Greatest Crime Writers Tell the Inside Story of Their Greatest Detectives*, ed. Otto Penzler (London: Quercus, 2010), 69–71. Macdonald's final Archer novel, *The Blue Hammer*, is referenced as the name of a coffee shop in Cambridge, Massachusetts in the US (but not the UK) edition of Connolly, *Killing*, 49.

dipping into it costs…Each time you use it you have to go a little deeper, a little further down into the blackness…The danger in diving into that pool, in drinking from that dark water, is that one day you may submerge yourself so deeply that you can never find the surface again. Give into it and you're lost forever.[81]

Through such self-aware scrutiny, Parker largely (and ethically) avoids using his empathy or his suffering as a flag of convenience under which to pursue revenge. Such reflective passages, layered across the books as they are, help develop the series' sense of empathy as an emotional parallel to the supernatural image of the honeycomb world, with its subterranean links that are felt more than understood. It is in no small part through this parallel that the series builds its emotional resonance, weaving together the world's hidden depths with both a supernatural framework and Parker's deeply personal commitment to the connections that constitute empathy, in all its ambivalence.

As suggested at the start of this section, Connolly's work helps model ways in which transnational Irish crime fiction with little overt Irish content can and should nonetheless inform our understanding of Irish crime fiction's full scope. In this regard, Parker's honeycomb world also offers a bridge to seeing Connolly's work in relation to other Irish writing, not just to the 'strong streak of anti-rationalism' that Connolly has seen in Irish literature, and not just to other Irish crime fiction, but also through analogues in Irish folklore.[82] Angela Bourke, for example, has given one account of the origin of fairies as fallen angels who took that form

---

[81] Connolly, *Killing*, 94.

[82] Connolly, 'No Blacks, No Dogs, No Crime Writers,' 54. Also of interest here is Richard Kearney's work on various aspects of Irish culture that show 'an intellectual ability to hold the traditional oppositions of classical reason together in creative confluence.' Richard Kearney, 'Introduction: An Irish Intellectual Tradition,' in *The Irish Mind: Exploring Intellectual Traditions*, ed. Richard Kearney (Dublin: Wolfhound, 1985), 9. Compare Kearney's sense of an Irish independence from reason's dominance to the following passage in Declan Hughes's fifth Ed Loy novel: 'At a certain stage, evil becomes a mystery, transcending all considerations of biography and motivation. … That doesn't stop people trying; books and newspaper articles appear, some content to detail the mere facts of the case, others attempting to provide some insight into the psychology of the killer's mind. The result: we know almost all the facts; we remain terrifyingly low on insight' (*City*, 301). Here, Loy's sense that some evil is not susceptible to rational explanation fits interestingly with Connolly and Glynn, and with Irish crime fiction's sense of the counter-rational, articulated above by Connolly. Glynn's work is not counter-rational in the way Connolly's is, and yet Glynn is clearly invested in a sense of how things exceed explanation and understanding.

when the rebellious angel Lucifer and his followers were expelled from Heaven, and God the Son warned God the Father that Heaven would soon be empty. Like figures in a film that is suddenly stopped, the expelled angels falling toward Hell halted where they were: some in mid-air, others in the earth, and some in the ocean, and there they remain.[83]

In Connolly's *The Black Angel*, we are similarly told that 'According to Enoch, two hundred angels rebelled, and they were cast down initially on a mountain ... Some, of course, descended farther, and founded hell, but others remained on earth.'[84] This sense of converging realms further underscores the physicality of the honeycomb world: this convergence is in the very nature of that world. In such ways, Connolly's and Bourke's accounts share a fundamental sense of in-between-ness, a sense that these beings have a powerful, real impact on the physical world not despite their shadowy presence so much as because of it. This sense arguably defines much about Parker himself, with all of his ambivalent otherness and his acute empathy, which is sharpened by his in-between-ness, much as Declan Hughes, Alex Barclay, Andrew Nugent, Jane Casey, and others have used the outsider experiences of immigrant and expatriate protagonists to focus particular issues in their fiction.

Given that Connolly references a wide range of research on mysticism and the supernatural throughout his work, it would be difficult and perhaps misleading to narrow such matters to an exclusively Irish influence. After all, as Bourke notes, the fairies' origin 'story is also found in the

---

[83] Angela Bourke, *The Burning of Bridget Cleary* (New York: Penguin, 2000), 31. Bourke's discussion of the ways in which fairies fleetingly but suggestively mark their presence offers further analogues to Parker's experience of the honeycomb world, as in *The White Road*: 'It was neither a dream, nor a reality. It was as if, for a brief moment, something that resided in a blind spot of my vision had drifted into sight, that a slight alteration of perception had permitted me to see that which usually existed unseen' (Connolly, *White*, 135). This is amplified a scant few pages later, when Parker's dog's 'eyes remained fixed on a patch of darkness in the corner, denied light by the thick drapes but darker yet than it should have been, like a hole torn between worlds' (Connolly, *White*, 137).

[84] Connolly, *Black*, 307. Strikingly, Enoch is also mentioned as part of the Traveling Man's cosmology in Connolly, *Every Dead Thing*, 251–2, 272, 276, 296. In particular, the character Rachel references an edition of Enoch by the Victorian scholar R.H. Charles (Connolly, *Every Dead Thing*, 252). In a gratifying example of coincidence, this edition was reviewed by M.R. James – described by Connolly as 'my favorite writer of supernatural fiction' (*Night Music*, 426) – who concluded that 'we can heartily thank Mr. Charles for what he has given us.' M.R. James, 'Charles's Translation of the *Book of Enoch*,' *The Classical Review* 8, no. 1–2 (1894): 44.

apocryphal Christian literature of the late Middle Ages, associated with the Harrowing of Hell,'[85] as it also is in the mystical Jewish texts of which Epstein speaks to Parker. In other words, it will not do to resort to allegorical readings that would merely cover Connolly's work in a thin veneer of green. Nor can one persuasively suggest that his real concerns, if you just look closely enough – and past the numerous American influences, from Ross Macdonald to James Lee Burke – are secretly Irish, certainly not in the sense to which the field of Irish Studies has grown accustomed.

At the same time, without greening the lily, it is worth noting that other contemporary Irish writers of varied genres have also addressed the forces discussed by Bourke, and, like Connolly, have identified deep cultural roots that contribute to an insistent mistrust of certainty, such as runs throughout the Parker series. The poet Paul Muldoon, for example, displayed in early works like 'Immram' (*Why Brownlee Left*, 1980) both an abiding comfort with uncertainty and a deep familiarity with Chandler and other noir writers. Muldoon has also written about fairy lore, suggesting that the 'idea of there being a contiguous world, a world coterminal with our own, into and out of which some may move' could 'be traced back to the overthrow of the Tuatha Dé Danann,' who

> are made invisible by virtue of the *féth fíada* or *ceo sídhe*, the magic mist or veil, a kind of world-scrim, that hangs about them…This idea of a parallel universe, a grounded groundlessness, also offers an escape clause, a kind of psychological trapdoor, to a people from under whose feet the rug is constantly being pulled, often quite literally so.[86]

Muldoon's observations here echo Connolly's explanation that he has 'difficulties' with more conventional mystery novels because of 'the simple fact that I don't share the beliefs on which they are based. The world is not rational and intelligible. Order is fragile, a thin crust upon the underlying chaos. Any answers we get will be partial at best and at worst will simply give rise to further, deeper doubts.'[87] This conviction, which parallels strands of Irish culture and of supernatural writing, is everywhere apparent

[85] Bourke, *Burning*, 249n8.

[86] Paul Muldoon, *To Ireland, I: The Clarendon Lectures* (Oxford: Oxford University Press, 2000), 7.

[87] Connolly, 'Charlie Parker,' 77.

in the Parker novels, from the detective's first appearance in *Every Dead Thing* through to *A Game of Ghosts*.

Of course, even with this vision of the 'thin crust' between 'Order' and 'chaos,' Connolly does construct a sense of mystery with a detective, villains, clues, crimes, and other familiar elements of the genre. Crucially, however, he does so in a way that reflects the idea that something fundamentally unknowable is at the heart of the series and of Parker's life, a quality that bears the marks of the varied genre, transnational, and religious influences I have been discussing and that does much to shape this unique detective. While it uses many of crime fiction's structures, then, this series does not rest on the belief that the world is ultimately or essentially knowable, that its mysteries are all only apparent mysteries, that every depth can be plumbed. Instead, a foundational uncertainty is central to – rather than at odds with – the Parker series, enabling the novels to extend the boundaries of both Irish writing and crime fiction as substantially as they do. In this, Connolly's work models some of the ways in which Irish crime fiction that does not deal in the familiar markers of Irish literature – and that is consequently less likely to be taken up in existing critical discussions about that literature – may nonetheless draw on deeper Irish structures, modelling both what crime fiction can reveal about Irish culture and what Irish writing can bring to crime fiction.

CONCLUSION

Through their integration of transnational elements – from the globalised exploitation in Glynn to the overseas settings of Hunt's *The Chosen*, Ryan's Korolev series, Connolly's Parker series, and Barclay's Bryce series – the novels discussed here demonstrate ways to find meaning and to be recognised as Irish texts without needing to represent Irishness in order to do so. This chapter's consideration of these transnational patterns identifies suggestive connections between these novels and Irish culture, connections that don't re-impose the familiar representational burden that these texts should be overtly *about* that culture. Not least among these connections is the integration of a fundamental uncertainty, one that links to both older Irish culture and to recent books by French, Glynn, and others discussed in Chapter 3.

An additional effect of sidestepping this representational burden is to highlight the complex relationships between genre fiction and Irish literature. Although much more work can and should be done on these relationships, the crime fiction examined here enriches our understanding not only of the genre but also of Irish literature in general. In doing so, these novels demonstrate that crime, transnational, and Irish literatures can all be linked, broadening our sense of what constitutes Irish literature and contributing to a process whereby that literature – in dialogue with both international crime fiction and Irish novels that signal their nationality in more familiar ways – can be seen anew.

References

Ascari, Maurizio. *A Counter-History of Crime Fiction: Supernatural, Gothic, Sensational*. Basingstoke: Palgrave Macmillan, 2007.

Banville, Vincent. *An End to Flight*. London: Faber, 1973. Reprint, Dublin: New Island, 2002.

Barclay, Alex. *Darkhouse*. New York: Delacorte, 2007.

———. *The Caller*. London: Harper, 2007.

———. *Killing Ways*. London: HarperCollins, 2015.

———. *The Drowning Child*. London: HarperCollins, 2016.

Beckett, Samuel. *Molloy*. Translated by Patrick Bowles in collaboration with Samuel Beckett. Paris: Olympia, 1955. Reprint, New York: Grove, 1955.

Binchy, Chris. *Open-Handed*. Dublin: Penguin Ireland, 2008.

Blake, Linnie. *The Wounds of Nations: Horror Cinema, Historical Trauma, and National Identity*. Manchester: Manchester University Press, 2008.

Bourke, Angela. *The Burning of Bridget Cleary*. New York: Penguin, 2000.

Bowen, Elizabeth. *The Heat of the Day*. New York: Knopf, 1948. Reprint, London: Penguin, 1986.

Burke, Declan. *Absolute Zero Cool*. Dublin: Liberties, 2011.

———. ed. *Down These Green Streets: Irish Crime Writing in the 21st Century*. Dublin: Liberties, 2011.

———. *The Lost and the Blind*. Surrey: Severn, 2014.

Carson, Paul. *Ambush*. London: Heinemann, 2004. Reprint, London: Arrow, 2005.

Casey, Jane. *The Stranger You Know*. London: Ebury, 2013.

———. *After the Fire*. London: Ebury, 2015.

———. *Let the Dead Speak*. London: HarperCollins, 2017.

Cavanagh, Steve. *The Defence*. London: Orion, 2015.

———. *The Plea*. London: Orion, 2016.

———. *The Liar*. London: Orion, 2017.

Charles, Paul. *I've Heard the Banshee Sing*. London: Do-Not Press, 2003.

Clark, David. 'Mean Streets, New Lives: The Representations of Non-Irish Immigrants in Recent Irish Crime Fiction.' In *Literary Visions of Multicultural*

Ireland: The Immigrant in Contemporary Irish Literature, edited by Pilar Villar-Argáiz, 255–268. Manchester: Manchester University Press, 2013.

Cleary, Joe. *Literature, Partition and the Nation-State: Culture and Conflict in Ireland, Israel and Palestine*. Cambridge: Cambridge University Press, 2002.

Colfer, Eoin. *Plugged*. London: Headline, 2011.

Connolly, John. *Every Dead Thing*. London: Hodder & Stoughton, 1999. Reprint, New York: Simon & Schuster, 1999.

———. *Dark Hollow*. London: Hodder & Stoughton, 2000. Reprint, New York: Simon & Schuster, 2001.

———. *The Killing Kind*. London: Hodder & Stoughton, 2001. Reprint, New York: Atria, 2002.

———. *The White Road*. London: Hodder & Stoughton, 2002. Reprint, New York: Atria, 2003.

———. *Nocturnes*. London: Hodder & Stoughton, 2004. Reprinted and expanded, New York: Atria, 2006.

———. *Bad Men*. London: Hodder & Stoughton, 2003. Reprint, New York: Atria, 2004.

———. *The Black Angel*. London: Hodder & Stoughton, 2005. Reprint, New York: Atria, 2005.

———. *The Unquiet*. London: Hodder & Stoughton, 2007. Reprint, New York: Atria, 2007.

———. *The Reapers*. London: Hodder & Stoughton, 2008. Reprint, New York: Atria, 2008.

———. *The Lovers*. London: Hodder & Stoughton, 2009. Reprint, New York: Atria, 2009.

———. *The Gates*. London: Hodder & Stoughton, 2009.

———. *The Whisperers*. London: Hodder & Stoughton, 2010. Reprint, New York: Atria, 2010.

———. 'Charlie Parker.' In *The Lineup: The World's Greatest Crime Writers Tell the Inside Story of Their Greatest Detectives*, edited by Otto Penzler, 63–79. London: Quercus, 2010.

———. *The Burning Soul*. London: Hodder & Stoughton, 2011. Reprint, New York: Atria, 2011.

———. *Hell's Bells*. London: Hodder & Stoughton, 2011. Reprinted as *The Infernals*. New York: Atria, 2011.

———. 'No Blacks, No Dogs, No Crime Writers: Ireland and the Mystery Genre.' In Burke, *Down These Green Streets*, 39–57.

———. *The Reflecting Eye: A Charlie Parker Novella*. Dublin: Bad Dog Books, 2012. An earlier version was published in the story collection *Nocturnes* (2004).

———. *The Wrath of Angels*. London: Hodder & Stoughton, 2012. Reprint, New York: Emily Bestler/Atria, 2013.

———. *The Creeps*. London: Hodder & Stoughton, 2013.

———. *I Live Here*. Dublin: Bad Dog Books, 2013. Expanded and republished in Connolly, *Night Music*, 399–443.

———. *The Wolf in Winter*. London: Hodder & Stoughton, 2014. Reprint, New York: Emily Bestler/Atria, 2014.

———. *A Song of Shadows*. London: Hodder & Stoughton, 2015. Reprint, New York: Emily Bestler/Atria, 2015.

———. *Night Music: Nocturnes 2*. New York: Emily Bestler/Atria, 2015.

———. Introduction. *The Wrath of Angels*, reprint edition. London: Hodder & Stoughton, 2015.

———. 'Author Introduction.' *Dark Hollow*, reprint edition. New York: Emily Bestler/Atria, 2015.

———. *A Time of Torment*. New York: Emily Bestler/Atria, 2016.

———. *Parker: A Miscellany*. Dublin: Bad Dog, 2016.

———. *A Game of Ghosts*. New York: Emily Bestler/Atria, 2017.

Connolly, John, Declan Burke, and Ellen Clair Lamb, eds. *Books to Die For: The World's Greatest Mystery Writers on the World's Greatest Mystery Novels*. London: Hodder, 2012.

Connolly, John, and Jennifer Ridyard. *Conquest*. London: Headline, 2013.

———. *Empire*. London: Headline, 2015.

———. *Dominion*. London: Headline, 2016.

Cook, Michael. *Detective Fiction and the Ghost Story: The Haunted Text*. Basingstoke: Palgrave Macmillan, 2014.

Coppola, Francis Ford, dir. *The Conversation*. San Francisco: American Zoetrope; Hollywood: Paramount, 1974.

De Lint, Charles. 'Books to Look For.' *Fantasy & Science Fiction* 110, no. 6 (June 2006): 28–9.

French, Tana. *Faithful Place*. New York: Penguin, 2010. Reprint, 2011.

Glynn, Alan. *The Dark Fields*. London: Little, Brown, 2001. Reprinted as *Limitless*, New York: Picador, 2011.

———. *Winterland*. London: Faber, 2009. Reprint, 2010.

———. *Bloodland*. London: Faber, 2011.

———. *Graveland*. London: Faber, 2013.

Grady, James. *Six Days of the Condor*. New York: Norton, 1974.

Graham, David. *Incitement*. Dublin: Andromeda, 2013.

Headrick, Charlotte. '"Where no kindness goes unpunished": Declan Hughes's Dublin.' In Mannion, *The Contemporary Irish Detective Novel*, 45–55.

Higgins, Jack. *The Eagle Has Landed*. New York: Bantam 1975.

———. *The Eagle Has Flown*. New York: Pocket, 1991.

Horsley, Lee. *Twentieth-Century Crime Fiction*. Oxford: Oxford University Press, 2005.

Hughes, Declan. *The Wrong Kind of Blood*. London: John Murray, 2006. Reprint, 2007.

———. *The Colour of Blood*. London: John Murray, 2007.

———. *City of Lost Girls*. London: John Murray, 2010. Reprint, 2011.

———. *All the Things You Are*. Surrey: Severn House, 2014.

Humaydan, Iman, ed. *Beirut Noir*. New York: Akashic, 2015.

Hunt, Arlene. *Vicious Circle*. Dublin: Hodder Headline, 2004.

———. *Undertow*. Dublin: Hachette, 2008. Reprint, 2009.

———. *Blood Money*. Dublin: Hachette, 2010.

———. *The Chosen*. Dublin: Portnoy, 2011. Reprinted as *Last to Die*, Ickenham: Bookouture, 2016.

———. Seminar discussion with the author and students. 'Irish Crime Fiction' undergraduate seminar. Trinity College Dublin, 11 March 2015.

James, M.R. 'Charles's Translation of the *Book of Enoch*.' *The Classical Review* 8, no. 1–2 (1894): 41–44.

Joyce, Joe. *Echoland*. Dublin: Liberties, 2013. Kindle.

———. *Echobeat*. Dublin: Liberties, 2014. Kindle.

———. *Echowave*. Dublin: Liberties, 2015. Kindle.

Kearney, Richard, ed. *The Irish Mind: Exploring Intellectual Traditions*. Dublin: Wolfhound, 1985.

Kelly, Aaron. *The Thriller and Northern Ireland Since 1969: Utterly Resigned Terror*. Aldershot: Ashgate, 2005.

Kerrigan, Gene. *The Rage*. London: Harvill Secker, 2011. Reprint, New York: Europa, 2012.

Kincaid, Andrew. 'Detecting Hope: Ken Bruen's Disenchanted P.I.' In Mannion, *The Contemporary Irish Detective Novel*, 57–71.

Leonard, Elmore. *Pronto*. New York: Delacorte, 1993. Reprint, New York: William Morrow, 2012.

———. *Riding the Rap*. New York: Delacorte, 1995. Reprint, New York: Delta, 1998.

———. 'Fire in the Hole.' In *When the Women Come Out to Dance: Stories*. New York: William Morrow, 2003. Reprint, New York: Dark Alley, 2004.

———. *Raylan*. New York: William Morrow, 2012. Reprint, 2013.

Lewis, Jennifer. '"Sympathetic Traveling": Horizontal Ethics and Aesthetics in Paco Ignacio Taibo's Belascoarán Shayne Novels.' In *Detective Fiction in a Postcolonial and Transnational World*, edited by Nels Pearson and Marc Singer, 135–155. Surrey: Ashgate, 2009.

Macdonald, Ross. *The Blue Hammer*. New York: Knopf, 1976. Reprint, New York: Vintage Crime/Black Lizard, 2008.

Mallo, Ernesto, ed. *Buenos Aires Noir*. New York: Akashic, 2017.

Mannion, Elizabeth, ed. *The Contemporary Irish Detective Novel*. Basingstoke: Palgrave, 2016.

———. '"Irish by blood and English by accident": Detective Constable Maeve Kerrigan.' In Mannion, *The Contemporary Irish Detective Novel*, 121–134.

McCarthy, Conor. *Modernisation, Crisis and Culture in Ireland, 1969–1992.* Dublin: Four Courts, 2000.

McGilloway, Brian. *Bleed a River Deep.* London: Macmillan, 2009. Reprint, London: Pan, 2010.

McKinty, Adrian. *Dead I May Well Be.* New York: Scribner, 2003.

———. *The Dead Yard.* New York: Scribner, 2006.

———. *The Bloomsday Dead.* New York: Simon & Schuster, 2007. Reprint, London: Serpent's Tail, 2009.

———. *Fifty Grand.* New York: Henry Holt, 2009.

———. *The Sun is God.* London: Serpent's Tail, 2014.

McKinty, Adrian, and Stuart Neville, eds. *Belfast Noir.* New York: Akashic, 2014.

Millar, Cormac. *An Irish Solution.* Dublin: Penguin, 2004. Reprint, 2005.

———. *The Grounds.* Dublin: Penguin, 2006. Reprint, 2007.

Muldoon, Paul. *Why Brownlee Left.* London: Faber, 1980.

———. *To Ireland, I: The Clarendon Lectures.* Oxford: Oxford University Press, 2000.

Murphy, Paula. '"Murderous Mayhem": Ken Bruen and the New Ireland.' *Clues* 24, no. 2 (Winter 2006): 3–16.

Neville, Stuart. *Collusion.* London: Harvill Secker, 2010. Reprint, New York: Soho, 2010.

———. *Stolen Souls.* London: Harvill Secker, 2011.

Nugent, Andrew. *The Four Courts Murder.* London: Headline, 2006.

———. *Second Burial.* London: Headline, 2007.

O'Brien, Flann. *At Swim-Two-Birds.* London: Longmans Green, 1939. Reprint, London: Penguin Classics, 2001.

———. *The Third Policeman.* London: MacGibbon and Kee, 1967. Reprint, McLean: Dalkey Archive, 1999.

O'Loughlin, Ed. *Not Untrue & Not Unkind.* Dublin: Penguin Ireland, 2009.

O'Sullivan, J.P. *Don't Hang Me Too High.* New York: M.S. Mill, 1954. Reprint, New York: Pocket, 1956.

Pepper, Andrew. '"Hegemony Protected by the Armour of Coercion": Dashiell Hammett's *Red Harvest* and the State.' *Journal of American Studies* 44, no. 2 (May 2010): 333–349.

———. *Unwilling Executioner: Crime Fiction and the State.* Oxford: Oxford University Press, 2016.

Phillips, Bill. 'Irish Noir.' *Estudios Irlandeses* 9 (2014): 169–177.

Pollack, Sydney, dir. *Three Days of the Condor.* Hollywood: Paramount, 1975.

Radcliffe, Zane. *London Irish.* London: Black Swan, 2002.

Reddy, Maureen T. 'Contradictions in the Irish Hardboiled: Detective Fiction's Uneasy Portrayal of a New Ireland.' *New Hibernia Review* 19, no. 4 (2015): 126–140.

Russell, Michael. *The City of Shadows.* London: Avon, 2012.

———. *The City of Strangers*. London: HarperCollins, 2013.

———. *The City in Darkness*. London: Constable, 2016.

———. *The City of Lies*. London: Constable, 2017.

Ryan, William. *The Holy Thief*. London: Mantle, 2010. Reprint, London: Pan, 2011.

———. *The Bloody Meadow*. London: Mantle, 2011. Reprinted as *The Darkening Field*, New York: Minotaur, 2012.

———. *The Twelfth Department*. London: Mantle, 2013. Reprint, New York: Minotaur, 2013.

Welcome, John. *Run For Cover*. London: Faber, 1958.

Wills, Clair. *That Neutral Island*. London: Faber, 2007.

Conclusion

Across the preceding pages, I have sought to engage with existing discussions in both Irish Studies and in crime fiction studies, neither of which has yet made much of a home for the body of fiction considered here. It is particularly unfortunate that Irish literary scholarship has had so little to say about this genre, an absence that speaks directly to some of the field's blind spots and habits. A fuller engagement with these materials, not just here but in the critical works that will surely follow and that I hope can build on this volume, will do much to enrich our understanding of Irish crime fiction. This process will expand the wider critical frameworks of Irish Studies in productive ways, allowing it to speak to a fuller sense of Irish culture. Irish crime fiction has significant audiences at home and abroad, and both Irish Studies and crime fiction scholarship will benefit from addressing these texts and their relationships to those audiences.

Towards that goal, these chapters have traced different elements of the genre's belated but accelerated development in Ireland. This does not make this book anything like a linear history, however. Instead, though this book does attend to such matters, the focus here has been on providing a substantial survey that can start the process of synthesising further discussions.

In weaving this survey, this book has attempted to follow something of a moving target in the ongoing wave of Irish crime fiction. That wave has produced a remarkable amount of excellent crime fiction, to an extent without real precedent in Irish culture. New material continues to appear

© The Author(s) 2018
B. Cliff, *Irish Crime Fiction*, Crime Files,
https://doi.org/10.1057/978-1-137-56188-6

at a daunting rate, not only with established series like those by John Connolly (who has just announced his sixteenth Charlie Parker novel, *The Woman in the Woods*, scheduled for 2018), Jane Casey (who has just moved to a larger publisher with her seventh Maeve Kerrigan book), Alex Barclay, or Adrian McKinty (who has just announced three more books in his Duffy series). This deep roster of established, active writers is in addition to the continually expanding group of newer writers, particularly women, Sinead Crowley, Kelly Creighton, Louise Phillips, and Liz Nugent among them. Faced with such an accelerated output, particularly one with for the most part scattered and isolated antecedents, no single study of Irish crime fiction can or should pretend to be fully comprehensive.

The reasons for this genre's seemingly sudden development in Ireland may perhaps clarify to some degree over time as more studies emerge, but any uniform consensus about those reasons seems unlikely. In this, Irish crime fiction has good company, as the origins and evolution of crime fiction in general remain very much under debate, exemplified in recent excellent works like Andrew Pepper's *Unwilling Executioner: Crime Fiction and the State* (2016), which offers persuasive revisions to standard accounts of the genre's genesis. Although they may account only in part for this growth, several contributing factors do carry some explanatory weight, whether they emphasise the socio-economic factors of the 'Celtic Tiger,' or the inspiration of 'Tartan Noir,' or the diversification of publishing models amidst corporate consolidations, or the ever-shifting tastes of the marketplace. These contributing factors are all the more difficult to pin down when the novels make such divergent uses of their contexts. Declan Hughes's first Ed Loy novel, *The Wrong Kind of Blood* (2006), for example, is set against the boom of the Celtic Tiger, and reflects in substantial ways on that era, but treats its characters as much more than ingredients in a pat allegory about a nation losing its sense of itself. Instead, as does the best writing considered here, the novel places its contexts and its characters in a sustained dialogue with each other, from which emerges a much deeper portrait of family, of community, and of the corruptions to which they give rise and by which they are undermined.

Amidst these competing explanations and eagerly heterogeneous narratives, a number of distinctive features stand out as recurring across the subsections of Irish crime fiction. One such feature emerges from Chapter 2 but echoes throughout the following chapters: early thrillers set in Northern Ireland, particularly during the Troubles, often seemed to rely on reductive binaries, not least in the distinction between politics and 'real life.' In recent decades, however, the best crime fiction from Northern Ireland is sharply attuned instead to the meanings that emerge from disjunction and contradiction, which in turn become the levers that move these books through insightful and empathetic narratives.

Indeed, familiarity and comfort with disjunction and uncertainty echo throughout much of the work examined in every chapter here, finding profoundly varying expressions on both sides of the border. This is most immediately apparent in the number of novels here that give the lie to assumptions about crime fiction *requiring* a conservative sense of closure and resolution. Instead of confirming those assumptions, these novels frequently end with a deep, abiding sense of uncertainty. Some of that unease – as in Alan Glynn's work, or Adrian McKinty's – reflects a changing society's persistent ambiguities and its complex political histories. Other modes, including the Gothic elements of French's novels, or the supernatural and anti-rational strains of imagination in Connolly's Parker books, add to this their own existential layers of unease and uncertainty.

Over the course of this book, an emphasis on uncertainty and disjunction emerges as one of Irish crime fiction's underlying patterns. This, along with the effect of the island's small scale on the kinds and shapes of crime narratives, is one of Irish crime fiction's distinguishing features. This profound familiarity with uncertainty exemplifies what these novels can reveal in and about Irish culture, and is in turn central to Irish crime fiction's contributions to the discussions surrounding contemporary international crime fiction.

FURTHER READING

Note: Crime novels are often republished in paperback or international editions with widely varying page numbers. In the following reading list, first editions are given and used wherever possible. Where a subsequent reprint has been used instead, the details of that reprint are also given. In all instances where a first and a later edition are listed, the later edition is the source for all quotations in the text.

Banville, John. *The Book of Evidence*. London: Secker & Warburg, 1989.
———. *The Untouchable*. New York: Knopf, 1997.
Banville, Vincent. *An End to Flight*. London: Faber, 1973. Reprint, Dublin: New Island, 2002.
———. *Death by Design*. Dublin: Wolfhound, 1993.
Barclay, Alex. *Darkhouse*. New York: Delacorte, 2007.
———. *The Caller*. London: Harper, 2007.
———. *Blood Runs Cold*. London: Harper, 2008.
———. *Time of Death*. London: HarperCollins, 2010.
———. *Blood Loss*. London: HarperCollins, 2012.
———. *Harm's Reach*. London: HarperCollins, 2014.
———. *Killing Ways*. London: HarperCollins, 2015.
———. 'How a line you hear, read or write can light a fuse.' *Irish Times*, 7 April 2015. http://www.irishtimes.com/culture/books/how-a-line-you-hear-read-or-write-can-light-a-fuse-1.2167392 (accessed 1 May 2017).
———. *The Drowning Child*. London: HarperCollins, 2016.
Bateman, Colin. *Divorcing Jack*. New York: Arcade, 1995.

© The Author(s) 2018   185
B. Cliff, *Irish Crime Fiction*, Crime Files,
https://doi.org/10.1057/978-1-137-56188-6

————. *Cycle of Violence.* New York: Arcade, 1995.

————. *Mystery Man.* London: Headline, 2009.

————. *The Dead Pass.* London: Headline, 2014.

Beckett, Samuel. *Molloy.* Translated by Patrick Bowles in collaboration with Samuel Beckett. Paris: Olympia, 1955. Reprint, New York: Grove, 1955.

Binchy, Chris. *Open-Handed.* Dublin: Penguin Ireland, 2008.

Black, Benjamin. *Christine Falls.* London: Picador, 2006. Reprint, 2007.

————. *The Silver Swan.* London: Picador, 2007. Reprint, 2013.

————. *A Death in Summer.* London: Mantle, 2011. Reprint, London: Picador, 2012.

————. *Vengeance.* London: Mantle, 2012. Reprint, London: Picador, 2013.

————. *The Black-Eyed Blonde: A Philip Marlowe Novel.* London: Mantle, 2014.

Black, Ingrid. *The Dark Eye.* London: Headline, 2004.

Blake, Nicholas. *The Private Wound.* London: Collins Crime Club, 1968. Reprint, London: Bloomsbury, 2012.

Bowen, Elizabeth. *The Heat of the Day.* New York: Knopf, 1948. Reprint, London: Penguin, 1986.

Bradby, Tom. *Shadow Dancer.* London: Bantam, 1998. Reprint, London: Corgi, 2012.

Brady, Conor. *A June of Ordinary Murders.* Dublin: New Island, 2012.

————. *The Eloquence of the Dead.* Dublin: New Island, 2013.

Brennan, Gerard. *The Point.* Hove: Pulp Press, 2011. Kindle.

————. 'The Truth Commissioners.' In Burke, *Down These Green Streets*, 201–210.

————. *Fireproof.* Edinburgh: Blasted Heath, 2012. Kindle.

————. *Wee Rockets.* Edinburgh: Blasted Heath, 2012. Kindle.

————. *Other Stories and Nothing But Time.* Edinburgh: Blasted Heath, 2012. Kindle.

————. *Possession, Obsession and a Diesel Compression Engine.* N.P.: Heebie Jeebie Press, 2012. Kindle.

Brennan, Gerard and Mike Stone, eds. *Requiems for the Departed.* Norrköping: Morrigan, 2010. Kindle.

Brophy, Kevin. *The Berlin Crossing.* London: Headline Review, 2012.

Bruen, Ken. *The Guards.* Dingle: Brandon, 2001. Reprint, New York: St. Martin's Minotaur, 2003.

————. *The Killing of the Tinkers.* Dingle: Brandon, 2002. Reprint, New York: Minotaur, 2004.

————. *The Magdalen Martyrs.* Dingle: Brandon, 2003.

————. *Calibre.* New York: St Martin's Minotaur, 2006.

————. ed. *Dublin Noir.* New York: Akashic, 2006.

Burke, Declan. *Eightball Boogie.* Dublin: Lilliput, 2003. Reprint, Kindle Original, 2011.

———. *The Big O*. Dublin: Hag's Head, 2007. Reprint, New York: Harcourt, 2008.

———. *Crime Always Pays*. N.P.: N.P., 2009. Kindle. Reprint, Surrey: Severn, 2014.

———. *Absolute Zero Cool*. Dublin: Liberties, 2011.

———. ed. *Down These Green Streets: Irish Crime Writing in the 21st Century*. Dublin: Liberties, 2011.

———. *Slaughter's Hound*. Dublin: Liberties, 2012.

———. *The Lost and the Blind*. Surrey: Severn, 2014.

Capote, Truman. *In Cold Blood*. New York: Random House, 1966. Reprint, New York: Vintage, 1994.

Carson, Ciaran. *Exchange Place*. Belfast: Blackstaff, 2012.

Carson, Paul. *Scalpel*. London: Heinemann, 1997.

———. *Cold Steel*. London: Heinemann, 1998.

———. *Ambush*. London: Heinemann, 2004. Reprint, London: Arrow, 2005.

Carter, Andrea. *Death at Whitewater Church*. London: Constable, 2015.

Casey, Jane. *The Missing*. London: Ebury, 2010.

———. *The Burning*. London: Ebury, 2010.

———. *The Reckoning*. London: Ebury, 2011.

———. *The Last Girl*. London: Ebury, 2012.

———. *The Stranger You Know*. London: Ebury, 2013.

———. *Left for Dead: A Maeve Kerrigan Novella*. New York: Minotaur, 2014.

———. *The Kill*. London: Ebury, 2014.

———. *After the Fire*. London: Ebury, 2015.

———. *Let the Dead Speak*. London: HarperCollins, 2017.

Cavanagh, Steve. *The Defence*. London: Orion, 2015.

———. *The Plea*. London: Orion, 2016.

———. *The Liar*. London: Orion, 2017.

Chabon, Michael. *The Amazing Adventures of Kavalier & Clay*. New York: Picador, 2000.

Charles, Paul. *I've Heard the Banshee Sing*. London: Do-Not Press, 2003.

———. *Sweetwater*. Dingle: Brandon, 2006. Reprint, 2007.

———. *The Dust of Death*. Dingle: Brandon, 2007. Reprint, 2008.

———. *Family Life*. Dingle: Brandon, 2009.

———. *Down on Cyprus Avenue*. Chester Springs: Dufour, 2014.

Childers, Erskine. *The Riddle of the Sands*. London: Smith, Elder, & Co., 1903. Reprint, London: Penguin, 1999.

Colfer, Eoin. *Plugged*. London: Headline, 2011.

Connolly, John. *Every Dead Thing*. London: Hodder & Stoughton, 1999. Reprint, New York: Simon & Schuster, 1999.

———. *Dark Hollow*. London: Hodder & Stoughton, 2000. Reprint, New York: Simon & Schuster, 2001.

———. *The Killing Kind*. London: Hodder & Stoughton, 2001. Reprint, New York: Atria, 2002.

———. *The White Road*. London: Hodder & Stoughton, 2002. Reprint, New York: Atria, 2003.

———. *Nocturnes*. London: Hodder & Stoughton, 2004. Reprinted and expanded, New York: Atria, 2006.

———. *Bad Men*. London: Hodder & Stoughton, 2003. Reprint, New York: Atria, 2004.

———. *The Black Angel*. London: Hodder & Stoughton, 2005. Reprint, New York: Atria, 2005.

———. *The Unquiet*. London: Hodder & Stoughton, 2007. Reprint, New York: Atria, 2007.

———. *The Reapers*. London: Hodder & Stoughton, 2008. Reprint, New York: Atria, 2008.

———. *The Lovers*. London: Hodder & Stoughton, 2009. Reprint, New York: Atria, 2009.

———. *The Gates*. London: Hodder & Stoughton, 2009.

———. *The Whisperers*. London: Hodder & Stoughton, 2010. Reprint, New York: Atria, 2010.

———. 'Charlie Parker.' In *The Lineup: The World's Greatest Crime Writers Tell the Inside Story of Their Greatest Detectives*, edited by Otto Penzler, 63–79. London: Quercus, 2010.

———. *The Burning Soul*. London: Hodder & Stoughton, 2011. Reprint, New York: Atria, 2011.

———. *Hell's Bells*. London: Hodder & Stoughton, 2011. Reprinted as *The Infernals*. New York: Atria, 2011.

———. 'No Blacks, No Dogs, No Crime Writers: Ireland and the Mystery Genre.' In Burke, *Down These Green Streets*, 39–57.

———. 'The Chill by Ross Macdonald.' In Connolly, Burke, and Lamb, *Books to Die For*, 297–304.

———. *The Reflecting Eye: A Charlie Parker Novella*. Dublin: Bad Dog Books, 2012. An earlier version was published in Connolly, *Nocturnes*.

———. *The Wrath of Angels*. London: Hodder & Stoughton, 2012. Reprint, New York: Emily Bestler/Atria, 2013.

———. *The Creeps*. London: Hodder & Stoughton, 2013.

———. *I Live Here*. Dublin: Bad Dog Books, 2013. Expanded and republished in Connolly, *Night Music*, 399–443.

———. 'Chapter 9.' In *Inherit the Dead*, edited by Jonathan Santlofer, 117–125. New York: Touchstone, 2013.

———. *The Wolf in Winter*. London: Hodder & Stoughton, 2014. Reprint, New York: Emily Bestler/Atria, 2014.

———. *A Song of Shadows*. London: Hodder & Stoughton, 2015. Reprint, New York: Emily Bestler/Atria, 2015.

———. *Night Music: Nocturnes 2*. New York: Emily Bestler/Atria, 2015.

———. *A Time of Torment*. New York: Emily Bestler/Atria, 2016.

———. *Parker: A Miscellany*. Dublin: Bad Dog, 2016.

———. *A Game of Ghosts*. New York: Emily Bestler/Atria, 2017.

Connolly, John, Declan Burke, and Ellen Clair Lamb, eds. *Books to Die For: The World's Greatest Mystery Writers on the World's Greatest Mystery Novels*. London: Hodder, 2012.

Connolly, John, and Jennifer Ridyard. *Conquest*. London: Headline, 2013.

———. *Empire*. London: Headline, 2015.

———. *Dominion*. London: Headline, 2016.

Coppola, Francis Ford, dir. *The Conversation*. San Francisco: American Zoetrope; Hollywood: Paramount, 1974.

Coughlan, Clare. 'Paper Tiger: An Interview with Tana French.' In Burke, *Down These Green Streets*, 335–344.

Creighton, Kelly. *The Bones of It*. Dublin: Liberties, 2015.

'Crime Fiction and Contemporary Ireland.' Panel Discussion with Paul Charles, Declan Hughes, Gene Kerrigan, Brian McGilloway, Niamh O'Connor, and Louise Phillips. 'Irish Crime Fiction: A Festival.' Trinity College Dublin, 23 November 2013.

Crofts, Freeman Wills. *The Cask*. London: Collins, 1920. Reprint, London: Penguin, 1952.

———. *Inspector French's Greatest Case*. London: Collins, 1925.

———. *Sir John Magill's Last Journey*. New York: Harper, 1930.

———. *Fatal Venture*. London: Hodder & Stoughton, 1939.

Crowley, Sinéad. *Can Anybody Help Me?* London: Quercus, 2014. Reprint, 2015.

———. *Are You Watching Me?* London: Quercus, 2015.

———. *One Bad Turn*. London: Quercus, 2017.

Dillon, Eilís. *Death at Crane's Court*. London: Faber, 1953. Reprint, Boulder: Rue Morgue, 2009.

———. *Death in the Quadrangle*. London: Faber, 1956. Reprint, Boulder: Rue Morgue, 2010.

Donoghue, Emma. *Room*. London: Picador, 2010.

———. *Frog Music*. London: Picador, 2014.

Ennis, Garth, and Steve Dillon. *Preacher*. Nine volumes. New York: Vertigo, 1996–2001.

Fitzgerald, Conor. *The Dogs of Rome*. London: Bloomsbury, 2010. Reprint, 2011.

———. *The Fatal Touch*. New York: Bloomsbury, 2011.

———. *The Memory Key*. London: Bloomsbury, 2013.

———. *Bitter Remedy*. London: Bloomsbury, 2014.

French, Tana. *In the Woods*. London: Hodder & Stoughton, 2007. Reprint, New York: Penguin, 2008.

———. *The Likeness*. New York: Penguin, 2008. Reprint, 2009.

———. 'Interview with Tana French.' Goodreads.com, July 2010. http://www.goodreads.com/interviews/show/536.Tana_French (accessed 5 March 2016).

———. *Faithful Place*. New York: Penguin, 2010. Reprint, 2011.

———. *Broken Harbour*. Dublin: Hachette, 2012.

———. '*The Secret History* by Donna Tartt (1992).' In Connolly, Burke, and Lamb, *Books to Die For*, 567–572.

———. *The Secret Place*. New York: Viking, 2014.

———. 'About the Author.' http://www.tanafrench.com/about.html (accessed 5 February 2016).

———. *The Trespasser*. New York: Viking, 2016.

Gaffney, Frankie. *Dublin Seven*. Dublin: Liberties, 2015.

Glynn, Alan. *The Dark Fields*. London: Little, Brown, 2001. Reprinted as *Limitless*, New York: Picador, 2011.

———. *Winterland*. London: Faber, 2009. Reprint, 2010.

———. *Bloodland*. London: Faber, 2011.

———. 'Murder in Mind: The Irish Literary Crime Novel.' In Burke, *Down These Green Streets*, 117–129.

———. *Graveland*. London: Faber, 2013.

———. Seminar discussion with the author and students. 'Imagining Ireland I' undergraduate seminar. Trinity College Dublin, 10 February 2014.

———. *Paradime*. New York: Picador, 2016.

Grady, James. *Six Days of the Condor*. New York: Norton, 1974.

Graham, David. *Incitement*. Dublin: Andromeda, 2013.

Green, F.L. *Odd Man Out*. London: Michael Joseph, 1945. Reprinted with introduction by Adrian McKinty, Richmond: Valancourt, 2015.

Gregory, Jarlath. *The Organised Criminal*. Norfolk: Salt, 2014.

Hammett, Dashiell. *Red Harvest*. New York: Knopf, 1929. Reprint, New York: Vintage/Black Lizard, 1992.

Higgins, George V. *The Friends of Eddie Coyle*. New York: Knopf, 1972. Reprint, New York: Picador, 2010.

Higgins, Jack. *The Eagle Has Landed*. New York: Bantam 1975.

———. *Touch the Devil*. New York: Stein and Day, 1982.

———. *Confessional*. New York: Stein and Day, 1985.

———. *The Eagle Has Flown*. New York: Pocket, 1991.

Hughes, Declan. *Plays: 1*. London: Methuen, 1998.

———. *The Wrong Kind of Blood*. London: John Murray, 2006. Reprint, 2007.

———. *The Colour of Blood*. London: John Murray, 2007.

———. *The Dying Breed*. London: John Murray, 2008. Reprint, 2009.

———. *All the Dead Voices*. New York: William Morrow, 2009. Reprint, New York: Harper, 2010.

———. *City of Lost Girls*. London: John Murray, 2010. Reprint, 2011.

———. 'Irish Hard-Boiled Crime: A 51st State of Mind.' In Burke, *Down These Green Streets*, 161–168.

———. *All the Things You Are*. Surrey: Severn House, 2014.

Hunt, Arlene. *Vicious Circle*. Dublin: Hodder Headline, 2004.

———. *False Intentions*. Dublin: Hodder Headline, 2005.

———. *Black Sheep*. Dublin: Hodder Headline, 2006. Reprint, 2007.

———. *Missing Presumed Dead*. Dublin: Hodder Headline, 2007.

———. *Undertow*. Dublin: Hachette, 2008. Reprint, 2009.

———. *Blood Money*. Dublin: Hachette, 2010.

———. *The Chosen*. Dublin: Portnoy, 2011. Reprinted as *Last to Die*, Ickenham: Bookouture, 2016.

———. *The Outsider*. Dublin: Portnoy, 2013.

———. Seminar discussion with the author and students. 'Irish Crime Fiction' undergraduate seminar. Trinity College Dublin, 11 March 2015.

Hunt, Arlene, Declan Burke, Jane Casey, John Connolly, Conor Fitzgerald, and Alan Glynn. 'Irish Crime Fiction Abroad,' panel discussion, 'Irish Crime Fiction: A Festival.' Trinity College Dublin, 23 November 2013.

James, M.R. *Collected Ghost Stories*. Edited by Darryl Jones. Oxford: Oxford University Press, 2011.

Joyce, Joe. *Off the Record*. London: Heinemann, 1989.

———. *The Trigger Man*. London: Heinemann, 1990.

———. *Echoland*. Dublin: Liberties, 2013. Kindle.

———. *Echobeat*. Dublin: Liberties, 2014. Kindle.

———. *Echowave*. Dublin: Liberties, 2015. Kindle.

Kelly, John. *The Polling of the Dead*. Dublin: Moytura, 1993.

Kerrigan, Gene. *Little Criminals*. London: Vintage, 2005. Reprint, New York: Europa, 2008.

———. *The Midnight Choir*. London: Harvill Secker, 2006. Reprint, New York: Europa, 2007.

———. *Dark Times in the City*. London: Harvill Secker, 2009. Reprint, New York: Europa, 2013.

———. *The Rage*. London: Harvill Secker, 2011. Reprint, New York: Europa, 2012.

———. 'Brutal, Harrowing and Devastating.' In Burke, *Down These Green Streets*, 249–263.

Kilroy, Claire. *The Devil I Know*. London: Faber, 2012.

King, Catriona. *The Keeper*. Belfast: Hamilton-Crean, 2015. Kindle.

Kitchin, Rob. *The Rule Book*. Brighton: Pen Press, 2009.

———. *The White Gallows*. Brighton: Indepenpress, 2010.

Leonard, Elmore. *Pronto.* New York: Delacorte, 1993. Reprint, New York: William Morrow, 2012.

———. *Riding the Rap.* New York: Delacorte, 1995. Reprint, New York: Delta, 1998.

———. 'Fire in the Hole.' In *When the Women Come Out to Dance: Stories.* New York: William Morrow, 2003. Reprint, New York: Dark Alley, 2004.

———. *Raylan.* New York: William Morrow, 2012. Reprint, 2013.

Lynch, Paul. *Red Sky in Morning.* London: Quercus, 2013.

Macdonald, Ross. *The Blue Hammer.* New York: Knopf, 1976. Reprint, New York: Vintage Crime/Black Lizard, 2008.

MacLaverty, Bernard. *Cal.* London: Jonathan Cape, 1983. Reprint, New York: Norton, 1995.

Madden, Deirdre. *One By One in the Darkness.* London: Faber, 1996.

McCabe, Patrick. *The Butcher Boy.* London: Picador, 1992.

McCarthy, Kevin. *Peeler.* Cork: Mercier, 2010.

———. *Irregulars.* Dublin: New Island, 2013.

———. *The Wolves of Eden.* New York: Norton, 2018.

McEldowney, Eugene. *A Kind of Homecoming.* London: Heinemann, 1994.

———. *A Stone of the Heart.* London: Heinemann, 1995.

———. *The Sad Case of Harpo Higgins.* London: Heinemann, 1996.

———. *Murder at Piper's Gut.* London: Heinemann, 1997.

McGilloway, Brian. *Borderlands.* London: Macmillan, 2007. Reprint, London: Pan, 2007.

———. *Gallows Lane.* London: Macmillan, 2008. Reprint, London: Pan, 2009.

———. 'McGilloway on the Run.' *Derry Journal*, 14 March 2008. http://www.derryjournal.com/news/mcgilloway-on-the-run-1-2122496 (accessed 30 May 2017).

———. *Bleed a River Deep.* London: Macmillan, 2009. Reprint, London: Pan, 2010.

———. *The Rising.* London: Macmillan, 2010. Reprint, London: Pan, 2011.

———. *Little Girl Lost.* London: Macmillan, 2011. Reprint, London: Pan, 2012.

———. *The Nameless Dead.* London: Macmillan, 2012.

———. *Hurt.* London: C&R Crime, 2013. Reprinted as *Someone You Know*, New York: Witness Impulse, 2014.

———. *Preserve the Dead.* London: Corsair, 2015. Reprinted as *The Forgotten Ones*, New York: Witness Impulse, 2015.

———. *Bad Blood.* London: Corsair, 2017.

McGowan, Claire. *The Lost.* London: Headline, 2013.

———. *The Dead Ground.* London: Headline, 2014.

———. *The Silent Dead.* London: Headline, 2015.

———. *A Savage Hunger.* London: Headline, 2016. Kindle.

———. *Blood Tide.* London: Headline, 2017.

McInerney, Lisa. *The Glorious Heresies*. London: John Murray, 2015.

McKinty, Adrian. *Dead I May Well Be*. New York: Scribner, 2003.

———. *The Dead Yard*. New York: Scribner, 2006.

———. *The Bloomsday Dead*. New York: Simon & Schuster, 2007. Reprint, London: Serpent's Tail, 2009.

———. *Fifty Grand*. New York: Henry Holt, 2009.

———. 'Odd Men Out.' In Burke, *Down These Green Streets*, 96–105.

———. *The Cold Cold Ground*. London: Serpent's Tail, 2012.

———. *I Hear the Sirens in the Street*. London: Serpent's Tail, 2013.

———. *In the Morning I'll Be Gone*. Amherst, NY: Seventh Street, 2014.

———. *The Sun is God*. London: Serpent's Tail, 2014.

———. *Gun Street Girl*. London: Serpent's Tail, 2015.

———. *Rain Dogs*. Amherst: Seventh Street, 2016.

———. *Police at the Station and They Don't Look Friendly*. Amherst: Seventh Street, 2017.

McKinty, Adrian, and Stuart Neville, eds. *Belfast Noir*. New York: Akashic, 2014.

McNamee, Eoin. *Resurrection Man*. London: Picador, 1994. Reprint, New York: Picador, 1995.

———. *The Blue Tango*. London: Faber, 2001.

———. *The Ultras*. London: Faber, 2004.

———. *Orchid Blue*. London: Faber, 2010.

———. *Blue is the Night*. London: Faber, 2014.

Millar, Cormac. *An Irish Solution*. Dublin: Penguin, 2004. Reprint, 2005.

———. *The Grounds*. Dublin: Penguin, 2006. Reprint, 2007.

Moore, Brian. *Lies of Silence*. London: Bloomsbury, 1990.

Muldoon, Paul. *Why Brownlee Left*. London: Faber, 1980.

———, screenwriter. *Monkeys*. Directed by Danny Boyle. Belfast: BBC Northern Ireland, 1989.

———. *To Ireland, I: The Clarendon Lectures*. Oxford: Oxford University Press, 2000.

Murray, Paul. *An Evening of Long Goodbyes*. London: Hamish Hamilton, 2003. Reprint, London: Penguin, 2011.

———. *Skippy Dies*. London: Hamish Hamilton, 2010.

Neville, Stuart. *The Twelve*. London: Harvill Secker, 2009.

———. *Collusion*. London: Harvill Secker, 2010. Reprint, New York: Soho, 2010.

———. *Stolen Souls*. London: Harvill Secker, 2011.

———. Seminar discussion with the author and students. 'Imagining Ireland IV' undergraduate seminar. Trinity College Dublin, 23 November 2012.

———. *Ratlines*. London: Harvill Secker, 2013.

———. *The Final Silence*. London: Harvill Secker, 2014.

———. *Those We Left Behind*. London: Harvill Secker, 2015.

———. Seminar discussion with the author, Christopher Morash, and students. 'Irish Crime Fiction' undergraduate seminar. Trinity College Dublin, 11 February 2015.

———. *So Say the Fallen*. New York: Soho, 2016.

———. [Haylen Beck, pseud.]. *Here and Gone*. New York: Crown, 2017.

Neville, Stuart, John Connolly, Declan Hughes, Brian Cliff, Fiona Coffey, and Elizabeth Mannion. Panel discussion at launch of Elizabeth Mannion, ed., *The Contemporary Irish Detective Novel* and Stuart Neville, *So Say The Fallen*. Glucksman Ireland House, New York University, 13 September 2016.

Nugent, Andrew. *The Four Courts Murder*. London: Headline, 2006.

———. *Second Burial*. London: Headline, 2007.

———. *Soul Murder*. New York: Minotaur, 2009.

Nugent, Liz. *Unravelling Oliver*. Dublin: Penguin Ireland, 2014.

———. *Lying in Wait*. Dublin: Penguin Ireland, 2016.

———. *Skin Deep*. Dublin: Penguin Ireland, 2018.

O'Brien, Flann. *At Swim-Two-Birds*. London: Longmans Green, 1939. Reprint, Penguin Classics, 2001.

———. *The Third Policeman*. London: MacGibbon and Kee, 1967. Reprint, McLean: Dalkey Archive, 1999.

O'Connor, Gemma. *Sins of Omission*. Dublin: Poolbeg, 1995.

———. *Falls the Shadow*. Dublin: Poolbeg, 1996.

———. *Walking on Water*. London: Bantam, 2001.

———. *Following the Wake*. London: Bantam, 2002. Reprint, New York: Jove, 2004.

O'Connor, Niamh. *If I Never See You Again*. London: Transworld, 2010. Reprint, 2011.

———. 'The Executioners' Songs.' In Burke, *Down These Green Streets*, 195–200.

O'Donnell, Mary. *Where They Lie*. Dublin: New Island, 2014.

O'Flaherty, Liam. *The Informer*. London: Jonathan Cape, 1925. Reprint, London: Penguin, 1937.

O'Higgins, Michael. *Snapshots*. Dublin: New Island, 2015.

O'Loughlin, Ed. *Not Untrue & Not Unkind*. Dublin: Penguin Ireland, 2009.

O'Neill, Louise. *Asking For It*. London: Quercus, 2015.

O'Sullivan, J.B. *Don't Hang Me Too High*. New York: M.S. Mill, 1954. Reprint, New York: Pocket, 1956.

Parsons, Julie. *Mary, Mary*. London: Macmillan, 1998.

———. *The Courtship Gift*. London: Macmillan, 1999.

———. *Eager to Please*. Dublin: Town House, 2000.

———. *The Guilty Heart*. London: Macmillan, 2003.

———. *The Hourglass*. Dublin: Macmillan, 2005.

———. *I Saw You*. London: Macmillan, 2007.

———. *Therapy House*. Dublin: New Island, 2017.

Patterson, Glenn. 'Butchers' Tools.' *Fortnight*, September 1994, 43–44.
———. *The International*. London: Anchor, 1999. Reprint, Belfast: Blackstaff, 2008.
———. *Gull*. London: Head of Zeus, 2016.
Perry, Karen. *The Boy That Never Was*. London: Michael Joseph, 2014. Reprint, London: Penguin, 2014.
Phillips, Louise. *Red Ribbons*. Dublin: Hachette, 2012.
———. *The Doll's House*. Dublin: Hachette, 2013.
———. *Last Kiss*. Dublin: Hachette, 2014.
———. *The Game Changer*. Dublin: Hachette, 2015.
Pim, Sheila. *Common or Garden Crime*. London: Hodder & Stoughton, 1945. Reprint, Boulder: Rue Morgue, 2001.
Pollack, Sydney, dir. *Three Days of the Condor*. Hollywood: Paramount, 1975.
Power, Kevin. *Bad Day in Blackrock*. Dublin: Lilliput, 2008. Reprint, London: Pocket, 2010.
Quinn, Peter. *The Hour of the Cat*. New York: Overlook, 2006.
———. *Dry Bones*. New York: Overlook, 2013.
Radcliffe, Zane. *London Irish*. London: Black Swan, 2002.
Reid, Christina. *Plays 1*. London: Methuen, 1997.
Ridgway, Keith. *Hawthorn & Child*. London: Granta, 2012.
Russell, Michael. *The City of Shadows*. London: Avon, 2012.
———. *The City of Strangers*. London: HarperCollins, 2013.
———. *The City in Darkness*. London: Constable, 2016.
———. *The City of Lies*. London: Constable, 2017.
Ryan, William. *The Holy Thief*. London: Mantle, 2010. Reprint, London: Pan, 2011.
———. *The Bloody Meadow*. London: Mantle, 2011. Reprinted as *The Darkening Field*. New York: Minotaur, 2012.
———. *The Twelfth Department*. London: Mantle, 2013. Reprint, New York: Minotaur, 2013.
———. *The Constant Soldier*. London: Mantle, 2016.
Spain, Jo. *With Our Blessing*. London: Quercus, 2015.
———. *Beneath the Surface*. London: Quercus, 2016.
———. *Sleeping Beauties*. London: Quercus, 2017.
———. *The Confession*. London: Quercus, 2018.
Sweeney, Anna. *Deadly Intent*. Surrey: Severn House, 2014. Originally published in Irish as Anna Heussaff, *Buille Marfach*. Inverin: Cló Iar-Chonnacht, 2010.
Van Dyke, W.S., dir. *The Thin Man*. Hollywood: Metro-Goldwyn-Mayer, 1934.
Welcome, John. *Run For Cover*. London: Faber, 1958.

Index[1]

[1] Notes: Page numbers followed by 'n' refer to notes.